UNDER THE BURDOCK WEED

BY

LEE CARL

northern liberties press

Philadelphia, Paris, London

Published by
Northern Liberties Press
Old City Publishing Inc.
628 North 2nd Street
Philadelphia, PA 19123, USA

This book is a work of fiction. Names, characters, places and incidents either are products of the author's imagination or are used fictitiously. Any resemblance to actual events or locales or persons, living or dead, is entirely coincidental.

ISBN 0-9704143-3-1 (hardcover)

Also by Lee Carl:

The White Squirrel

To Kathy
and my nephews,
Jim, Joe, Jay and Jeff

and

To Spork
for a thousand and one reasons.

ACKNOWLEDGEMENTS

The author is grateful for the publication and promotion efforts of Ian Mellanby and Guy Griffiths, and for the skillful copyreading and perceptive editorial suggestions of Fred Maher. He also gives thanks to his brother-in-law, Len, for finding the Bluebird.

Chapter One

Marjorie Worth had lived in the same house her entire life—that is, until they took her away. Rob Putnam had seen his reclusive aunt only twice—once in his early teens on a fateful day that still haunted him, then again on that traumatic moment of her departure. He would never forget either encounter even if the dreams vanished.

Built about 1900, the Tudor-style house was set far back from the road. Its steeply sloped roofs, leaded-glass windows and dark-wood beams were well hidden from neighbors by dense growth—overgrown shrubbery, vines, giant oaks and feathery hemlocks.

Rob stood on the uneven walkway, its blocks of concrete lifted here and there by tree roots. He sighed as he thought of restoring the neglected property that was suddenly his. The unexpected gift was welcome, given his impending marriage, but thoughts of the work that lay ahead staggered him. His eyes moved to a chimney barely visible amidst the hemlock branches, then to the high walls of the enclosed garden on the east side of the house—walls covered with ivy whose twisted trunks were as thick as those of the wisteria that had long ago squeezed to death an aged oak. Surely this secret garden had been a part of Aunt Marjorie's life. She had never ventured from her house and garden, according to the gossipers who really knew nothing of her life. Rob's mother had filled his head with tales of Marjorie's twisted childhood, only later to refuse to acknowledge her sister's existence.

Rob could not help but wonder what he might find once he began his cleanup. He was intrigued by thoughts of searching through Aunt Marjorie's closets and drawers, of venturing into her attic and cellar.

He wanted to be alone on this first visit to the vacated house, because a step into that living room would be a step into his past. Surely that staircase would evoke that haunting vision from his youth. Jackie, his fiancée, had begged to come along. But tomorrow was soon enough for that.

Rob walked slowly toward the heavy wooden door, almost in awe of the property that was now his. Dressed in jeans and a T-shirt, he had prepared himself for work, but expected to do more looking than anything else on this Saturday in mid-summer, a day that would turn scorching hot by early afternoon. Already the shrill sounds of cicadas resounded through the trees.

Six-feet tall and slender, Robert Putnam was almost handsome. The mischievous twinkle in his blue-gray eyes had captured Jackie at first stare. His major worry until now had been the premature receding of his ebony hair—wavy hair that was giving way much too fast for a man of 27 years. But Aunt Marjorie's house had made him forget such worries. Strange that his newly found fortune should both delight and trouble him. He had never owned much of anything before. His five-year-old car took him to and from a decent job. Making the commitment to marry Jackie had been somewhat traumatic. Now this. He stood still for a moment before digging into his pocket for the key.

After unlocking the door, Rob pushed it open slowly and stepped into the house. A flash from his youth raced his heartbeat and hampered his movement. He tried to shake off the feelings, then moved his feet, but only after giving conscious thought to forcing steps. The room was like—yet unlike—the way he remembered it. The flowered wallpaper was streaked with brown stains and dark age marks, and the dusty pinkness was more dusty, having faded and grayed with time and dirt, and the many wingback chairs seemed smaller. In truth, while the room was large, it was not as grandiose as he had pictured it. But then a 27-year-old man of today did not see or feel as a teenage boy of yesteryear.

The stairs to the second floor were not as mighty as he remembered them, but they twitched his heart anyway, and he looked away, gazing instead at the portrait of his grandmother above the tiled fireplace. He walked to the baby grand piano and wrote his name in the dust atop the dark mahogany. It was as though he were claiming his rights to the piano and all that surrounded it. He was proclaiming the property his, trying to convince himself, telling his head and his heart that he was truly here. He leaned against the piano and looked about, his eyes seeing more as they adjusted to the dim light that entered through grimy windows. His eyes were drawn from an ornate vase on a piecrust table back to the flight of stairs, and again he turned away.

Brightness pulled Rob into the dining room where light from outdoors splashed across the room and lit a heavy coating of dust on the mahogany table and cast a dull shine on a tarnished silver tea service. Despite the dust, a crystal chandelier danced with sparkles of light, its prisms reflecting rainbows among the rosebuds on the soiled wallpaper. The sunlight came from the walled garden. It poured over the east and south walls and through small panes of glass in wide double doors that opened onto an overgrown patch of flowers and weeds. Tree branches hung over the north or front wall, the inside of which supported trellised vines of clematis twisted with bindweed that strangled tall spikes of delphinium.

Rob sighed again as he surveyed growth that had overrun the flagstone walkways, weeds that were crowding out clumps of pink phlox and yellow daisies. Dandelions grew between the bricks of the walls, sucking nourishment from small deposits of earth.

A push, a pull and a kick finally enabled Rob to open the doors. Dust fell from the molding above, causing him to sneeze as he stepped into the outdoor heat.

"God help me," Rob mumbled, realizing that the garden alone was a summer of work. He strolled about the winding walkways, now and then pulling and tossing a clump of tall weed or grass. At one point he grasped a giant burdock as if about to strangle the worst of his enemies. Anger took charge of his expression as he gritted his teeth. Perhaps to Rob this burdock represented all of the undesirables he would purge from his wedding house. The big-leafed weed finally gave way, coming up with a weighty hunk of soil. Rob tried to toss it over the wall, but it hit the bricks and fell into a mass of spider flowers. He glanced down at the hole he had made in the earth, and a curious sight grabbed his attention. At first he wasn't certain of what he saw. He reached for it, lifted it from the hole, frowned and tipped his head, then brushed dirt from it. Without question, it was a human skull, minus its lower jaw—a small one for sure, but a human skull, the skull of an infant, perhaps a newborn infant. Holding it at arm's length, he kept staring at it, brushing it with his fingers. Slowly he drew it toward his face and gazed into its eye sockets.

Rob hurried from the garden, cradling the skull in both hands.

In the kitchen, where modern-day appliances had been added to turn-of-the-century cabinet work, Rob glanced quickly from stove to refrigerator to sink, then gently placed the skull in the sink and turned on the water. He lifted it, holding it under the faucet. As the water rolled over it, he kept asking himself how it could have found its way into Aunt Marjorie's garden—a garden accessible only through the house or from over high walls.

When the skull was as clean as he could make it, Rob turned off the water and placed his finding on the drainboard. He stepped back from it, and remained there staring until seconds gave way to minutes. Suddenly his eyes rolled as more thoughts raced through his brain. An impulse sent him dashing back to the garden where he kneeled at the hole and began enlarging it with his hands. Within seconds he found the jaw, then other small bones.

Chapter Two

The car was an ordinary, four-door, blue Chevy without extras, bouncing along more quickly than it should in a residential neighborhood. In fact, the young woman in the tennis shorts and top, holding on firmly in the front passenger seat, was annoyed with the nervous driver.

"You just went through a stop sign!" she exclaimed, aiming her small upturned nose at Rob. Jackie Harwood was a trim, sandy-haired, green-eyed, girlish 23-year-old who easily grabbed a man's attention. "Cute" and "pretty" described her better than "beautiful," but no one denied that she was eye-catching, partly because she knew what to do with her strong points, her eyes among them. Little by little she had learned to defend herself against Rob's quick wit and crazy antics, and was reaching the point where she could punch out retorts and one-liners almost as fast as he could toss them. Her mother had taught her never to be outdone by a man. A graduate of Bryn Mawr College, she often reminded Rob that the quality of her schooling was a notch above his education—achieved at State College where he majored in fraternity beer-drinking. "What's with you, anyway?" she continued. "First you don't want me to tour the house until tomorrow. Then you pull me away from my writing in mid-sentence."

"I'd rather show you than tell you," Rob responded. "So just hold on."

"I started the letter three times. I can't believe they sent the wrong flatware. That woman on the phone tried to tell me I was wrong."

The car tires scraped the curb as Rob choked the motor off in front of the house. His quick leap from the car told Jackie that she was supposed to hurry. Despite her effort, Rob grasped her arm and pulled her up the long walkway.

"Let's move it."

"Rob! Stop it!"

Jackie was used to Rob's quick moves, sudden decisions, impatience and sometimes irrational decisions, but his pushing and pulling were a bit much this time. Inside the house, she slowed her pace in an effort to look around the living room, the piano among items catching her eye.

"No. Not now," Rob insisted as he hurried toward the kitchen. "This way. Come on."

"What a beautiful picture. Is that her?" Jackie slowed while gazing at the gold-framed portrait above the fireplace.

"No. That's her mother. My grandmother. Later. Come on."

Before entering the kitchen, Jackie stopped. "Let me guess. You found money. Lots of money. The old gal had papered the kitchen wall with it."

"Damn it, no."

Rob took Jackie by the hand, led her to the center of the kitchen, stood behind her with his hands on her shoulders, and aimed her toward the sink.

"There. On the drainboard."

Jackie stared quietly for a moment, then questioned, "A skull?"

"Yes. A human skull. So small it has to be the skull on an infant. I found it in the garden. In a shallow grave. Very shallow. Under a patch of weeds, next to a clump of iris. The rest of the bones are in that bag." Rob pointed to a brown grocery bag next to the skull. "They were entwined with the iris tubers."

"Are you saying a baby was buried in the garden?"

"That's right."

"But how did it get there?"

"Damned if I know."

"You don't think Aunt Marjorie planted it there?"

"Hell, I don't know what to think."

"Well, call the police. That's what you're supposed to do when you find a body, no matter how old it is. I mean, who knows? It might be murder or something. Don't you have to call the police?"

"I suppose. But I'm not going to. Not yet, anyway."

"Why not? You want trouble?"

"I want to know more first. I mean, my God, Aunt Marjorie never left this house! And I doubt that she ever allowed anyone in."

"You don't know that. Maybe your aunt wasn't what people thought she was."

"That's absurd!" Rob stepped to the sink and picked up the skull. "No one ever saw the woman. She was a freakin' recluse." He turned the skull around and around in his hands. "I know what you're thinking." He faced Jackie. "But that's impossible. No way could this be her baby. Marjorie having sex with someone would be like..." He couldn't think of a parallel. "Like... Like some cloistered nun..." But the image didn't mesh with Rob's vision from boyhood, and his expression was almost that of a man in shock as the word "nun" passed his lips. The staircase flashed into his mind. Anyway, even if he had wanted to swallow his words—and he didn't—it was too late now.

"Maybe it's not a human skull. Maybe it's a monkey's."

"This is no monkey." Rob stepped toward Jackie and handed her the skull. "I studied physical anthropology, and I think I know a monkey's skull from a human one. Besides, Aunt Marjorie didn't have a monkey running around her house." He couldn't help but laugh.

"Someone else could have buried it there, I suppose." Jackie frowned as she pondered the thought.

Rob's smile disappeared. "Over those walls? Are you kidding?"

Jackie fingered the skull. "So maybe it was put there before the walls were built."

"Before the Twentieth Century? No way. Those bones aren't that old. And they were hardly buried. Just below the surface."

"So, call the police and let them find the answers."

"No, I said!" The idea seemed to irritate Rob more than it should have.

"What is it, Rob?" Jackie looked up from the skull and stared into her fiancé's eyes.

7

"If this involved my aunt I don't want the police looking into it. Understand?"

"No. Not really."

"She's my aunt. It involves my family."

"Protecting the family? Come on, now, Rob. Your mother broke with the family years ago. She pretends Marjorie didn't even exist. You told me so yourself."

"If this involved my aunt I don't want the police looking into it."

"Since when did you become so protective of Aunt Marjorie? You never said a kind word about her."

Rob said nothing as he turned away from Jackie. But within seconds he spun around and took the skull from her.

"What happened to its chin?" she asked.

"The jaw bone? It's in that bag." Again he examined the skull closely.

"So you didn't answer my question. You're afraid the cops will go chasing after your auntie? Is that it?"

Rob was deep in thought as he placed the skull on the drainboard. He frowned, bit his lip and pinched his chin before lifting his head and looking at Jackie. "We haven't even searched this house. We haven't looked into the closets or the attic. I simply think it's important to find out more about Aunt Marjorie before we do anything else. I'm not sure why. But I think we should. Who knows. It just might be the proper way to go, for her sake. Don't you think? Bear with me for a little while. Okay?"

Jackie, being somewhat of a romantic, found all sorts of thoughts dashing about in her head. "Maybe Aunt Marjorie had a secret lover," she said. "Can you imagine?"

"No, I can't."

"Maybe we're on the threshold of uncovering a great story of love. Maybe her baby was stillborn, and she carried it into the beautiful garden and buried it under a patch of blue iris while tears streamed down her face."

Rob fingered the knobs on the stove one by one and verified four times over that the gas had yet to be turned on. As he opened the oven door and looked inside he asked, "How would a woman who never left her house find herself a lover?"

"Someone had to come inside here to install that dishwasher."

"Now you're getting silly."

"She had to have food delivered, and a lot of other things, let's face it. Maybe she fell for the mailman, or the gas man. Maybe a handsome hunk came to read the water meter and fell for her. Maybe they made mad passionate love. You told me she was beautiful."

"She was. In a strange, cool, quiet way." Rob's eyes stared far into the distance as his memory carried him back to his youth. He could actually feel his heart increase its beat.

"Are you okay?"

Rob looked away, but within seconds turned his eyes back on Jackie and nodded.

"You haven't told me everything, have you, Rob?"

"What do you mean?"

"I don't know. There's a look in your eyes sometimes."

He forced a quick smile and kissed her check.

Jackie held him at a distance and looked into his eyes. "You okay?"

"Sure."

"Tell me, Rob, how did your auntie pay for all her deliveries?"

"I don't know." He took her by the arm and led her toward the dining room.

"A wealthy recluse hides her money, doesn't she?"

Rob failed to answer as his eyes wandered.

Chapter Three

"**M**y God!" exclaimed Jackie while sorting through clothes in a walk-in closet off the master bedroom. "I can't believe these things! Honestly, I just can't believe... Look at this! A blue chiffon ballroom gown. What in the world did she do with it? Why would she have it? Where did she dance, in front of a mirror?"

"Maybe," answered Rob, who squatted cross-legged on the floor of the bedroom, a mammoth pile of papers heaped before him—papers he had pulled from several drawers and a chest. "You won't believe these letters either. None is addressed to her. They're all addressed to men, but they were never mailed. They weren't even put into envelopes. Do you think she just made up these names? Maybe they're a bunch of guys she fantasized about."

"You won't believe this. A satin top covered with sequins. And these night clothes!" Jackie kept pushing hanger after hanger along the bar in the deep closet. "I wish I could afford so many beautiful nightgowns and negligees. And the colors! Look at this peach one! It's gorgeous! What in God's name was she doing with all this stuff? Where did she get it all?"

"It's all yours now, if you want it." Rob leaned back against the foot of the bed—a four-poster whose wood matched the mahogany of a handsome chest and dresser that shared the pale blue-walled bedroom with a white vanity and oversized mirror. Oil paintings of blue and white snow scenes decked the walls. "Listen to this. 'Dear Earl, I want to remember you as you were. Please don't let them hurt you. I know the truth. I wish I had known you years ago, when you were a boy. Love, Marjorie.' And that's it. Short, like so many of the others. Most of them are like quick thoughts strung together. It's like something suddenly hit her, and she dashed off a quick letter."

"You should see this fur-trimmed bed jacket. It's unreal."

"I think she lived in a dream world. Dressing up for men she never met. Writing letters to men she never met."

"Well, then, how did that baby get into the garden? She must have met at least one man." As she spoke, Jackie stepped from the closet, holding a slate-blue dinner dress close to her body. She hurried to the mirror and looked at herself. "Oh, I like this. But you know, I'd really like to know more about her before I start wearing her clothes. I mean, maybe she was really creepy. But she sure did have good taste for a woman who never left the house. Not to be too critical of your mother, mind you, but she could have picked up a clue or two from her reclusive sister. Frankly, if I didn't know better, these clothes would tell me that Marjorie was the worldly one."

"Listen to this. 'Dear Clark, Carol is not the woman for you. Believe me, I know. I knew it even before last night when I held my finger over your mustache. You look so boyish with a clean upper lip. I can picture you as a boy. Love, Marjorie."

"Look, Rob, what do you think of this?"

"Yeah, it's pretty." He looked down quickly and read another letter. "Jesus, these are strange. No matter who she writes to, she keeps referring to his boyhood."

Jackie tossed the blue dress on the bed and began examining the makeup on the vanity. "All kinds. And the very best. Enough for years." She pulled open a drawer and gasped. "Oh, Rob, you should see the jewelry. Costume stuff, I guess, but there's so much and it's so beautiful. Look at these." Jackie held dangling rhinestones to her ears and faced Rob. "Look."

A quick glance up was followed by a look down as he went on reading. "Pretty. Very pretty. But get this letter. It's addressed to Tyrone. And here's one to Robert. It refers to his widow's peak. I think I've figured it out. These are all addressed to movie stars of decades ago. She fantasized about these guys. She wrote them letters and pretended to mail them."

"But if she didn't go to the movies, I don't get it." Jackie held a triple strand of pearls around her neck.

"Maybe she read about them." Rob looked up. "Those pearls don't quite go with your tennis shorts."

Jackie smiled, returned the pearls to the vanity and leaped at Rob, took his hands and tried to pull him to his feet. Instead, he pulled her to the floor and pecked kisses on her cheeks, forehead, nose and lips. She kissed him back, and then they rolled about, teasing and wrestling like a couple of kids. When she lay on the floor out of breath, he held himself above her, looked into her eyes with love, and asked, "Will you be comfortable in this house?"

"Once we make it ours I will."

"We'll make it ours. Don't worry. We'll make it ours in every way."

"By exorcising the ghosts of Aunt Marjorie?"

"Aunt Marjorie isn't dead yet. She's just gone."

"No, she's still here. She's everywhere in this house."

"We'll sweep the corners clean of all menacing dust."

Jackie squirmed out from under Rob, pushed the blue dress aside, and sat on the bed. "Come here."

He kissed her, then lay beside her. "It's all so crazy. Aunt Marjorie is one hell of a mystery. I wish we could find a diary."

"What good would it do? You wouldn't know truth from fantasy."

Rob thought about that for a moment. "Maybe. But it would give clues, I'm sure."

"Do you think we'll ever have this place fixed up? I mean, before the wedding?"

Rob laughed. "Maybe in time for our first anniversary."

"It'll be fun showing it to everyone."

"Not to my mother. She'll hate the changes we make, and she'll dread the parts that remain the same, because they'll remind her of things she wants to forget."

Rob's mind wandered back to that day of his childhood—that day he was brought to this house to stay with an aunt he had never before met. He could picture Aunt Marjorie, standing on that staircase, dressed in black, her eyes holding him transfixed.

"What is it, Rob?"

"Nothing. I was just thinking."

Jackie saw it again—that look on Rob's face. Several times since he had fallen into ownership of the house, she had seen it—that drifting into a somber distance. She was used to a happy, fun-loving, gregarious, optimistic Rob who had kept her floating even higher than her usual buoyant self. She had always smiled often, but not as broadly as Rob. She had always liked to dance, but not as wildly as Rob. She had always laughed with gusto, but not with a roar such as Rob's. She had often sung a favorite tune, but not with sudden loud bursts such as Rob's. Little by little, however, she had caught up and conquered. Now she even shook a hand more firmly than the average women, but, unlike Rob, didn't hold on for an extra vise-like squeeze followed by a high-five and maybe a slap on the back. She would point with pleasure at a bright red cardinal perched in an oak, while he would scare the bird away with his gestures and shouts. She would comment with sparkling energy after a good movie; he would raucously rave. Both spoke often of their love for each other. They had fun together.

"Is it the skull?" Jackie asked. "Or is something else troubling you?"

"Did you ever have a funny feeling that you can't quite put your finger on? Kind of a squirmy feeling from childhood. Maybe from a day you were left alone. Or from a time you didn't have control and felt spooked for some reason. It's like an uneasiness that you can't fully fathom."

"Like when my parents first left me with a baby-sitter. Even today I get a strange feeling when I think of it."

A haunting smile crossed Rob's face as he began to brush away his thoughts. He allowed it to grow into a grin, turned on Jackie and tickled her about the ribs and under the arms. "Now I gotcha, gotcha, gotcha!"

"Stop it!"

Chapter Four

Rob Putnam and Ty Scott ate together almost every lunchtime during the work week, except, of course, when one or the other was on the road, or when Jackie beckoned her beau. They were both public relations men for Pure-Pup Pet Food, Inc. They were good friends, though far different. Ty often drowned under the waves of Rob's exuberant personality. He was small, quiet and boyish. Hard as it was to believe, he was more than two years older than Rob, but looked many years younger.

"I know Tuesday is an odd time to start a vacation, but they said I could do it," Rob explained as he and Ty seated themselves at a table in the company cafeteria.

"You mean tomorrow?" Ty asked.

"Right. Wish I could have started today. But at least this gives me time to clean up a couple of things first. I finished that piece for *Puppy Journal* this morning."

Unlike Rob, who fit the stereotype, Ty didn't look or act the part of a PR practitioner. He was an excellent writer, but his chief skill was in layout and design. His true desire was to someday scrap graphics for pure art. He believed a great painter was buried inside of him.

A fine arts graduate of Muhlenberg College, Ty was hired by Pure-Pup the same year that Rob joined the firm, and was assigned to the office across the hall from his friend. Drawn together by timing and proximity, they had been buddies ever since, despite the fact that the soft, little man with the blond hair and the teenage face was often pressured by his outgoing partner and confidant. Rob fretted because Ty wasn't outgoing enough, didn't socialize enough, didn't date enough. His efforts to match him with one woman after another never paid off, mainly because Ty never followed through. He recalled only one attachment, and he viewed it as an obsession, something that plagued Ty for month after month. The fixation stemmed from a chance meeting with a deaf girl at the county fair, someone Ty finally stopped talking about after more than a year. But that episode was unreal and long gone, as far as Rob was concerned. Now, the fact that Ty had passed his 29th birthday alarmed Rob, yet failed to faze Ty—at least openly. The only response to Rob's constant reminder of Ty's upcoming 30th birthday was a boyish grin and a lifting of the eyebrows, signals that made Rob sigh in frustration.

"So, for four solid weeks I'm going to work on that house without giving a thought to dog food," Rob said. "You wouldn't believe that place. I don't know where to begin." He was so tempted to tell Ty about the garden bones that he looked down at his tray in hopes that his mind would be captured by the chicken salad that he quickly stuffed into his mouth.

Ty spooned his vegetable soup and wondered why the company didn't hire a better cook. But he liked Pure-Pup, probably because the boss liked his work. He didn't even mind eating in the company cafeteria—a sterile room that resembled a school cafeteria. For a change, however, he and Rob sometimes traveled cross-town to their favorite oyster bar. He and Rob knew the town well, having been born and reared in its suburbs. Graduates of the local high school, they had both landed jobs after college at one of their hometown's few corporations. Pure-Pup was important to the area—a region of fewer than 100,000 residents off the northeast extension of the Pennsylvania Turnpike, about 60 miles north of Philadelphia.

Ty and Rob had not been boyhood buddies and barely knew each other in high school—Rob being a sophomore when Ty was a senior. Rob was grateful for their close relationship, realizing that gregarious types were sometimes looked upon as skimming the surface of life, trying to grab a little of this and that, and not getting deeply personal with anyone. The truth was, Rob was more introspective than many believed, and he yearned to share his innermost thoughts and feelings. In fact, he and Ty played on each other when it came to soul-searching, each pulling from the other. They had a special place—Marty's Tavern—for late-night pouring-out, something they called Ty-Rob talk. A call from one to the other asking for "tyrob" at Marty's signaled a need for unloading. Rob had once told Jackie: "Ty really listens and reflects. So many people don't. I know I could share any confidence with him. A guy doesn't find many friends like that."

Then why didn't he share the tale of the skull? Rob wasn't quite sure, but he knew he would in time. He kept telling himself that he had to explore more first and try to erase some haunting feelings.

"Are you okay, Rob?"

"What's that?" Rob tried to clear his mind. "Sure. I'm fine. I was just thinking of the house."

"You said it's on the west side?"

"In the Mulberry section." Rob's thoughts wandered again.

"I know that area well. I delivered papers there from age twelve to seventeen. Some beautiful old houses."

Rob barely heard Ty's words. He made an effort to focus his thoughts, then said, "It's a Tudor-style house. Can't wait to show you. I'll give you a tour soon, after I get a few things brushed up." Rob could see the skull on the kitchen drainboard. He could feel it in his hands and envision the shape of its eye sockets as he rolled a piece of lettuce around the remainder of his chicken salad. Abruptly breaking his thoughts, he forced a smile and reminded Ty: "As best man you'll be hanging on the arm of Sally Lake coming down the aisle."

"Don't start again with Sally Lake."

"She's good to look at."

"And a total bore. I've never forgiven you."

"You didn't try. You were still fantasizing about that deaf girl."

Ty's muscles tightened and he looked away, then down at his soup bowl. Gathering his wits, he forced eye contact with Rob and said, "My vacation will be work, too. I promised the playground people I'd help put the kids' leagues together, and I signed up for the Rescue Fund food drive."

Although Rob thought Ty's need for cause after cause was excessive, he still saw his friend as a true humanitarian, not a feigned do-gooder. To him, Ty's efforts to supply pets to residents of nursing homes or design a sliding board for kids were never for recognition. And it was Ty's love for children that made Rob push harder in his match-making efforts. Time and time again he had said: "Damn it, Ty, you'd make one hell of a daddy!"

"Getting back to the wedding," said Rob.

"Oh, no. Not Sally Lake again."

"No. I just want to remind you of your duties."

"Duties?"

"As best man, you have certain duties."

"Such as?" A teasing smile played about Ty's lips and added a glint to his eyes.

"Come on, now. You're supposed to protect me. Don't let them get to my suitcases. Or my car. I don't want Limburger cheese spread on my Chevy engine. And I don't want any dildoes popping out of Jackie's traveling bags."

"Hey, it's payback time, isn't it?"

Chapter Five

The attic stairs were crowded with boxes, picture frames, old lamps, books, curtain rods, flower pots and other items that had never made it to the attic, all piled on one side, leaving a narrow passage of steps that were difficult to navigate. Rob tried to make his way to the top, but was pushed back, not by the clutter, but by the heat. Unable to turn around, he backed all the way to the second-floor hallway and into the arms of Jackie, who had been standing at the door watching him and preparing to follow.

"Pardon me if I strip, but these clothes have to go," Rob said. "It must be a hundred and ten degrees up there." He tugged and pulled off his shirt, tossing it to the floor of a hallway decked with ornate emerald-colored urns and family portraits. Quick of motion, he unbuckled his jeans and stumbled out of them after struggling to pull them over his sneakers.

Jackie eyed him up and down and liked what she saw. Rob, dressed only in sneakers and white briefs, was a force strong enough to make her forget the chores. She wanted to pull him to the floor right then and there.

"Let's go." Rob was quick to mount the crowded steps again, leaving Jackie with weak knees and a pounding heart.

After a deep breath, Jackie peeled off her blouse and wiggled out of her shorts. She began her climb stripped of all but panties, bra and tennis shoes. Smooth, pale flesh contrasted with that tanned by the summer sun.

Rob and Jackie found the attic so heavy with boxes, furniture, books and other objects that they stood in awe.

"My God!" Rob exclaimed. "Look at this stuff. It's a wonder the ceiling below hasn't cracked a thousand times over." As he glanced about, his eyes fell on Jackie and stayed there. "Oh," he whispered. "I suppose before we get all sweaty..." He wrapped his arms around her and pecked kisses here and there. She held tightly as minute gave way to minute and their bodies grew moist and slippery.

"We either go down to the bedroom, or we fight it off and get to work," Jackie whispered into his ear. The scorching heat and the perspiration should have been enough to kill the passion, but not quite so in the amorous bodies of Rob and his fiancée. Finally, it was Jackie who won the battle against lust. "We came here to hunt, so let's hunt and save the other for later. It'll be our reward."

"I can't save it."

"Yes you can." She pushed him away and eyed the bulge in his briefs. "This will be a test."

"There's nothing new about this test."

"Yes there is. We know there's a big bedroom below us in a house that's all ours."

"Stop it, you sadist."

"Look over there." She pointed in an effort to distract him and turn off his libido.

Rob turned and faced a pile of old phonograph records—9 and 12-inch, 78 RPM recordings from the 1940s and 1950s. He knelt and fingered them. "God it'll be fun to play some of these. Look. Crosby, Sinatra, Jolson, Pat Boone, Fred Waring. What's this? Yma Sumac? Wow! 'Jealousy' and 'The Ritual Fire Dance.' Oh, my God, 'The Bluebird of Happiness.' Dad never talked to me about much, but he would sing the 'Bluebird' and explain how he and his boyhood friends would tune in at midnight and hear it played on some Philly radio station. They would..."

"Rob. Look over here. Can you believe it?" Jackie stared at a pile of dolls in the alcove of a dormer window.

"Jesus! That's a lot of dolls."

Jackie stepped to the pile, which was higher than the window sill, and picked up a doll dressed in dirty pink—a doll with tiny bow lips and big blue eyes that opened and closed. "I used to have one like this." She brushed away dust and held the doll to her cheek.

"Maybe dolls were very important to Aunt Marjorie," said Rob.

"The clothes have been ripped off a lot of them. Don't you think that's odd?"

Rob's eyes caught sight of a stack of photograph albums. "What have we here? Hey, these should teach us something." He squatted and began to leaf through an album. "Come look."

Jackie continued to finger the doll. She gazed on it with affection while attempting to straighten its little dress. With care she placed it atop the mound of dolls and stepped back. An eerie, squirmy feeling pervaded her body as she gazed on the pile of mostly naked dolls— overlapping arms and legs pointed in all directions.

"Come here," Rob called. "Look."

Jackie couldn't break her stare

"Hey, what's with you?" asked Rob. "Come look. Here's a picture of my grandfather. When I was a kid, I can remember hearing Mom talk about him. I don't think she liked him very much. I used to sit at the top of the steps and listen. My father would get annoyed, and sometimes Mom would cry. She'd tell him about Marjorie's temper tantrums, and the gifts her father would shower on Marjorie. How he would always favor her, cater to her, spoil her."

"Maybe he bought her all these dolls."

"Maybe."

Jackie stepped to Rob's side, stroked his wet shoulders, then knelt. "Let's see."

"Here. And this is my mother at about six years old. I think this is Marjorie, several years older. That's my grandmother pushing Uncle Jack on the swing."

"You never mentioned an Uncle Jack."

"I don't remember him. I'm not even sure I knew him. Mom's got pictures tucked away. She never gets them out anymore."

"Where is he now?"

"I don't know. He was a black sheep, I think. Something strange must have happened. He was forced to leave, or something like that. Mom doesn't talk about him. Not since my father walked out when I was a young teenager." Rob closed the album. "We can look at these later."

"You know something? This attic could be very attractive if ever finished off. I love the sloped ceilings and the dormer windows."

"The house is already too big for us."

"Well, if we ever have a large family. I could do a lot with this."

"Large family? What are you talking about—large family. Hell, there are five rooms on the second floor. Anyway, you never said you wanted a lot of kids. I just might decide not to marry you."

Jackie giggled.

"One or two kids, and that's it," Rob proclaimed emphatically.

Jackie wrinkled her nose, then spun about and took in more of the sights. "I love that old end table. Look at the carvings around the edges."

"My God, look here. More movie magazines. Stacks and stacks of old movie magazines like the ones we found in the hall closet. She probably dashed off a letter every time she read one, pretending she was part of Flynn's life or Gable's life."

"Rob, here are some of the most beautiful Christmas decorations I've ever seen." Jackie stooped and opened box after box. "All kinds of little figures of people and animals. Houses and trains. Some of these tree ornaments are old. They don't make them like this anymore. Look at this one." She lifted a cluster of silver grapes. "It's heavy. Must be solid."

Rob thought that his heart had stopped beating as his body's electricity lifted his hair. His mouth opened as if to call out, but nothing came. What he sighted looked like a mummy—a small mummy the size of an infant. It lay in an Easter basket, among other baskets, far to one side, where the sloped ceiling met the floor. As he stepped slowly toward it, a vision of the garden skull flashed into his mind's eye. As he moved, he had to bend his neck, then his back, then his knees. He was crawling when he reached for it and lifted it from its bed of Easter grass.

"Jackie" he whispered timidly. "Jackie, I've found something."

She caught a touch of fear in his voice and quickly turned toward him and watched as he backed up until he could stand. He faced her, holding the object in both hands as if presenting a sacrifice to the gods.

"What is it?" Jackie asked.

Rob failed to answer as he began to peel off the cloth wrappings. Around and around he unraveled the material, which ripped now and again because it had been weakened and turned brittle by the years. Jackie was held speechless and motionless until Rob sighed and gave out a nervous laugh of relief.

"It's only a doll," he said.

"Dear Lord."

"I thought for sure..."

"But why would anyone wrap up a doll like that?"

"I don't know. Maybe she was preserving a doll that died."

"You know, Rob," said Jackie as she faced the pile of dolls, "your Aunt Marjorie must have been a very lonely woman."

Rob said nothing. He simply tossed the "mummy" onto the heap of dolls and then circled about, glancing at old glassware and china, stuffed animals, bundles of clothes, his grandfather's law books and broken lamps.

"Well, well, look at this old radio," he said, running his fingers around the curved wood that formed its top and sides. Picking up a book, he said, "A copy of 'Pilgrims Progress.' What do you know."

"I've got to go down." Jackie's bra and panties were soaked, and the bra straps were turning her skin red. Sweat was burning her eyes.

"Go ahead. I'll join you in a minute." Rob's hair was plastered to his forehead, and his body glistened. His wet briefs clung to his buttocks. "I can't take it either."

"Shout hallelujah if you find her hoard of cash," Jackie said from below. "Your auntie didn't live on air alone."

Minutes later, as Rob stepped from the attic stairs carrying five photo albums, he found his fiancée lying prone and naked on the hallway carpet, her wet panties and bra tossed aside. As he looked down on her, he smiled warmly and placed the albums on the floor. "The water's on, you know," he said, remembering his calls to the utility companies.

"What are you suggesting?"

"It's time we tried the shower to see if it works."

"You know it works."

He knelt, picked up his T-shirt and used it to wipe perspiration from her back. "Well, we don't know if it works with two people under it."

"I think it will."

"Let's find out for sure."

Chapter Six

Rob paced back and forth in his mother's living room—a room dressed up in Early American, not in a Spartan way, but with plenty of frills and ruffles. As if possessed, he circled around and walked among the waxed pine and the stuffed chairs slipcovered in colorful prints.

"I don't want little parts and pieces," he insisted. "Unload what you know. I'll tell you this, Mom, I'm not leaving here until I get a better picture of Aunt Marjorie and that house. And a better idea of what your childhood was like. Maybe you should try to explain what the hell my grandparents were up to while nurturing you and Marjorie. And, of course, Uncle Jack, who's also a big mystery, I might add. He's only a name to me—a name with no substance, no meaning."

Emily Putnam, who had been standing at the newel in her housecoat listening to her son, spun suddenly and stalked into the adjoining dining room—a room that carried out the theme of the living room.

"I don't want to hurt you, Mom," Rob continued. "I'm not stupid. I know there's a lot of pain inside of you. But maybe that's because you never tried to resolve it. Maybe that's because you never opened up."

"Oh, I opened up," Emily said as she seated herself at the dining table and gazed at her vague image in the polished pine. "I opened up so much that I drove your father away. All the words—the words, words, words. They don't resolve anything. Each one cuts a little deeper."

"Don't you think that I deserve to know about my family?"

"You don't understand."

Rob walked up behind his mother and put his hands on her shoulders. She started, looked up and stared blankly toward a hutch decked with pewter cups and willoware. Her house was meticulous because restless energy kept her dusting and polishing. If the portrait of Martha Washington hung crooked by a quarter inch, she would quickly fix it. Her house and her weekly bridge game had become her way of life to a large extent. It was as if she had retreated to protect herself.

"I thought maybe you came to have breakfast with me for a change," said Emily, a trim woman of 60 years—a woman who had only recently allowed her hair to turn gray, who dressed in plain but tasteful clothes, who no longer liked her Early American frills but wasn't about to redecorate.

"Mother." Rob's tone revealed impatience.

"You know you got me out of bed, don't you?"

"I'm sorry. But I've got a big day ahead of me, and I didn't want to get started while so many questions raced around in my head."

"Let me fix you some eggs."

"I'm not hungry, Mom."

"I have some of those sticky buns you like so much."

"No, really, Mom, I'm not hungry. Understand? Not hungry."

"Well, you have to eat something."

"You're trying to avoid the subject. Tell me about your sister."

"I don't have a sister."

"Oh, Jesus, let's not play that game."

"How about some French toast?"

"Mom! Don't, please." Rob walked to the other side of the table and faced his mother. "Okay, we won't call her your sister. Tell me about Marjorie, the woman who lived in my house."

"You should be grateful that you have that house. Isn't that enough?"

"Hey, I'm grateful. God knows I'm grateful. But I'm curious as hell." Rob pulled a chair out from the table, sat, joined his hands together by interlocking his fingers, and stared directly at his mother. Lowering his voice he said, "Mom, you always said we could talk, but we never really have. Sure, I could share my problems, and you always listened. And you would sometimes unload your frustrations about trivial things. But the truth is, you would never open up about certain things from the past. You know what I mean."

Emily turned her eyes away from Rob and said nothing for many seconds. She tightened her lips as her expression betrayed heavy thinking. Finally she looked at her son, slowly parted her lips, and said, "Only because it hurt so much to talk about those things. I didn't want to feel the pain again. I don't want to now."

"That's not healthy, Mom."

"I guess I don't want to remember." She stood and stepped to a bay window that held pots of ferns and begonias. Gazing into the distance, she fingered a leaf and quietly said, "Everything changed when Papa forced Jack to leave. For awhile, it seemed no one spoke. It was then—after Jack left—that Marjorie would no longer leave the house. Papa started to over-indulge her. He'd bring gifts for her, but not for me. I was only eight years old, and he hurt me so much. She was thirteen, five years older, and she got the dolls. I didn't." Emily kept staring out the window, hiding her quivering cheeks and lips from Rob. "Mother said we weren't allowed to talk about Jack. I loved my big brother." Her voice cracked.

Rob joined her at the window and put his arm around her. "Are you okay, Mom."

She didn't answer his question, but in time said, "I hated Marjorie. I hated her so much." Pulling away from Rob, she sat in a Boston rocker near the hutch, put her head back and closed her eyes.

"I remember her as being very beautiful. She was, wasn't she?" As soon as his words popped out, Rob regretted them, fearing that his uneasiness had caused him to say the wrong thing.

Emily kept her eyes closed and began to rock.

Rob tried to gather his wits. Within minutes he plunged ahead: "Why was Uncle Jack forced to leave?"

"He was only nineteen years old." Emily's words were slow and soft. "I never saw him again."

"But why? Why did he leave?"

"They never told me. But I know." She opened her eyes and looked down at her hands, which were cupped in her lap.

"Tell me."

"Jack did something terrible." Emily stopped rocking.

Rob stood still, watching his mother as a cat watches a bird. When she failed to continue, he stepped away from the window and toward the rocker and finally nudged her with the words: "Go on."

"He used her. You know what I mean."

"He forced himself on her?"

"He had a wonderful laugh, my brother. I still hear it." Emily began to rock. "Even after all these years, I still hear it." Again she closed her eyes. "He and his friends used to shoot marbles in the back yard and I would watch from the window. He was a good player, and every time he'd win, he'd give out with that wonderful laugh."

"Did you blame Marjorie for taking away your brother?"

"Yes, but I know that's not fair. Strange. Logic and the heart never go together. I guess I blame Papa more. I was in my room, but I could hear. I heard him order Jack out of the house. He said terrible things. Things I didn't even understand at the time."

Rob placed a chair in front of the rocker and sat facing his mother, his eyes fixed on her face. "Are you okay, Mom?"

She opened her eyes and smiled sadly. "When your father left us, he blamed my angry obsession with my family." Her smile disappeared. "He said I took my hostility out on him. I was hard on him, I guess. Maybe I did drive him away."

"Do you miss him?"

"Sometimes I do." She smiled again. "You look so much like him."

"I know. You've told me." Rob lowered his eyes. "I don't think about him often. Maybe I don't want to. Maybe I push away the thoughts." Fleetingly, he recalled the 'Bluebird of Happiness', then tried to redirect the conversation: "Did Marjorie have friends? Did anyone visit her?"

"No."

"No one at all?"

Emily pushed herself from the rocker and returned to the window. "I must water my ferns. They like a lot of water."

Rob was quickly on his feet, but stayed at a distance. "What about school? Surely Marjorie was educated."

"A tutor came."

"Then she did have visitors?"

"A tutor. When she would accept him. Sometimes she wouldn't see him. She'd pull a temper tantrum." Emily's words seemed distant and unemotional, but in truth caused her to keep her back to Rob and her eyes focused on the garden outside. "She would lock herself in her room, and they would beg her to come out. I know I should have pitied her, but I couldn't." Emily tightened her lips, breathed in a bit of strength, turned and faced Rob. "Looking back on things, I suppose we can say that Marjorie crawled right inside of herself and stayed there."

"Well, I'm not sure about that," said Rob, thinking of the skull and the other garden bones.

"What do you mean?"

"I'm not really certain. It's just that the house holds so many secrets."

"Like what?"

"If I knew, then they wouldn't be secrets."

"Now you're the one who's playing games. Tell me what you mean."

Rob fought for the right reply and finally said, "Expensive evening clothes, for example."

"Ordered by catalog."

"I'm sure you're right. We've found stacks of catalogs."

"She never went out of the house." Emily's tone revealed her anger.

"What is it, Mom?"

"Even as a teenager she danced in front of the mirror when she thought no one was watching, her lips bright red with Mama's lipstick."

"It seems strange that a girl so traumatized would dance, even by herself." Rob didn't necessarily believe his words. He was probing.

"She was always pretending." The very thought made Emily turn away again and gaze through the window.

"To escape?"

"I suppose. Sometimes she'd lie on her bed and just stare at the ceiling for hours. I used to think she did it on purpose so Papa would buy her ice cream. But Mama said it was the black bile of melancholy."

"Why didn't they get help for her?"

"And tell the world about the dirty family secret?" Tears welled in Emily's eyes.

Rob pondered his mother's words. But instead of offering comfort, he asked, "What about money? She was obviously well fixed."

Emily's face reddened and her lips quivered. Unable to speak, she turned and walked from the room as Rob tried to reach out to her, regretting his last question.

"Mom," he called out. "Did I say something wrong? I'm sorry."

Chapter Seven

Jackie allowed her yellow VW beetle to knock bumpers with Rob's car as she parked it at curbside in front of the house that was to become her dream house once the memories of Aunt Marjorie were washed away. Her father could have bought her a much more expensive car, but that wasn't the style of Alex P. Harwood, self-made man. In his thinking, cars and houses were earned.

Picnic basket in hand, Jackie scampered up the walkway. Her intention was to place the chicken salad in the refrigerator before the heat of the day did any damage. Mother had always warned her about mayonnaise and poultry.

Jackie's mother was a good cook, but not a homebody. She had created many a dinner party for her husband's business needs, but was just as adept at cocktail conversation at the country club. She had helped her daughter prepare today's lunch only because her scheduled luncheon at the Art Alliance had been canceled. Jackie had suggested a bit of this and a little of that, acting very much like a woman in love who wanted to please her fiance. Anne Harwood worshiped Rob, finding him an excellent choice for her daughter. Jackie's father, on the other hand, was anything but exuberant, having a father's need to hold on to his little girl. The fact that Jackie was an only child didn't help much either, but he had reconciled himself to the inevitable—his only child, a wee bit spoiled, would not only marry, but end up with a big house long before she or Rob deserved it. After all, it had taken him, now a marketing executive, many years before earning enough money to own property. There was something wrong—in his way of thinking—about simply inheriting a house.

Jackie placed the picnic basket on the porch while struggling to open the door. "Rob, are you in there?" She turned the knob again and again, then pushed hard, opening the door and sending herself flying into the living room. She caught herself before a stumble. "Rob, where are you?" Within a moment, she returned for the basket. "Rob!" After a deep breath, she stood in the doorway glancing around the room, making plans for the walls and floor space. She smiled slightly as ideas jumped about in her head. The piano, she decided, would stay where it was.

When her thoughts returned to chicken salad, Jackie was again on her way, carrying the basket to the kitchen through the dining room where she paused only briefly to gaze at the overgrown, weed-infested garden. Thoughts of the skull sent her quickly to the kitchen where she was pleased to see that human bones no longer rested on her drainboard.

"Rob, where are you?"

Jackie placed the basket on the drainboard, opened it, and drew forth a bowl covered with aluminum foil. She carried it to the refrigerator and balanced it in her right hand while opening the door with the left.

"Aaaah!" she screamed.

There on a lower shelf of the refrigerator was the skull and its lower jaw, staring right at her. "Oh, my God! In the refrigerator?"

"That you, Jackie?" came a call from the cellar.

"I'll be damned if I'll put this salad in there with that thing," mumbled Jackie as she saw the bag of bones in the very bottom of the refrigerator, under the shelf holding the skull.

Rob clumped up the cellar steps, pushed open the door, and greeted Jackie: "Hi, sexy! Have you brought food for your famished man."

"Why are those bones in the refrigerator?" She shot daggers at him with her sharp green eyes.

"Seemed the best place. Cool and out of sight."

"With the food?" She let the refrigerator door swing close and handed the bowl to Rob.

"You're being silly." He peeked under the foil. "Looks good! Oh, am I hungry."

"Actually, my mother made it. But I helped, I'll have you know."

Rob opened the refrigerator and placed the bowl on the top shelf. "Before we eat, I have something to show you in the cellar. Okay? Then we'll have a picnic at the dining table."

After pecking a kiss on Jackie's cheek, Rob took her hand and led her through the cellar doorway and down the old wooden steps—steps that felt unsafe because of a loose railing, steps that were blackened by years of coal dust followed by oil scum.

"I don't like this," Jackie complained. "It's dark down here."

"Watch your step."

A single light bulb, hanging over a rusty washing machine, barely illuminated the crowded cellar. Large, dark objects loomed here and there in Jackie's unclear vision. She closed her eyes again and again in an effort to adjust them to the darkness and the glare of the single, naked bulb.

"Don't let go!" she protested as Rob tried to pull away his hand after seconds of standing on the damp concrete floor—damp despite rainless days of heat. "Give me a minute."

"This way."

"What's that?"

"Just a bunch of moldy cartons."

"And that?"

"Now that may have been a fine specimen once upon a time."

"It looks like a giant bird from prehistoric times, now dead and rotting away."

"Not quite. It's a peacock chair. And you're right. It's dead and rotting away."

"A peacock chair?"

"When Aunt Marjorie no longer wanted something, it found its way up to the attic or down to the cellar. It seems that the bigger pieces came down." Rob lifted Jackie's hand and pointed. "Over there. That was a grandfather's clock, now dead or dying."

"A grandfather's clock? What a pity!"

"And there's no way Aunt Marjorie, the recluse, could have carried that clock down those cellar steps alone. No way."

"What are you suggesting? That a secret admirer sneaked into the house late at night and helped a reclusive spinster move furniture, before bedding her down?"

"Maybe."

"And how, pray tell, did this gentleman come to know his fair lady—a sick woman who never left her house?" Jackie's eyesight improved, so she dropped Rob's hand and began to maneuver among piles of stuffing from crates and boxes.

"Maybe her mailman was a voyeur who watched her dance before her mirror, and then came calling."

"Your imagination is on a rampage."

"And don't tell me yours doesn't run a little wild when you look around this place." He put his arm around her waist. "Come look at this." He led her by bundles of old newspapers to three brick archways that once fronted coal bins used before the heating system was converted to oil. "Look in there."

Jackie held tightly to Rob as she leaned forward and looked through the center archway, expecting perhaps some mummified remains. "What is it? It looks like a huge pile of rubbish, with a giant tree fungus growing out of one side of it."

"That tree fungus is a parasol, once a beautiful parasol, I suspect. But now soiled, discolored, moldy."

"More clothes? I can't believe it. And in the coal bin?" Jackie stepped closer. "I can see it now. A big pile of rotting clothes, surrounded by little piles."

"But very special clothing. I think more special than those evening gowns and negligees. Look closely. Peel off layers as I did to make those little piles, and you get all the colors and textures of Degas, soiled by mildew and decay. Rob leaned over and pushed part of the large heap aside. The sheer material was so rotted that some of it fell apart. "No matter how deep you dig, it's Degas over and over again."

"Degas?"

"All of his pastels, layers and layers of them, turned dirty. Look. Ballet dresses, slippers and ribbons. Layer after layer."

"Costumes?"

"I suppose you might say so."

"Maybe the dancing clothes of little girls."

"Not so little, I'm afraid."

Jackie stepped back while Rob continued to poke around in the pile of putrefying satins and chiffons. "Maybe Aunt Marjorie danced for her secret suitors. Or maybe she sneaked out at night and performed in the local music halls."

"We're going to start a list, Jackie—a list of all persons who might have knocked on Aunt Marjorie's door."

"You're out of your head!" Jackie put her fists on her hips. "You're a freaking loony tune! I'm beginning to think you're as weird as the rest of your family."

"Now, what's that supposed to mean?" Rob turned around and stepped toward Jackie.

"I'm beginning to wonder what I'm marrying into."

"You mean you wouldn't want me if I were a little kooky?"

"Well, I don't know. It depends on how kooky, I guess."

Rob smiled fiendishly. "Do you really want to hear about my wicked ways?"

"Stop it, Rob!" Jackie burst into laughter.

"Hey, I'm serious."

"You can't even pretend to be wicked."

Rob grinned, took Jackie into his arms, and began to suck on her neck as Dracula might. His efforts at metamorphosis failed, however, and he slipped quickly from vampire to a normal but passionate male who kissed fervently on neck, cheeks and lips.

Jackie melted. When she finally broke away, she said, "I suppose I wouldn't mind if you were a tiny bit wicked."

"You'll help me, won't you?"

"Help you do what?"

"You know. Make the list."

"You're not serious?"

"Yes I am."

"Rob!" Exasperation filled her voice.

"We'll call the utility companies, the department stores, the Post Office. We'll check their records back through the years. We want the names of mailmen, truck drivers, oil men, water-meter readers, food delivery men, anybody and everybody."

Jackie was ready to explode, but bit her lip until she was under control. With hard-won restraint she said, "We have this house to fix up and a wedding to plan. Are you forgetting?"

"Everything will get done. Don't worry." He kissed her cheek.

"Damn you!"

"We'll make a game of it."

"Game? You won't make a game of it, and you know it. I mean, I see this as some sort of compulsive behavior. You're being driven by the ghost of Aunt Marjorie."

"Aunt Marjorie isn't dead."

"Well, she might as well be."

Rob walked away from Jackie and began rooting through a pile of papers, folders, magazines and books. "First we have to find out how old those bones are. If we can pinpoint their age, we'll only have to search for people who served Marjorie during a short span of time. That'll cut our work. I want to know everyone who visited this house nine months before that baby was born."

"This is crazy!"

"Aunt Marjorie kept every receipt she ever got. Her desk, her chests, closets, file drawers are full of them. They can help us zero in on delivery times. We have to clean out all that stuff anyway."

"You're the one who said it would take ages for us to get this place in shape."

Rob stepped close to Jackie and whispered: "But you're the romantic. You're the one who first talked about Aunt Marjorie's secret lovers. You helped build ideas in my mind." He rubbed his nose against hers. "You want to find out. I know you do."

"I'd rather find out where she hid her money. Of course, maybe she had a secret sugar daddy who was also her lover. Maybe he bought her pretty clothes and jewelry and showered her with money."

Chapter Eight

Ty Scott lived in a basement apartment on Elmwood Avenue, a shady street in the town's north end. His was the largest bachelor's apartment in a 10-unit building—a brick structure dating back to the 1940s, but perfectly maintained and attractively trimmed with white window boxes crowded with red geraniums and pink petunias. He needed the extra space because of his many projects. One room held his drawing board, workbench, tools, brushes, boxes of supplies and a dozen half-finished projects, including an assortment of kites he was making for the Hampton Boys' Home. But his apartment was far from cluttered. He kept the work and storage areas cut off from his living section, neat but creative quarters accented by his graphic art designs framed in polished steel and an original Ty Scott oil painting depicting a row of tattered children sitting on a curb in front of a graffiti-splattered wall. Because the apartment was below street level, it provided high windows with deep sills where Ty had placed odd-shaped plants whose lower stems and vines hung down the walls. His modern sofa and chairs were upholstered in cream and black, and his tables and ornaments were predominantly glass. A foot-high clear-glass rooster stood alone at one end of his coffee table.

As the sun lowered itself, removing a few degrees from the day's high of 92, Ty busied himself outside, in front of the apartment building, at curbside where his shiny blue van awaited its evening run.

After-work hours were usually busy ones for Ty. Within a few days, for example, he would take an evening drive to the Boys'

Home with a van full of kites. Tonight, he would visit the Methodist Home with an important cargo aimed at putting a smile on the face of Hortense Williams, an 88-year-old widow.

Ty was about to open the driver's door when Rob's car came toot-tooting down the street and pulled to a screeching halt.

"Come join us," yelled Rob. "We're heading over to Luigi's for pizza."

Jackie smiled and waved. She was clinging all over Rob.

"Can't," Ty replied. "I got a bundle to deliver to the old ladies' home. Hop out and take a look." Ty stepped to the rear of his van. "He's a cute little fellow. Just picked him up at the animal shelter."

Rob and Jackie joined their friend in time for the door opening.

"Ta-dah!" Ty called out as he presented a fluffy pup who stood inside at the very edge, wagging his tail and tipping his head. The dog was a mixture of terrier breeds and owned plenty of whiskers. His eyes were the beseeching kind that weakened the strongest of hearts. Rob and Jackie poured out "Ahhhh" at the same time.

Excited by the attention, the dog was about to turn his wiggles into a leap when Ty grabbed his collar and held him back. "He's going to visit old Mrs. Williams for a little while tonight. Aren't you Whiskers?" Ty scratched him under the chin. "And I can't wait to see her smile."

"Oh, he's so cute!" Jackie exclaimed. "May I hold him?"

"Sure. Come on, Whiskers."

Jackie took the dog into her arms and cuddled him against her breast. "Oh, you're so nice. Yes you are."

While Jackie petted and nuzzled, Ty rattled off a few details of office business to fill in his vacationing friend, then changed the subject: "Hey, when am I going to see that house of yours?"

"We're far from anywhere at this point," Rob explained. "The work's going to take a lot longer than we figured. So you might as well come take a look. I can't hold you off forever. What say I swing by for you on Saturday?"

"I'm working the Little League that morning."

"I'll pick you up for a late lunch. How's one o'clock?"

"Make it half-past."

"I'll treat you to a burger and a shake, then show you the legacy of dear Aunt Marjorie."

"It's a deal."

"So what's going to happen to Whiskers?" Jackie asked as she returned the dog to the van. "He's adorable."

"I hope Whiskers will visit many of my friends. In the long run, I don't know what will happen to him."

The little dog tipped his head again and kept wagging his tail, even as Ty closed the back of the van.

"See you Saturday," Rob said as he and Jackie climbed into his car.

"Enjoy your pizza," Ty called out while springing eagerly behind the wheel of his van. A smile stayed on his boyish face as his friends sped away. He was a quiet buoy that kept bobbing— outwardly serene but experiencing the swells. His feelings of excitement were usually contained.

Rob kept honking until Jackie pulled his hand off the horn. "You can't do anything in a quiet way, can you? You should take lessons from your friend back there."

Ty's van bounced through suburbia and into farmland. Whiskers barked as a few Holstein cows crossed the road, lowing as they headed for pasture after late-day milking. Ty waited impatiently for the last cow to cross, then gunned his engine. The winding highway divided alfalfa from the stubble of winter wheat already harvested. A few hills and valleys led Ty from countryside into Norton, a community that offered a hospital, a cemetery, a lumberyard and the Methodist Home along the highway leading into town. The home for elderly women, set far back from the road, was well hidden by tall evergreens of great breadth.

Ty had his favorites among people on his van routes, and Hortense Williams was certainly one of them. But his thoughts were not on her as he approached the home. They had drifted elsewhere, as they did so often after seeing Rob with Jackie. That repeating voice within his brain kept telling Rob that his do-good projects were not substitutes for women, that he was not trying to escape Rob's fun-time socializing, that his after-hour travels gave him deep, inner, self-contained excitement. Besides, he still had Amy in his heart after all this time. He knew Rob wouldn't understand, would call it fantasy, would even call it sick. "But you don't understand, Rob. You just don't understand."

Pebbles from the curved driveway leading to the home pounded the bottom of the van and returned Ty's thoughts to the Widow Williams. He parked near the entrance and dashed to the rear of the van.

Ty perched the pup on his right shoulder, securing him there with a solid grip that projected his elbow into space, so that he might add drama to his entrance. He knew that the slight, hunched, four-foot-eleven woman was already downstairs prepared to greet him. Hortense always insisted on receiving her visitors in the lobby, never in her room. For a woman of 88 years, she owned vigor that generated itself when some event, no matter how small, entered her otherwise uneventful life. She would spend hours readying herself, dressing up in a pink or yellow dress that was too youthful for her, powdering her cheeks with a puff from her musical powder box, lining her lips with pink lipstick. Ty pictured her standing in the entrance hall—a spacious area with a high, intricate, inlaid wood ceiling, dark woodwork, and a dominating staircase with walnut banisters that curved to form a high balcony on the second floor.

In truth, Hortense was not standing. She was seated on a Victorian love seat near the foot of the stairs, having been there for more than a half hour. Several other women had gathered on the balcony above, each looking down in anticipation.

When Ty made his entrance, Hortense rose slowly, her eyes fastened on the pup. Her smile grew until it spread wide and brightened her entire face.

Ty smiled, too, as he looked at her tiny frame fitted in pink, a white bow under her chin, ringlets of gray-white hair atop her head. She reached out with gnarled hands, unable to keep them steady. Ohs and ahs from above echoed throughout the hall as a half dozen elderly women peered down from the high balustrade.

Hortense, who well remembered each of her beloved terriers from days long gone, was speechless. A tear rolled over her powered cheek as Ty placed Whiskers in her arms. She held the little dog tightly and allowed him to lick her face.

Chapter Nine

T artar sauce oozed from Ty's fish sandwich as he took his first bite.

"You're sloppy as hell!" Rob proclaimed as his eyes brightened with mischief. He and his friend sat in the sunlight of another hot day, up against a wide window overlooking a McDonald's play-yard for kids.

Ty wiped his lips and returned to the subject of his lunchtime discourse—Hortense Williams and the fluffy pup. "I mean, it was beautiful. I mean, I won't forget it. That's what it's all about, you know?"

"I know. I know." Rob knew only too well, having heard all the details of Whisker's visit to the Methodist Home. In fact, Rob was well acquainted with Ty's turn-ons.

"She'd laugh when Whiskers would run from her, turn around, and come dashing back wagging his tail." Ty's enthusiasm, low-keyed by most standards, was at an unusual peak because of his defensiveness. Surely he was trying to tell Rob that his needs were met. "And when Hortense held Whiskers to her cheek, letting him lick her face, all the other ladies giggled."

Rob munched on his Big Mac, swallowing quickly, hoping to talk again before Ty launched another sentence about canine capers at the old women's home. He saw good causes as vital, but not as substitutes for high living, parties and dates. "Wait until you see my overgrown garden," Rob said, tossing his words out as quickly as he could. "I've got iris tubers that must weigh five pounds each, and a trumpet vine that's pulling bricks from the wall. It's a case of survival of the fittest, with the vines and weeds winning."

Ty finished his sandwich, wiped his lips again and asked, "What street did you say?"

"Street?"

"Your house. What street is it on?"

"Juniper. Do you know Juniper Lane?"

Abruptly breaking eye contact with Rob, Ty focused on a helix-shaped sliding board in the play-yard. Slowly he said, "Yes... yes, I know Juniper Lane." He paused as his thoughts searched. "That's quite a sliding board, isn't it. Funny, I never see anyone using it."

"You'd use it, wouldn't you? If you had a kid. You should have a kid of your own."

"Don't start, Rob." Ty's eyes shot daggers at his friend. "Let's get out of here."

* * *

"Handball at the usual time?" Ty asked as the car carried him and Rob past evenly spaced maples on each side of a winding lane.

"Not this week, Ty," Rob said while turning the car from the Maplewood section of new houses into the well-established Mulberry section where Aunt Marjorie's house—now the property of Robert Putnam—rested among stately homes of assorted architecture on spacious lots heavy with shrubs and trees.

"Uh-oh, I knew it. And you said marriage wouldn't change anything."

"I'm not married yet."

"That's the point."

"I'll put handball in my marriage contract. Honest. One night out, every other week, for handball with Ty. How's that?"

Ty laughed. "Fat chance."

The car glided along, hugging the curb as it neared Rob's house.

"This is it," Rob announced as he brought the car to a halt. "On the right."

Ty, whose boyish face was already fair skinned, became suddenly ashen as if a giant leech had sucked away his blood, turning his lips cold despite the summer heat.

Rob hurried from the car, slammed the door and raced around

the front end as he motioned to Ty. "Come on!" He started up the walkway, only to stop and look back when Ty didn't follow. "Hey, aren't you coming?" After staring at his friend for a moment, he stepped back toward the car with puzzlement bringing ridges to his forehead. "Are you okay?" As he spoke, his eyes asked the same question. "Ty, what is it?"

"It's nothing." Ty's words were hardly audible. His lips barely moved.

"What?"

"It's nothing." Ty forced a smile and stepped from the car. "I guess I didn't quite expect this."

"Expect what?"

"This house."

"What do you mean?"

"Well, it's a very nice house. It's big. It's more than I expected."

"You sure you're okay?

"I'm fine. I just wanted to take it all in for a moment." Ty's word were not in sync with his expression. "I just wanted an overall look."

"Well, come on." Rob hurried toward the door. "Wait until you see the inside."

The word "inside" seemed to immobilize Ty. He stopped abruptly, as if his feet were stuck in wet concrete. The beads of sweat on his forehead and upper lip were not from the summer heat.

Rob unlocked and opened the door, then looked back. "What the hell is it with you?"

Ty gained a modicum of control and stepped forward.

"You look ready for the undertaker," Rob said. "Are you sick?"

"Yes. I think I'm sick. It's my... It's my stomach. Something I ate, I guess."

"Can I do something?"

"No. Well, maybe I could use a drink of water. It's the heat, y'know."

"Come on inside. The trees keep the house cool."

Ty followed Rob, but once inside the house he heard little of what the new homeowner had to say. His eyes were fixed on the staircase as if held there by a ghostly vision.

"I'm going to put bookshelves here and there, on each side of the fireplace." Rob spoke with fervor, suddenly wrapped up in the excitement of his remodeling projects. "I've started to paint over here. See? I'm using oyster white on the walls. It'll give a nice background for paintings—maybe one of your paintings, eh?"

Suddenly aware that he was getting no meaning from Rob's words, Ty tried to tune in to the rantings about paint, wallpaper and carpet. "Sounds nice," he said, not really tying his response to anything in particular. He didn't want to ask Rob to repeat the details of colors and textures that he had vaguely heard. "About that water?"

"There's a glass on the sink in the kitchen. Help yourself."

Rob walked to the dining room where he stood admiring the table while waiting for Ty. The wait was longer than it should have been, but there were plenty of thoughts to occupy his mind.

"Look at this table," Rob said as Ty joined him. "Isn't it a beauty? Jackie waxed it yesterday. She polished the silver, too." He pointed to the tea service that captured bright luster from the garden. "The house is full of treasures." He stepped to the double doors. "Come look at this overrun garden."

Ty tried to concentrate on Rob's enthusiastic chatter. He grasped words here and there between and among his thoughts. Joining his friend, he looked out at the garden.

"Can you believe that?" Rob asked. "What a jungle. I've started to pull weeds at the far end. But you'd hardly know it." He opened the doors and stepped into the hot sunlight. "I want you to take a look at something I dug up."

Ty followed Rob to a peach basket next to a clump of pink phlox in the center of the garden. He watched as Rob reached into the basket and lifted a large, dark cluster of warty growths, remindful of stubby, gnarled cigars and deformed potatoes, all stuck together.

"What is it?" Ty asked.

"It's the largest I've ever seen." Holding the massive cluster in both hands, Rob examined it closely and then extended his arms as if offering it to Ty. "It must weigh five pounds."

"But what is it?"

"Tubers of a single iris plant."

"A root?"

"You can have it if you want it. Plant it at the old ladies' home. They'd love it. They could watch it grow."

Ty forced a smile.

"I'll put it in the sink until we leave. Okay?" Rob moved quickly into the house as he said, "It's not the only thing I've pulled from the garden." He was tempted to tell Ty about the skull, but held back. His anxious expression changed when he walked into the living room and found Ty at the foot of the stairs. "Go ahead. Go on up."

Ty didn't respond.

"Are you okay? " Rob could not decipher the peculiar look on Ty's face.

Ty awoke from his thoughts. "I really should go."

"Don't you want to see the second floor? Come on. I'll show you the room I'm camping in. It's a mess, but I sleep well after pushing myself all day."

"I told Doc Anderson I'd stop to see a deaf girl who refuses help."

"I thought you had the afternoon free?"

"I do. In a way, I do. It's just... Well, I forgot about the girl. If I could squeeze it in. You know?" Ty rattled off disjointed words. "Tomorrow's not good."

Rob still couldn't decode Ty's strange expression. "What is it with you? I've never seen you like this."

"I guess I... I guess I really would like to see the upstairs." Ty had suddenly shifted gears. He began a fast climb, taking two steps at once, deciding to avoid eye contact with Rob and move quickly from room to room.

Chapter Ten

Rob and Jackie decided on a picnic in the park instead of another one on the living room floor. It would be a pleasant change, they were sure. They even switched from work clothes to clean white shorts and jersey tops. Despite Jackie's protests, they did, however, take cartons of Aunt Marjorie's secrets with them so they could keep sorting through materials while sitting on the grass under a big oak tree near the duck pond.

The evening of the picnic came one day after Rob had packed a small bone chip, a pottery fragment and an Indian arrowhead in a padded envelope and mailed it to his fraternity brother, "Skinny-dip" Jones, now Dr. James Harrington Jones of the Anthropology Department at Cornell University.

As they drove to the park, Rob explained: "Sending the pottery chip and the arrowhead is pure subterfuge. It's a ruse. It's my diversionary tactic. In fact, I've had that arrowhead since I was a kid. I don't know much about carbon-fourteen dating, if that's what they use today to determine age. Actually, I figure they have much more sophisticated methods now. Whatever the case, 'Skinny-dip' is good at that stuff. That's his field."

"Will he know that the bone is human?"

"I don't think so. It's just a tiny fragment. I don't think he'll give it a second thought. He'll just run time tests on three things I supposedly dug up in the garden."

A Canadian cold front had pushed the daytime high from yesterday's 92 degrees to today's 78. Evening picnic time in the park was cooler yet, much to the delight of Rob and Jackie. A breeze stirred the maples as Rob parked the car near the edge of the pond. Before unloading the boxes and the picnic basket, the hungry twosome stood at the side of the car and let the breeze blow their hair and refresh their bodies.

They placed the blanket under their favorite oak tree on a slope overlooking the pond where lily pads and mallard ducks floated on shimmering water. As Jackie opened the basket, Rob returned to the car for another box of Aunt Marjorie's letters and clippings.

They ate first, relishing every bit of their potato salad, ham sandwiches and hard-boiled eggs—all purchased at the deli for lack of preparation time. Hours of work at the house and only coffee at noon, not to mention the cooler weather, had nearly doubled their appetites.

Jackie pushed away a box of Aunt Marjorie's hoardings as she stretched out on the blanket. Her actions sent several messages to Rob: That she wanted nothing to do with Marjorie, that she felt pleasantly relaxed after filling her belly, that she was ready to tease, tickle and toy.

"We have work to do," Rob said.

"Not yet." She took his hand and kissed it.

He leaned over her and kissed her on the cheek, then the lips. "I love you."

"Not as much as I love you."

Rob gazed down into her eyes. "More."

"That's impossible."

He smiled broadly, then lay next to her, taking her hand in his. Each time he squeezed he sent a silent message that she returned.

A crow, perched atop a distant pine, called out as it surveyed its territory, cawing and cawing to warn against intrusion.

The sun was low and the shadows long by the time Rob began to sort through a carton of Aunt Marjorie's papers.

"More letters to movie stars," he commented as he rooted quickly through the box, hoping to find something more revealing. "I think these are all addressed to Tyrone Power. Can you believe that?"

Jackie sighed as she pushed herself up from the blanket. "I'm not in the mood, but you're nudging me into it. Shove that one over here." She pointed, then reached out and grabbed the smallest of the boxes—

a shoe box tied with a faded blue ribbon. With effort, she slipped the ribbon from the box and lifted the lid. But before starting her perusal, she yanked a flower stalk from a plantain weed and tickled Rob's ear with it. She giggled as he swatted himself, then she tickled his neck.

"I know it's you," he said. "Cut it out and get to work or I'll toss you in the pond."

"You wouldn't dare."

"Try me!"

She bit the back of his neck.

"Ouch! You're asking for it!" Rob leaped to his feet, picked up Jackie and started toward the pond, only to drop her quickly.

"God, you're heavy!"

"I am not!"

He embraced her with fervor, kissed her hard, then took her by the hand and led her back to the blanket where he pointed to the shoe box.

"Okay," she said contritely.

Jackie sat cross-legged on the blanket, forced a serious expression in an effort to set a serious mood, and began to sort through clippings from the shoe box. Her legs tired quickly, and she wondered how Indians sat that way. After shuffling and wiggling her way back to the tree, she leaned against the trunk and stretched her legs all the way to Rob, who was reading Aunt Marjorie's department store receipts. She kicked off her flats and was tempted to rub Rob's back with her toes. But instead she sighed again and began concentrating on her reading assignment.

Within seconds Jackie said, "Rob, this is strange."

"What's that?"

"All the clippings on top are about the same thing."

"What?"

"A baby left at Willowood Hospital."

"Let me see." Rob pushed himself close to Jackie.

"Here, look. And here's another. And this one, too. Why would she keep all these? Listen to this. 'A newborn male infant was found early this morning on the steps of Willowood Hospital by a Westside nurse as she arrived for duty.' And get this headline from a follow up. 'Police have no clues to Baby Willow's mom.' Baby Willow?"

"This one says the baby was probably only a couple days old."

"Rob, are you thinking what I'm thinking?"

"I'm not sure. What are you thinking?"

"That maybe Aunt Marjorie had more than one baby."

"We don't know that Aunt Marjorie had any babies."

"Maybe she sneaked out of the house at midnight and carried the baby all the way to the hospital."

"Don't jump to conclusions. And don't let your imagination run wild. Maybe she was deeply taken by this newspaper story. Maybe it had nothing to do with her. Maybe she was moved by the thought of a little baby being deposited at a hospital door."

"This clip has a date on it. September, 14, 1979. How old was Marjorie in 1979?"

"Fourteen years ago? I don't know. In her late forties, I guess. Women don't have babies in their late forties."

"Some do." Jackie looked up into the tree branches as her mind wove tales. "Was she still beautiful then?"

"Oh, yes!" Rob was fast to answer even though he was engrossed in reading. "I saw her in her forties. She was more than beautiful." He put aside the clippings and focused on distance as his thoughts traveled back. "I was only in my early teens, but I remember. I could never forget."

"Did you have sex with her?"

Rob shot a fiery glance at Jackie. "Why would you suggest such a thing? Of course I didn't have sex with her. She was my aunt. I was only a kid."

"Love-starved old maids have been known to use young teenagers."

"You're sick! Anyway, it didn't happen. I wouldn't lie to you about something like that."

"But something happened. I see it in your eyes every now and then. Did she try to seduce you?"

"Hell no!"

"Are you sure?"

"Yes."

"Really?"

Rob didn't answer. He simply played with a blade of grass.

"You're not sure, are you?"

"You've got a vivid imagination." He began to tickle her, then kissed her about the neck—an effort to change the mood, and maybe the conversation. "Come on." He sprang to his feet, grabbed her arm and pulled. "Race you to the pond."

The orange-red sun was slipping beneath the horizon, turning a few streaky clouds on fire and reflecting brilliance in the pond water—brilliance broken by ripples as mallards paddled north to south. Tall pines were but silhouettes against the glowing sky.

Rob and Jackie ran to the edge of the pond, and a few ducks turned toward them in search of food. Dragon flies flew their jerky stops-and-starts among the water lilies, and fireflies flashed here and there as the night grew dark.

Chapter Eleven

Auburn hair? Deaf? Dr. Anderson's description was so exact. It perfectly fit the image that Ty had carried for such a long time. No matter what it took, he had to find out if he and the doctor had encountered the same blue-eyed lass. He parked his van near a thicket of sassafras and sumac along winding Redrock Road west of town. Despite a late evening haze, he could see the Harrison house in the distance, around the next curve, set far back from the road, just as Dr. Anderson had described it. Though poorly paved and patched, the county road was actually in better condition than many arteries serving Redrock Township, the area's worst pocket of economic depression. The houses along Redrock Road were well separated, often by small patches of truck farmland or scrubby brush, occasionally by junkyards or scorched earth.

Puzzling over strategy was nothing new for Ty. In his quiet, thoughtful way he usually wove a web that worked. At the moment, however, he was stumped. He first blamed his inability to plot a plan on interference from thoughts that had been stirring a storm in his brain—thoughts from the past that disturbed his sleep. But in time he came to realize that his state of mind was a weak excuse, and that maybe no adequate approach existed. He argued with himself over the right to enter another man's home, the right to force his will. His best answer was that justification lay within his own moral code.

This was different from his other causes because of his deep emotional involvement—in Rob's way of thinking an obsessive involvement, a fantasy now long gone. It was different in that Ty couldn't predict the outcome as he could with other causes, those that gave him that internal satisfaction, that buoyancy.

Ty had never found it so difficult to park in front of a house, leave his van and knock on a door. He was well aware that while he was a man on a mission, he was a small man short on credentials. He represented no school, no medical center, no government agency.

Something gave him the spark to start his van and slowly move it toward the Harrison driveway. Again he parked it along the road, somewhat fearful of alerting Sam Harrison by driving right up to the porch. The van leaned toward a roadside gully, for the shoulder was soft and crumbling, but Ty left it there, hoping it would not continue to tilt. He began a hesitant walk toward the house, wondering what part curiosity played in his current quest. Surely he wanted to see for himself if Amy Harrison was indeed the blue-eyed lass with the auburn hair who had caught his eye at the county fair.

Ty's eyes glanced from window to window as he examined the wooden house and its crooked porch. The weatherworn clapboard had once been white, and the red-brick chimney had once been aligned with the roof and missing no mortar.

He scolded himself for thinking that perhaps he was the knight-on-white-horse who could rescue a fair maiden imprisoned in a badly blighted area. That was not his current mission, he told himself. Though he was never the patronizing type, he warned himself about showing the least touch of condescension. If Harrison was the hostile father he had met at the county fair, then perhaps the man was proud as well as stubborn.

Lights flashed on downstairs in the two-story house as Ty neared the splintered steps, causing his heart to increase its beat.

Again hesitating, Ty was slow to lift his fist and knock on the door. He tapped lightly at first, then added a touch more force. Stepping back as the door opened, he immediately recognized Sam Harrison from their brief encounter at the fair. The tall, gaunt man with receding salt-and-pepper hair stood staring at Ty. He had intense eyes, especially for strangers. He said nothing.

"Mr. Harrison?"

"Yes?" Cigarette smoke and years of work at the Nettleton Wallboard and Insulation Company had marred Harrison's deep voice with the sound of scratchy grit. The outlawing of asbestos had come too late to save his lungs.

Ty searched closely for any indication that Harrison might recognize him. "My name's Ty Scott. I'm a volunteer with a couple agencies in town, and I was wondering if I could speak with you about your daughter."

"Who sent you here?"

Ty's eyes had adjusted enough so that he could see the features of a man who looked far older than his 45 years. Despite the backlight that nearly turned Harrison into a silhouette, Ty saw hollow cheeks, high cheekbones and well-arched brows. He saw a man whose bony shoulders held underwear straps that widened into a soiled undershirt that covered a concave chest and bulging belly. And he grew certain that Sam Harrison did not recognize him.

"I came on my own." Ty tried to be forthright, but his soft voice falsely portrayed meekness.

"Anderson sent you, didn't he?"

"Not really. I know Dr. Anderson well because of my volunteer efforts, and he told me about Amy. But I came on my own. Please let me explain. May I come in?"

"Anderson had no right to send you. He had no right to talk to my neighbors. He had no right to touch her ears. Now you get off my porch."

"But you don't understand. With an operation she might be able to hear. There's no guarantee, but..."

"It's up to God, mister. Not some doctor." Harrison began to close the door. "Now you get off my porch."

"Wait! Please."

"You got no business here." Harrison opened the door again and stepped toward Ty in an effort to force him toward the steps. "Now you leave us alone."

As Ty moved back he caught a glimpse of auburn hair. Amy appeared in the living room, standing near the steps to the second floor. Ty's look was brief, but her stature, her shape and the flow of her hair made him certain.

"You got some gall, mister," Harrison uttered. "I don't take kindly to strangers comin' knockin' on my door. I don't like do-gooders, 'specially those tryin' to tell me how to run my life."

"I'm sorry, Mr. Harrison. I came because I care, because I want to help."

"We don't need your help."

Ty turned slowly and walked down the porch steps. As he made his way along the dirt driveway, he felt empty inside and shamefully incompetent. He could feel the pounding of his heart and told himself that it was not only his confrontation with Harrison that had quickened the beat; it was also his brief glimpse of Amy.

Midway along the drive he glanced back and saw the dark image of Harrison on the porch. He continued his steady pace, refusing to hurry, though he was anxious to crawl into his van and feel secure behind its wheel. As he neared the road, he jumped when something stirred in a patch of weeds and rustled the leaves. A jolt sent a shiver through his body, and he stood still for a moment at the end of the driveway, trying to convince himself that it was just a toad or garter snake.

Gathering his thoughts, he stepped toward his car, wondering why the fair Amy, so perky yet soft, should live in such a house. He would never have guessed, and could not reason why.

Once in the van, Ty was quick to start the engine, sending pebbles flying as he drove west on Redrock Road. Though he was heading away from home, he didn't care, for he wanted time to think.

Sam Harrison remained on his porch long after Ty vanished from view. Though Ty had caused Sam's anger to peak again, it often flared and was always there, an undercurrent within him. Bitterness had ingrained itself in him long before the death of his wife, a woman of breeding who had married far beneath her station, a woman disowned and disinherited by her family. His failures, his slippage through the years, his descent into a life far lower than humble had bred a strange mixture of self-hatred and false pride cloaked in self-righteousness. His protection of Amy was fanatical and justified in his mind by his rigid religious beliefs.

Ty drove toward the hazy streak of salmon-pink on the western horizon, barely noticing occasional house lights widely scattered on each side of the county road. Stubby trees were now dark images against a darkening sky.

Having seldom experienced emptiness, Ty didn't like the feeling. He knew that his ineptitude at the Harrison house had pulled him down, but something beyond that was draining his spirit. He was certain that his 30th birthday played a role, but only because it coincided with Rob's upcoming wedding. No matter how many times he scoffed at the idea, Rob's getting married was giving him a strange, unfamiliar case of loneliness. The feelings kept intruding despite a heavy work schedule and busy after-hours overloaded with do-good efforts.

And, on top of all that, came a traumatic dose of haunting recollections—images resurrected from his days as a newsboy.

Ty glided his van to a halt at the side of the road, near a pile of rubber tires. He leaned his head on the wheel and tried to tell himself that the waves that had always buoyed him were not subsiding. Unconvinced, he whispered, "Fuck."

Chapter Twelve

Rob had arranged a dozen stacks of receipts on the dining room table hours before the letter arrived. Each pile represented a different delivery service—department store, utility, food market, heating oil, whatever. The chart on the oversized pad of paper in front of him listed assignments for Jackie and himself—assignments that could now be carried out thanks to the letter from "Skinny-dip" Jones.

Waiting anxiously, Rob occasionally drummed on the table with his fingers while watching the shadows of the stacks grow longer as the late-day sun sank behind the garden wall.

When the front door slammed, Rob pulled the letter from the pocket of his paint-splattered shirt, and when Jackie entered the room, he waved it at her and said, "Sit down and listen."

Although Rob's eagerness aroused curiosity in Jackie, she took time to compliment him: "The walls look great. Nice paint job." She sniffed the smell of latex.

"Come on, now. Sit down and pay attention."

"Okay! Okay!" Jackie took the seat opposite Rob and gave him a kittenish smile. "You could have said something nice about the sparkling prisms." She glanced up at the chandelier.

"They're fine," he snapped. Immediately realizing his brusqueness, he spoke with more feeling: "They're beautiful. You did a great job."

Jackie had spent hours polishing the prisms, after days of debate with Rob over whether to keep the chandelier. They had finally decided to live with it awhile before launching another debate.

Rob unfolded the letter and read: "Dear Moon... "

"Moon?"

"They used to call me Moon."

"Who?"

"My fraternity brothers."

"Why?"

"Jackie, please! I'll tell you later." Rob didn't hide his annoyance. "Come on, now. Will you listen?"

"Moon? You don't want to tell me, do you?"

"God damn it, Jackie! Swallow your tongue for a minute!"

Jackie folded her hands together, placed them on the table, struck a pose of obedience, and gave her undivided attention to Rob.

"Dear... Dear so-'n-so: Nice to hear from you. Congrats on your upcoming wedding. I hope to be there to tie your socks in knots and soak your underwear in toilet water. Now to the point of your letter. The piece of pottery you sent is modern-day terra cotta, only a few years old. Sorry. No big find there. The arrowhead dates back to circa fifteen hundred. I'm sure it's Iroquois, but I'm not certain which tribe. That's your only old piece. I'm afraid the bone is of recent origin, probably only a dozen years old, maybe fifteen, and that's partly testwork and partly guesswork. But I'm usually accurate. I haven't made many mistakes. Sorry I don't have more exciting news for you."

Rob stopped reading and looked up at Jackie. "Now we can get to work and seek out those who served Aunt Marjorie during the late seventies and early eighties. I've given you one department store. I'll take the other two. I've divided the utilities."

Jackie's eyes flashed suddenly, but not from eagerness to take on the work that lay ahead. "Rob, those years! Don't you realize?"

"What?"

"Twelve to fifteen years ago. The late seventies and early eighties. Think about it."

"Well, let's see." Rob counted on his fingers. "That's when I was twelve to fifteen years old, or something like that. And Aunt Marjorie was in her late forties."

"Damn, Rob! Don't you see? The clippings about the baby dropped at Willowood Hospital. They were dated September of seventy-nine."

"I'll be damned!"

"Both babies were born about the same time."

"Twins, do you think?"

"Maybe. But maybe not. They could have been born a year or two apart. That is, if Skinny-dip is anywhere near accurate in his dating. Jesus. I wonder."

"There's a connection, I'm sure."

"Maybe. Maybe not. We might be letting our thoughts run wild."

Chapter Thirteen

Ty had switched supermarkets when the new Great Deal store opened at Maple and Overbrook streets. The lower prices were worth the extra mile drive.

Standing between the cereal shelves and the coffee display, he tried to concentrate on his late-day shopping. He was annoyed with himself for allowing troublesome feelings to tamper with his brain. Cursing his self pity, he told himself to practice the upbeat lessons he so often preached to others. But reason failed to override his emotions.

Ty glanced at his list, then pushed his cart toward the dairy section, unaware of the shoppers around him until a flash of auburn hair jolted him.

Forgetting about milk and eggs, Ty left his cart in mid-aisle and took off after a young woman who disappeared around the end of the pickle display. He glanced down the next aisle, but saw no auburn hair.

It couldn't have been her, he told himself. Obviously his mind was playing tricks, a sure sign that recent happenings were messing with his head. Anyway, he had never seen her shopping before. But then this was only his third visit to the Great Deal market.

Ty started toward the next aisle, then stopped abruptly, chastising himself for his foolishness. He walked back to the dairy foods, telling himself that he had seen nothing, or perhaps hair similar to Amy's, or maybe a flash of auburn in his mind's eye.

He looked at his list, put cartons of milk and eggs into his basket, and tried to concentrate on his shopping. But his brain wouldn't allow him total freedom, and by the time he pushed his cart toward the checkout counters, he had scrapped his list and made some hasty choices, including a bottle of clam juice and a jar of pickled okra. He fidgeted as he waited in line behind a well-rounded woman whose cart was heaped well above the brim.

Suddenly Ty's heart muscles twitched and his scalp tingled. There, to his right, at the next checkout counter, was Amy Harrison. She had just paid her bill and was lifting a bag of groceries into her arms. Briefly, she glanced his way, but apparently looked beyond him. Her eyes were as pure blue as he remembered, and her skin was fair and smooth.

Trapped in line between the big woman and an impatient teenager, Ty was frustrated beyond reason. He shifted nervously as the skinny, long-haired male behind him popped gum. The equally skinny checkout woman with the frizzy blonde hair was as slow as a pregnant slug. Ty could desert his cart and push his way out, but how would he communicate with Amy anyway? He thought about all sorts of signals, expressions and motions, but realized that such frantic efforts would probably chase her away. His annoyance with the cashier and the large woman grew as they debated the price of a cantaloupe. Finally, with no progress in sight and Army leaving the store, Ty left his groceries and pushed and excused his way to the exit.

Outside, Ty watched Amy as she looked this way and that, obviously seeking someone. He suspected she was searching for her father, and he kept his distance as he tried to fathom an approach. Timidly he stepped toward her just as a pickup truck turned from among the parked cars and aimed itself at them. Instinctively he stepped back as his heartbeat quickened. His frustration reached a new high, intensified by his inability to act and by the intrusion of Sam Harrison.

Ty watched as Amy, her pale blue dress rippling in the early evening breeze, struggled to place the grocery bag in the truck, hoist herself and take her place next to her father.

Inside the store, Ty continued to watch through the plate glass until the truck was gone. He then sought his cart, eventually finding it shoved up against a display of paper towels. Tempted to push over the precarious pile of towels, he bit his lower lip, thought better of it, and grabbed the cart handle with unnecessary force, hurting his fingers as he squeezed the metal. He looked about, fearful that he had displayed his vexation.

As Ty waited in line again—this time behind a trim nurse with a light load—he wondered about Amy: Did she remember him from the night at the fair?

* * *

Later, while driving his van, Ty was still fixated on Amy. His mind kept flashing pictures of the county fair: the Ferris wheel, the blue-ribbon pigs, and Amy trying to win a stuffed panda at the dart booth.

"Let me try for you," he had urged, not aware of her deafness. When she ignored him, he tried again. "Please. I'm pretty good at hitting balloons." Not until her father appeared and pulled her away as she struggled quickly with sign language did Ty realize. He stood there gaping. Then, with adrenaline pushing up his blood pressure, he tossed money at the bald dwarf in the booth, grabbed the darts, and fired at the balloons as if he were attacking red and yellow demons from outer space.

As he drove along Overbrook Street, houses flashing by at left and right, Ty allowed the images of the fair to repeat again and again. He remembered running through the crowd, gripping the panda in one hand, searching for Amy from one end of the fairgrounds to the other—near the tumblebug ride and the whip, at the pie-and-cake display, by the freak show, near the exit gates.

Then suddenly, there she was, auburn hair bobbing in the throng beyond the cotton candy booth, shimmering in the colorful midway lights that increased their glow as daylight faded. He wanted to run right up to her and toss the panda into her arms, but hesitated because of her father. Instead, he watched and followed, hoping that in some way, for some reason, she and her father would become separated.

Ty trailed them for more than an hour, praying for a moment when he might slip her the panda. He watched them eat hot dogs, followed them in and out of cattle and sheep barns, saw them taste prize-winning pies, and looked from afar as they rested on a bench.

It was near the Ferris wheel that Ty watched them go their separate ways, into the men's and women's toilets. His emotions peaked. He could barely contain his anxiety as he stationed himself just outside the women's room, realizing only too well that men usually exit before woman. But fate was with him. Amy was first to appear.

Ty thrust the panda at her, bringing fear to her eyes. But within seconds his smile turned her shocked expression into a warm glow. She hesitated, then took the stuffed animal and held it against her breast.

Hoping she could read lips, Ty carefully pronounced his words: "Who are you? Where do you live?"

She smiled and tipped her head.

"Please tell me who you are," Ty begged. He looked into her eyes, and tried to take her hand, but she pulled away. He stepped toward her and reached out again, touching her fingers and feeling a surge from his belly and weakness in his knees.

She shook her head, stepped back, yet continued to offer a warm smile.

"What do you think you're doing?" barked Sam Harrison as he pushed through the crowd. He seized the panda and shoved it at Ty, then grabbed Amy by the arm and pulled her away.

"But you don't understand." Ty tried to explain, but it was too late. Amy looked back twice and smiled timidly as her father pulled her away.

That was three years ago when Amy was perhaps 18 or 19 years old. Today, Ty still could not believe his assertive actions that night. The girl-of-the-fair remained a part of him, but as time passed thoughts of her became doubly suppressed—first because of Rob's constant but well-meant harassment, then because of Ty's fear that she was forever gone from his life.

Ty parked his van in front of his apartment, but remained in the driver's seat as images continued to occupy his mind. When his thoughts finally returned to the present, he told himself to telephone the library and inquire about books on sign language. Better yet, he could call the Society for the Deaf. Or, why not use tomorrow's lunch break to drive to the Deaf School?

* * *

Hours later, in the darkness of his room, he struggled to capture sleep. He knew a heavy workday lay ahead. A deadline loomed for a brochure on a new puppy formula. The pieces and parts wouldn't fall together, even after days of playing with shapes, sizes and colors. He had always tested his sketches and layouts on Rob, so he felt justified in blaming his buddy's absence for his lack of decision. No doubt other factors impaired his efficiency—Rob's house and upcoming marriage, not to mention Amy.

Sleep came by 2 a.m., but it was racked by disturbing dreams, visions of two women—one a sultry beauty in black chiffon, looking down from a staircase, her black hair flowing to a point below her shoulders, a slight smile on her moistened lips, a look of come-hither in her eyes; the other an auburn-haired lass with china-doll complexion, in a pale blue dress, fearfully darting from doorway to doorway in a vacant, maze-like house without windows. First one, then the other. One dominant and aggressive, even when motionless. The forceful figure kept erasing the transient one, always returning just as Ty reached toward the auburn hair, always destroying a chance meeting, always standing in the way, and finally weakening Ty to the point where he had little energy for the chase.

Ty woke exhausted and wet with sweat at 4:10 a.m. He stumbled from bed, felt his way in the dark, bumped into a hassock in his living room, yet didn't turn on a light until he reached his kitchen where he opened the refrigerator door and grabbed a can of beer. As he drank, he played with the idea of giving up sleep for his drawing board, since ideas sometimes jelled in the wee hours. But he knew that might totally wipe out the coming day, so he opted for bed, finished his beer, and groped his way back to his moist sheets.

Again slumber came slowly, and again it brought dreams. The provocative woman on the staircase beckoned Ty to her bedroom. There, he saw her image in the vanity mirror. When the reflection blurred, he tried to crawl into the mirror to chase the fleeting figure of a girl with auburn hair. But the image of the dark-haired woman reshaped itself, and the frightening allurement once again controlled the moment.

Chapter Fourteen

The Green Acres Nursing Home was a square slice of pound cake (with windows) plopped on a treeless stretch of dry land that once sprouted corn and oats. The summer heat had burnt the newly planted grass, turning it to dust. A pair of stunted junipers, both slightly scorched, marked the entrance to the unimaginative structure of cream-colored concrete. Rob's car rested on a patch of asphalt that had lifted and lowered itself often during the summer heat, and now, with September approaching, was an expanse of bumps. This was his first visit to the nursing home, and his first feeling of guilt since inheriting Aunt Marjorie's house. There was something wrong about her being here and his being there, but he placated the feeling by telling himself that the house had been purchased by his grandfather, not by Marjorie. Anyway, he would move his aunt to a better home when and if he found her money. Of course, if she had used up all her father's saving, then whose fault was it anyway? Get off the guilt trip, he told himself. After all, Aunt Marjorie had never meant anything to him— anything but an unshakable image from a curious night that unleashed particular feelings in his teenage body.

Rob stood waiting in a beige sitting room supplied with inexpensive, modern, squared-off, beige chairs and a beige sofa on a beige rug. He finally sat on one of the chairs, next to a large plastic plant—a split-leaf philodendron—one of several that decorated the room. The nurse, or whatever she was, had told him to wait until the end of "feeding time"—words that suggested the zoo or a cattle barn. He pictured someone shoving mushy feed into Marjorie's mouth while she driveled. Such thoughts carried him back to that unforgettable day when piled-up newspapers and junk mail had led police and him to Marjorie, who was on the toilet, her head in the sink, an American flag wrapped around her breasts, a rhinestone tiara in her hair, drivel on her lips and chin.

Major among Rob's hopes was that his aunt would have a lucid moment or two during his visit. But the nursing home director had given him little hope, explaining that only twice had his staff recorded what appeared to be brief lucidity.

Rob stood again, then sat and crossed his legs, only to uncross them seconds later. He looked at his watch. Forty-five minutes had passed since he entered the building.

"She's ready to see you now," said the big, broad-shouldered, mannish woman as she stepped into the room. Dressed in an oversized, white uniform, the woman was built to lift and move immobile patients. "We've moved Miss Worth into the solarium so that your visit might be comfortable."

Rob followed the care-worker down a hospital-white corridor, past doors at left and right, most of which were closed or only partially opened. Just once did he see far enough into a room to catch a glimpse of a patient—an old woman, prone on a metal bed squeezed into scant space. No wonder they moved Aunt Marjorie to the solarium, he thought.

The big woman left Rob at the end of the corridor, backed off, and hurried away.

Rob stepped into the bright solarium, where sunlight streamed through the windows and straggly begonias struggled to grow on the sills. Lounge chairs formed a semicircle, and a porch rocker owned a corner all to itself. But Rob saw little other than Aunt Marjorie, who had been placed center-stage for his convenience. He stepped right up and took a hard look at a woman strapped into a wheelchair, her head hanging to one side, a nervous twitch moving her lips and fingers. The curves and lines of her facial features were still those of a beautiful woman, but crow's-feet told her age—somewhere in the early to mid-sixties, if Rob's calculations were correct. Her eyes were empty. But the most striking change, one that disturbed her nephew, was her short, unevenly cropped hair, dark but gray at the roots. Without long hair, she simply wasn't Marjorie Worth. Rob also sensed that the white terry cloth robe would not have been her choice. Never would she have wanted to be seen this way, he told himself as he looked about for a chair.

Choosing the rocker, Rob moved it close to the wheelchair, sat and rocked for more than a minute before he flatly stated, "I'm your nephew Robby."

Marjorie failed to react. Her eyes focused on nothing within the solarium.

"I'm Robby, your sister Emily's son. Do you remember me?"

His aunt remained unresponsive.

"Do you remember your sister Emily? Do you remember Jack— your brother Jack?"

Rob thought he saw a slight change in Marjorie at the mention of Jack, but he wasn't certain. He was almost sure that her cheek twitched. Shifting the rocker, he placed himself in a better position to watch her eyes. "You remember your brother Jack, don't you?"

Her eyes remained the same.

"When I was in my early teens, I came to your house. I knocked, while my mother waited on the walkway. No one answered, and I can still remember my mother saying, 'Go on in. Go on in.' I pushed the door and it opened. I looked back as my mother walked away. I stepped inside and saw you standing on the staircase, dressed in something soft and black. You smiled at me. Do you remember?"

Marjorie's eyes seemed to move slightly.

"I didn't know why I was there. But you were kind to me."

Her neck muscles tightened, and Rob wondered if she were trying to lift her head. He was certain he saw a flicker of light in her eyes.

"Now you've given me your house. I don't know why. But thank you. Thank you very much." Rob felt uneasy, and he looked down at the floor. "I'm about to get married. So, it's a wonderful wedding gift."

Marjorie's eyes focused on Rob, but he was unaware of it until he lifted his head and again looked into her face. Her lips, drawn down to one side, had parted slightly.

"You do hear me, don't you?" He sensed that she wanted to respond. "Your father gave you a lot of dolls, didn't he? Did he bring you a new one every night?" Then suddenly, Rob blurted out the haunting question: "Did you bury a baby in the garden?"

Fear flashed in her eyes but for a instant. Then her eyes were blank again, and Rob knew that he had lost her, and he damned himself for his impatience.

Chapter Fifteen

Again Ty parked his van along the gully on Redrock Road, across from the dirt driveway leading to Sam Harrison's weatherworn house. But this time it was early morning, not evening. Gray skies hid the rising sun and threatened rain. As Ty waited, he took one last look at the book on sign language, concentrating on a few hand symbols that he had tried to memorize over the past few days. Then he closed the book and slid it under his suit coat on the passenger seat, and once again picked up the letter that had taken him hours to complete at his drawing board—a letter of beautifully drawn signs copied from the book. Dressed for work, he loosened his blue necktie, then unfolded the letter for the seventh time, studied it, folded it again, and slipped it into his shirt pocket.

Just as he was about to reach for the book again, he heard the roar of an engine. His body quaked, then stiffened as his eyes turned toward the house and searched the landscape. When he saw the pickup truck bouncing down the driveway toward him, he slouched low in the seat, hiding himself from view. Within seconds he heard the motor race by him. He waited, then lifted himself in time to see the truck disappear in the distance.

Without hesitating, he reached behind his seat and grabbed the stuffed panda that he had kept hidden in his closet for three years.

He strode boldly at first as he walked toward the house, only to waver slightly about halfway up the drive. At the porch steps he tapped his shirt pocket twice to make certain that the letter was still there, then began to puzzle over how he would draw Amy to the door if she couldn't hear him. Telling himself that she would probably feel the vibrations of heavy pounding, he transferred the panda from his right to left hand, mounted the steps, crossed the porch, and knocked on the door before allowing any doubt to stifle his newborn courage.

No one responded to his knocking. He stepped to a window, tried to peer through the translucent curtains, but saw no one. Again he knocked on the door, pounding heavily with his right fist. He kept it up, causing not only the door but the walls and windows to vibrate. In time he added his foot to his fist and stamped as he knocked. His thumping became rhythmical, surely the kind of beat that would arouse the deaf. At one point he thought he saw someone move a curtain. He stopped pounding, certain that Amy knew he was there, but simply wasn't going to answer. Moving to the window, he held the panda against the screen for a full minute, then backed away and turned. As he began to step down from the porch, he heard the door open, stopped with his foot in the air, teetered, caught his balance and turned. Amy stood in the doorway wearing work slacks and a soiled blouse. Her wide eyes pleaded for answers to questions that creased her brow.

"Hello," Ty said, well aware that Amy couldn't hear him. He grinned and held up the panda.

Amy smiled hesitantly. She pointed at Ty, then at the panda, then at herself.

Ty nodded. "Yes. It's for you. I won it for you at the fair." He moved his lips with precise care. "You do remember, don't you?" His beaming expression brought sparkle to his eyes.

Amy's smile broadened, but slipped away when Ty moved toward her. Sensing her fear, he stepped back, then reached out, holding the panda in both hands. Her frown deepened and she shook her head.

Ty felt a surge of frustration, not only because Amy wouldn't accept the panda, but because his thoughts raced around in his brain refusing to mesh as he struggled for a means to communicate. A moment later he tucked the panda under his arm and reached out with the letter. She hesitated, then took the folded paper, hurried into the house and closed the door.

Although late for work, Ty refused to leave, tried to open the door, found it locked, but kept jiggling the knob until Amy pulled the door open wide enough to expose her head. As her eyes pleaded with him to go, Ty finally used the few sign-language gestures that he had spent days trying to memorize. Over and over he awkwardly gave the signs for "friend" and "care." He was even so bold as to sign "love" just as Amy closed the door. It was flashed in desperate haste as she disappeared, and he was uncertain as to whether she had seen it.

Ty stepped into heavy mist that became a drizzle as he walked toward his van. Bending his shoulders, he increased his pace and held the panda against his chest to keep it dry. The droplets grew to full-fledged rain by the time he crossed Redrock Road. His wet shirt clung to his shoulders and back, but he didn't fret, for Amy had taken his letter.

Inside the van, he carefully placed the panda on the floor behind his seat, then wiped his wet brow with his handkerchief. A distant rumble of thunder announced the start of a downpour.

Chapter Sixteen

Jackie didn't like her assignments. She was especially displeased when she had to make visits in the rain. Considering herself a forthright and independent woman, she wondered why she hadn't simply told Rob to go to hell. After all, other thoughts did occupy her mind. Wedding plans, for example. The final fitting of her gown was also scheduled for this rainy day. And she had to find time to resume her arguments with her mother, mainly about who to include on the guest list. But here she was in her VW beetle, parked under a sycamore tree, waiting for a break in the downpour so she could rap on a stranger's door and feel foolish and uneasy while asking vague questions.

The sky brightened slightly, and Jackie squinted at the rain. Deciding it had let up enough, she opened the car door and thrust out her umbrella. No way would she allow her blue-gray summer suit to get wet. It gave her the businesslike look of a professional woman, as did other parts of the disguise—thin-rimmed eyeglasses (pure window glass) and a narrow briefcase.

Crossing the street toward a row of brick houses, Jackie held the umbrella in one hand, the leather portfolio in the other, and assumed the proper posture for the mission—head up, shoulders back, pace brisk. Concrete steps led her to a stoop and a white door marked number 46. She rang the bell and waited.

She was taken aback when a child answered. The little boy, dressed in yellow shorts and a Donald Duck T-shirt, blew from her mind the spiel she had rehearsed for an adult. He contorted his face by biting his lower lip with his buck teeth, pushing up his nose with his forefinger, and crossing his eyes.

Jackie gathered her wits and asked, "Is your mommy or daddy home?"

The four-year-old replied with a juicy Bronx cheer that didn't stop spluttering until a harassed woman appeared behind him, a dishtowel flung over her shoulder.

"Johnny, you stop that this minute!" she yelled "That's not nice!" The frail, dark-eyed woman with the wispy hair looked at Jackie while pulling and pushing the boy from view. "I'm sorry. It's just one of those days. May I help you?" The woman was obviously young, despite the weary look about her eyes.

"I'm sorry to bother you," Jackie began. "I'm looking for a Mr. Harry Hedgepeth. Does he live here?"

"That's my husband's father. Why do you want to see him?"

"I believe he used to deliver mail in the Mulberry section. We're investigating an inheritance matter for a family there, and we're hoping that Mr. Hedgepeth can give us some information."

"What kind of information?"

"Well, I'd rather explain that to him."

"Don't see how he can help you." The woman yanked the towel from her shoulder and folded it twice. "All he did was deliver mail."

"May I speak to him?"

The woman tightened her lips and inspected Jackie from head to toe.

"Is there some reason you don't want me to see him?" questioned Jackie, suddenly annoyed with herself for asking. Be careful, she warned herself. Say the wrong thing, or come on too strong, and you're out of here.

"Johnny," the woman shouted, "go get Pop Pop. Tell him there's a lady here to see him." Then, looking into Jackie's eyes, she whispered, "He's a bit... a bit... I can't think of the word. An odd fellow, I guess you'd say."

"Eccentric?"

"That's it exactly. He's eccentric."

Jackie glanced up at her umbrella.

"Well, come in out of the rain. Can't be too careful these days about who you let into your house." The woman backed up and turned. "He'll love to talk to you. He likes visitors. He'll talk your ears off."

Jackie closed her umbrella and leaned it against the iron railing. Inside, she found a living room of begged and borrowed unmatched pieces. The stuffed chairs and sofa sagged, and the plaid upholstery clashed with the flowered wallpaper.

"Take a seat," urged the frail woman as she adjusted her hair.

"I'll wait for Mr. Hedgepeth." Jackie remained standing near the doorway.

"Suit yourself."

Jackie couldn't help but wonder what she was getting into this time, recalling yesterday's visit to a tree trimmer turned latter-day, proselytizing Jesus freak, or Wednesday's interview with a grisly delivery man with a fast-paced come-on.

"Well, what have we here?" asked 72-year-old Harry Hedgepeth as he came down the steps. Harry was a broad-shouldered, white-hair man with a neatly trimmed mustache. He had obviously continued to take care of his body after retiring from years of hiking with a mail pack. Without hesitation, he marched right up to Jackie, took her hand, and led her to the sagging couch. He lowered himself into a wing chair opposite her and motioned to his daughter-in-law to leave the room. Just then Johnny plunged down the stairs, only to back up after a glance from Pop Pop.

Jackie figured that Pop Pop ruled the roost, perhaps to the chagrin of his daughter-in-law. She couldn't miss his boots—fancy, leather cowboy boots. Other than that, she found nothing eccentric about his dress.

Within seconds Jackie was alone with the retired letter carrier, and she was quick to thank him and explain: "It's kind of you to see me, Mr. Hedgepeth. You might think my visit rather strange. Frankly, I'm hoping to learn some facts about a woman who lived on your mail route in the Mulberry section. The courts have awarded my client her house because of her infirmity. She's little more than a vegetable today. This whole thing may seem odd, but we're simply hoping that you might remember something about the woman that might help fill in some gaps." Jackie suddenly realized that she was repeating herself and rattling off too many words too quickly. She straightened up as best she could, considering the sofa's broken springs, and lowered her voice while speaking more slowly: "Do you remember Marjorie Worth at twelve Juniper Lane? Tudor-style house with lots of shrubs and trees."

"My dear young lady, do you realize that you haven't even told me your name?" A teasing smile brought a glint to Harry's eyes.

"Oh, I'm so sorry." Jackie prayed that Harry Hedgepeth wasn't flirting with her. "I'm Jacqueline Harwood, and as I said, my client has taken possession of..."

"May I get you a cup of tea, Miss Harwood? It is Miss, I presume?"

"Yes... yes, it's Miss. No, not really. Any tea, I mean. I'd just rather we talk. Perhaps you could tell me, Mr. Hedgepeth, if you remember the woman who lived in the Tudor house on Juniper Lane. I was told at the Post Office that you delivered mail there."

"For fifteen years I delivered mail in the Mulberry section. Retired seven years ago. I'll tell you something, young lady, I remember those houses so well I could count them like sheep while falling to sleep. I remember the old Colonial at Juniper and Maple. Mrs. Parker always gave me a generous Christmas gift. Then there was that fieldstone house on Locust Place. Vicious dog growled at me every morning. I just hoped and prayed he'd never get loose. Mean looking animal. Then there was Mr. Hartman. Lived alone in a big brick house. Retired gentleman. He liked to talk football."

"But Mr. Hedgepeth, surely you remember the house at..."

"Oh, yeah. I remember the Tudor house. But I never saw that woman. Not in fifteen years of delivering her mail, the heaviest load on the block. In fact, the heaviest load in the Mulberry section. Magazines, packages, junk mail, all sorts of stuff. But I never saw that woman. I was in her house, though."

"You were?"

"Sure was. I'll never forget it."

Jackie drew a pen and a pad of paper from her briefcase. "Please tell me about that, Mr. Hedgepeth."

"Why do you want to know? What good will that do anybody?"

"I represent Miss Worth's nephew, the owner of that house. My client knows little about his aunt and is seeking any information available."

"I'll never forget that morning." Harry was obviously anxious to tell the story. "I always pushed some of her mail through the door slot. There just wasn't enough room in the box. Well, this time a brown envelope was taped over the slot. It was addressed to me. Not to Harry Hedgepeth, but to the mailman. Figure she didn't know my name. Anyway, it was for me, and I opened it. I can still see that hundred dollar bill, clear as can be, like it happened yesterday. One hundred dollars. And a note written on a little piece of yellow paper. Tell you something, Miss Harwood. I was built strong in those days, and I guess she must've seen me coming and going. So she figured I could do the job. So she left me this hundred dollar bill and this note that said..."

Chapter Seventeen

Rob and Jackie had agreed to meet at his mother's house at 7 p.m. to exchange information. Having arrived early, Rob sat at the kitchen table, across from his mother, while each drank coffee and forked down pineapple cheesecake. The surroundings were neat and trim, like the rest of the house, products of Emily's nervous energy. Cafe curtains trimmed the windows, tie-back cushions decked the chairs and a deacon's bench, and a well-polished hurricane lamp marked the center of the knotty pine cobbler's table.

"Papa loved his garden, but little by little he began to plant Marjorie's favorite flowers," explained Emily, whose defenses were weakening as a result of Rob's persistent probes. She was opening up and speaking more freely about her reclusive sister. "Marjorie was hung up on iris."

"Iris?" Rob was sure his heart skipped a beat.

"You know. Blue flags, we used to call them. Of course they come in yellow and pink, too. One time I watched her undress a doll and lay it among those tall sword-like leaves of the iris plants. I figured she was playing Baby Moses or something."

Rob breathed deeply, gulped coffee, and shifted directions: "Tell me more about Uncle Jack. You didn't blame him, did you? You blamed her. You wanted to believe that your sister seduced her big brother, didn't you?"

Emily said nothing. She stared at her son for an instant, then looked away.

But Rob didn't let up: "If Jack meant so much to you, then why didn't you try to keep in touch? Why didn't you chase after him, try to find him, or something?"

Emily examined her fingernails. "I did. When you were a boy, I wrote to him. There just wasn't any reason to tell you about it. Anyway, I had my own cross to bear and didn't want to get into that part of it with your father, who was closing me out because of my constant obsession with my family. The truth was, I kept on writing to Jack until you started college. Then I lost contact. The letters came back unopened."

"Did he answer any of your letters?"

"Yes. For awhile. Then his letters stopped coming."

"Did you keep his letters?"

Finally Emily looked at Rob. "Oh, yes."

"Could I see them?"

She looked away again, stared toward the windows, and said nothing. "Mom?"

"No, Rob. I don't think so. Don't push that far. Please."

Rob folded his hands, sat quietly, and looked down into his coffee cup. In time, he glanced up at the copper clock above the stove and said, "Jackie's late." He uttered the words simply to break the silence.

His mother followed with more small talk: "Finish your cheesecake. There's plenty more."

Rob picked up his fork and toyed with a piece of the cheesecake. Seconds passed before he asked, "When Jack's letters stopped, did you try to locate him?"

"The Post Office had no forwarding address. At least, not by the time I contacted them. His company... well, they wouldn't tell me anything."

"You didn't try hard enough."

"I didn't know how, really. And without your father's help..." Her words trailed off.

"He was a salesman, right?"

"Air conditioning and refrigeration."

"Well, air conditioning specialists often go from cooling company to cooling company, right?"

"I don't know. I never thought about that." Emily looked toward the windows again. "Anyway, he obviously didn't want to keep in touch. And I think that was my fault. I kept dredging up things he didn't want to hear, things that hurt him." Her eyes moistened. She tried to speak, but couldn't.

"There aren't that many air conditioning and refrigeration companies," Rob said, unaware of his mother's tears. "I bet you could count them on one hand. Maybe two hands."

Emily carried her cup and plate to the sink and stayed there, keeping her back to Rob. Her neck twitched, and her son suddenly realized how much she was hurting. He rose from the table and was about to put his arm around her when the doorbell rang.

"I'll get it," he said. "I'm sure it's Jackie."

Emily wiped her eyes, turned from the sink and watched Rob hurry from the kitchen, unaware that compassion had mollified his obsessive preoccupation. She pondered a thought—that Rob displayed a touch of insensitivity. But within an instant she blamed herself for never having given him the facts on which to build fully developed insight. She had suffered alone, keeping secrets deep within her bosom. Maybe that had been just as unfair to Rob, she thought, as it had been to herself. Her mind was elsewhere as she carried Rob's dish to the sink and then busied herself rearranging items in the refrigerator until Jackie entered the kitchen.

"Look at what I brought you from my folks' garden." Jackie held up a foot-long green squash, then pecked a kiss on Emily's cheek. "See, I didn't forget. You told me how much you liked zucchini."

Emily disguised her mood with a bright expression as she greeted her future daughter-in-law. "With cheese and oregano," she said as she wiped her hands on a towel. A broad smile and an embrace were her ways of saying she approved of Rob's choice. "How are you, dear?"

"Tired, to tell you the truth."

Emily fingered the zucchini as she carried it to the refrigerator. "This'll go well with tomorrow's fish and tomatoes. Have you eaten, Jackie?"

"I stopped home and caught the end of mother's dinner. Gulped some stew from the bottom of the pot. Dad was grumpy because I was late, but insisted I sit there and eat ice cream."

"How about a slice of my pineapple cheesecake?"

"I'm afraid it wouldn't fit in my tummy." Jackie sighed, sat at the table, and hung her head in her hands.

"This'll wake you up." Emily poured coffee. "You want another cup, Rob?"

Standing in the doorway, Rob shook his head while drumming on the doorjamb with his fingers. Within seconds he was pacing the floor. He finally curbed his motion by sitting on the deacon's bench and gripping the seat with both hands.

"Don't worry Rob; I'll leave you two alone," said Emily, misreading her son's behavior, construing his nervous preoccupation as impatience.

"Don't run off because of him," Jackie insisted. "Come on. Have coffee with me."

"It's my bridge night at Martha Greene's, so don't fret, Jackie." Emily returned the pot to the stove. "There's enough coffee here to keep you going. And if you get hungry, there's plenty to eat in the refrigerator." She pinched Rob's cheek, winked at Jackie, and walked from the room.

As soon as the front door slammed, Jackie shifted gears from a sleepy low to a testy high. "You didn't have to put your mother out of her own house." Adding sarcasm, she went on: "We could have discussed our secret investigation at our house, where Aunt Marjorie's spooky presence might have given us a helping hand." She hardened her stare. "I can see that you're ready to pounce on me for results. Well, you're going to be disappointed. And, frankly, I've had it! No more of these ridiculous visits with strangers. Not for me. You have no idea how foolish I felt today, and, on top of that, I was late for my fitting, damn it. This thing has gotten out of hand, and I don't want to be a part of it."

Rob realized that he had become highly keyed up in anticipation of discussing the day's findings, and he understood that Jackie was tired and touchy. Without care, the mixture could explode. So, against his nature, he forced deliberate calmness as he said, "Take it easy, now, and listen to me. First of all, this is Mom's bridge night. If I hadn't known that, I wouldn't have suggested coming here. Second, I needed information from her.

Third, I'm not playing a silly game. In fact, it's not just the skull that's pushing me."

"I know. It's an obsession."

"You don't understand."

"Then explain it to me."

"There are a lot of things I need to know, a lot of things I have to find out about my family, and about my own feelings. I didn't realize until minutes ago that Mom blames herself for a lot of things. And that, along with so many hurts, is why she's held so much inside and filled her days with busy work." Rob reached out and took Jackie's hand. "Look, you don't have to make any more visits if you don't want to. I'll try to finish the job myself."

"It's just that it seems so... so... hit and miss. Even when we find someone, there's no payoff. Today I made a woman cry. I asked for her husband, who installed downspouts on Aunt Marjorie's house. Holy hell, the man is dead! He fell off a roof and broke his neck! The woman stood there blubbering, tears streaming down her face. How do you think I felt? I didn't know what to say." Jackie sipped her coffee, then shook her head in disgust. "And, as for that delivery man who once worked for Nettle's Department Store, that Clarence what's-his-name—well, the house he lived in was torn down years ago. Neighbors think he moved to Detroit, and I'm not heading for Detroit. Then there's the mailman, Harry Hedgepeth. Had a long talk with him. He doesn't like to stop talking. In fact, if he had bedded down your Aunt Marjorie he probably would have told me all about it in great detail. Anyway, he never saw the woman in fifteen years of carrying mail to her house."

"But we don't know if he's telling the truth."

"That's the problem, Rob. No one's going to admit the things you want to hear. So what's the point of it all?"

"The point is, we gather clues and string them together. Eventually, some sort of picture will emerge."

"Anyway, I believe the old guy, despite his chivalrous ways and his fancy cowboy boots. He admitted being in her house. Get this. She left him a hundred dollar bill in an envelope. Why? To move that grandfather's clock into the basement. She knew he had the shoulders to do it. So she must have been watching him. Probably peeked out at mail time every day for years. Strong back or not, he was feeling his age, and struggled with the clock. It slipped and fell the last few steps. So, he didn't want to take the hundred bucks. He stood in the living room, calling out to her, telling her why. Finally left the money on the piano. He found it in the mailbox the next day. This time he took it."

"But he never saw her?"

"If he had, I think he would have told me. He probably would have described her in detail." Jackie pushed herself up from the table and reached for the coffee pot. "So, that's it."

"Hey, you did fine."

"Stop playing nice guy. It's annoying as hell."

"You're trying to pick a fight."

"I know," Jackie admitted while pouring coffee for both of them. "I'm as bitchy as a pregnant wart hog."

"Well, I had good results today."

"That's because you pick the easy assignments, like pumping your mother and visiting hospitals."

"Don't forget I checked out gas and electric. Tomorrow I'll try again to reach the water meter reader. Now, sit down and listen." Rob waited until Jackie was back in place and focused on him. "I found out that Willowood Hospital shipped Baby Willow to Children's Services, a state adoption agency in Philadelphia. I called them. They wouldn't tell me where he is today, but apparently he was never adopted for some reason. Anyway, I have an appointment with a Mrs. Wood next Thursday."

"You'll be back at work next week. Did you forget?" Jackie's eyes flashed a warning. "Hey, you're not sending me to Philadelphia!"

"I'll take a day. I'll get sick. Or something."

"With Ty out? Didn't you say Ty was starting his vacation next week?"

"Yeah, I asked him to push it off, but he wouldn't. I'm pissed at him anyway, damn it. He knows I broke my apartment lease and that I'm moving more of my stuff into the house this weekend, but he hasn't offered to help. It's not like him. I could sure use his van. Strange that a guy who likes to help little old ladies can't find time to help his buddy. I don't get it. He hasn't stepped foot into our house since I showed it to him. Frankly, he hasn't acted so freakish since he became fixated by that girl he met at the county fair three years ago."

"Maybe he can't handle your getting married. Ever think of that?"

"That's ridiculous." Rob drank the last of his coffee and came down hard with the cup.

"Don't break your mother's china."

"You know what I did today? I played some of those old records we found in the attic."

"Are you telling me you entertained yourself while I worked? You sat around playing records?"

"No, no. I sorted through another heap of Aunt Marjorie's receipts for purchases and repairs while I listened to the music."

Jackie gave forth another long sigh. "You know, Rob, it doesn't matter how many receipts we examine, we're not going to locate all of the people who touched Marjorie's life. Who cleaned her windows? Who cleaned the snow off her walkway? Who tried to collect for this cause or that charity? She didn't get receipts for everything. We even forgot about her paper boy. Who delivered her newspapers? Who collected the money? How?"

"I can check that one easily enough by calling the circulation department. That is, if they kept records that long. I suppose I don't see a neighborhood kid as the answer. Maybe I'm hung up on the stereotyped image of the woman who flirts with the meter reader."

"You know, something's happened to us, Rob. We've created Marjorie in our own minds—a Marjorie that maybe never existed. You once accused me of being a romantic, of turning Aunt Marjorie's tale into a heart-throbbing love affair. But what you've done is worse. You've turned her into a licentious seducer of the gas man. And I think your teenage visit with Aunt Marjorie— something you don't like to talk about—plays a role in all of this."

Rob looked at his fingernails.

"And one more thing," Jackie said. "Don't be too hard on Ty until you know everything."

Rob reached out and took Jackie's hand again. "I love you, even when you're bitchy."

"I was nasty, wasn't I?"

"Yes, you were terrible. But you can make it up to me." Rob's eyes danced.

"What now?" Her expression denoted wariness.

"Come roller skating with me."

"Roller skating?" Jackie pulled back her hand. "You've got to be kidding."

"No. I'm serious. There are several pairs of skates in my toy chest in Mom's basement. We can skate right down the street and into the cemetery, like I did when I was a kid. Right now. Let's go."

"You're nuts! You're absolutely nuts!"

Rob laughed. "We could skate around and around in the cemetery while I teach you the words to 'The Bluebird of Happiness'."

"You're insane. I'm beginning to wonder about your whole family. Except maybe your mother. She's a nice lady."

"When's the last time you went roller skating?"

"We've been sitting here having a tense, tiring discussion following an exhausting day, and you suggest skating? Is this another one of your silly jokes?"

"Do you think I'd joke about a thing like that?"

"I know your mother's coffee is strong, but..."

"I'll tell you what. You won't have to go skating with me tonight if you give me two things in return."

"Something tells me I'm being had. I mean, what kind of a deal is that? Let me get it straight, now. You want me to agree not to do something I don't want to do in return for doing two things that I may not want to do."

"Something like that. I want passionate rapture on Mom's living room rug in return for not roller skating. And, in addition, I want the 'Bluebird'."

"I'm too tired for passion."

"No you're not. You've gotten your second wind, thanks to Mom's coffee. I can see it in your pop-pop-popping eyes."

Jackie giggled, gave Rob a kittenish smile, batted her eyelashes, and ran from the room while trying to chirp like a bird.

"And what's that supposed to be?" Rob called out as he took off after her.

"A birdie."

"That's not exactly what I had in mind," he said softly as he caught up with her in the living room, grabbed her from behind, and wrapped his arms around her waist. He kissed her savagely on the back of her neck and behind her ears, then whispered, "I'll tell you about the 'Bluebird' later." He turned her around and kissed her on the lips.

In time, she broke away, ran behind the couch, and mimicked, "Tweet, tweet, tweet."

Rob looked one way, then the other in trying to decide his direction of attack. A fiendish expression twisted his facial muscles.

"Do you think most lovers do silly things like this?" Jackie asked.

"Of course. When no one's watching. And especially after a pot of wicked brew that pops the eyes." He jumped north, then turned south around the back of the sofa. "Gotcha!" Lifting Jackie into his arms, he carried her to the center of the room where he placed her on the carpet. "Wow! you sure are..."

"Don't say it! I'm not heavy, and I have a perfect figure, and you know it."

Rob knelt next to her and gazed into her eyes. "Well, now, I guess you are pretty special." He pecked a kiss on her nose, then planted a earnest one on her lips. When he lifted his head again, he smiled and whispered, "I really do love you."

* * *

An hour later, Rob and Jackie were still on the living room carpet, stretched out next to each other, gazing toward the ceiling, and talking about their lives together.

"And I'll always make you a big breakfast before you go to work," Jackie said, "no matter how busy my schedule."

"No you won't. Not a liberated woman like you. Don't make any promises you can't keep."

"We'll never sleep in twin beds like some old couples, will we?"

"It depends on how loudly you snore. I might move to another room, and you can have Marjorie's room all to yourself."

"Don't call it Marjorie's room! Not anymore. Anyway, I don't snore!"

"But you might someday."

"Men snore louder than woman, anyway."

"Who says?"

"Everyone knows that."

"Hogwash! But don't worry. I'll always put up with you."

Jackie frowned, as if something puzzling had just stirred her brain. "What's this about bluebirds?"

"Those old records that I played today—one was 'The Bluebird of Happiness'. And I decided that someone can sing it at our wedding."

"What? Is this another of your silly jokes?"

"No. You made a promise, now."

"I made no such promise!" Jackie sprang to a sitting position.

"I don't want 'Because' or any of those other cliches. I want the 'Bluebird'."

"You're crazy!" She leaped to her feet and stood with her hands on her hips, glowering down on him. "Anyway, it's not up to you. The bride decides things like that."

Rob began to sing off-key but with dramatic gusto: "So be like I, hold your head up high, till you find the bluebird of happiness."

She kicked him in the upper thigh.

He feigned pain, but sang on: "You will find, greater peace of mind, knowing there's a bluebird of happiness."

She kicked him again.

Trying to control his laughter, Rob moaned and moaned again, then sang on: "For every cloudy morning, there's a midnight moon above."

"If you're trying to tell me something—believe me, I don't need a Pollyanna lecture right now!"

This time Rob grabbed Jackie's foot before she could kick, then gave forth yuk-yuks of laughter as he pulled her down into his arms.

Chapter Eighteen

"Yes, is Mr. Samuel Fletcher at home, please?" Dressed in a navy blue suit, Rob stood at the door of a brick duplex among a row of two-family dwellings on Washington Avenue in the south end of town.

"There's no Samuel here," responded the big-boned blonde with the protruding chin and prominent cheekbones. "I'm Sam Fletcher, if that's who y' want—Sam for Samantha."

"Oh, I'm sorry. Do you work for the water company?"

"For more than twenty-five years."

"I don't know why, but I expected a man. I'm looking for the Sam Fletcher who read meters in the Mulberry section in the late seventies and early eighties."

"That's me. And I'm still doin' it. Hell, it pays some of the bills."

"Well, my firm is investigating a former property owner at twelve Juniper Lane. I wonder if we might step inside and talk."

"If you've got somethin' to ask me, mister, ask it right now, out here."

Rob wasn't about to challenge the big women whose broad shoulders blocked the doorway. "Okay. Do you remember the woman who lived at number twelve?"

"Who is it you said you represent, mister?"

"Well, my legal firm—that's Putnam, Harwood and Jones—is gathering information for a client who has come into ownership of the property."

"And you want information from me, a meter reader? You gotta be a phony, mister. What do you really want?"

"No. Please. Please hear me out." Rob was forced to back down the steps as the woman stepped out onto the stoop. "I simply need some information on Marjorie Worth. Perhaps you remember her house. A Tudor style. Number twelve. The lady was rather reclusive. She kept to herself."

"Oh, yeah. You just rang a bell, mister. I remember her. She was a spook—a real spook."

"You saw her?"

"How 'bout some identification, mister?"

"I don't have my business cards with me." Rob backed across the sidewalk while digging into his pants pocket. "I stupidly left without them this morning. But, here, I can show you some other identification." He pulled out his wallet and opened it to show several cards—driver's license, credit cards, medical and membership IDs—and immediately plunged into questions to distract the woman. "Did you say you once saw Miss Worth? Few people did, you know. Were you ever in her house?"

"She left the cellar door open for me like clock work. She knew just when I was comin'."

"Then you never really saw her?"

Sam sat on the stoop, pondered for a moment, looked up and down the street, then smiled ever so slightly. "I shouldn't really tell you this. I got so damn curious. So, one day I snuck into the bushes and peeked through a window. God damn, there she was with some piece of flimsy material draped over one shoulder and twisted around her naked body. She was waltzing around and twirling, putting on a big show for nobody."

Rob waited for more. "And?"

"You can sit here, mister. I don't like t' see you standin' like that. Take one of them steps."

Rob, tired of shifting his weight, welcomed the chance to sit and rest his legs. "Thanks." He sat on the second step, feeling a bit more certain that Sam trusted him.

"I don't mind talking about that weirdo," she offered. "I just didn't want to be talkin' to no neighborhood spy. Folks around here, they don't like Effie and me. They don't like our kind."

Rob showed no reaction to Sam's words. He waited and hoped she would say more about Marjorie.

"I'd like to see some of them come out and see you sittin' here with me. That's what I'd really like. That'd shake 'em up a bit."

Now, all of a sudden, Rob worried that Sam was going to act out some scenario to confuse the neighbors. What he didn't want was a lot of extraneous talk. He decided to try to push her back on track. After all, she did say she didn't mind talking about Marjorie. "So, did you see anything else through that window?

"What's that?"

"Through that weirdo's window, on Juniper—what else did you see?"

"She danced and danced and danced. But the strangest thing was this... this doll. There was this doll in a chair. She picked it up and rocked it in her arms. And then, well, I ain't seen anything quite like what she did next. She nursed the doll."

"What do you mean?"

"You know. Her boobs"

"Do you mean she held the doll to her breasts?"

"Yeah. She held the doll there. She'd cradle it in her arms, then hold the head and press the lips against her nipple."

"Jesus."

"I think Old Lady Hopkins, across the street... I think she's watching us. I think I saw her move the curtain."

"Did you see anything more. Did Aunt Marj... I mean, did that weirdo do anything else?"

"I felt embarrassed. I had this squirmy feeling inside of me. I got out of them bushes."

Despite her protests, Rob figured that Sam had enjoyed watching his Aunt Marjorie.

Chapter Nineteen

John Alan Worth had moved up from sales and was now vice president of the Heat Pump Division of Fairbanks Industries, Inc. His desk stretched almost from wall to wall in a spacious office that held rich appointments—intricately carved wooden shelving, volumes of leather-bound books on engineering and marketing, deep red draperies and carpeting, gold-framed ink drawings of 19th Century factories, and an oil portrait of Willis Carrier, the father of air conditioning.

Shuffling papers when the intercom buzzed, he responded by pushing a button and asking, "Yes, Marianne, what is it?"

"Mr. Putnam is here to see you."

The vice president glanced at his watch. "Okay, send him in." He pushed aside some papers and leaned back in his swivel chair.

With practiced control of himself, Rob was almost expressionless as he entered the office, though his eyes took in everything. Jack Worth was not what he had expected. Rob had not envisioned a man of such bearing—a regal air immediately evident when the white-haired executive stood and offered his hand. For a man beyond retirement age, Uncle Jack was an imposing, well-built, well-groomed figure with a firm handshake and a smile that brightened his blue eyes. Well trained in proper body movements, he knew how to control the moment with stance, posture and gestures as he looked down on Rob.

"Please have a seat, Mr. Putnam. How was your flight?"

Rob decided to speak before he sat. "The flight was fine. I appreciate your seeing me on such short notice."

"Friday afternoons are generally bad. But you sounded so urgent. Something about a multi-million dollar heat-pump contract? Please pull up a chair, Mr. Putnam, so we can both sit down."

This time Rob reached for a chair—a black leather one that he placed directly in front of his uncle, who slipped back into his swivel chair. The two men sat staring at each other for several seconds. Finally Rob broke the silence: "I lied."

"I beg your pardon?"

"I lied about the contract. That's not why I'm here."

Although Jack Worth was well accustomed to handling crises with calm assurance, his eyes showed surprise and annoyance. "Why are you here, Mr. Putnam?"

"Well, for one reason, I wanted to get a good look at you."

"Is this some sort of jest? Because, if it is..."

"No, no, no. I'm serious, Uncle Jack."

"What did you call me?" The brow below Jack's thick crop of white hair was creased by a sudden frown.

"Uncle Jack."

"Who are you?"

"I'm your nephew. I'm Emily's son."

Jack sat still. Not a squeak came from his swivel chair. His eyes remained fixed on Rob. In time, he lifted his left hand and rubbed his chin, then asked, "My sister Emily?"

"Yes."

The big man revealed but a moment of perplexity, quickly concealed under a businesslike facade. He pushed the button on his intercom and said, "Marianne, please hold all my calls for the next hour." Within an instant he changed his mind. "No, Marianne, on second thought, tell Fredrickson I can't see him this afternoon. Cancel everything. Mr. Putnam and I will be at the Velvet Lounge. You can get me there in an emergency."

* * *

Overhead Tiffany lamps reflected on dark, polished wood in the Velvet Lounge, a meeting place where deals were set. The richly furnished barroom was frequented by young upwardly mobile types in navy blue blazers and senior executives in pinstripe suits. Its massive bar, broad woodwork, sturdy tables and chairs were ornately carved in Victorian style. Double-globe lamps topped the tables, and mock gaslights protruded from walls decked with red velvet-like embossments.

Jack had led Rob to a table in a deep corner where they both drank Scotch on ice.

Lifting his glass in what was almost a toast, Jack drank a third of his whiskey without taking his penetrating eyes off his nephew. "Now tell me, how did you find me?"

"That was the easy part." Rob sensed he faced a master of perception. He felt invisible antennae reaching out and grasping insight through every sound, sight and touch.

"Oh?"

"I just kept calling air conditioning companies until someone told me where you were. I started with Trane. Then I called Lennox, then Carrier, and so on. You used to work with a man named Herman Belfield at York. Remember?"

"Good old Hermie. He moved up when I left. I'm sure he was glad to see me go." Jack finished his Scotch, looked for the waitress, gave a hand signal, and then fixed another stare on Rob. "Well, now, my resourceful nephew, what exactly do you know about your Uncle Jack? And why did you fly hundreds of miles to get a look?"

Rob realized immediately that the questions were far from incidental. Uncle Jack was jockeying for a starting position.

"I know enough of the family history, if that's what you're asking."

"I see. Then perhaps you've come to blackmail me." Jack was matter-of-factly cool. "Is it money you want?"

"My God no!" Rob, who had been trying to hide his emotions, was seized by incredulity that sent sparks into his eyes.

"I didn't think so. But I had to test the waters. Now I know I have to wade into the mud."

"Maybe. Maybe not. It depends on how much you can tell me about Aunt Marjorie without getting your feet muddy."

"Marjorie? You want me to talk about Marjorie? No, I'd rather talk about your mother. How is she?"

"She's holding her own. I found out only days ago that she

actually misses you. I had no idea. You were never part of my life, so I didn't know you were still part of hers."

Jack waited, then said, "And?"

"What can I say? She's okay. Inside, a lot of shit from the past chews her up. But I don't want to talk about that. I want to know about Marjorie."

"Why the interest in the mysterious recluse of Juniper Lane? A craving to know about your family? A fear that you may have strange genes? A hope that you might inherit her money? You should try knocking on her door. She might surprise you and let you in."

"The house is mine. Aunt Marjorie doesn't live there anymore."

Rob's words froze Jack with his glass halfway to his mouth. Within a moment, he breathed freely, then slowly moved the Scotch-flavored water to his lips. After a sip, he said, "Strange. I can't picture her anywhere but in that house. I figured she would die in that house."

"She's in a nursing home. She's nearly a vegetable. The courts awarded me the house because she was judged incompetent and I was listed to receive the house in her will."

A knowing expression spread Jack's lips into a weak smile. "But of course," he proclaimed. "And the will was written before your grandfather died, and witnessed by him. Right?"

Rob's eyes showed confusion.

"Marjorie had no business sense," Jack said, "and would never have thought of a will. Her daddy controlled her—that is, controlled everything but her urges. He gave me nothing, and, of course, made sure she left me nothing in her will. Your mother? No, not poor Emily. He wouldn't have considered that. After all, you're the young living heir. You were a child when he died. You weren't old enough to make mistakes. Not old enough to displease or disappoint him."

"Then it wasn't Aunt Marjorie's idea?"

"To give you the house? I doubt it. Marjorie only takes, she doesn't give."

Rob's eyes focused on infinity as his thoughts drifted. "I never considered the date on the will. I just saw it briefly, and the lawyer never mentioned it. I thought..."

"What is it, Rob?"

"Wow."

"What?"

"I thought maybe she remembered me. From a night. Years ago."

Jack's discerning eyes searched Rob's face. "I see. You know Marjorie better than I thought."

Rob forced himself to be pragmatic in an effort to close out certain memories: "The will said nothing about her money."

"Ah-hah! Then you are looking for money."

"Not really. It's just strange. There seems to be none. No bank statements come to the house. We haven't found hidden cash under the floorboards."

"The old man probably knew she'd spend it all. Frankly, I'm glad he cut me off. I'm glad I didn't get any of his filthy bundle. If I had, I probably wouldn't have made it. I wouldn't have scratched and clawed my way up. I wouldn't have started night school at age thirty-five." Jack frowned and looked for the waitress. "Where the hell are our drinks?" He signaled impatiently. "Are you married, Rob?"

"I will be come October. The house came just in time."

"What's her name?"

"Jacqueline. We call her Jackie."

"Is she pretty?"

"Oh, yes!"

"Do you have fun together? It's important to have fun."

Rob laughed. "No doubt about it. We like a lot of the same things, and we compromise on the others. She thinks I'm a little crazy. But she plays along. She can start things, too, and be a real tease. But I love her—so much."

Jack's eyes showed warmth. "You know, Rob, I'm nearly seventy years old, and my wife and I still have fun. She helped me through some brutal times. I thank God for her sense of humor." He studied the touch of surprise that had seeped into Rob's expression, then went on: "We have two married children—a son, and a daughter with two kids. So, I'm a grandfather."

"You're not at all what I expected," Rob said quietly as a petite, sandy-haired, dimpled waitress placed fresh glasses of Scotch on the table.

Jack waited until the waitress was out of earshot, then whispered, "You mean I don't look like an incestuous rapist?"

For a moment, Rob couldn't find the right words. He sputtered, then said, "To tell you the truth, I didn't know what to expect. My mind didn't link you with a wife, children, a plush corporate office."

"I know. I should look like Bela Lugosi, or Lucifer with little horns on my head."

"It's really weird. I want to like you, but feel I shouldn't." Rob gulped his Scotch faster than he should have. His face reddened as he coughed.

"I'm surprised your mother told you. She was always the secretive one who held everything inside. I used to think her heart would grow so big it would burst. More than anything, I wish you'd tell me more about my little Emily."

"Like I said, she's fine. She's happy about Jackie and me." Rob finished his drink and wiped his lips. "She and I are talking about things we never talked about before. I'm glad. It wasn't right for her to hold everything inside. As for me, I just need to find out some things, to fill in some gaps."

"When I'd get into trouble with the old man, Emily would always try to patch things up. But he treated her like she wasn't even there, like she didn't exist."

"And Marjorie?"

Jack motioned for drinks again, then looked directly into Rob's eyes as he said, "She was a vamp at age thirteen." Anger tightened his eyelids to a squint. He lowered his voice, but not his intensity. "And I fucked her because I hated her, and because she begged for it."

Rob was taken aback by the words of John Alan Worth, vice president. His lips parted as if he were about to speak, but nothing activated his voice box.

"You don't understand, do you. I mean, how could an eighteen-year-old boy do that to his thirteen-year-old sister? That's the lowest of low. Only pieces of scum do such things." Jack stopped talking abruptly when he saw the waitress approaching with fresh drinks. When she was gone, he poured the Scotch whiskey down his throat and allowed anger to invade his facial muscles. "You see, I know that no one would ever believe me. Do you believe me when I tell you that she never let up, that there wasn't a day when she didn't come after me?"

Rob didn't answer.

"She would open the shower curtain, stare at me, then step under the water. She would crawl into bed with me. She would grab me and play strange games. She begged me to show her how. Then later, when she got mad at me, she told her daddy." He paused for another taste of Scotch. "Okay, I'm still the guilty one, right? Excuses just don't mean much when it comes to incest. I'm well aware that I wanted to hurt her. It was like I was saying, okay, here it is, take it, take it, take it. She laughed when it was over, like she had finally trapped me into it. And I guess she had. The way I see it, she stole from me. She stole away my family."

Jack was not a man to lower his head. But this time he did, and he stared at the table for several seconds before he looked up and said, "My anger helped me. I was determined to make it, no matter what. And I did it, goddamnit! I know what I am today. I have no guilt. I won that battle long ago. My only sorrow comes from not having kept in touch with your mother. In some ways I miss her letters. In other ways I don't. She didn't mean to hurt me. But she kept reminding me of things at a time when I was trying to free myself."

In steady but quiet tones Rob asked, "Did Marjorie have a baby?"

This time the corporate executive was taken aback. "No. Of course not. What a strange thing to ask."

"Not as strange as you might think." Rob was almost certain that the skull and bones could not have come from a baby born so many years ago. Besides, if that were the case, "Skinny-dip" Jones was three decades off in bone-dating—something that Rob figured was mighty unlikely. Another thought: a baby born to a teenage Marjorie might have scandalized the family, but would not have resulted in an improper funeral under the stern and holy guidance of Grandfather Worth.

"Are you trying to tell me something?" asked Jack after downing the rest of his Scotch.

"Don't worry. I have no news of an inbred imbecile hidden in some far-off institution."

"I doubt that the family would have protected me from that. I'm sure my father would have followed through with his threat to castrate me."

"Don't look at me so strangely. I'm not trying to add drama to our conversation just for the sake of drama. I found an infant's skull buried in Aunt Marjorie's garden. I had a fragment dated. It goes back about fifteen years. I have no proof that Marjorie gave birth. But what you've told me makes me wonder even more."

"Holy shit."

Chapter Twenty

"But why wouldn't he lie?" asked Jackie, who, dressed in her white tennis outfit, was perched atop a tombstone in the cemetery not far from Rob's mother's house. "He certainly wasn't going to admit that he was at fault. Or totally at fault, anyway. You know what they say. Some people can hold good jobs, be pillars of the community and wonderful neighbors, yet have secret lives and do things no one ever suspects."

Dressed in jeans and a T-shirt, Rob sat on the grass at the base of the tombstone, now and again looking up at Jackie. "I don't know. There was something in his eyes that made me believe him. On top of that, there's the way Mom reacts when she thinks of him. I feel the vibes, you know? Inside, she has this yearning for the big brother she once knew."

Orange light from the setting sun filtered through the cemetery trees. A gentle breeze carried a touch of September and tossed the hair of Rob and Jackie. The end of his vacation also gave Rob the feeling of autumn's approach. It was Sunday evening, and tomorrow would bring his return to work. A trace of school-day melancholy from days past was overridden by happiness in both of them. Love's rapture also overrode annoyances from wedding plans and the continuing saga of Aunt Marjorie. Without question, the cement of joy held together the bricks of battle.

Jackie talked on: "I mean, you hear about it all the time on television. Some neighbor will say, 'Oh, I can't believe it. He was such a wonderful person. Everybody loved him. I just can't believe that he murdered his mother and his wife and all of his kids. I just can't believe he slit the throat of his pet dog and set his father on fire.'"

"That's different. I'm not talking about someone who suddenly cracks and goes berserk. This guy has really established himself. He's a vice president. He has married kids and grandchildren."

"That doesn't mean a thing. We hear about vice presidents who embezzle. We hear about well-established preachers who sleep with prostitutes, well-established priests who fool around with altar boys, well-established congressman who have gay lovers, well-established fathers who rape their teenage daughters. I'm just saying, don't be fooled by a big office and a look in the eyes. There are a lot of good actors out there who can spin believable tales. If that weren't true we wouldn't have so many con artists who talk little old ladies into handing over thousands of dollars."

"Well, maybe we'll never know the full truth." Rob leaned back against the tombstone, placed his cheek on Jackie's calf, and wrapped his arm around her legs. "But I'm beginning to think that Marjorie, even at thirteen, had the power to entrap her eighteen-year-old brother."

"Remember, Rob, that many a person changes a story, adds to it, exaggerates, twists it, whatever, as the years move on. People don't even realize they do it sometimes. They rationalize. They have to justify their actions, and sometimes even lies become the truth in their own minds."

"Yes Professor Harwood. Is your lecture over?"

Jackie freed herself and kicked Rob in the ribs. Quickly, Rob grabbed her legs again, this time pulling her from the tombstone.

"Aaaaa! Stop it! You're hurting me!"

Though Jackie was the vocal one, it was Rob who doubled up in pain when she landed on his lap. In fact, the sharp twinge in his groin caused him to bend over and squeeze Jackie, who reacted to his moan by freeing herself and jumping to her feet. He doubled up more tightly and continued his low groan.

"Well, it serves you right." Jackie thought better of her words. "Are you hurt?"

"What's it look like," he muttered. "We may never be able to have children." He moaned again.

"Aren't you overdoing it?"

His eyes shot daggers at her.

"Sorry." She put her hand on his shoulder as he leaned back against the tombstone. "What can I do."

"Not a freakin' thing! It'll pass. I'll live."

Jackie sat next to Rob, put her head on his shoulder, and waited for him to recover. In time, they snuggled securely.

It would be October before brilliant reds and yellows would come to the cemetery trees, but already a touch of color was splattered among the maples and oaks. The wind even sent a few leaves twirling to the grass, a harbinger of things to come. The gray squirrels were a shade bushier. Rob and Jackie watched a pair of them scamper about, up and down the oaks, here and there burying acorns near the tombstone flower beds where the earth was soft. The sun had fallen below the horizon, but a band of light in the west, blocked here and there by tall evergreens, gave enough light to the cemetery to nearly erase the evening's first flashes of fireflies.

A musing mutter came from Rob: "Jeez, I don't know."

"What?"

"Uncle Jack didn't have to tell me anything. He could have denied it all."

"Rob! I thought we were finished with that subject."

"I can't seem to shake it loose."

"I can tell." Jackie nestled more tightly. "Keep in mind, he might be the biggest phony this side of the Mississippi." In a mocking tone she said, "Poor, poor Jack—he couldn't resist his thirteen-year-old sister." Then, into Rob's ear she whispered, "That's pretty hard to swallow."

"But like I said. He could have insisted nothing happened."

"Would you have believed him?"

"No."

"Of course not. And a good con artist would know that. So, maybe he was playing games with you. Anyway, he knew your mother told you something. Who were you going to believe, him or your mother?"

"Oh, shut up."

"You started it again."

Rob tickled Jackie's ear with his tongue, then pressed his lips long and hard on her mouth, only to interrupt his kissing with the words, "I figured it out."

"Rob!"

"I got it. I can hear your mind ticking."

"What are you talking about?"

"You don't want Marjorie to be a bad person. Because if she turns out that way, then the romance is gone. You're still looking for that Romeo you think came knocking on Juliet's door."

"Stop talking and kiss me."

"You know something?"

"What now?"

"I think we should send a wedding invitation to Uncle Jack."

"Are you kidding? I don't want a molester at our wedding."

"Fifty years ago the guy made a mistake. He was only a boy."

"It's touchy enough with your father coming. Have you talked with your mother about that yet?"

"No. I will."

"They're going to have to sit in the same pew. Up front."

Rob started to hum the "Bluebird of Happiness" as if to escape from the thought.

"Kiss me."

He followed her command. They stretched out on the grass and cuddled until the mosquitoes drove them from the cemetery.

As they followed the sidewalk outside the graveyard wall, Rob burst into song: "So don't you forget, you must search till you find the bluebird..."

"Oh, no," Jackie protested.

". . . You will find peace and contentment forever if you will (At this point Rob lifted his voice to a crescendo.) be like I, hold your head up high, till you see a ray of light..."

Jackie cringed, looked toward the houses across the street in fear that someone had heard, then glanced into the cemetery as if concerned for the dead.

Chapter Twenty-One

Rob changed his plans because Ty's call sounded so urgent. His first day back at work had been busy. And it had followed a restless night. Still, he had planned to spend the evening arranging books in his study-library—the last of the downstairs rooms to be refurbished. Living in the house had been helpful, but proved even more useful now that he was back at Pure-Pup. His goal was to have the entire lower level and part of the second floor—at least the master bedroom—completed by the time Jackie moved in after the honeymoon.

So he had mixed feelings about Ty's call: pleasure in the fact that his buddy had finally reached out; displeasure in the fact that he probably would lose a night's work at the house. The tone of Ty's telephone conversation had added nothing but mystery to what Rob considered strange behavior, and Ty's words had offered no clue to his virtual disappearance over the past three weeks.

Rob left Jackie's parents house at 7:15 p.m., after downing Mrs. Harwood's veal fricassee, and arrived at Ty's apartment 10 minutes later. Two knocks on the door, and Ty was quick to answer.

"Come in."

Ty backed up, and Rob immediately felt more drama had been added to what was already an apartment with artistic flare.

"I feel something different," Rob said. "You've made some changes."

"I switched some of the graphics, that's all. Figured those pinwheel designs better fit my mood."

"You moved your painting of the street kids."

"Now you can see it when you enter. And take a look at this rattail cactus. See how it hangs down the wall."

Suddenly both men stopped talking and simply stared at each other as if to ask: What are we doing?

"How are you?" Rob asked as he offered his hand.

Ty embraced his friend while Rob said, "I stopped calling because you seemed too busy for me. I guess you were busy redecorating."

"No, it's not that." Ty placed his hand on Rob's shoulder and squeezed. "Come on. Sit down." He sat at the glass coffee table and motioned to Rob to sit across from him.

When Rob was secure in his seat, he studied Ty's expression and said, "You sounded urgent on the phone."

A strange look, including a smile of embarrassment, spread across Ty's face. "Do you think a person can be in love with someone he doesn't really know?"

Rob thought for a moment. "Well, I've heard it said that we don't truly know someone until we've lived with that person awhile. And maybe we never get to know them fully."

"That's not what I'm getting at. I mean, can we be in love with someone we've hardly met, someone we know mainly from afar, someone we've communicated with only briefly?"

"Are you trying to tell me you're in love?"

"Come with me. I want to show you something." Ty darted around the end of the coffee table and scooted to the door of his studio—that oft-used workroom, always cluttered with a vast assortment of unfinished projects.

Rob followed. When he entered the room, his eyes were immediately drawn to three large easels that dominated everything else in the studio. They held massive canvases covered by white sheets. Rob stepped toward the easels, which were arranged side-by-side and blocked the view of all objects at the south end of the room. "You've been painting, I see." Rob reached out, grabbed a corner of a sheet and began to lift.

"No!"

Rob recoiled, dropping the sheet.

"Please," Ty said. "Not that one. It's not ready."

"Sorry."

"This one. Over here. But before I uncover it, please stand back."

Rob retreated.

"A little more," Ty urged.

Stepping backward almost to the door, Rob could feel a certain tension in the room, high-keyed vibes from his friend. Ty pulled on the sheet, and it fell to the floor to expose a portrait of an auburn-haired girl—a breathtakingly beautiful oil painting meticulously brushed to create dramatic contrasts. The blue eyes of the young woman, portrayed at the age of 18 or 19, seemed to plead as they asked questions. Behind her, against the night sky, stood a Ferris wheel, its ring of tiny, bright lights forming a distant halo above and beyond the auburn hair that captured the midway lights, giving it a bewitching illumination against the blackness of the night. Rob knew at once that this was the mysterious Amy of the county fair. He also knew that the portrait, was, without question, the finest piece of artwork that Ty had ever created. He said nothing while trying to pull together his thoughts.

"Well?" Ty asked as his eyes begged for a response.

"It's beautiful. No. It's more than that. It's spellbinding."

"Do you really think so?"

"Of course I think so."

"It's the girl..."

"I know who it is. I didn't know she was still on your mind. It's been years."

"No it hasn't. It's been since yesterday. Only yesterday."

"What are you saying?"

"She's been part of my life all along. But now she's really back into it again."

"Literally or figuratively? Do you mean you've actually seen her again?"

"Oh yes. Again and again. Twice in the supermarket. Several times at her house, but often just a glimpse."

"Ty, we went through this before. You feel sorry for this girl."

"She's a woman now."

"Okay. You feel sorry for this woman, and you mistake your feelings for love. And, damnit, if you're stalking her like it sounds, you're really asking for trouble. What's with you?" Rob gave a noisy sigh of exasperation. "It's true that people get crushes on strangers. Obsessions, that's what they are. Like frustrated old maids who get hung up on movie stars." His words threw him for a second, but he caught himself and brushed off the image of Marjorie. "Or like that Hinckley dude who shot Reagan because he craved Jodie Foster after seeing her in a movie."

Ty refused to respond. He turned and walked from the room. Again Rob followed, and again they sat opposite each other at the coffee table, both silent, both looking down, both picking at their fingernails.

"I'm sorry, Ty." Rob spoke slowly and softly. "I know you're not going to shoot the president. It's just that we've been friends for a long time now, and I've watched you in action. We've spent nights out together. We've gone to a lot of parties together. I've introduced you to scads of women. You always shy away. Even when you date, you never follow up. But you fall in love with this deaf woman, from afar, no less. An image. Something almost intangible. Someone you don't have to fear. Someone who's weaker than you. Someone you can never have. Someone who's not perfect and needs care like so many of the other people in your life. Don't you see what you're doing?"

"I know what you think. But believe me, I'm not mistaking pity for love. Besides, I don't pity her because she's deaf. Being deaf might be an advantage in her life for all I know. It's true I'd like to free her, because she's in the hands of a religious fanatic who keeps her a virtual prisoner. And I don't crave her simply because she's someone I can't have. Believe me, I'd love to be with her. I'd love to hold her in my arms."

"To comfort her."

"No, to love her!" Ty looked at his buddy in a beseeching way as if praying to be understood.

Rob studied his friend's face. "You're really hurting, aren't you?"

"It's like a big dash of hurt tossed into a blissful stew. Feeling like I do is... well, it's wonderful and beautiful, but so fucking painful."

"If you're in that kind of shape you're not going to listen to me no matter what advice I give."

"Maybe. I guess what I want is for you to listen to me."

"Okay. I'll listen." Rob gave a smile of reassurance. "In fact,

I'm curious as hell to find out how you found her again. In the supermarket?"

"No. Doc Anderson led me to her." A disturbing feeling flashed into Ty's mind as he recalled that afternoon in Rob's house, near that haunting staircase, when he mentioned the physician and "a deaf girl who refuses help." To distract himself and Rob, he said, "Let me get you a beer." He darted to the kitchen. "You didn't fully answer my first question—about loving someone you barely know."

"I think your question is rhetorical. You don't want to hear about physical attraction, idol worship, crushes. You've already made up your mind and you're looking for approval. You want your ol' buddy to back you up. Hell, I guess you're the expert now."

Ty stood in the kitchen doorway, holding two bottles of beer. "Are you telling me to trust my own feelings?"

"I'm not telling you anything. But it comes down to that, I guess. Let's face it, you're not going to accept any advice from me unless it agrees with your own feelings. So, that's what you're left with—your feelings."

Ty forced a silly grin as he walked toward his friend. "God damn, you're a big help."

"Hey, I'm pulling for you. There've been times in my life when I've followed my instincts against advice. There've been times when I've been hurt, too. But, I suppose that's part of living."

Ty handed a bottle of beer to Rob, seated himself and mused for a moment. "Some say that Elizabeth Barrett and Robert Browning fell in love before they met. Through their writings."

"An interpretation by the romantics, I'm sure."

"I wrote to Amy in sign language. It was painstaking work. I expressed my feelings as best I could. Yesterday she slipped me a note, written in English. She thanked me and told me she would keep my letter hidden in a little wooden box under her bed. But she asked me to stay away. She said her father was a good man, and that they believed if God had meant her to hear she would hear." Ty took a lengthy swig from his bottle of beer. "I can't stay away from her, and I don't care whether she can hear. I just wanted her to know she might have an option, and I told her so in my letter. Doc

Anderson says they can do great things today. They actually have ear transplants. They can replace the cochlea when the hair cells have died. It's amazing. It's like putting a tiny snake inside a seashell. And a computer can tell if the implant transmits sound."

"You told her this?"

"Yes, but with care. I didn't want to give her false hopes. But I guess that doesn't matter anyway. Her old man has her convinced that only God should cure, and only when He wants to." Ty drank more beer. "Doc Anderson had a chance to examine Amy when he was making a call on Redrock Road. Amy was there helping a sick neighbor."

Rob wiped his lips after a gulp of beer, then asked, "So what did the doc find out?"

"An operation might work. That's all he could say. He warned me that a transplant is not for every deaf person. Some people should stay in the deaf culture. He said sometimes making a change is like living in two worlds—using sign language and thinking in English—and it's not for everybody."

For a moment, neither man spoke. Rob was first to break the silence: "Well, now I can see why you haven't been in touch. Frankly, I was pissed. I needed your help."

Ty looked down at his bottle of beer. He knew only too well that Amy was not the only reason he had kept his distance from Juniper Lane. His lack of response to Rob's remarks filled him with discomfort. Finally he pushed himself into saying, "Let me know what I can do."

"Maybe you should call when you see some open time during your vacation."

"There's something else," Ty blurted out, "but I'm not ready to explain."

"Oh?"

"Hey, you need another beer." Ty seized Rob's empty bottle with excessive force and was immediately on another fast run to the kitchen.

Puzzlement pushed Rob to the verge of an interrogation, and the probes began to form in his mind. But he thought better of it. Suddenly his instincts told him to back off. In fact, they told him it was time for something else: "If Amy is filling you with artistic fervor... well, that's great. Really great. That painting of her is absolutely beautiful."

Ty immediately sensed his buddy's effort to restrain himself and yield to an upturn in conversation. It took little to push Ty in that direction, for he was eager to explain his driving force. So, on his return to the coffee table with cold, moist bottles of beer, he spouted out, "Maybe she's an obsession, but that's okay. How many times did I say I could have become a first-rate artist if I had ever set my mind to it? But I just kept turning out brochures for dog food. All the time we hear, 'I could have been a great actor, but...' or 'I could have been a great writer, but...' or 'I could have been a great musician, but...' So many people lack drive, and sometimes drive comes from an obsession, from pain, from love or lust, from all sorts of hang-ups, from the need to overcome or prove something."

"Holy shit!" Rob was struck dumb. Never before had he heard his mellow friend unload so much at one time.

Ty opened his mouth to begin anew.

"Are you going to keep on spewing?"

"You bet, damn it! If Van Gogh hadn't had a burning desire for human affection, and a craving for that London girl, maybe we would never have seen his sunflowers."

"You're not planning to cut off your ear for Amy are you?"

Ty ignored the remark and drank beer to moisten his lips for more talk. "Coleridge fought the madness of opium. Beethoven had an over-active libido that gave him syphilis. Whitman released some of his closeted lust into 'Leaves of Grass'."

At a loss for words, Rob simply guzzled beer.

"Don't get me wrong, Rob. I'm not placing myself among the greats. Hell, no! It's just that so many of them were pushed by passions of all sorts. So what the hell, a little guy like me can have his passion, too. Right?"

"And the pain?"

Ty smiled. "Don't fret. I won't cut off my ear."

Rob held up his beer bottle, and with a touch of whimsy said, "To Vincent's ear!" Then, a curious frown changed his expression.

"I hope you'll forgive me for saying this, but I've always felt you lacked passion."

"For women, you mean? Why should I take offense? You've expressed it a thousand times over. Sometimes simply with a look. I'm not stupid." Ty leaned forward to launch a serious thought: "I'm not devoid of experience, like you think. But, in a way, I was almost imprisoned by it. I pulled it inside of me and held it there."

"Can't you tell me?"

"Oh, yes. But it's a long story, and it can wait for a night of heavy 'tyrob' talk at Marty's Tavern. Let me get you another beer."

Chapter Twenty-Two

"She's more lucid than ever. She spoke several times this morning."

That was the telephone message that sent Rob fleeing from Pure-Pup as if his office were ablaze, shouting to his secretary: "I'll get back when I can."

But now disappointment was growing as Rob rocked at Aunt Marjorie's side in the solarium at Green Acres. To him, she seemed no different than before, except that her hands shook more rapidly. Already he had tried to stir her memory more than a dozen times with meaningful words and phases, but her lips returned nothing but twitches.

"Remember your garden?" he asked for the third time. "Remember the iris that bloomed in your garden? And remember your dolls? You would get all dressed up and dance for your dolls. Do you hear me, Aunt Marjorie? I'm Robby. I'm your sister Emily's son. Remember the night I stayed at your house? I was just a kid. You came to my room, remember?"

The latest physician's report on Marjorie's condition had been as varied as all the others, somewhat contradicting the previous report, and giving Rob serious doubts about the doctors' opinions. The latest word: "She's recovered somewhat from her stroke—that is, her last and more serious one—but either Alzheimer's disease or a series of previous, small strokes has had its effect, not to mention the debilitating results of Parkinson's disease and the malfunctions of some major organs."

After another 10 minutes of rattling off names and situations, Rob decided to keep his mouth shut and just rock. It was then that he noticed her eyes. They seemed to follow him—back and forth, back and forth. Though uncertain, he also thought that her head wasn't tipped as far to one side, and that her lips were straighter, no longer down to the right. He watched her closely, paying particular attention to the muscles of her neck, jaw and mouth. But it seemed she made no effort to form words.

Rob glanced at his watch when he heard distant chimes, confirming the arrival of noon. He had been at Green Acres for 40 minutes. In frustration, he said, "Damn it, Aunt Marjorie, speak to me!" A moment later he sighed, stood and started to leave.

"I... I... I re—mem—ber." Marjorie's broken words were barely audible. But Rob heard them.

"My God, was that you, Aunt Marjorie?" His wide eyes rolled. "Oh, Jesus, say something more." He leaned over her, placing his ear almost against her mouth. He heard nothing but quick, uneven breathing. "Oh, please, Aunt Marjorie," he whispered. "Please try. Tell me about Jack. Tell me about your brother Jack."

"He..."

"Yes, yes. Go on."

"He hurt... hurt me." Her words were hardly audible.

"He hurt you? Is that what you said? He hurt you?"

Marjorie failed to respond, and Rob decided to try again: "Tell me about your dolls. You had a lot of pretty dolls. Do you remember them?"

"Ba... by."

"What?"

"Ba... My babies. I paid him t... t... t... take my baby."

* * *

Rob couldn't wait any longer than the first telephone booth. His car bounced onto the macadam of a service station at Marshall and Elm streets, swung around in a semicircle and came to a screeching halt at a pole holding the phone box.

Leaving the car door open, Rob kicked a beer can and tripped over his own feet as he rushed to the telephone. "Bitch," he muttered as he searched his pockets for a quarter. Fumbling at first, he finally managed to drop two dimes and a nickel into the slot and dial Jackie's number. After two rings he let out, "Come on!"

"Hello."

"Jackie, its me. Listen. She talked. And she mentioned babies. That's babies, plural."

"You're kidding."

"And I didn't mention the word 'baby'. In fact, I deliberately avoided it this time, so I wouldn't plant the word in her mind. She said it. All by herself. I asked her about her dolls, and that led to it."

"Well, maybe she meant her dolls when she said 'babies'. Lots of little girls call their dolls babies."

"But they don't say a man took the baby."

"Did she say that?"

"Damn if she didn't! Now we have to find that guy. She definitely said 'he', so we can skip the women. We'll go back to all the men we talked to—the oilman, the gasman, everybody—until we find out who picked up that baby."

"Maybe you will, but I won't! Anyway, you're jumping the gun again. You're making broad assumptions."

"Well, it makes sense that she didn't carry Baby Willow to that hospital. She paid somebody to do it. Just like she paid people to do other things."

"Baby Willow could have been born to a distraught, pregnant teenager or some other unhappy soul."

Rob ignored Jackie's suggestion and talked on, fast and loud: "Let's think about it. Who could've done it? Who's the most likely candidate? Not the baby's father. No way she would have paid the father to do it. And I don't think she would have trusted that strange little meter reader from the gas company. No way was it peeping Sam from the water company, unless she had a sex-change operation. And it sure wasn't that repairman who said he never got paid."

"Maybe Harry Hedgepeth, the mailman. After all, she paid him a hundred bucks to move a clock." Jackie was more facetious than serious.

Rob was silent as his thoughts raced. "Why not! It's possible. If she selected him once, why wouldn't she select him again? She trusted him to come into her house. If she trusted him once, why not trust him again? And she offered him good money. And moving a baby is worth a lot more than moving a clock. Hell, it makes sense. It really makes sense."

"Will you slow down? Damn it, Rob, stop doing that! You're rushing into your world of illusion again. Don't ever criticize me for..."

"Hey, if we don't talk off the top of our heads sometimes, we might not put things together. Just thinking aloud, thinking aloud."

"So, what happens tomorrow?"

"Collins gave me the afternoon off to go to Philly, providing I do business while I'm there. Mrs. Wood said she couldn't see me until late in the day anyway, so it works out. Why don't you come with me? I'll spring for dinner at Bookbinders."

The automatic, recorded operator interrupted: "Please deposit five cents..."

Chapter Twenty-Three

Despite early afternoon sun glare, the city skyline captured Jackie's wandering eyes and held them. Rob, on the other hand, focused on things nearby, including the rear of a silver tank car whose mud flaps danced to the tune of humming tires and growling engines. He drove with one hand on the steering wheel, the other around Jackie's shoulders, and followed the curves of the highway that hung above and west of the Schuylkill River, whose shimmering waters flowed to the southeast. The skyline grew closer with every swerve.

"How it's changed," Jackie said while nestling closer to Rob.

"What's that?"

"The new buildings thrusting above the others."

Heavy green growth darkened the river's edges, contrasting with the water's reflection of a sunny September day. Across the river valley, houses seemed stacked upon each other on steep slopes. Farther south, V-shaped ripples trailed scattered racing sculls.

Highway construction forced Rob's car into a single lane between concrete barriers and slowed traffic to under 30 miles an hour.

"Damn it! Might have known."

Jackie could feel his body tense. "Remember your philosophy about rolling with the punches. We could sing songs to pass the time. Or you could tell me about your efforts to find that retired cashier from Wilson's Department Store."

"Ah, I forgot to tell you. I located her. The store manager found her for me. She lives alone in Scranton. I got through by phone late this morning. And, believe it or not, she remembered Marjorie Worth, only because no one else sent large amounts of cash through the mail. Mrs. Ellis said there was no way she'd ever forget the wads of bills. Auntie never paid by check. It didn't matter how much she owed, she'd just toss greenbacks into an envelope— sometimes one of those large padded envelopes. I figure she paid all her bills that way."

"And probably lost a lot of money," Jackie added.

"And probably didn't care."

After several rounds of "Row, Row, Row Your Boat," Rob switched on his directional signals and turned the car onto an exit ramp.

* * *

Tending to chores in mid-city Philadelphia meant double parking on busy streets, with Jackie nervously waiting in the car as Rob ran the errands. They distributed Pure-Pup press releases to newspapers, then delivered pet-care public service announcements to radio stations, then rode up and down one-way streets until they found the brownstone row house that held Children's Services. Weatherworn gargoyles and relief art marked the facade of the four-story building, once the home of a department store heiress. Decay and misuse had taken its toll on the once handsome entranceway. The iron railings and footscrapers were gone, and the brownstone steps were flaked and uneven. Stained glass windows in the heavy oak doors had been replaced by common plate glass.

Rob proclaimed "The gods are with us!" when he found a parking place in front of row houses a block south of the agency. His struggle to maneuver the car into the tight spot ended with a sigh of victory. He kissed the steering wheel, then kissed Jackie on the neck with a loud sucking pop that she feared might cause a hickey.

"Don't!" She bit his ear in return.

They quickly settled themselves into a forced calm after Rob nudged Jackie and nodded toward a bare-topped teenage boy in jeans standing on the curb across the street.

"Behave yourself. We're being watched."

"Look who's telling me to behave!"

He glanced at his watch. "It's nearly three. Let's go."

* * *

The spacious downstairs rooms of the brownstone house had been cut up into small, modern offices. Rob and Jackie waited in the front space—a 10' X 10' cubicle remindful of a physician's waiting room. They sat on a maple bench that matched other chairs in the simply furnished area. Gone was the high ceiling of yesteryear, replaced by composition blocks only eight feet above the floor. The walls held two certificates and a framed sketch of a woman cradling a child in her arms.

Jackie toyed with Rob's thumb as she said, "So all you found out from the woman in Scranton was that Aunt Marjorie paid her bills in cash, is that it?"

"That's just what I wanted to verify. It explains a lot of things." Rob stretched his legs to shake off the cramps of travel. "We knew she paid her utility bills that way. Now we know she paid her big bills that way—bills for expensive clothes, jewelry and furnishings. That helps explain the lack of bank statements and canceled checks. It explains why my inquiries with area banks came to zero."

"But it doesn't tell us where she hid her money."

"You money-hungry freak! You're still hoping to find that loose board in the floor."

"You know I'm not money hungry, Rob. If we find nothing, we find nothing, and we live happily ever after. But you can't tell me you don't get turned on thinking there might be a cache somewhere in that house."

"I figure she spent every cent of grandpa's money, then decided to waste away."

Rob pulled in his feet and stood when a tall flat-chested, black-haired, hook-nosed woman entered the room. Dressed in a gray suit and wearing horn-rimmed glasses, the woman introduced herself as Thelma Wood, drew up a chair, and told Rob to "Please sit down."

"It's kind of you to see us," Rob said.

"As I understand it, Mr. Putnam, you have some interest in John Willow Doe?"

"Yes. The child tagged Baby Willow by the press."

"Well, as I told you on the phone, I can't open his files to you. We're governed by a lot of city, state and federal regulations. So, frankly, I don't know what I can tell you. But you were so persistent that I agreed to see you. I suppose I can give you a few non-restricted facts and impressions off the top of my head."

Jackie edged away from Rob and propped herself in the corner of the bench as Rob asked, "You said the boy was never adopted?"

"He's in a foster home. He's been in several." Mrs. Wood's expression grew more serious. "But before we go on. May I ask you again about your interest in John Willow? What exactly do you want, Mr. Putnam?"

"Well, frankly, I have evidence—very circumstantial, mind you—that he might have been born to someone I know."

"If that's the case, you should take your evidence to the police." Mrs. Wood turned her eyes on Jackie, then looked back at Rob. "Most John Doe cases stay on the books for a long time. The Willow Case is still open."

"I can't go to the police. Not yet anyway. I need more facts before I can involve others." Rob shot a warning glance at Jackie, then asked, "Why wasn't the boy adopted? Is there something wrong with him?"

"Oh, no. He was a beautiful child?"

"Was?"

"Well, I haven't seen him lately. He must be thirteen or fourteen years old. I suspect he's still a good-looking boy. He always seemed younger than his age. Sort of a baby-faced blond."

"Blond?" Rob had pictured a dark-haired youngster, one with rich, silky, dark hair like Marjorie's. After gathering his thoughts, he asked, "Why wouldn't someone want such a boy?"

"Oh, he was wanted, all right. Couple after couple wanted him. We kept a waiting list. But when it comes to John Does the situation can be pretty sticky, especially if the police are still hunting. At one point they were about to close the case when a letter arrived, starting the hunt all over again."

"A letter?" Rob sat on the edge of the bench. "What letter?"

"Well, again, you'd have to check that with other authorities. The police, I presume. All I know is that we had to put a hold on the adoption process."

Rob glanced at Jackie and muttered, "Holy shoot." He looked back at Mrs. Wood and asked, "When was this? When did the police get this letter?"

"I don't remember for sure. I think the boy was five or six years old."

"And you don't know who the letter was from?"

"Nor do the police, I understand. But you might find out more up your way. If I were you I'd check with your local authorities."

"I'll be damned."

Mrs. Wood stood and said, "If there's nothing more. I've had a busy day and still have several calls to make."

"Please, Mrs. Wood. Can you tell us anything about the contents of that letter."

"No. I didn't see it. That's strictly a police matter."

"But wait. One more thing, please. May we see the boy? Could you tell us where he is?"

"Oh, I'm afraid that's out of the question."

"Why? Can't you tell us the names of the foster parents? We won't do or say anything. Just so I could get a quick look at him."

"No. I'm sorry." Mrs. Wood turned and started to leave the room.

"Wait. Do you have a picture of him? Could you show us a picture?" Rob sprang to his feet and followed Mrs. Wood until Jackie grabbed the back of his coat.

"Don't push, Rob," Jackie whispered. "That won't get you anywhere, and it might spoil things for later."

Chapter Twenty-Four

Again Ty stopped his van on Redrock Road as the sun rose and the birds chirped, but this time he parked it farther from the Harrison driveway, fearful that Amy's father might get suspicious if he saw the van too many times. Nestled close to a straggly mass of mulberry, the van was nearly hidden from anyone turning left from the Harrison driveway and heading northwest on Redrock Road as Sam Harrison did almost every morning. The orange glow from the early sun turned yellow-white by the time Ty heard the pickup truck's engine sputter and race—a sound he had come to know well. He waited until the rat-a-tat-hum grew steady and faded in the distance before deciding whether to drive or walk to the house. Leaving his coat and tie in the van, he again chose to walk, reasoning that he could hide himself better than he could hide the van if Amy's father should return for a forgotten lunch box or something.

While quick-stepping along the road and up the dirt driveway, Ty could feel his heartbeat race as his glands pumped him full of all sorts of emotions. He carried the panda in his right hand, not realizing that he had a strangle hold around its neck.

As usual, Ty began knocking timidly on the door, only to increase the pounding to cause vibrations. Wearing a soft blue dress as if expecting company, Amy came to the door more quickly than before and offered a smile. Ty was immediately plagued with that feeling again—the feeling that Amy was out of place in the Redrock environment, that she belonged somewhere else, that some other influences had molded her.

This time Amy took the panda without hesitating, held it against
her cheek, said thanks with her eyes, then motioned to Ty to stay on
the porch. She was gone in an instant. But Ty paced back and forth
for only a few moments before she returned with an even broader
smile. She stepped onto the porch, closed the door, took Ty's hand
and pulled him down the steps and around the west side of the
house where long, early morning shadows darkened piles of wood
obviously gathered from dead and dying trees and fallen branches.
Guiding him around the heaps, Amy led the way to a backyard
cluttered with old auto parts and rabbit cages. She freed her hand
from his and ran toward the northwest, turning and motioning to
him, urging him to follow. Excited eagerness radiated from her as
she danced across the stubble of undernourished corn.

Ty was nonplused, but his astonishment did not slow his pace.
He caught up with Amy as she pointed to a patch of woods across
the field. It became obvious that she was leading him, in a
beseeching way, to the trees. She took his hand again, and together
they scampered toward the wooded tract where flecks of autumn
colors were beginning to show amidst a full range of greens. First
the field gave way to scrubby brush—sumac and goldenrod, tall
grasses gone to seed, wild mustard and giant mulleins. Then came
the underbrush—huckleberry, wild grape and woody shrubs that
thrive in the shadows of young locust and sassafras trees. Ty and
Amy kicked their way through the thickets and hurried into the
darkness of the tall oaks, maples and pines. Here and there a tulip
tree rose like a straight pole pushing through the dark canopy
above, and an occasional beech bulged its roots and displayed moss
on its smooth, gray bark.

Amy became excited when a patch of light shone through the
evergreens that had begun to outnumber the leaf-bearing trees. She
tugged on Ty's arm, tried some quick sign language and pointed
ahead. Ty followed Amy's twists and turns among the pines and
hemlocks. As the brightness grew closer, the trees became burdened
with vines. Hanging curtains of wild grape gave way to
honeysuckle at the clearing. Amy pushed through the vines,
spreading them left and right, and unveiling her special place—an
oasis in the woods, an opening where a small, wandering stream

flowed around rocks, splashed down falls, and rippled over smooth stones and pebbles of all colors. At the water's edge, arrowhead plants and touch-me-nots sucked strength from the moist earth. There, too, was a broad, flat rock of obvious importance to Amy, for she became animated as she pointed to it and spoke with her hands. It didn't take long for Ty to grasp her meaning. This was her rock, her seat, her smooth piece of granite from which to dangle her feet into the bubbling waters of the cool brook.

Ty smiled broadly as he watched Amy, then used his hands and fingers to tell her about his crash course in sign language—a steady drilling of himself for weeks at all hours, and a double devotion to the task during his current vacation.

Suddenly Amy giggled and pointed to Ty's trousers. He looked down and saw nettles and burs clinging to his pants. "Oh jeez," he muttered as he started to pull the stickers off one by one. She knelt and helped him. Her closeness aroused him, and he pulled back. She glanced up with surprise and tried to read his expression. He turned away and busied himself pulling at the burs.

Amy touched Ty's shoulder to get his attention, just as he rid his trousers of the last prickly seed. He gazed into her eyes, saw that she was pleading to be "heard," tried to decipher her hand signals, but failed to grasp every word. "Happy place" and "beauty" and "peace" and "escape" were among the signs he understood. They were enough to tell him that this was Amy's place for breaking free of the humdrum. Here, he figured, she found a touch of splendor and fantasy.

Shedding her shoes, Amy sat on her rock and lowered her feet into the stream. Ty yanked off his shoes and socks, rolled up his trousers and hurried to her side. They smiled at each other, wiggled their toes, and kicked the water, splashing it on nearby rocks. As time passed, Ty realized that Amy's purpose in bringing him to her secret place was simply to show him her special hideaway, an escape that obviously made up an important part of her life, perhaps the most important part. There was little question about her naivete and innocence, made apparent not only by her free abandon, but by the very fact that she had led a man to such an isolated retreat.

Ty had come prepared with pad and pencil, knowing too well

that his fingers and hands had yet to be fully trained. When communication became complicated, as it did when "talk" turned to Amy's deafness, he pulled the small pad and stubby pencil from his pocket and scribbled notes. He wrote about man's free will, God-given choices, and advancements in medicine that were gifts not to be ignored. But Amy's eyes grew fearful as she shook her head and tried to close out such thoughts. When she stopped reading his notes, Ty realized he had pushed too far, so he turned the "conversation" back to birds, trees, ferns, mosses and lichens.

When Amy's eyes once again danced with fun and innocence, Ty kissed her on the lips. She withdrew and her smile vanished. The courage that he had mustered slipped away fast, his face reddened, and a sheepish embarrassment controlled his expression. Amy's sensitivities immediately told her that she had hurt him. Suddenly she felt terribly wrong. When sadness in her eyes began to drift away, she placed a kiss on his lips—a short kiss that helped him recover and sent a tingle through his body. Yet moments passed before he kissed her again. She took it in, and offered back. The kiss grew long while intoxication permeated their bodies.

A slight breeze stirred the touch-me-not leaves and bent the stems of the arrowheads. From a distant treetop came the call of a warbler.

Chapter Twenty-Five

Rob and 72-year-old Harry Hedgepeth sat on the stoop in front of Hedgepeth's red-brick row house, their knees spread wide. It was nearly dinner time, and Rob was still dressed in his office clothes—a navy blue suit and deep red necktie against a white shirt. Harry wore a plaid shirt to go with his cowboy hat and boots. He chewed tobacco and occasionally spit over the iron railing into a juniper bush.

The five o'clock sun was but a hazy glow behind thin clouds.

A calico cat wandered by, looked up at Rob and Harry, then scurried off.

The old man talked about the crash of the dirigible Hindenburg, soup lines during the Great Depression, Allied troops landing at Anzio during World War II, and a dozen other recollections from the 1930s and '40s. Jackie was right, thought Rob, he likes to talk, and he's definitely a bit peculiar.

Anxious to return the conversation to Aunt Marjorie, Rob waited patiently for a break in the reminiscences. When it came, he plunged right in: "What else did you carry for Marjorie Worth?"

Harry was taken aback. "What?"

"Well, I know she trusted you. She wasn't going to trust just anyone. Surely she asked you to do more than carry a clock."

"Well, not really, I don't think. Nothing that comes to mind."

"Come on, Mr. Hedgepeth. Anybody who can recall the things you remember about your mail route and the war surely can remember carrying a baby to Willowood Hospital."

Harry started. Rob could see and feel the recoil, and he knew at once that he had guessed right.

"Baby? What do you mean, baby?"

"It's okay, Mr. Hedgepeth. Really. What you did was a good thing. You can't get in trouble for it. Anyway, it was a long time ago. Please. Tell me about it."

Harry revealed his discomfort. He shifted his buttocks, spit out his entire tobacco chew, and looked up into the air.

"Please," Rob repeated. "Marjorie Worth is my aunt and I'm living in her house. I have to know. It's important."

Harry looked at Rob. For seconds he just studied the young man. In time he spoke: "That baby might be related to you?"

"That's right. That baby might be my cousin."

The old man pulled out his package of tobacco. "Okay. It was like the other time. She left me an envelope with instructions and money." He paused, bit off a wad of tobacco, and chewed for awhile as his thoughts gathered. "I never saw a thousand dollar bill before. No, you're right, I couldn't forget. I'll never forget that thousand dollar bill. And I'll never forget that little baby." He spit over the railing. "I went back to the house late that night, like the instructions said. The baby was in one of those old wicker laundry baskets. Tiny thing. All wrapped up in a blue blanket on a soft pillow." Harry spit into the juniper bush again, shook his head a couple times, then went on: "The basket was in a patch of shrubs, just like she said. I carried it to my car and put it on the back seat. To tell you the truth, I was scared. The little fellow started to cry, and I closed the doors fast and made sure all the windows were up." He cleared his throat, put his little finger into his ear and shook it fast, then looked down at his feet.

"Please go on."

"Well, I drove to Willowood. It was the closest hospital. I parked near one of the entrances and waited. And, when I saw no one going in or out, I put the baby at the door. It was real late. The baby started to cry. And I took off fast."

Chapter Twenty-Six

"He didn't chew tobacco in front of me," Jackie said while trying to slow the old, metal porch swing that was being powered by Rob. He fought her with every push, getting a childish delight out of forcing the squeaking swing to overextend itself.

"That's all you have to say?" asked Rob, who had rattled off every detail of his meeting with Harry Hedgepeth as soon as he joined Jackie on her parent's back porch—a wide Victorian porch with pillars topped with gingerbread; a porch edged by a railing that enclosed pots of geraniums and begonias; a porch that overlooked an old-fashioned backyard heavy with perennials. Phlox and Shasta daisies shared the deep garden with clumps of rhubarb and horseradish. A pear tree held a rope swing, and an arbor of vines yielded grapes in season.

"No, I have more to say." Jackie tickled his ear. "But only if you swing more gently."

Rob smiled comically as he slowed the swinging. "So, now. Give me your reaction to my success as a sleuth."

"Oh, you're about to take all the credit, is that it? Keep in mind that I led you to Mr. Hedgepeth."

"But without belief."

"Damn you!" She squeezed his nose. "I was the first to say Baby Willow was Marjorie's kid. I was the first to think she might have given birth to two babies. Remember that night in the park?"

"But you didn't keep the faith, baby." He stuck his tongue into her ear.

"Stop it!"

"But I thought you liked that. You used to say it tickled your tummy."

"Not when you talk to me like that."

"Tell you what. Tonight we'll go skipping."

"Skipping?"

"When's the last time you went skipping down the street?"

"I don't know. When I was twelve years old, I guess."

"Isn't that a shame? What happens to us when we grow up?"

"Well, I think we'd look mighty silly skipping down the street."

"But skipping would make us laugh, giggle, smile, and feel free—free like that 'Bluebird of Happiness'."

"And we think Hedgepeth is eccentric! God, you top him by a mile."

"In a far, far different way. Come skipping with me and you'll see."

"You're nuts! Can you imagine what the neighbors would think of us?"

"That's the point. We shouldn't care what the neighbors think. Don't you get a deeper meaning from what I'm saying?"

"Ah, let me put on my thinking cap and interpret the deeper meanings of skipping."

A stir in the bushes caught Rob's attention. "Here comes your father."

Coming out from under the grape arbor and walking toward the porch was Alex P. Harwood, marketing director for Mayberry Jacobs, Inc., manufacturer of synthetic fibers—a man whose handsome, evenly chiseled features helped him climb the corporate ladder, a man whose thick dark hair was becoming even more of an asset as it grayed at the temples. He carried a basket of tomatoes freshly picked from his vegetable garden at the far end of the yard, near his compost pile. The 50-year-old executive had yet to shed his gray pin-stripes and white collar.

"He seems so out of place," Rob commented. "This rustic yard always reminds me of an old grandmother's domain. Your folks seem too cosmopolitan."

"Dad likes both worlds. He says a home should be a retreat. Won't our home be our special sanctuary, our retreat?"

"I hope so. It should be, what with a walled-in garden and the memories of a recluse."

"I could do without the latter."

"I think your old man's beginning to accept me," Rob whispered. "At least he doesn't keep pointing out how long it took him to own a house. And he's stopped calling me a 'dog-food flack'."

"But what if he knew of your craving to skip?"

Rob laughed, then quickly forced a more serious expression as Jackie's father mounted the porch. "Good looking tomatoes."

"They could win blue ribbons," said Alex. "Look at this." He held up a fully ripened tomato that more than covered his hand. "Must weight two to three pounds." He looked at Jackie. "I'll get your mother to slice it up for dinner."

A waft of roast beef aroused hunger in Rob when Alex entered the pantry, allowing kitchen aromas to escape.

"I can taste your mom's cooking already," Rob said as his thoughts drifted to his mother. "Guess where my mom went today?"

"Where?"

"To see her sister."

Jackie sat up straight as her eyes popped. "You're kidding?"

"Nope. Haven't heard the results. But she went. I suppose some sort of guilt pushed her there. I guess she wanted to see Marjorie before the old gal died."

"I'll be damned. Why didn't you tell me?"

"I meant to."

"Who would have thought."

"I stopped by at noon, and she was all in a tizzy. She kept changing dresses and rearranging her hair, chattering fast, and flitting about."

"God. After all these years." Jackie moved closer to Rob and put her head on his shoulder. "Life takes strange turns, doesn't it. Sometimes I thought you pushed her too hard, came on too strong. But you did get her to open up. I guess that's good. At least it should be, in the long run." She allowed her eyes to drift about, taking in the arbor, the stump of an old wisteria vine, and the swing on the pear tree. "You know, I've lived in this house since I was little. I get these kind of funny feelings when I think of leaving it." She clung more tightly to Rob. "Will you promise me something?"

"What?"

"Make me a swing, like the one on the pear tree?"

Rob kissed her cheek. "You betcha. I'll fix you a super swing. And I'll push you whenever you want."

"Well, I don't know about that."

"What do you mean?"

"You can't be trusted. You'd probably swing me right up over the tree branch. What made you that way, anyhow?"

Rob laughed and rubbed his nose on her neck. "Exactly what way do you mean?"

"What made you such an idiot? Was it that fraternity house at State College?"

"I was always a tease, even as a little brat. Maybe it was some sort of defense mechanism, but to me it was just kidding around and having fun." He tickled her under the arm, then he whispered, "Shouldn't you be helping your mother?"

"Yes. But she told me to get out of her kitchen. Come to think of it, I'll probably be glad to have my own kitchen." Jackie pulled away from Rob, put her head back, and let her mind travel. "You know, Rob. This house has a lot of special parts. When I was a little girl I loved going up and down and around and around that back stairway. None of my friends had dark, circular stairways leading up from their kitchens. There's something about a tall Victorian house. It gave me a lot of places to play, a lot of secret places to hide and talk with my dollies."

"H'm. Shades of Aunt Marjorie."

"No! Don't you dare compare!" Jackie glowered at him. "Sure, I had my dolls like most little girls. And I could share my childhood woes with some of the special ones. Maybe that's what dolls are all about. I bet you fed your troubles to a teddy bear."

"To a little yellow dog with blue-button eyes."

"So maybe your Aunt Marjorie needed a lot of dolls."

"Speaking of Marjorie. I've been thinking about that letter—the one Mrs. Wood mentioned. I've been trying to figure out how we might unearth some facts about it without going to the police. If that case was opened up again because of that letter, there had to be some press coverage. One of the police reporters is bound to know something. Clarence Scutter has been covering the cops for the local *Times* for fifteen years or more. But I don't want to alert the press unless there's no other way. First, I think we should check back copies of the *Times*. There might have been a story or two."

"That means hours of looking at microfilm."

"I know." He put his arm around her. "And I was wondering if..."

"No! Absolutely not!" She freed herself and pushed him away. "How could you even ask?"

"Well, you didn't give me a chance to ask. Now listen to me, will you? This is how we'll do this."

"If you think I'm going to sit at one of those stupid machines for hour after hour, you're crazy! I mean it, Rob!" She leaped from the swing and turned her eyes on him.

"Okay. Okay." Rob assumed the role of a martyr, showing it in tone and posture. "I'll do it myself. That means, of course, that you'll have to shop alone Saturday for those upstairs curtains. And for the back-room wallpaper. And for that bedroom rug."

Jackie gritted her teeth while continuing to stare at him.

"Cat got your tongue?" Rob asked.

"That's a stupid expression. It's also a very irritating one right now. You see this potted begonia? How would you like it in your lap?"

Rob instinctively protected his groin with both hands, bringing a smile to Jackie's lips and a sparkle to her eyes. A change that ignited a laugh in Rob. Soon they were both laughing and pawing over each other.

"Isn't love wonderful?" Rob asked, prompting Jackie to hit him on the top of the head.

Rob's return attack was a fervent kiss on the lips, accompanied by a firm embrace. Jackie was pushed back against a corner porch-post, her arms tightly wrapped around her fiancée, when the pantry door opened and her mother announced, "Soups on!" Anne Harwood was a trim 48-year-old woman with closely cropped, soft brown hair—a woman who worked to keep her belly flat and her thighs thin, not only for her own well-being, but to aid her husband's climb toward a corporate vice presidency. She stared directly at Jackie and Rob, did not apologize for the interruption, and flatly stated, "You'll have plenty of time for that later. Right now we're going to eat before my food gets cold." A forthright woman, she had always been the family's key force. Her face showed strong character—a solid chin, straight nose, high cheekbones and sharp but discerning eyes.

Rob and Jackie stood hand-in-hand looking at her as a monarch butterfly winged its way across the porch, slowing its zigzagging flight again and again to flutter in mid-air.

Chapter Twenty-Seven

Jackie chose the city library over the newspaper morgue, simply because she was more familiar with it. The microfilm machines were lined up against the wall on the library mezzanine. Of the six stations, only one other was occupied. A studious-looking Japanese youth sat with his chin in his hand and gazed into the machine at the far end, five down from Jackie.

Hours of reading images of newspaper pages from a TV-like screen was wearing on Jackie, and she rubbed her eyes often. At 1 p.m., four hours after she had entered the library, she pushed her chair back and closed her eyes in hopes of reducing the pain in her head. She resumed her efforts five minutes later, only to stop again when her stomach growled. It was time to sneak a few bites of her peanut butter crackers. (Food was forbidden in the library.) After some secret munching, she was again staring at the images.

The Japanese student left at 2:10, smiling and nodding at Jackie as he passed by. Now it was time for her to fold her arms in front of the machine and rest her head kindergarten-style. As the ache in her head subsided, her thoughts drifted to Rob and how extraordinary it felt to be in his arms and how incredible it was to realize that she would spend the rest of her life with him. Such reflections gave her enough energy to return to work. But another hour passed before a small one-column headline grabbed her attention:

Police Reopen
'Baby W' Case

Jackie was quick to absorb the lead paragraph of the news story:
Police today reopened the Baby Willow case after receiving a letter
from someone claiming to be the mother of John Willow Doe, an
infant boy left on hospital steps more than five years ago.

After seizing her pen, Jackie began to write on her pad of
yellow paper.

* * *

Forty minutes later Jackie was outdoors speaking to Rob from a
telephone booth in front of the concrete steps and Greek columns of
the library. Again and again she glanced at her pad as she rattled off
parts and pieces of 1984 news reports.

"So the letter was really an effort to reach the kid when he was
about five or six years old, and the only way she knew how was
through the police. She was obviously trying to tell the boy that she
cared, that she loved him. This first story and a follow-up the next
day indicate that the police were trying to track the letter and find
the writer. Apparently they didn't succeed."

"Well, if Marjorie wrote the letter, it's strange they didn't track her
down through Harry Hedgepeth," Rob said. "He must have known her
handwriting. Hell, if Auntie never left the house, he probably posted
all her mail. And let's not forget the notes she wrote to him."

"If Marjorie wrote it, she was smart. It was a clip-and-paste job. The
kind kidnappers put together from printed words. Neither article says
anything about the envelope. She could have printed on that. Maybe she
even had someone else mail it. Like the grocery boy or the paper boy."

"Does either story give the location of the kid at that time?"

"No, but the follow-up gives an important lead that will excite
your bones, Mr. Putnam. The reporter did some tracking of his own
and quotes Baby Willow's foster father—that is, of course, the kid's
foster father back in the early eighties. Chances are that guy no longer
has the boy, but he just might be able to lead you somewhere."

"Where's he from?"

"That's the trouble. It doesn't say. But his name is Clinton Cuthbert. I figure there can't be too many of them around. Anyway, I think the Cedar Valley area is the place to start looking."

"Why do you say that?"

"Because the second-day story says a copy of the letter was turned over to Lieutenant Albert Gibbons of the Cedar Valley State Police Barracks for delivery to the kid through his foster parents at an appropriate time."

"Bravo! You get a dozen Brownie points for one hell of a job!"

"You owe me a steak dinner at Smilies. A total spread, from soup to nuts."

"Fair enough."

Chapter Twenty-Eight

For the fourth morning in a row Ty sat next to Amy on her special rock in her special place. Both wiggled their toes as they wet their feet. Each day since his first visit to Amy's glistening retreat in the woods, Ty had dressed more casually—and on this day wore blue shorts and a blue-and-white striped crew shirt. Boyish clothes went well with Ty's boyish looks, and his vacation days and the warm September weather gave him a relaxed spirit. His socks and sneakers hung from the branch of a nearby sassafras.

But his preparations this time had been more than the selection of clothes. Increasingly puzzled about Amy's background, he had used breakfast-time to write questions on index cards—questions he had meant to ask before, but couldn't or didn't for one reason or another. No longer would he allow timidity, preoccupation or fear to hold him back.

Ty found Amy particularly attractive in her yellow shorts and white top, and when settled on the rock he wrapped his arm around her waist without hesitation—and without her rebuff. As they wet their feet, Amy busied herself teaching Ty more sign language. In time, Ty grasped her hands, telling her to stop. The pad of paper slipped from his lap into the water, and he let it float away despite her protests. He pulled a card from his pocket and handed it to her. She read: "Did you always live in that house?"

Amy shook her head and signed "bigger" and "better"—hand movements that Ty understood. Then she took the pencil from him and wrote on the card: "Before mother died."

Ty drew another card from his pocket, and Amy read: "Have you always lived with your father?" She signed "grandparents" and "deaf school," but Ty failed to understand. She wrote words on the card and handed it to him.

By the time Amy had read and answered all the questions on the index cards, Ty had learned—or at least thought he understood—that Sam Harrison had fallen from rung to rung down a ladder of inadequate success that his wife had tried to push him up, with no help from her well-to-do parents. Ty also learned that Amy's mother had taught her politeness and manners. And he discerned that Amy had boarded at deaf school as a child and stayed briefly with her grandparents after her mother's death; that her father had found her, taken her from the sins of high living, and saved her for Christ.

Ty found it harder and harder to concentrate on the signs, symbols, drawings and words, mainly because he was next to her, touching her, wanting her. After a few more struggling attempts to understand, he took her chin in his hand, turned her face toward his, and looked into her eyes. As silent messages moved from eyes to eyes, blissful feelings spread through their bodies and held them transfixed until Amy broke the spell by looking away. Using sign language, she told him that "peculiar feelings" pervaded her body. She patted her chest rapidly to indicate palpitations.

Again Ty turned her chin and gazed into her eyes. He ran his finger gently down her nose and across her cheek. Then he touched her lips.

Suddenly Amy's eyes moistened. Pushing and pulling emotions caused confusion, and her expression showed perplexity. She lifted her feet from the water, stood, turned her back, and stepped away. After walking but a few steps, she hesitated, partly because of her bare feet, partly because of her desire to be held in Ty's arms.

Ty sensed her ambivalence. He had seen it each day—the vacillation, the tug-of-war. Each time he had responded differently, but always gently. This time he walked up behind her and touched her softly, placing his hands on her shoulders. Within seconds his hold grew firm, and he pulled her back against his chest and pressed his cheek against her head. He stayed with her, holding her, swaying her slightly.

In time Ty led Amy back to the rock where they sat quietly, her head on his shoulder.

Later, when the sun was high enough to send flickers of light through the treetops, Amy began to use her hands rapidly, giving sign after sign. He grasped enough meaning to understand her need to tell him about her unfamiliar feelings, the newness of her emotions.

Their ability to communicate, not only with sign language and pencil, but with eyes, touch, lips and intuition, grew steadily as the morning waned. Time had sped by, and suddenly Amy showed alarm, looked toward the sky, and leaped to her feet, sprinkling Ty with water. She pointed toward the house, and indicated her need to return home quickly. Her anxiety showed as she scampered about, grabbing her socks and shoes and stumbling as she slipped into them. Ty moved fast, bending the limb of the sassafras as he pulled down his sneakers.

* * *

After clearing their way through the woods and brush, Ty and Amy started to walk hand-in-hand across the stubble of the cornfield. They were barely a third of the way to the house when Ty felt Amy stiffen. Her hand squeezed his with unusual strength. He looked up and immediately saw what Amy had sighted: her father's pickup truck parked at the side of the house.

"Oh, my God," Ty muttered. He looked into Amy's worried eyes, then placed his hand on her shoulder and pressed tightly to comfort her. He tried to disguise his fears, and, with a firm hold, attempted to tell her that they would face her father together.

Amy kept pointing to the sun, then toward the house. Ty soon grasped her meaning: noontime was near; her father sometimes came home for lunch.

They were more than halfway across the field when Sam Harrison appeared in front of the house. He looked down the driveway, then turned and scanned the northern horizon. When he searched the fields to the northwest he saw Amy and Ty coming toward him. He made no effort to walk toward them. Instead, he kept his eyes on them, wavering not one iota, and secured his footing as if building a bulwark against attack.

Amy began using sign language frantically as she and Ty neared her father, but Sam ignored her and fixed his stare on Ty. "What do you think you're doing with my daughter?" he asked. His tone was harsh as he continued: "Why are you here? What do you want?"

Ty's first words were not what he, himself, had expected: "I love your daughter, Mr. Harrison."

"Love her!? You don't even know her!"

"That's not true."

"I don't know what your game is, but I don't like it." Tall, lean and gaunt, Sam towered over Ty. "You and that Dr. Anderson—schemin' an' plottin' against my daughter's beliefs."

"No, you don't understand."

"You're damn right I don't understand. You get away from her." Sam grasped Amy's wrist and pulled her from Ty. "Where'd you take her. Over t' them woods?"

"We just wet our feet in the stream. Please, Mr. Harrison, let me explain. As strange as it must seem to you, I really do love your daughter."

"You're trespassin'. You don't belong here." He pushed Amy toward the house and pointed forcefully at the door, but she refused to leave, backing up only a few steps. Again turning to Ty, he yelled, "I'm a peaceful, God-fearing man, and I never hit no one—never. But I will. To protect her. To protect her I will, and God will know why."

"I don't want to fight with you. But I'm not afraid to tell you that you're being unfair to your daughter."

Rage reddened Sam's bony face. "Don't you try to tell me how to raise my own flesh-and-blood."

"I know you mean well, but..."

"Get out of here!"

"Please, Mr. Harrison."

"If you don't get out of here, there's goin' t' be plenty of trouble."

Ty tried his best to overcome his soft nature. He refused to back up when Sam stepped within inches of him and looked down on his boyishness. He forced a steady stare into Sam's grim face and said, "Amy and I feel a wonderful joy when we are together, and I don't care if she can hear or not, if that's bothering you. I don't care. I just know how I feel."

Amy tried to force herself between the antagonists as the look of anger increased in her father's eyes. The men side-stepped away from Amy, and Sam harshly insisted, "Y' can't love someone y' don't even know." He kept staring at Ty as if the young man were the devil incarnate. "I've met evil men before and I know they come in all shapes and sizes."

"You've got it all wrong."

"Did you touch her? Did you hurt her?"

"I would never hurt Amy. I could never hurt her." At this point Ty shocked himself by shouting, "I'm not leaving here without her."

Sam reached out with his trembling hand and grabbed Ty's crew shirt and tightened it around his neck. Noises of panic and fear came up from Amy's throat. She thrashed her arms widely, then took hold of her father's arm and tried to pull it from Ty's throat. She began to weep. When her weeping grew to heaving and sobbing cries, her father let go of Ty and backed away horrified by his own violence.

Amy used sign language, her lips and her eyes to ask Ty to leave. Again and again she pleaded with him. Finally he nodded and backed off. He kept looking at her, then at her father, who seemed immobilized as he glared at them. Ty kept backing down the driveway. In time he turned and walked away.

Chapter Twenty-Nine

Pepperville wasn't even on the map. In fact, it was not a legal municipality. It was one of those clusters of houses called communities, having formed around a general store and a service station at a crossroads within a township. Actually, the trip to Pepperville was a bucolic treat, offering pastoral scenes aplenty. Rob hadn't informed Jackie of their destination when inviting her for a country drive on Sunday afternoon. To ensure her acceptance, he had promised her a dinner at the Mohawk Inn on the way home. Although, in truth, he still owed her several dinners for the 15 interviews she had conducted before balking. Her presence in Pepperville was vital to his plan. Rob was well aware that a young couple could elicit child-care or adoption information more easily than could a man on his own. Jackie, being far from stupid, suspected there was more to Rob's invitation than a ride through rolling hills of alfalfa. Both had scores of chores before the wedding, and a leisurely Sunday drive was way off the base path.

They had driven no farther than the third herd of milking cows when Jackie reminded Rob: "Okay, I know you're up to something. But remember. No more interviews for me. You promised."

"Just be with me, okay? And we'll order the blue-plate special at the Mohawk."

"That makes me more suspicious than ever. Besides, you promised me lobster and steak after my fruitless treks to Allentown and Wilkes-Barre department stores, whose delivery idiots didn't know Marjorie from a gopher. Come on. Fill me in. What plot is unfolding today?"

"Maybe I just want to show you the Appalachian foothills of Lockwood Township."

"Sure. And I want to show you the teats on a cow's udder."

Rob laughed. "You mean tits, don't you?"

"I was being genteel."

"You know, as fillies go you're pretty smart."

"If you weren't driving, I'd twist your gonads."

"My, another euphemistic quip. What have you become?"

"Fast but urbane. To keep up with you, but on a higher plane."

"How poetic!"

"Now, let's cut the prattle." She pulled on his ear.

Rob sucked in a deep breath and exhaled slowly. "Okay. This is how it shapes up. I'm going to ask you to take part in a big white lie."

"I don't like the sound of that. How white is it?"

"As the driven snow. So help me."

"I'm listening."

As Rob gathered his thoughts, his car bounced over a railroad crossing and sped between newly plowed fields ready for winter wheat. Pine groves broke the openness. Then came fields of soybeans, and a distant combine, its paddles raising dust.

"We're on our way to visit Mr. and Mrs. Clinton Cuthbert in Pepperville at the northern tip of Cedar Valley. Over in the hills on the western side of Lockwood Township."

"You're telling me you located Cuthbert, right?"

"Thanks to you and a couple Cedar Valley phone books. Nothing to it." Rob slowed the car on a no-passing curve through a wooded stretch. "I told him we got his name from that adoption agency. He thinks we're a childless couple interested in adopting the boy. I said we were struggling with our decision, and we wanted some input from him and the other foster parents."

"You call that a white lie?"

"Hey, I had no choice. I couldn't figure any other way. And no one's getting hurt. Good might come of it. Doesn't that make it white?" Rob took a fast look at Jackie's expression of perplexity, then said, "Just keep telling yourself it's for a good cause."

"To tell you the truth, Rob, I've never been sure of the cause."

"Trust me."

"I'm beginning to wonder."

"Oh, come on. Detectives use subterfuge all the time."

"You're not a detective."

"You'll have to admit we've become pretty good at it."

"At lying?"

"No. At investigating. Hell, you don't want your microfilm scanning to go for naught, do you?"

Jackie was quiet as she pondered the thought. She slid down in her seat and grimaced while the car traveled through open country. The two-lane road, like a twisting ribbon, could be seen for miles ahead as it dipped into a valley of patchwork-quilt farmland and rose into the distant hills.

As the car sped downhill, Jackie shifted in her seat, sat upright, cleared her throat and proclaimed, "Our marriage isn't going to work."

"What?"

"I can't marry a man who isn't open and honest. And I feel funny about my own pretense with so many of those people. I can imagine some of the lines you used."

"Holy shit! You're too much! Look, I'll write to Cuthbert later on and confess. Okay?"

"That's just part of what I mean."

"Oh?"

A truckload of hogs rumbled by, shaking Rob and Jackie and forcing a wave of wind against the car. As the stench of swine dung dissipated, Jackie said, "I'm also thinking about the way you treat me. The way you hold back. Like today. Why didn't you tell me everything first?"

"Oh hell, Jackie, I just put it all together. Anyway, you know how I like to play games. Besides, I thought you liked surprises."

"It's not just this. You've been keeping secrets. We shouldn't have secrets from each other."

"Secrets?"

"Like... Well, like Moon. You never told me why they called you Moon."

Rob almost drove off the side of the road at the next turn. "Oh for God's sake! I was embarrassed to tell you, that's all. We all had nicknames at the fraternity house." He gunned the engine and sent the car on a bouncing fly over a span that bridged a narrow stream for watering cattle. "Dear Abby says there's no need to share everything from the deep past."

Jackie tightened her lips and slid down again.

"Okay!" Rob exclaimed. "I used to throw moons."

"Throw moons? You mean drop your pants and toss your butt?"

"All in fun."

"You don't do it anymore, do you?"

"For you, I might."

A smile finally came to Jackie's lips, but it slipped away fast. "What about your overnight visit with Aunt Marjorie when you were a young teenager? Don't you think it's about time you told me about that?"

Rob failed to respond as they drove through a rural community— assorted clapboard houses on each side of the road, a small white church with a high-reaching steeple, a post office, veterans memorial, variety store and a one-pump service station. He stopped the car behind a hay truck at the town's only traffic light.

When the green light flashed, Rob fed gasoline, but was forced to crawl behind the truck. A half-mile out of town he made his move and passed the truck by crossing the double line. Quick acceleration gave Jackie a touch of whiplash, but she said nothing, fearful of distracting Rob from the thought she had implanted in his mind. She waited with hidden impatience.

His response finally came: "It's something I never talked about. But it always plagued my mind. I suppose I was never sure. A kid that age can experience something, then look back on it when he's much older and see it differently. Even today I keep struggling with it. A friendly touch, a warm hug—I'm not certain what they were. Or maybe I am, almost. I guess I wanted to find out more about her before I let myself believe. If she was what she might have been, then maybe she did touch me in the wrong places. I guess I'm not making much sense."

Jackie said nothing as the Chevy sped along the winding road, slicing between rolling slopes of bird's-foot trefoil ready to be baled as hay for winter feeding. Rob swerved the car to avoid a dead opossum.

"I'll never forget walking into that living room. At first I saw no one. Then..." Rob hesitated. "Then... there she was. On that staircase. In that black see-through negligee or whatever it was. The image of her on those stairs has been with me ever since. Her skin was so smooth and white, like flesh untouched by the sun's rays. And her black hair was soft and flowing with a luster I'll never forget. But I think it was her dark eyes that held me motionless. I didn't move until she called me to the stairs. Her voice was almost a whisper."

Off to the left, a white farmhouse and a cluster of white barns and silos reflected the afternoon sunlight, while on the right, Holstein cows grazed on pastureland.

"I remember how she put her arm around me and led me to my room. She was gentle and kind, and held me close. I looked up at the portrait of my grandfather, and she stood behind me, her breasts against my shoulder blades. For a moment I felt smothered. I couldn't breathe. Then she left me alone. In that room."

Rob slowly brought his car to a stop at a railroad crossing. The red warning lights and the freight train had been visible since the Chevy crested the last hill. Now the clanking of the boxcars silenced him. Realizing the length of the train, he turned the ignition key, cutting off the engine. Neither he nor Jackie spoke as flatcars loaded with scrap metal and spools of cable rumbled by. When the end neared, Rob started the motor and pumped the pedal nervously. The car leaped forward just as the red lights stopped flashing and while the ding-ding-ding still cut the air.

Time passed, as did fields of stubble from grain long since harvested. But this time Rob did not return to his rambling discourse. Eventually Jackie felt compelled to lead him back to Marjorie.

"Did you see her again that night?" she asked.

"Yes. She came to my room with a tray of cookies and milk. We ate together at a small table in the bay window. She was still dressed... well, the same way. I wasn't very hungry. I still didn't know why I was there. I still didn't know that my father had walked out on Mom." Rob fell silent again, but within a few moments he quietly explained, "After that, she led me to her room and told me to sit on her bed. She sat beside me and talked about my hands."

"Your hands?"

"Yes. She said they were nice. And firm. And strong. Then she told me she was glad I had come to visit her."

"Did she touch you?"

"A little. Then she hugged me and told me to go to my room. I couldn't sleep. I must have lain awake for hours before I fell off. At some point I saw a light in the hallway. She was standing in my doorway. I could see her silhouette, but pretended I was asleep. I didn't move a muscle. Even though I closed my eyes, I knew she walked into the room. I could feel her hovering over me. She touched me, and I felt strange. But I'm not sure when I was asleep and when I wasn't. I had my first wet dream, I think."

"Oh, Rob. I'm sorry." Jackie gently ran her fingers through his hair.

"Don't be. I'm not certain of anything. In a way, I feel compassion for her. A lonely woman. In need of another human being. Maybe just someone to touch."

"You're forgetting the babies."

"No I'm not. That's why I need answers. I just have to put it all together."

"And what about Uncle Jack's story?"

Rob thought for a moment. "We just don't know, do we?"

Chapter Thirty

Myrna Cuthbert, an obese middle-aged woman who waddled when she walked, swayed slightly as she stepped out onto the green-painted wooden porch where late-day sunlight brightened the flowered tent-like blouse that hung low enough to cover the top of her wide black pants. She did not welcome Rob and Jackie into her humble house. Instead, she pointed up the driveway. "He's back there. Do y' like ice tea?"

Rob and Jackie nodded, then walked along the side of the one-story house, constructed by Clinton Cuthbert himself and fronted with a fake-brick facade. The side walls were concrete block. A wooden pantry was tacked on at the rear.

"I have a feeling she didn't want us inside," whispered Rob as he and Jackie followed stepping stones along a wire fence that supported a twisted mass of bindweed. Rob had parked his car in front of the vacant lot on the other side of the fence—a lot overgrown with weeds, tall grass and scrawny locust trees strangled by poison ivy.

They were welcomed to the backyard by a barking dog—a pit bull tied by rope to a tool shed. The dog pulled, choked, growled and slobbered.

"How y' doin' there?" greeted Clinton Cuthbert, who appeared from around the corner of the pantry.

Rob felt the name didn't fit the man. He reached out and shook the hand of Clinton, a broad-shouldered, bull-faced, handyman-type equipped with tools and pencils in the breast pocket of his overalls. Ruddy-faced and bur-haired, Clinton held a monkey wrench in his left hand and wore paint-splattered brogans on his big feet. He compressed Rob's knuckles and kept shaking his entire arm for several seconds.

"It's kind of you to see us, especially on a Sunday," Rob said. "This is my fiancée, Jackie Harwood."

Clinton looked at Jackie and smiled broadly enough to expose a gold tooth—an upper bicuspid, left side. "Nice t'meetcha."

While Jackie made small talk about the weather, Myrna shuffled slowly from the pantry with a tray of iced tea and biscuits. Taking painfully sluggish steps, the puffy-cheeked, fuzzy-haired woman eventually joined the others at a cluster of plastic lawn chairs and tables in the shade of a sugar maple.

"Call me Myrna," she said while handing a drink to Jackie. "This is where we used to have picnics with Johnny. Every time we ate outside we'd call it a picnic. He loved the picnics, once he stopped being so headstrong and started to trust us a bit."

"By Johnny I presume you mean the boy we've come to talk about?" Rob asked.

"They called him John Doe, so we called him Johnny," explained Clinton, who noticed that Rob was staring at the swing, sliding board and seesaw at the back of the yard, not far from a collection of work projects behind the tool shed. "We got them things for Johnny, Mr. Putnam. You probably figure we're not too well fixed. But we always did well by the kid, didn't we Myrna. We was sorry t' see 'im go."

Myrna placed the tray of biscuits on the closest table and squeezed herself into a chair as she said, "He was a nice little boy, once he settled down. They took him away when he just turned seven."

"They was gonna bring us a little girl after that," Clinton explained. "But then they decided we wasn't gonna get any more kids."

"Why's that, Mr. Cuthbert?" Rob asked.

"You can call me Clint. Everybody 'round these parts calls me Clint."

"Okay, Clint. And you can call me Rob."

"Tell 'em about the room, Clint," Myrna urged.

"They said the kid's room was too small. But it was a mighty nice room. We fixed it all up. Even put in bunk beds so's Johnny could have a friend over, but he never did." Clinton frowned and looked toward the house. "I built this place all by myself." Then he smiled, looked from Jackie to Rob, and lightened his tone. "So, you folks are thinkin' about adoptin' Johnny?"

"Yes, can you tell us something about him?" Rob asked.

"Like we says, he was a nice boy. Kinda suspicious at first. Kinda quiet. Kinda shy. Nice smile, though. We haven't seen 'im in seven years, mindja."

"If he's anything like he was, you'd like 'im," Myrna added. "Surprised you folks want a boy that old. Most young couples want babies. How'd y' find out about Johnny?"

Jackie sensed that Rob was struggling for an answer, so she jumped in with, "We know something about the history of the boy."

Clint and Myrna kept their eyes on Jackie, expecting more.

"Well... well, you see, we suspect he might be related to someone we know."

Rob didn't like the direction of the conversation. "But we want him anyway, whether or not he's related to this person. At least we think so. We just wanted to follow up on his history."

"Have y' seen the other foster folks?" asked Clint.

Rob was quick to say, "Not yet, but we're going to. You're first on our list."

"Y' mean y' ain't seen the boy yet?" Clint looked puzzled.

Suddenly Rob realized he had worked his way into a trap. And he tried to squirm his way out: "We didn't want to do that until we learned more about him. You know how it is. One look, and we might decide, not really knowing what we should know." He gulped his iced tea.

"I don't get it," said Clint. "Y' want this kid, but y' never seen 'im? I thought y' was interested 'cause y' liked 'im."

"We do," Rob insisted. "We do. From what we've learned so far. And pictures. We've seen pictures, and read reports."

Jackie was not only uncomfortable; she was angry. She tried not to show it, though Rob sensed it.

Looking at Jackie, Myrna finally mustered courage to ask the question that had whet her curiosity from the start: "Can't y' have kids of your own?"

Unwilling to lie with her tongue, Jackie shifted in her seat and pointed to Rob, figuring that a lying finger was somehow less sinful.

"Oh, yeah," blurted Rob, who was even willing to say he was sterile if it would change the direction of the conversation. "Right. It's me. I'm the one. I've got the problem." Quickly switching the subject again, he said, "So, tell us more about Johnny."

Clint offered no response in words, but an expression of puzzlement continued to grow about his eyes.

Myrna drank some tea and then said, "Well, Johnny wrote to us a couple years back. Told us all about the animals at the Philadelphia Zoo." She munched on a biscuit.

A gray squirrel dashed through the yard, causing the pit bull to bark and run until the rope yanked him back. Darting again, the struggling animal choked as he yipped and yelped. Jackie turned her eyes on the dog, but Rob was too intent on following up on Myrna's remark.

"Where is he?" Rob asked. "I mean, at the time he wrote, where was he?"

"Over in Maywood," Myrna said. "With the Oswalds. Johnny didn't say nothing bad about them. Is he still livin' there? Or did they move 'im again?"

Jackie used coughing as a diversionary tactic, hoping to give Rob time to think before answering. Her coughing spasm choked to a finish as she reached for her drink.

"Are you okay?" Myrna asked as Clint and Rob focused on Jackie.

After sipping tea, Jackie said, "I'm fine. I'm fine. Sorry. I must have swallowed wrong."

It didn't take Clint long to remember Myrna's question. He looked at Rob and was about to repeat it. But Rob was quick to react, turned to Myrna, and spoke first.

"Yes, Johnny's still with the Oswalds. We're scheduled to drive over to Maywood tomorrow night."

Chapter Thirty-One

"Why the hell are you acting that way?" Rob asked as his car sped and bounced through rolling dairy country. He flipped down the visor as the highway turned west before swinging southwest again. The setting sun was an orange glow that tinted the fields and the distant trees. Beyond a white plank fence at left, a lone Guernsey, her brown coat warmed by the evening sunlight, joined a dozen Holsteins at a watering hole.

"What way?" Jackie asked.

"You know what way. You've barely said a word since we left Pepperville."

"You didn't know what the hell you were doing back there. And the whole thing made me very uncomfortable."

"We got what we wanted, didn't we?"

"If you think I'm going to Maywood with you, you're crazy." Jackie slipped lower into her seat.

Neither spoke for the next mile.

Finally, Jackie's thoughts—the ones that kept intruding and going around and around in her head—got the best of her, and she said, "I keep thinking of the men we interviewed and wondering which one, if any, is the father."

"Believe me, I know the feeling. It's beating my brain all the time."

"I wish I could turn it off."

Rob and Jackie were silent for another half mile. Then, as they passed thick clumps of goldenrod, Rob spoke quietly, meditatively: "I don't think it was any of them."

"Why's that?"

"None of them were fair-skinned, blue-eyed blonds. We didn't go far enough."

"You're forgetting your genetics. Dominant genes can hide recessive genes. Blue-eyed blonds can be born of dark-eyed parents."

"But look at the odds. There are no blonds in my family. So, the father either has those recessive genes tucked away, or he's blond. I'm guessing he's blond. From the description of the kid, I'm guessing he's very blond."

"Maybe the father was just a stranger who came aknocking one night."

"A blond stranger."

"Okay. A fair-haired Nordic knight."

"On a white horse, of course."

"Well, we did find plumbing bills, and you never checked with plumbers. Someone had to cut the grass. And then you never called the local *Times* about the newsboy."

Rob said nothing as the car curved through a wooded area. But when the trees were gone and the highway cut between fields of alfalfa, he blurted out, "God almighty, why did I ever think I had to check with the *Times*."

"What do you mean?"

"I know the newsboy."

"You do?"

"He told me. One day in the company dining hall."

"What are you talking about?"

"Ty. Ty was the paperboy. He told me he served the Mulberry section." Rob chuckled. "I can just see little Ty sleeping with Aunt Marjorie. What a joke. I think he's afraid of women. Except for that deaf girl who can't speak."

"But he is blond."

Rob said nothing for several moments, then forgot to feed gasoline. The Chevy began coasting to a stop.

"What are you doing?" Jackie asked.

Rob resembled a zombie by the time he brought the car to a halt at the side of the road near a patch of sumac.

Jackie touched his shoulder and asked, "What's wrong?"

Rob said nothing at first, then mumbled something about "taking a leak." Slowly, he opened the door, stepped from the car and found his way to the far side of the sumac. He peed on a barbed wire fence.

When too much time passed, Jackie called, "Are you all right?"

Seconds later, Rob appeared from behind the sumac. His expression showed disbelief. He moved robot-like, occasionally shaking his head. Once again in the car, he simply stared forward, showing no inclination to start the engine.

"Rob!?"

"How could I have been so blind," he muttered.

"Do you mean Ty? Is it Ty?"

"That day when I took him to the house. When he saw it, he turned white."

"Like you, right now."

"He said it was his stomach, something he ate. But he didn't want to get out of the car. And then, in the house, he kept staring at the staircase. That staircase. The one that always haunted me."

"Let's not jump to conclusions, Rob. We've done that before."

"But there's more. He didn't want to go upstairs. Suddenly he wanted to leave. Then, when he did go up, he went directly to the master bedroom, to her bedroom. He just looked. He didn't say anything. And then he backed away. I was so preoccupied with my own thoughts, so excited to show him everything, I just didn't give much credence to his actions. I did think it strange that he moved so fast from room to room, and didn't look me in the eye—not even once. But now, looking back on it..."

"Of all people. Ty. That's hard to accept. He would've been so young. Just a boy."

"There's more. That night when he showed me his painting of the deaf girl. He told me that something had happened in his life, that there was a woman. He wanted to explain, but said he needed time. But he really wanted to tell me. He just couldn't. Not quite yet."

"They said John Willow looked younger than his years. Just like Ty."

"I'll be a fuckin' sticky banana. I can't believe this. Jesus. We were just too close. What is it they say? We couldn't see the forest for the trees?" Rob kept shaking his head. "Holy shit! Can you picture little Ty—about sixteen years old, but probably looking fourteen if not twelve—screwing Aunt Marjorie? Maybe he was younger than that. Hell, I think he served newspapers for about five years."

"I just thought of something, Rob."

"What?"

"All those boxes of un-mailed letters, the ones we thought were addressed to Tyrone Power. Dear Ty, Dear Ty, Dear Ty. There were so many. We pushed them aside. We didn't bother reading them. They way outnumbered the Clark Gable and Robert Taylor letters."

"My God. Do you think?"

"Maybe."

"I'll be a fuckin' mongoose."

"What are you going to do?"

"Look at the letters, of course."

"No. I mean after that. Are you going to tell him?"

"I want to find the Willow kid first. I want to look at him. I want to see his smile, his eyes, his hair, his skin."

Jackie put her hand on Rob's chin and turned his face toward her. "Look at me. How and when are you going to tell him?"

Rob thought for a moment, sighed, and then said, "I'd like him to tell me first—that is, about Marjorie. It just seems better that way—better than my telling him I know he laid my aunt. I'd like to find out from him, first, if he knows there was a baby. Or two babies. I guess it's time for some serious rapping at Marty's Tavern."

"I doubt that he knows about the boy. After all, she got Harry Hedgepeth to carry the baby to the hospital. Besides that, Ty's too compassionate a man not to have sought out his child. Hell, he'd be taking care of that boy today if he knew. You know I'm right."

Rob sat still, his mouth down, his eyes focused on infinity as a truck rumbled by.

After two more trucks and three cars, Jackie started the conversation again: "Well, I think this proves the seduction theory. I might even be willing to accept your Uncle Jack's story. This might even explain the way you've viewed Ty through the years—as asexual or whatever. Who knows, Marjorie might have traumatized him. Maybe now he needs a woman who he can come-on-to and feel secure with."

"Like a deaf woman, who's probably inexperienced and over-protected?"

"Maybe."

"Are we guessing too much? Are we putting together a jigsaw puzzle before we have the pieces?"

"Circumstantial evidence has won many a case for many a lawyer."

"It's hard to fathom why I didn't see all this before. Yet it's difficult for me to believe even now. So, on the other hand, I can understand why I didn't see it." Rob took in a deep breath, then exhaled a long sigh. "Well, before anything else, I'm going after a big piece of the puzzle—the kid, Baby Willow, Johnny Doe, or whatever his name is."

A blue-and-white police car pulled to a stop alongside Rob's Chevy. "You folks all right?" yelled a blond, long-faced state trooper.

"Yeah, we're all right, officer," Rob responded.

Chapter Thirty-Two

Dressed in gym shorts and a tank top, Ty was on the floor of his apartment, between the shoved-back sofa and his coffee table, doing sit-ups at unnecessary speed in an effort to work off his frustrations. He had accomplished only 15 sit-ups by the time he pushed himself to his feet and again paced back and forth and around and about. But moments later he was back on the floor, racing his heartbeat with speedy sit-ups. Fifteen more huffs and puffs, and he was back on his feet, gritting his teeth and locking his jaw. He sat on the couch, loosened the laces on his sneakers, stretched out his legs, stared at the ceiling, and muttered "Fuck."

Two days without Amy, and he was beside himself. He had made trips to the supermarket at appropriate times, but without success. He knew he could hold out no longer. His only choice was to drive to the Harrison house, no matter what the consequences. But darkness had set in, for the September days were growing shorter, and Ty realized this was not the hour to try. But the pull was horrendous. It racked his body with anxiety. His desire to hold Amy, his need to comfort her, his fear for her well-being—all this and more churned his body and mind into fitful emotions.

He considered, but ruled out, downing shots of whiskey. He ruled out jogging because it would simply take him back to the supermarket for more frustration. He ruled out television because it offered nothing strong enough to capture his attention. And he ruled out masturbation. That left more sit-ups, or maybe push-ups this time. After punching the couch, he tied his sneakers, flopped to the floor, tried a couple push-ups, then collapsed and lay prostrate.

Rapid tapping jolted Ty at about 9:30 p.m. He pushed himself up and hurried to the door as the rap-rap-rap continued, growing louder and faster with each second.

"Hold your breeches on!" Ty shoved hair from his forehead, then opened the door.

There stood Amy, dressed in a pale blue dress, a look of helplessness and fear coming from her red and puffy eyes. She whimpered as she reached out for Ty.

"Amy, what is it?" Ty wrapped his arms around her and held tightly.

Seconds later, he held her at arms length, and, with his lips and eyes, sought an explanation, all the while wondering how she had found his apartment.

With rapid movements of her fingers, hands and arms, Amy tried to explain, again and again forming the signs for "fight" and "father."

"Did he hurt you?" Ty asked, using his hands as he spoke.

Amy shook her head decisively, then pointed to her heart as she nodded, and Ty knew her hurt was inside. He led her to the couch, sat beside her, and put his arm around her. In time, he inched away from her, fixed his eyes on hers, and used symbols to ask how she had found her way. He recognized her sign for "walk," and realized at once that she had traveled five miles by foot. Although he had described his apartment to her, he still wondered how she had located it. Her symbols for "telephone" and "book" helped him understand.

The big question was "why," and she answered that by depicting a bitter clash with her father—an argument about "lust" and a "father's right to protect" and "God's laws."

Again he embraced her, and tried to comfort her with squeezes. He rocked her slightly, then used his hand to put her head on his shoulder. As the moments passed, he toyed gently with her hair while wishing she could hear his thoughts.

* * *

Hours later, Amy and Ty, both dressed in men's blue-striped pajamas, were stretched out on a bed that had sprung from the living room couch—a convertible sofa for Ty's overnight guests, his bedroom having but a narrow single bed. The coffee table, now cluttered with empty cola bottles, ice cream dishes and a bowl of pretzels, had been moved aside to accommodate the bed. Atop the sheets, Ty and Amy held each other tightly, as if fearful that breaking the hold would somehow carry them apart. Their heads lay on a single pillow, their cheeks pressing against each other.

Midnight came and passed. The time was 2:20 when knocking startled Ty, causing him to break his hold and spring from the bed. His actions frightened Amy, who sat up and followed him with her eyes as he stepped toward the door, hesitated, then took a few more steps.

"Who's there?" he called out.

"It's the police. We'd like to talk with you."

Ty motioned to Amy and pointed to the bedroom. She responded quickly, leaped from the bed and ran from the room.

"Just a minute." Ty knew he had no time to close the bed, but he dashed to the coffee table, gathered up the bottles and dishes, and slipped them under the bed. "I'm coming." He opened the door to find two policemen—a stocky, pug-nosed man with the jowls of a bulldog, and a slender, round-faced redhead splattered with freckles. "What's the problem, officers?"

"Are you Mr. Tyrone Scott?" asked the stocky, dark-eyed man.

"Yes, I'm Ty Scott. What can I do for you?"

"May we come in?" asked the redhead.

"Oh, sure. Sure." Ty backed off, allowing the officers to enter.

"We're looking for a young deaf woman named Amy Harrison," continued the redhead as he and his partner observed the rumpled sheets on the bed. "Her father suspects you may be holding her against her will."

"That's crazy!" A barely apparent quiver altered Ty's words. "Her father's been keeping her a virtual prisoner most of her life. She's over twenty-one. She can come and go as she pleases."

"Is she here, Mr. Scott?" asked the pug-nosed officer, showing impatience.

Ty hesitated, then said, "Yes. I'll get her." He went to his studio-workroom first and grabbed two sketch pads and pencils from his drawing table, then hurried to the bedroom. He held Amy's hand as he led her to the policemen.

"Are you Amy Harrison?" asked the freckled officer.

"You're forgetting that she can't hear," Ty said in a critical tone. He handed a pad and pencil to the redhead and gave the others to Amy.

The officers examined Amy with their eyes, glanced at Ty, then looked at each other, obviously taking note of the matching pajamas. Seconds later the slender policeman began writing. Amy was quick to follow. As they passed questions and answers back and forth, the stocky sergeant pulled Ty aside and quietly but sternly asked, "How did you get her here?"

"She came on her own. She was frightened. In fact, she walked five miles to get here. I tried to comfort her."

"I bet you did." The officer's sarcasm was obvious.

"You don't understand. I love her. I want to marry her. Her father has no right to keep her a prisoner." Ty shocked himself with his own words. For the first time he had told himself, aloud, that he wanted to marry her.

Turning to his partner, the redhead said, "Bill, come here. Look at this."

Together, the officers read Amy's notes, and together they looked up at the young couple in the blue-striped pajamas. Ty and Amy held each other as they stared pleadingly at the policemen.

"Sorry we bothered you," apologized the redhead. He looked at Ty. "I don't know what you should do. But I'll tell you, her old man is a raging bull right now."

"How did you get here? How did you find us?"

"Your license plate," said the stocky sergeant. "Her father has your license numbers. He poured out a clear description of you, spitting venom with each word."

"Good luck," offered the redhead as he and his partner turned to leave.

* * *

In time, Amy completely melted against Ty's body, giving herself in pure trust. And although Ty had been in long-term pursuit, a barrier rose each time the ultimate neared. As they lay together, he held back when impelled to push his pulsating hardness against her. To him, she was the most beautiful flower in his garden of life. But a delicate one with fragile petals. So unlike the sultry black tulip that had seeded him with teenage lust.

The apex came only because of Amy's trustful giving—pure giving of her virgin self. It dissolved the barrier.

He entered with care, despite his unequaled passion. He hurt her slightly, but her rapture buried the sting in overwhelming joy. What was the first ever for her, was the first of a kind for Ty.

* * *

Later, as they lay next to each other, Amy was troubled by tears in Ty's eyes. But her frets were eased by the warmth of his smile.

* * *

Ty woke early the next morning, despite few hours of sleep. A streak of sunlight brightened the two sets of pajamas that lay piled on the floor. Lifting his bare torso, Ty looked at Amy, who slept peacefully. The sight of her fair face and soft hair on the pillow stirred his emotions. He told himself that last night's lovemaking was genuine, not solely Amy's rebellion against her father. Surely she would not feel guilt when she awoke, for last night had been so pure and unencumbered. How he hoped her total giving had freed her. How much he wanted to tell her that she had freed him, but he knew he couldn't.

Seconds after Amy opened her eyes her face became radiant and she reached out to him. Questions vanished from Ty's mind as he took her in his arms and felt her naked breasts upon his chest. Again they gave of themselves.

* * *

After the passion, they lay serene, first holding each other, then stretching out, gazing into infinity, their thoughts racing.

* * *

Much later, Ty began thinking of the special breakfast he would create for Amy. But first came something much more special. Ty rolled and stepped from the bed, slipped hurriedly into his pajama bottoms, motioned to Amy to stay where she was, and raced to his workroom.

While Amy's return to earth was slower, she managed to sit up in bed, showing afterglow modesty by pulling the sheet up over her breasts.

Ty stepped back into the room holding the portrait of Amy in front of him. He peeked around the side of it to see her expression. The look on Amy's face was one of disbelief. Her eyes grew wide. Her mouth fell open. She dropped the sheet and began to shake her head. Finally she used her hands to say that the portrait was far more beautiful than she.

"Oh no!" said Ty, shaking his head vehemently.

A beaming smile spread across her face, and tears rolled down her cheeks.

Chapter Thirty-Three

Rob shed his suit coat, loosened his necktie, and drove directly from work, bringing his car to a screeching halt in front of the tall, curlicue-trimmed, Victorian-style house of the Harwoods. Jackie, in gray slacks and a blue jersey top, had been waiting at curbside for several minutes, now and then glancing at her watch. She wrinkled her nose and made funny faces as Rob leaned across the seat and pushed open the passenger-side door.

"Hurry up!" he shouted. "Get in!"

No sooner had Jackie slid into the Chevy and slammed the door than Rob gunned the engine and sent the car leaping forward with a chugging jerk that tossed Jackie's head.

"Hey!" she exclaimed. "I want to live until tomorrow!"

"We're pressed for time."

"If I don't like the mission you can drop me at Sally Lake's."

"Your maid of honor can wait. Believe me, you'll like this mission."

"Remember. You promised dinner—again."

"We'll grab a burger on the way."

"Oh no!"

"Stick with me, Jackie. This is it. Do you hear me? This is it!" Rob turned the car onto another residential, tree-shaded street as he aimed for Locust Boulevard and the Eastside Ramp to the Interstate Highway. "Besides, when do you get a chance to see the Hornets play the Yellowjackets? Hell, it's going to be a real battle of the bees!"

"Explain yourself, Rob, before I stamp on your brake!"

"We're on our way to Maywood."

"Well, I figured that." As Jackie waited for more, Rob began to hum "The Bluebird of Happiness." She glowered, then snapped, "Rob!"

"So be like I," he sang, "hold your head up high, till you find the bluebird of happiness."

"A little birdie's gonna pinch off your private parts if you don't cut it out! What's with the hornets and yellowjackets?"

Rob lowered his voice and got serious: "I talked to Chester Oswald—one of four Oswalds in the Boyd County phone book. He was nice at first. But said tonight wasn't a good time to visit because the boy would be playing for the Hornets."

"Baseball?"

"No, soccer. Baseball's a spring game, dummy."

Jackie took a quick look at Rob's expression. "That's it, show your teeth. You'd better smile when you call me a dummy."

"Oswald's language sort of surprised me. But maybe I didn't hear right over the phone. Considering his neighborhood, he must be a man of some stature. Anyway, he grew suspicious and clammed up. He wouldn't let me schedule for tomorrow or any other day. So I called the school superintendent, the Community Y, the municipal building and the Maywood police before I found out that the Hornets play the Yellowjackets on the north field at the Maywood Middle School."

"I don't like this."

"We're just going to take a look. That's all."

Rob turned the car onto the ramp and yielded to a truck on the Interstate before gunning the engine again. As the Chevy accelerated, he aimed for the inner lane, weaving the car in and out of rush-hour traffic until it was speeding alongside the medial strip.

"Take it easy, okay? You're uptight and flying high."

Rob ignored her. "Guess what? Mom visited Marjorie again."

"Oh?"

"For the third time. Can you beat that?"

"And?"

"She never says a thing. Just walks around the house looking grumpy after each visit. Even when I pump her, she won't talk about it. She walks out of the room."

"Give her time. She'll resolve whatever it is." Jackie decided it was her turn to change the subject, especially since she had something to confess: "I moved the skull and bones."

"You what?" Alarm sharpened Rob's words.

"Don't fret. They're safe. I just didn't want them in the refrigerator anymore."

"Damn it! They weren't hurting anything there."

"I put them in your handball bag and hung them in the cellarway."

"And how the hell am I supposed to play handball?"

"You haven't played in ages."

"That's because Ty doesn't call."

"You wouldn't have time, even if he did call. Besides, do you call him?"

"No. He's afraid to call me. And I'm not ready to call him. But he'll be coming back to work next week. And there's no way we'll be able to avoid each other." The thought sobered Rob and darkened his expression.

* * *

The Maywood Middle School was somewhat remindful of Independence Hall—red brick with white trim and a clock tower. The school and its sports fields were surrounded by single residences on well-landscaped lots on avenues shaded by maples. Maywood was a prosperous borough of white-collar and executive types who commuted to the city. While primarily a bedroom community on a Conrail line, it had its other side—a cluster of sub-standard houses between the rails and the river. As for its old-time residents, most of the blue-bloods who once owned estates on the north side had long ago sold out to the nouveau riche.

"Helluva good-looking building," Rob said as he drove slowly along Maple Avenue, in front of the well-groomed school, replete with shrubs and grass. He turned north along the side of the school, and, within seconds he and Jackie saw a playing field dotted with boys in bright green and yellow-and-black uniforms. Light from the setting sun poured across the field, turning the uniforms aglow. Wooden bleachers held crowds of shirt-sleeve fans. The September night was warm.

"I guess the kids in yellow and black are the Yellowjackets," Jackie commented as Rob struggled to parallel park in a tight space.

"That means John Willow Doe is wearing green."

With the Chevy squeezed into bumper-to-bumper space, Rob was quick to exit, slam the door and hurry to a chain-link fence along the field. He peered into the sunlight, squinted his eyes, used his hand as a visor, and tried to examine each kid.

"Look, that's him," Rob said as Jackie reached the fence. "That's got to be him." Rob pointed, then quickly dropped his arm. "He's the only blond kid out there in a green uniform. He's just a little guy. Just like Ty." Rob shifted back and forth as he attempted to get a better view.

"Calm down," Jackie whispered. "You're like a caged lion."

"We've got to move around to the other side. I want to see him when he runs off the field." Rob checked his watch. "I'm sure they didn't break for the half yet."

"Look! That boy just got hit in the head by the ball."

"No, Jackie. He hit the ball with his head."

"They do that?"

"They just can't touch it with their hands. Come on. Let's move."

"Settle down. These people—all these moms and pops and kids—are going to wonder who the hell we are. They probably all know each other. I feel out of place."

"Don't be so self-conscious. Come on." He tugged at Jackie and began a fast walk toward the bleachers. "We'll stand near the crowd. Then, when the boys run from the field, we'll move toward the sidelines and get a close look."

Jackie felt all eyes were on them as they hurried along the fence. She was thankful for a Yellowjacket goal that drew shouts and cheers from the crowd. Rob quickened his pace. With Jackie straining to keep with him, he worked his way to a position near the bleachers, all the while keeping his eyes on the slight youngster with the sun-bleached blond hair.

* * *

At halftime, the boys ran from the field. The small, blond boy was the last to reach the sidelines. Rob and Jackie stared directly into his face, getting a perfect view before the boy turned and moved to the far end of the bench where he stood alone, several feet from the other boys.

"Oh my God!" Rob whispered in disbelief. For a moment he froze, stunned by what he had seen. "Christ almighty," he mumbled, just before gaining enough energy to step back. He kept stepping back, turned, and walked behind the bleachers and stared toward the street, astonishment owning every whit of his expression.

Also numbed by the sight, Jackie was slow to find her way to Rob. She kept glancing back at the boy as she moved away. When he was out of view, she hurried to Rob's side and took his arm.

"Can you believe that?" Rob asked.

Jackie simply tightened her hold.

"Did you ever see such a likeness? He's a clone if I ever saw a clone."

"A thirteen-year-old Ty," Jackie whispered.

"Exactly. The spittin' image. I've never seen anything like it. You're right. Ty must have looked just like that in his early teens. It's hard to believe."

"I thought I saw sadness in his eyes. Then again, maybe I put it there. Maybe it was all in my head."

"No. I saw the same thing. I wonder why he didn't join the other boys. Why did he stand off to the side like that? Do you think he doesn't mix well?"

"Maybe it just happened this way—this time. Let's not read anything into that. Not yet, anyway. Hell, if he didn't mix well, why would he have joined the team in the first place?"

Rob glanced up and saw a woman staring down at them from the top of the bleachers. "Let's go back and watch the game for a little while. I want to get another look at the kid."

* * *

Ten minutes later, Rob and Jackie were back in the car driving up and down the streets of Maywood—shaded streets with Georgian, Dutch Colonial and Tudor style houses mixed with those of contemporary design, all on landscaped lots abundant with evergreens and dogwoods tinged with autumn crimson. As they drove on, they discovered more modest homes. And after crossing the railroad tracks, they found a small section of weather-worn, poorly maintained, frame houses near the river.

"I hope he doesn't live in one of these," Jackie said.

"We're looking for Pine Lane," Rob repeated for the third time. "Number twenty-two Pine Lane."

"Why don't you stop and ask someone? Why is it that men don't ask? They simply wander on and on."

"We'll find it."

Rob drove west on Lincoln Avenue and crossed the tracks again. Within minutes his car was back among those shady maples and spacious properties, moving slowly as he looked left and right. Lights went on here and there as dusk fell over Maywood.

"It's getting late," Jackie said. "I think we should start home. Besides, we look like spies or burglars or something, inching along like this, stretching our necks."

Rob flicked on the headlights as he slowed the car even more. "I just want to get a look at where he lives. Just a quick look, that's all." He turned the car at the next intersection and headed north on Slippery Lane.

"I don't like this crawling along. I mean it, Rob. It makes me uncomfortable. I don't know how I get trapped into these things. What if the police see us? They'll think we're casing these houses."

"There it is!" Rob braked the Chevy suddenly. "Pine Lane." He turned the car left and fed little gasoline as he searched for number 22.

"We're in the low numbers. I just saw number ten. It'll be on this side of the street."

"Keep looking."

"We just passed eighteen"

"I bet it's this corner house."

"God. Do you think so? That's quite a house."

"Check the curbing. Sometimes numbers are on the curbs."

"It's on that fancy lamppost. See? Written in wrought-iron script—twenty two. Well, I'll be. This house is a far cry from the Cuthberts' place in Pepperville. In fact, I think I'd use the word elegant to describe it."

A brick walkway and steps led to a stately yellow-painted brick house with white trim. The architecture was Georgian of the Palladian style—formal, to say the least. A heavy, paneled, white door held a massive brass knocker. Carefully manicured shrubbery and grass revealed the touch of a professional landscaper. As Jackie and Rob gaped, lights went on inside the house, on the first floor, and filtered through soft curtains that appeared to be framed by heavy draperies.

"Someone's home!" Jackie exclaimed. "Let's go."

"No, not yet." Rob turned off the headlights.

"What are you doing?"

"Just hold tight. Don't get excited." Slowly, he began to back up the car, then allowed it to slide to a stop along the curb under a maple tree. Few cars were parked on the street, since most of the houses had garages.

"Why are you parking?"

"I'm not sure yet."

"Rob!"

"Calm down." Rob opened the driver's door.

"Now what are you doing?"

"I'm still not sure."

"Rob! Close that door, and take me home!"

"Follow me."

"I will not!"

"Let's walk by the house and get a closer look."

"No way! If you're going out there, I'm staying right here."

"Alone?"

"Don't you leave me!"

"Come on. We're just a couple of lovers taking a stroll."

"You can see from here what the house looks like. You don't need a closer look. Now let's get out of here."

Rob stepped to the street, closed the door and hummed "The Bluebird of Happiness" as he nonchalantly walked around the front of the car. He opened the passenger door, and, with a sweeping gesture, offered his hand to his fiancée.

"Only because I don't want to sit here alone," Jackie whispered as she reluctantly stepped to the sidewalk. "This is stupid." She took his arm.

As they neared the corner house, Rob nudged Jackie and said, "Look up the driveway."

"What am I supposed to see?"

"Look."

"I am. I don't see anything but a garage."

"An open garage."

"So?"

"With no car in it. I figure that means Chester Oswald is not at home."

"Rob! That's a sexist assumption if I ever heard one! Maybe Mrs. Oswald is out. Maybe they're both out. Maybe someone else turned on the house lights. Or maybe they have one of those automatic timing devices."

As they neared the lamppost, Rob said, "No. I think he's out, probably buying the boy ice cream after the game. Or maybe pizza. That's what they do after kids' games."

Rob and Jackie passed the entrance walkway and turned the corner. After a few more yards, he stopped suddenly, held her back, turned and pulled. "Come on. Let's make another pass."

"Only if we head right for the car."

"Take a look at this place, will you?"

"I am. I am. It's not exactly the kind of house I expected. Neither was that homemade house of the Cuthberts. But this is at the other end of the spectrum. Of course, I don't know much about foster care and how they pick the people." Lifting her eyes and taking a wide sweeping look at the house, Jackie added, "But I suppose the Oswalds can do a lot for the boy. Maybe he's very happy here."

"He didn't look happy on that soccer field."

As they arrived once again at the lamppost, Rob stopped walking, grasped Jackie's hand and whispered, "I have to knock on that door."

"No you don't!" Jackie yanked her hand free.

"Yes I do."

"Are you crazy?"

"We're here. And I can't leave without finding out more."

"Rob, what's wrong with you? Mr. Oswald doesn't want to see you. Remember? You told me so yourself."

"But his wife might."

"And if he's home?"

"I'm sure he isn't."

"But if he is?"

"Then, the most he can do is tell us to leave." Rob started to walk up the brick pathway. "Come on."

"No!"

"I can't do it without you. We've got to look like a couple. Mrs. Oswald might be more open to a woman. A man alone might scare her to hell." Rob kept walking, hoping his fiancée would follow.

"Damn you," Jackie muttered. She remained at the lamppost until Rob was in reach of the knocker. Then she sighed in frustration and walked toward him. Seconds later she shuddered as she heard the striking blows of the knocker. When the door opened, she was standing behind Rob, slightly to one side.

The woman in the half-open doorway was as well manicured as the grass and shrubbery outside her house. Perhaps 38 or 40 years of age, she was hard to place in years because of obvious care that could almost summon the adjective "stunning"—but only at first glance. Her blonde hair was meticulously coiffured, and her blue eyes were outlined and shadowed with engineering skill. She wore a yellow, one-piece, clinging, knit dress with a deep V neckline, just-for-show buttons all the way down one side, and a 20-inch slit up from the bottom. "Yes? What can I do for you?" she asked in tones as cool as her eyes. Her fair-skinned attractiveness was marred by a hard chin.

"Mrs. Oswald?" Rob asked.

"That's right."

"My name is Rob Putnam, and this is my fiancée, Jackie Harwood. Please forgive us for not calling first. We're from upstate, and we believe we've discovered important facts about your foster child. In fact, we think he may have been born to a relative. And we may know his father."

Jackie was surprised by the truth of Rob's words. She had expected one of his lengthy "white lies." Stepping to his side, she linked her arm with his, and began a closer inspection of Lana Oswald. Something about the woman's stance told Jackie to substitute the word "crass" for "stunning."

"Why are you telling me?" Lana asked. "You should take your story to the proper authorities." Despite her words, Lana could not hide her curiosity. A calculating expression suddenly controlled her eyes.

"We will. In time. But the father is a friend, and he doesn't know yet. We're just putting the pieces together. Please. May we ask you some questions?"

"I don't think there's much to tell you."

"Please?"

Lana stared quizzically at Rob, then at Jackie. Finally, she stepped back. "Okay. Come in."

Inside, Rob and Jackie found a classical, formal, elegant setting that showed high regard for "correctness" rather than comfort. They found a spacious central hall, an elaborately turned stair balustrade, and paneled walls painted in shades of peach and cream. Hallway furnishings were highlighted by twin Chippendale settees and a pedestal table holding a Ming vase.

Lana backed up to the center of the hall, turned, and firmly established her footing as if to say: This is it. You can go no farther.

"Now, what's this all about?" she asked.

Rob realized that they were not going to be offered seats in the adjoining living room. Jackie, always discerning when it came to women, was still picking up clues. Lana's pose, her right hand on her protruding hip, and her garish rings on all fingers confirmed Jackie's suspicion that Lana didn't know a Ming vase from a plastic cup.

"I have good reason to believe—in fact, I know without doubt— that the boy is my cousin and the son of my best friend," Rob said. "We've told no one this. In fact, I didn't expect to tell you when I came here. It just happened."

Lana showed little emotion, other than a peculiar gleam in her eyes, as she said, "I really don't think this concerns me as much as it does my husband and the authorities in Philadelphia."

Still picking up vibes, Jackie's intuition told her that Lana was enjoying every bit of Rob's revelation.

"The boy is living with us," Lana continued, "simply because my husband insisted that he have a son at no expense and little bother."

Lana's frankness stunned Rob and Jackie.

"I don't understand?" Rob questioned.

"And you couldn't without knowledge of my life, Mr...."

"Putnam. Rob Putnam."

"Yes, Mr. Putnam," Lana said in her cool tones. "You couldn't understand unless you understood my personal life. And, frankly, that's none of your business. I will tell you one thing, however. That boy is unresponsive and ungrateful. He does what he's told, but seems to enjoy nothing. When he first arrived he was a nasty little bugger. Now he's sullen most of the time."

"I have a feeling you don't like him," Rob said.

"Let's just say he's an intrusion. Anyway, he's the property of my husband." Lana noticed a strange, revealing look in Rob's and Jackie's eyes. "No, no. You're getting the wrong idea. My husband doesn't get a hard-on for boys, if that's what you're thinking." She shifted to a defiant pose, and presented a cynical smile. "His problem is quite the opposite."

"Oh?" Rob questioned.

"If you're asking me something, forget it. I think it's time for you to leave."

"But about the boy?" Jackie asked.

"I've told you all I know about him. He comes and goes. He doesn't smile. He obeys orders. And, frankly, I don't know where he is right now. But I'm sure my husband's not with him."

"You didn't know he was playing soccer tonight?"

"Come to think of it, Chester did mention something like that. I hope he's not keeping the poor boy waiting in the dark. But then the kid can find his own way home if he has to." Lana forced a smile that was deliberately meant to be recognized as fake. "Now, I think you should go."

Dusk had darkened to where the sky's remaining light was but fading streaks in the western sky—streaks barely reflected on the houses of Pine Lane.

"Watch your step," Rob cautioned while holding Jackie's elbow as they walked down the brick path and tried to adjust to the darkness. When the door behind them closed, a yellow glow vanished from the walkway. Ahead of them, under the lamplight, a young boy yanked the leash on his spaniel as the dog lifted his leg and sprayed the post. "Come on!" the youngster urged. He pulled the dog and hurried off.

"Could you believe that woman?" Jackie whispered. "I've never experienced anything like that. Unbelievable! I mean, unbelievable! What kind of a person is she anyway?"

"Cold and calculating to say the least," Rob said softly. "In fact, I might describe her as a bitch. She was playing games with us, you know. The truth is, she was glad to see us, because she sure doesn't want that kid around. Once she realized why we were there, she tried to set us up. She actually wanted us to know her husband cheats on her."

A flash of light blinded Rob and Jackie for an instant as a car turned the corner and sped west on Pine Lane. After darkness returned, Jackie said, "I can't believe her cold-hearted attitude toward the boy. It's unconscionable."

"I think she'd love us to take the kid away."

"Well, I'll tell you, that boy shouldn't be in that house."

"She probably put a tail on poor ol' Chester. Frankly, I'd like to catch his act, whatever it is."

"Here's hoping John Willow isn't part of it."

Jackie and Rob hurried away, but took one more look at the Oswald's house before sliding into their car seats. Seconds later, with high beams on, Rob U-turned the car at the intersection. As it moved west its beams drenched a boy in light—a boy in a bright green soccer uniform, crossing the street about 50 feet ahead.

"That's him!" Rob exclaimed as he braked the car.

"What are you doing?"

"Hold tight." Rob rolled down the window. "Pardon me," he called as the boy quick-stepped over the curb and onto the sidewalk. "Can you direct me to the Interstate?"

The youngster stepped from deep shadows to the glow of a streetlight. "What's that?" he asked.

"The Interstate. Can you direct me to it?"

Timidly, the boy moved toward the car. "Take the next right, then drive till y' see the signs."

Rob stared directly into the sad eyes of the youth.

"Thank you," said Rob as he and Jackie watched the boy hurry off in the direction of the Oswald house.

"God it's hard to believe," Rob muttered. "This whole thing is hard to believe. That youngster is hard to believe. Jesus." After turning the car right, Rob continued: "When I first saw that house I thought, 'Wow, this kid's got it made.' I figured maybe he was well off and we were making a mistake by intruding. That bitch sure changed my mind. Hell, we gotta get him out of there."

"It looks like neither of them watched him play soccer. Do you think Oswald is really using the boy to get out of the house?"

"Seeing John Willow come home alone makes me think Chester's out there pumping some tootsy somewhere. That doesn't mean he didn't want a son. It just might mean that he found the kid to be an unexpected convenience."

"You're being too kind. Anyway, that woman of his should give him all the action he needs."

"Hell, she's hard as nails. I'd be afraid to get into bed with her. She might bite where it hurts."

"You're not supposed to think of things like that."

"You've got nothing to worry about, my little bluebird."

Jackie growled, then slid down in her seat as she often did when in deep thought. "So, when are you going to tell Ty?"

"Soon."

"How soon?"

"Very soon. Maybe tomorrow."

"How?"

"I don't know. Like I said before, I want him to open up first. I might have to push him into it. Some heavy 'tyrob' talk at Marty's Tavern is long overdue anyway."

Chapter Thirty-Four

S am Harrison seldom ventured into the town's north side. The
years had given him little call to do so. But here he was,
driving his pickup truck on Elmwood Avenue at about the time that
Rob and Jackie were speeding along the Interstate. He looked left
and right, searching through the darkness and the limbs of the shade
trees for the building so clearly described by police on the night of
Amy's disappearance. His anger, intensified by police inaction, had
not dissipated since that night.

Driving slowly, he passed the brick apartment building, only to
stop his truck suddenly as the white window boxes made a delayed
impact. Shifting gears, he slowly backed up the truck, then sat quietly
studying the building in detail, even down to the pink petunias yet to
be zapped by the first frost. Gripped by determination, he parked his
pickup across the street from the building.

The tall, gaunt man strode rapidly across the street, his mouth
turned down, his eyes squinting with rage. His grease-stained
workshirt, soiled workpants and denim cap seemed out of place on
Elmwood Avenue. He stood still for a moment on the apartment-
house walkway, then made his move when he determined that the
entrance to the basement apartment was at his left. His spindle legs
moved him quickly to the concrete steps and black iron railing. He
held onto the rail as he awkwardly stepped down toward the door,
his ill-health revealing itself even before a spasmodic cough bulged
the blood vessels and muscles in his neck. After several deep
breaths he rang the bell and pounded on the door. He allowed only a

few seconds to pass before pounding again, stopping when the light above his head flashed on.

Wearing a deep red bathrobe, Ty opened the door partway, exposing his mussed hair to the outdoors. He was about to speak, but the sight of Sam Harrison took away his words.

"I know she's in there." The gravel-throated harshness of Sam's utterance was not as frightening to Ty as the man's intense eyes— eyes that seemed to cut Ty's soft flesh. Sam's countenance would have been menacing enough without the overhead light that deepened the hollows in his face. "Bring her out here, or I'm comin' in t' get her."

Ty finally put his tongue and lips in working order: "Mr. Harrison, please. She wants to be here. She wants to be with me."

Rage bulged Sam's neck. His temples pulsated and his nostrils widened. "Get out of my way!" He shoved the door, ripping it from Ty's grasp and sending it crashing against the inner wall.

"You have no right, Mr. Harrison. You can't come into my home like this." Ty found himself taking the stand of his life. "Now, step back."

"Don't you tell me my rights!" Sam yelled as loud as his scratchy throat would allow. He shoved Ty, but the younger man bounced back and held his own, securing himself firmly in the doorway by gripping the frame on both sides.

"You'd better leave, Mr. Harrison," Ty said with strength, despite a quiver in his voice. "Right now."

Amy's father shoved Ty, but the boyish man shoved back and Sam lost his balance and fell backwards, his head hitting the iron railing and the concrete as he collapsed onto the steps. Blood gushed from his left temple, ran down his cheek and over his ear and dripped to the concrete. Ty immediately knelt and examined him. He felt for a pulse in Sam's wrists and neck, listened for a heartbeat, and turned the gaunt man's head to slow the bleeding. Suddenly Ty heard a guttural cry. He looked up and saw Amy standing there in his white terry robe, hovering over them, her hands and arms moving wildly, more throaty sounds coming from her mouth. Disbelief and fear in her eyes made Ty try frantically to explain. But she would accept no sign or signal from him, scratched and clawed at him until he stood and backed off, and then threw herself at her father.

Chapter Thirty-Five

Emily Putnam had readied herself for bed and had come downstairs in her pale yellow housecoat to fix a cup of warm milk to help her sleep—something she did often, but needed more than ever on this night of sadness and anger. Her cheeks quivered as she started toward the kitchen, only to be stopped by tapping on the front door. She turned, and guessed that no one but Rob would come rapping at such a late hour. Anyway, she recognized the rhythm of his drum beat. Rob seldom announced himself with a commonplace knock. She locked her teeth to strengthen her chin, walked directly through her living room of Early American ruffles, and opened the door.

Rob's expression turned grim as soon as he looked into his mother's eyes. "What is it, Mom?" he asked as he stepped into the room and closed the door. "What's wrong?"

Emily turned her back toward him, moved slowly to the center of the room and said, "Your Aunt Marjorie died a few hours ago."

"Oh, God, you're kidding?" He knew she wasn't. "Holy shit! And you were with her, weren't you? Jesus, I'm sorry."

"Damn her, she didn't even talk to me." Turning, Emily faced Rob and continued: "I'm glad she's dead. She's gone from our lives now."

Rob saw the quiver in his mother's cheek and the mixture of sorrow and anger in her eyes. "Don't, Mom. Please don't."

"Don't what? Don't express my anger? Is that what you're telling me? I didn't tell her I loved her. I couldn't. But I told her I wanted a sister. I looked right into her eyes tonight, and I told her I wanted a sister. But her eyes didn't even flicker. Oh, how I hate her." Tears rolled down Emily's cheeks as she reached out for her son. She embraced him and held him tightly. She sobbed as she said, "I thought maybe at the very end... But even then she wouldn't try. I hate her, Rob. Why didn't she try? I hate her."

"No you don't. You're angry because it wasn't the way it should have been. It never was the way it should have been. It couldn't be fixed at the very end, just because you wished it."

"Why didn't Papa love me? It was like I wasn't even there. It was always Marjorie—his Marjorie."

"Maybe he thought she needed him more than you did."

"No. She tricked him." Emily pulled away from her son and again turned her back toward him. "I needed him. And I needed Mama, too. Marjorie took them away from me." After wiping her eyes, Emily faced Rob and steadied her expression. "I love you, Rob."

"I know that, Mom. I'm lucky, because I've always known that. You gave me what your folks couldn't give you." He kissed her on the cheek. "And I love you, Mom."

"They took her body to the Rosemont Funeral Home. Will you go there tomorrow and make arrangements?"

"Of course. Don't think of that now."

"I'll be okay, Rob. It's just that all those years keep racing by in my mind. Each time I think of something I ask, 'Why did it have to be that way?' I tell myself it's in the past and can't be changed. But it doesn't seem to help. I keep blaming her. To me, it's always seemed that she destroyed so much."

"Think of her as being sick."

"And the sick can rule, right? They can rule your world."

"Why did you take me there that night?"

"What night?"

"When Dad left us. Why did you take me to Marjorie?"

Emily started to answer, then turned and walked away. Rob waited, then followed her into the kitchen where he found her pouring milk into a saucepan. He sat at the table, but kept his eyes on her.

"Your father walked out." Emily stirred the milk and kept her eyes on the pot. "I didn't know where he had gone. When he phoned from a Wilkes Barre motel that night, I took off after him. I had no place to leave you."

"But to dump me there, at that foreboding house. With her."

"I couldn't think straight. I was all mixed up, and I didn't know how long I'd be gone. I had no time to think. Anyway, I was ashamed. I was so ashamed, and I didn't want to see anyone. Who could I ask? That house was still my home. The grass had barely grown on Mama's grave next to Papa. I came for you the very next morning."

"I never told you about that night." As soon as Rob spoke, he regretted his words.

Emily turned and looked at her son. "What do you mean?"

"No, don't get me wrong. It was strange, that's all. I've never been able to forget her."

Emily waited for more, but Rob failed to continue. "I shouldn't have left you there."

"No. I'm glad you did. Otherwise I'd know her only as a twisted, mute woman wrapped in an American flag, her tongue sticking out of her mouth, her hands trembling as they carried her away. And as a dying woman in a nursing-home wheelchair."

Emily poured her warm milk into a cup. "Can I get you something to drink?"

"No thanks."

"Are you hungry?"

"God, no."

She sat at the table across from him, tried to smile, sipped her milk, then said, "I drove your father away. I can't really blame him for leaving. I was angry with them and I took it out on him. He grew tired of hearing it. Said I was possessed by my childhood, and figured I married him to get away from it all. Maybe I did. The trouble was, I didn't leave it behind. I brought it all with me into my marriage."

"It's weird, the things we never ask our parents. We just go on living, never knowing." He looked down at the table, then up at a high corner of the room, then at his mother. "I'm glad we can talk." He smiled kindly at her. "And I'm glad I know more than I did."

"Knowing doesn't always help. Sometimes I look back and wonder why I couldn't have changed things, especially with your father."

"Do you still love him?"

"I'm not sure I ever loved him as I should have." She sipped her milk.

"You blame yourself too much."

"Marriage seemed like a way out. But it really wasn't. I am to blame."

"And so is he. After all, he wasn't a father to me. Why hasn't he written to me in years? More than that, he didn't just leave you. He left me, too."

"He sent you postcards for a long time. Remember?"

"They stopped on my twenty-first birthday. It was as if he were saying, 'You're a man now. You can go it alone.' Hell, I think about him once in awhile, and I get a little tug in the gut. But to tell you the truth, there aren't many memories, except that stupid 'Bluebird'. Jackie sent a wedding invitation to his last address, but I'm not sure I want to see him. Then again, maybe I'm lying to myself. Do you think he'll show up?"

Emily's back stiffened.

"Don't worry," Rob said. "I don't think he will. He probably won't even get the invitation. And if he does, I doubt that he'll come."

"Weren't you going to tell me?"

"Sure. I just hadn't gotten around to it."

Emily thought for a moment, then said, "I guess it's only right. He is your father."

"I keep telling myself I don't care."

"Then you probably do." She smiled warmly. "Do you push away thoughts of him?"

"All the time. Except for the 'Bluebird'."

"What's this bluebird?"

"'Of Happiness'."

"The song?"

"I found a recording of it in Marjorie's attic."

"Don't call it Marjorie's. It's your house now."

"I can't seem to get used to that."

"It never should have been her house anyway." Emily's eyes watered. "Damn her!"

"I played the 'Bluebird' over and over until I learned every word."

"Why?"

"I don't know."

"Because it's a piece of your father?"

"I'm not sure. I joke about the song all the time. I'm never serious when I sing it."

"Even when you were little you would hide your serious side beneath a facade of fun."

"My way of coping? Is that what you're saying? Strange the games we humans play. I suppose I do want to hold onto something that was Dad's. And what about you? Denying that Marjorie was your sister—was that your way of coping?"

Emily simply lifted her eyebrows and tightened her lips.

"I've learned a lot about her," Rob said. "She left pieces of a crazy jigsaw puzzle all over that house. I'm still putting them together."

"I don't want to know." Emily shook her head. "Not everything. Not now. Maybe some parts and pieces someday."

"The good parts. Maybe pieces about your brother Jack? If the jigsaw keeps cutting the right curves, I just might find out that I have an uncle I like. He might have serious defects, mind you. But, for the most part, your instincts about him might be right."

Emily's lips parted and her eyes began to plead when the phone rang, startling her. A barely audible cry came from her throat as her head jerked back.

"Want me to get it?" Rob asked.

"No. I'll get it." She pushed her chair back and hurried to the wall phone near the refrigerator. "Who on earth would call at this hour?"

Rob yawned and rubbed his eyes. He was tired. The trip with Jackie to Maywood and the emotional experience of seeing John Willow Doe had exhausted him, especially after a full day at the office. He was not sorry, however, that he had extended the night by visiting his mother. For an instant he regretted not being with her when Marjorie died, but then realized that she would have forbidden it. His mind closed out his mother's words on the telephone. But suddenly he was alert to them.

"What is it?" she asked. "What's wrong? Yes, he's here. Wait. I'll put him on." She faced Rob. "It's Ty. He sounds strange. Really disturbed. He wants you to meet him at Marty's Tavern. Here. Talk to him."

"Oh, boy. Put on a pot of coffee. Make it strong. This could be a long night."

Chapter Thirty-Six

Marty's Tavern would not be special to those who did not make it special. It was simply a corner bar on the fringes of downtown, frequented by local residents and dart players. The front wall inside the narrow, dark barroom held two dartboards—one English, one American. The bar and its stools stretched along the north wall, booths along the south wall. A few tables and chairs fell in between. The rear wall held two doors to the rest rooms—one marked "Gents" and the other blemished by an unpainted splotch from a missing sign. As for decorations, the tavern walls offered only a few framed black-and-white photographs of bantam-weight prizefighters and group shots of local high school football players. A mirrored wall behind the bar reflected a multitude of liquor bottles.

Rob and Ty had been introduced to Marty's by a dart-throwing fanatic who worked for Pure-Pup. Obligation had taken them to a championship match between the Southside Woodpeckers and the Oaklane Steel-Pointers. Long after the contest and many beers, the twosome had stayed on alone at the far-rear booth, unloading thoughts from deep within. From that time on, Marty's Tavern was their special place for gutsy talk. The very feel of the bench and table, the smell of beer and the shadowy reflection of lamplight—all this and more set the mood and opened up Ty and Rob.

Lifted somewhat by three cups of his mother's coffee, Rob pushed his way into the tavern and immediately glanced toward the rear to assure himself that Ty was there. He couldn't mistake his friend's blond hair. Fast-stepping through the room, Rob paused but briefly to nod to the chubby, bald bartender. The midnight hour found the bar with few patrons—three old men on stools, two young men tossing darts.

"I took the liberty of ordering you a mug of draught," Ty said as Rob approached. "There's still a little foam on it." Ty gulped from his mug. "Drink up. I'm way ahead of you."

Rob slid into the booth and drank beer before he said anything. He wiped his lips, then spoke: "Time for a little 'tyrob' talk, eh? It's long overdue."

Ty looked down at his beer. "There's a lot I've been meaning to tell you. There's a lot that should have been said long ago. But that's not why I called you. There's something more immediate." He looked up at his friend. "Something terrible happened, and I'm not thinking straight."

"What is it?"

"Amy came to me. She stayed overnight with me. Tonight her father found us. I hurt him, but I didn't mean to." Ty's words were quick and broken. "It all happened so fast. He's unconscious in the hospital. She won't believe me. She won't even listen."

"Slow down, Ty. You're not making sense. Start from the beginning."

"Let me get us a couple more brews." Ty hurried to the bar.

"Come on, Mr. Bluebird," Rob mumbled to himself. "We need you."

When Ty returned with two frothy mugs, he began to talk as soon as he slid onto the bench: "I love her so much. And now she acts like she hates me."

"Ty, please. Back up, damn it."

Both men poured down beer, then Ty fastened his eyes on Rob and explained, "Her father came knocking on my door. When he answered, he demanded to see Amy, but I wouldn't let him. He tried to push his way in, but I shoved back, and he fell on the steps. The side of his face was all bloody." Ty stopped talking and again stared into his mug.

"Go on!"

"He gashed his head badly on the railing and the concrete. I tried to help. I could feel his pulse." Ty lifted his head and looked at his friend. "Amy got hysterical. She wouldn't let me near him. I called the cops."

"He's in the hospital now?"

"Over at Lakeside. The police ambulance took him. I told the cops what happened. They seemed to understand, but Amy didn't. She got the nurses and doctors to keep me away from him in the emergency ward. Every time I went near, she went crazy. She made these awful noises and kept throwing her hands in the air. She kept using signs to tell me that her father never hits people. She wouldn't believe me. I tried to explain. She's got this idea that I attacked him."

"Give her time. Her reactions are normal."

"She's so special, Rob. She's always telling me about the things her mother taught her—things that couldn't become part of her life with her father, yet became part of her, inside. When she was little, her mother nursed her through a terrible sickness that she doesn't remember. Maybe that's when she became deaf. She doesn't know. There are so many things about her that I guess I will never know. But I don't care."

"What happened to her mother?"

"She was killed in a car crash commuting from Allentown at night. She was working to pay Amy's way through deaf school. Her parents disowned her because she ran off with Harrison while in high school. She tried to mold him and fit him into a white collar job, but he couldn't handle it. He kept slipping until he was packing sheets of wallboard. Each time something went wrong in his life, he'd tighten his fanatical religious noose around himself and Amy. God was slapping him down for his mistakes, so he condemned himself and paid the penance by tightening the chains. At least that's the way I see it. I'll have to admit, I put the pieces together and added my own interpretation. Amy was brainwashed by him, but she loves him. Yet there's something deep within her. She learned too much from her mother. This undercurrent, this something else—it's there."

"Her mother's family was well-to-do?"

"Apparently. They took her in when her father went berserk after her mother's death. But they really didn't want her. Somehow her father got her back. I suspect he just came and took her. I'm sure he saw his wife's death as another of God's punishments. Now Amy probably sees me as a hand of the devil."

"If she's bright, she'll figure it out in time. She'll see. She'll know. Just wait. She'll come around."

"I don't know." Ty examined the grain in the table top. "You didn't see her. The look in her eyes... I can't shake it off."

"Ty, look at me." When his friend lifted his eyes, Rob went on: "You give advice all the time to kids and little old ladies. I mean, all the time you're solving other people's problems. Now, it's time to sort out your own situation. So, slow down and think."

Ty held tightly to his mug and tensed up even more as he said, "What if he dies? She'll never forgive me."

"Your emotions are getting in your way."

"That's right. They are. Because I love her." Ty's eyes moistened. "Do you understand? I love her. Do you believe me?"

"Yes. Yes, I believe you."

"You do?"

"Yes. I believe you. I really do." Rob tightened his fix on Ty's eyes. "The truth is, I never really knew you. Not completely."

Ty kept staring at Rob, but said nothing.

"I know you better, now," Rob said, almost whispering.

"You don't know everything."

"I know more than you think."

A strange look crossed Ty's face. "What do you mean?"

"Why don't you tell me?"

"I was going to tell you something tonight. But it's something you couldn't possibly know."

"Try me."

Ty showed anger as he said, "Goddamnit, Rob, this isn't a night for games."

"Sorry. I'm out of line. I know you're hurting."

"Hey. It's okay. I'm touchy, that's all." Ty poured down the rest of his beer. "I'm going to surprise the hell out of you." He focused on Rob. "I knew your Aunt Marjorie years ago."

"I know."

Ty didn't move a muscle, but his eyes questioned deeply. "You couldn't know. How could you know?"

"She left clues around the house. It took me time to put the pieces together. How old were you when it started. Sixteen?"

"When it started? What do you mean by it?"

Rob said nothing. He simply gave a knowing look.

"This is crazy."

"Hey, you're not the only kid seduced by an older woman. It could have happened to me."

"I don't understand. How could you know?"

"I'll give you a play by play account of the greatest sleuth job since Sherlock Holmes. But later. Okay?"

"I was going to tell you tonight."

"I thought you might."

"You're impossible. I don't believe you." Ty forced a crazy, crooked smile. He moved his fingers around the rim of his mug as his expression grew serious, then he looked toward a far corner of the barroom. "Yeah, sixteen. It started right after my sixteenth birthday. I'll never forget." After focusing back on Rob, he said, "You obviously know something, Rob. But you won't really understand until I tell you."

"I'm sure that's true." Rob dug his fingernails into the table as he quickly and matter-of-factly said, "Aunt Marjorie died today."

Ty's lips parted, but he could say nothing. Finally he struggled with "I'm sorry."

"No, no. Please don't. She obviously was tied more closely to you than to me."

"She was part of my life for a long, long time. Long after I last saw her. She'll always be there, I guess. But it's not the same now."

"Does her death free you in any way?"

"Amy freed me."

"I had that figured out, too."

"You did?"

"Once I began to understand."

"In my dreams, the beautiful woman on the staircase would chase away the girl of the midway lights. But I don't dream that anymore. Those dreams, they're gone. Now it's something else, and it's not a dream. It's real. Amy's a part of me. She's inside of me. She's part of my very being. I relish every little thing about her.

Like the time she wore the pale blue dress for me—a dress that didn't seem to belong on a girl from Redrock Road. She had made it, because her mother had taught her how. I cherish the way she feels about the birds and the flowers and her special place in the woods. She told me that even when she polished the furniture in that shabby house, she kept the pieces the way they should be, the way her mother taught her to care for them. She has her own treasury of memories inside of her. Some relate to things that seem so mundane or common, but to her they're special. She cherishes whatever life gave her to cherish, which to us doesn't seem like much, I suppose. I know that her night with me was beyond her dreams. But then it was beyond mine, too. But now I'm frightened. I can't lose her. No way. I just can't."

"You won't. Believe me. Not if she loves you. Give her time."

Ty's eyes darted about as his mind played with thoughts. Suddenly they turned on Rob. "Marjorie is dead." It was as if the realization suddenly jelled. "Please forgive me, Rob. But she's been dead. Do you understand what I'm saying? She was as she was way back then. The Marjorie of the past was the only Marjorie within me. She never changed. The woman who died today, I never knew. I want to show you something." Ty pushed himself from the booth. "Come on."

"But I've only had a couple beers."

"It's important. I have to show you. Come on."

Chapter Thirty-Seven

Ty almost knocked over the crystal rooster on his coffee table as he sped through his living room to the kitchen entrance. "Wait!" he demanded of Rob, who stopped abruptly, looked quizzically at Ty, then sat on the arm of the cream-colored sofa and watched his friend grasp the wall telephone and push buttons.

"Emergency room, please." The pause was long. "Yes, would you please give me the condition of Mr. Samuel Harrison. He was brought in a few hours ago with a head injury." Ty waited. "No, I'm not a relative, but... Well, could you at least tell me if he's gained consciousness?" Ty grimaced while he listened. "Damn it!" He hung up, then hurried to his studio door, put his back against it, and looked at Rob. "You wait right there. Okay?"

"If you say so."

After opening the door, Ty switched on the light and glanced at the three easels—two shrouded, one (the portrait of Amy) at center and uncovered.

"Okay. Come on."

Rob followed. Just inside the door, Ty grasped his arm.

"What is it?"

"Stay here." Ty walked to the easels.

"You showed me the portrait of Amy. It's beautiful. It's your best work."

"That's not it." Ty covered the painting of Amy and stepped to his right. "Don't move. Stay back there. Are you ready?"

"Ready."

Ty pulled the cover from the right-side easel, dropped it to the floor, and slowly stepped back.

Rob said nothing, but the beat of his heart quickened. His lips parted as a flash of heat flushed his face. His wide eyes were transfixed by the painting. Not until moments after Ty stood at his side did he utter words: "I don't believe what I'm seeing."

Ty was silent.

"I'll be damned. It's truly beyond belief. Incredible. Uncanny. It's just as I remember her."

Both men kept staring at the portrait of Marjorie Worth on the staircase—Marjorie in soft, flowing black, her beauty as it was when Ty and Rob were teenage boys. A radiance came from the portrait, yet so did mystery. Ty had captured the enigmatic, sensual, beauteous, yet foreboding nature of the woman. The pale skin colors contrasted sharply with the ebony hair and the deep red lips. A smile was not quite there, but come-hither danger was. Light focused on her face and cleavage, and her breasts were almost apparent through the sheer, black, embroidery that covered her nipples. She stood halfway down the stairs, her flowing gown vanishing behind the banister that held her smooth, left hand. It seemed she stared directly at Ty and Rob as she had looked down on them from that staircase years ago.

"It's remarkable," Rob whispered. "No, it's beyond words. But it's so eerie. It's just as I remember her. It's the picture my mind has carried since I was a young teenager. How did you do it?"

"It's as I saw her first. On the staircase."

"But it's exact. How could you..."

"She stayed with me. Every detail. I saw her over and over in my mind."

"Maybe you were trying to exorcise her from your mind."

"I don't know. But it was a vision that I had to put on canvas."

"It's more than amazing. It's more than incredible. I can't believe what I'm seeing. I know what it's like to carry a vision for years. I never told you. But that's exactly where she stood when I first saw her. I remember walking slowly into the living room, and then I looked up. I froze. I was unable to move. Then she beckoned me."

"Did you..." Ty hesitated, struggled with his tongue, then blurted out, "Did she take you to her room?"

"Go ahead. Ask. Say it straight out. You want to know if she taught me how to use my little teenage tool. The answer is, not quite. Certainly not fully. Almost, maybe. Sort of. To put it bluntly, I didn't screw Auntie Marjorie. But I did have an experience that night. She either brought me off, or set me going. Maybe I've blocked it out of my mind. I'll never know for sure. Maybe it was simply my first wet dream. But I do know this—dreaming or not, an intense feeling set off my launcher."

"Damn."

"After that night, I never saw her again until they carried her away." Rob studied Ty's face. "I have a feeling that you don't hate her."

"My God, no! I don't hate her in the least."

"Will you tell me about it?'

"Not while she's looking at us." Ty walked to the portrait, picked up the shroud and covered Marjorie.

Rob continued to stare at the easel as if he could see through the cover. The image stayed in his mind's eye, and he remained standing just inside the doorway even after Ty left the room. He finally backed out of the room, turned and found Ty in the kitchen entranceway, hanging onto the telephone again and pushing numbers. "Don't," he said. "Let me." With his usual sureness, Rob grabbed the phone.

Ty stretched out on the sofa. He gazed upward, but worrisome thoughts took the focus from his eyes.

Rob wondered why the hospital operator was so slow to pick up at 1:45 a.m. But in truth, only seconds elapsed before a woman answered: "Lakeside Hospital."

"This is Quigley from the *Times*," Rob said. "Connect me with public relations, please."

"Sorry, Mr. Quigley, but there's no one in that department now."

"Well, who's handling night-time press calls?"

"One moment, please. I'll connect you with Lyle Humphrey in emergency receiving."

Rob turned toward Ty as he waited. "Pour me a brew, will you. Or something stronger if you have it,"

"Humphrey here."

"Quigley at the *Times*. I'm doing a piece on an altercation over on Elmwood. I need a condition update on a Sam Harrison."

"Hold on."

Ty pushed past Rob and then rattled bottles under the kitchen sink.

"Mr. Quigley?"

"Still here."

"Harrison is in the Intensive Care Unit. He's gained consciousness, but they're still monitoring his heartbeat. Officially, he's listed as serious. The next hour will determine whether they put him on the critical list."

"Anything else you can tell me?"

"That's it."

As Ty brushed by, Rob grabbed a glass of bourbon and ice. "Thanks," he said into the telephone before hanging up.

"So tell me," Ty pleaded as he stood nearby, ready to gulp beer from a can.

"Not to worry. He's not on the critical list."

"But still unconscious, right?"

"No, he's conscious. Don't fret. He'll be okay. He's in the ICU where they know what they're doing."

"And Amy is hating my guts." Ty sat on the sofa and hung his head. "Strange, isn't it. Just when I was so happy. It's like the Old Guy up there was saying, 'Hey, you're feeling too good. We gotta burst that bubble.'" Looking up, Ty tried to catch his buddy's reaction. "Rob, you can't imagine what it was like to be with Amy. I wish I could explain."

"Euphoria? Is that the word you want?"

"That and more."

"I think I understand." Rob sat across from Ty. "You found someone to love, and that's wonderful. But more than that, you found something that had been stolen from you."

"What do you mean?"

"Well, I figure dear Aunt Marjorie had cut off your essence, so to speak."

"My essence? Now you're mincing words. You mean she cut off my dick, don't you?" Ty tried to tell Rob something with his eyes. "It's not like you think. I never really felt seduced or misused. Does that surprise you? I suppose today they'd say I was sexually abused. But, in my mind, it was never that way. Like I said, she died long ago, yet lived on as a dream, as a haunting vision." He glanced toward the door to his studio-workshop. "And as an image."

"Yes, a haunting vision," Rob whispered. "I know." Then he sought the right words and said, "So, tell me about the woman in your portrait—as she was, when she lived."

"I don't know where or how to begin."

"You've already begun."

"Not really." Ty finished his beer, then toyed with the can. "It started when I found a note on collection day. It was October. I remember kicking the leaves as I walked up the pathway, and I remember..."

Chapter Thirty-Eight

Sixteen-year-old Ty Scott, looking younger than his years, kicked leaves as he strolled up the walkway toward the front door of Marjorie Worth's house. Dressed for the coolness of the October day, Ty wore high-top sneakers, gray corduroy pants and a bright green Philadelphia Eagles football jacket. His blond hair jutted out from under the peak of his Eagles cap. At one point his kicking caused him to trip as his right sneaker caught on a piece of raised concrete. But he managed to catch himself and turn his near-fall into a boyish spin. An autumn breeze and the thick ground-cover of leaves infused a carefree feeling in Ty as he neared the hemlock-shrouded house. The oaks rustled, for they had yet to shed their russet-colored leaves of deep red and burnt yellow.

As he mounted the steps, Ty pulled his collection book from his jacket pocket and checked his records, something he did at each doorstep every Saturday afternoon. Actually, he already knew that this customer owed but one week's charge. Miss Worth never forgot to put his money in her mailbox. Ty had never seen her, but on two occasions had sensed her presence when window curtains moved.

The sun broke through the clouds as Ty mounted the steps of the Tudor-style house. The imposing doorway and heavy wooden door formed a mysterious portal that, in his mind, was off limits. Again he looked away from the forbidden entryway as he reached into the wrought-iron mailbox and took hold of his envelope.

Ty was down the steps and partway down the walkway before he ripped open the envelope and reached for the money that was not there. He found, instead, a note requesting his help: "Dear Paperboy, Please come into my house. You'll find the door unlocked. I need your help in replacing a closet pole that fell. You'll find your money on the piano."

The boy froze after his sneakers skidded to a squeaky stop on the walkway underneath the leaves. He read the note again. Then, he turned slowly and looked at the house. He stood still, read the note a third time, lifted his head slowly, and stared at the doorway. Seconds passed before he stepped hesitantly toward the house. Gone was his carefree gate. He kicked no leaves, and he skipped no steps as he climbed toward the heavy door. His eyes moved from knocker to bell button and back to knocker.

Within seconds of reading the note again, Ty folded the paper, slipped it into his jacket pocket, and then placed his right hand on the doorknob. At first, his effort to turn the knob was too weak, but he tightened his grip and tried again. The knob turned, the lock clicked, and the door opened inward. The quick beat of his teenage heart held him back briefly, but within a moment he pushed the door until he could see into the room. It took courage to enter the home of a woman so often whispered about—a woman who supposedly never had visitors.

Ty's first steps within the house were timid. He walked to the center of the living room—a poorly lighted room, despite the brightness of the day. Little light filtered through the curtains between the draperies. A globe lamp on a piecrust table near the newel post at the foot of the stairs reflected light on the banister. The wingback chairs and sofa, the tiled fireplace, the piano, and the gold-framed portrait of a woman were images burned indelibly into his brain—images that would appear years later in his dreams. The strong fragrance of lavender, though he had no name for it, seemed to go well with the dusty pinkness. It was a scent that would quicken his heartbeat in later life, that would haunt him and bring sweat to his armpits in department stores and gift shops, that would turn him away from boudoirs, that would flash a multitude of images in his mind.

Stepping to the piano, Ty reached for a white envelope that lay on the broad surface of the baby grand, near the curved edge of the harp-shaped mahogany. His fingers barely touched it when he heard movement on the stairs. Turning quickly as his heart jumped, Ty focused on the woman who stood halfway up the steps. His eyes widened and his lips parted as he gawked at Marjorie Worth—the enigmatic, sensual, beauteous, foreboding woman in soft, flowing black; the woman whose likeness he would one day paint in oil on canvas in minute detail from an image branded into his brain.

Light from the globe lamp near the newel post reflected on her smooth, pale skin, casting shadows that deepened and accentuated the contours of her face and the cleavage of her breasts that were barely covered by sheer, black embroidery. Her ebony hair and red lips contrasted sharply with her flesh tones.

Marjorie lifted her hand from the banister and motioned to Ty as her eyes also urged him to approach. A smile was almost on her lips, yet not quite, stirring mixed feelings within Ty—feelings of come-hither risk yet desire, of the pull to approach and the push to flee. But he knew that whatever his fears, he would not flee. He seemed to sense what she wanted, despite his tender years, his inexperience, his naivete. Stepping toward the newel, he revealed his innocence and apprehension in every whit of his expression. Libidinous instinct moved him despite weakness in his knees, unsteadiness that caused him to reach for the newel and hold on, ever so briefly. Sixteen-year-old manliness pulled him quickly from the post. He locked his jaw and tightened his fists in an effort to secure his wobbly legs, and looked up at her from the foot of the stairs.

"Come on," she urged in a soft yet deep whisper. She seemed to float up the steps and drift as she turned at the landing and vanished. Ty heard nothing more, but sensed that she waited atop the stairs.

Like most teenage males, Ty had been taunted by boys who boasted of conquests never achieved. But none of that had anything to do with this. His "decision" to climb the stairs was no decision at all. The feelings within him were all pervasive, erasing logic and replacing any rational thought with blind drive, excitement and wonder. He tiptoed up to the landing, turned and looked up to see Marjorie standing against the hallway wall next to a large emerald-colored urn. Her eyes beckoned him.

"Come on," she repeated before disappearing again.

Twitches in his calf and thigh muscles failed to stop Ty from mounting the rest of the steps. At the top, he looked to his left and saw Marjorie slip quietly from the hallway. He hesitated, then walked slowly to her bedroom doorway. When he peered into the room, he saw her standing at the side of the four-poster bed, and he watched as she dropped her soft, flowing negligee to the floor. Now posing in only black lace underwear, she lifted her hand and used her forefinger to summon him.

Ty sort of oozed into the room, sliding slowly around the doorjamb, keeping his back to the wall. His eyes never left Marjorie. They were transfixed on the black lace and creamy flesh of a woman three times his age. Marjorie's long-secluded body had been pampered through the years, protected from sunlight, oiled with lotions and shaped by ballet pirouettes before the mirror. Objects within the room were mostly vague images on the edge of Ty's vision. Blue and white surrounded him, but his steady stare turned the mahogany furniture into dark forms against light colors. He was not conscious of the blue-and-white snow scenes that decked the walls, or of the vanity and oversized mirror in the alcove where Marjorie so often primped and preened herself.

Smiling seductively at Ty, Marjorie sat on the edge of the bed and patted the blue satin spread with her hand. "Sit here," she whispered.

Ty's muscles reacted, but failed to move his body.

"Don't be afraid," she said. "Come on."

The word "afraid" caused manliness to prick Ty again, for he did not intend to show fear. He walked to the bed and sat beside Marjorie, yet gazed straight ahead at the wall and kept his knees together.

"Relax," she said. "It's okay. Really. Here. Let me take off your jacket." Starting from the top, she unfastened his Eagles jacket one snap at a time. She pulled it from his shoulders, slipped it from his arms, and tossed it to the floor. Then she removed his cap and rumpled his hair. "Move over here. Lean back. Here. Up against the pillows."

Ty shifted, stretched out, and wiggled his way into place. He lay in the middle of the bed with his head on a pillow.

Marjorie grasped another pillow, shook it, and put it under the boy's head. "Let me fix that for you. There. How's that?"

Ty spoke his first words since entering the house: "I never... I mean, I never before..."

"I know. I understand. Just relax. I'll show you." She began to unbutton his shirt, moving slowly from the top down, pausing now and then to gently touch his cheeks and lips with her forefinger. After freeing the last button, she spread open his shirt and fingered his smooth, firm, boyish, hairless chest. Soon she felt his legs shaking and tried to calm them by massaging his thighs, deliberately avoiding the swelling between his legs. When the quivering subsided, she unbuckled his belt and unzipped his corduroys and fondled him.

Within minutes she feared that he was reaching a peak of excitement too quickly, so she paused, looked into his eyes, smiled ever so slightly, and then slipped her straps from her shoulders, fully exposing her breasts.

Chapter Thirty-Nine

Sunday afternoon, only one day after Ty's visit with Marjorie, brought the 16-year-old back to Juniper Lane. The street alone filled him with excitement and anxiety. His heart pounded long before he pedaled his bicycle past the house. The feelings could not be contained. They possessed him.

U-turning his bike, Ty sped past the house again. He pedaled but a few hundred feet and circled once more. After slowing near the house, he accelerated, then coasted to the next intersection and turned the corner. Within seconds he pressed the brake and stopped the bike at curbside where he leaned against an old mulberry tree. He shook his head and rubbed his eyes. The past night had brought him little sleep. He had risen early, served his newspapers, and returned to his parents' modest, white clapboard house before his mother and father awakened. He had gone directly to his bedroom and stayed there until called, and had become annoyed when his mother—a slight, blonde, soft-spoken woman who looked old enough to be his grandmother—insisted that he eat his breakfast. "What's wrong with you?" she had asked. "You haven't touched a thing."

In church he had heard nothing that the minister said, and fidgeted enough to annoy his father, a quiet, little, balding, nondescript man who rarely scolded his only son, born years late and unexpected.

Later, Ty had forced a bit of lunch while being questioned by his mother—as his father listened and watched—about his silence, preoccupation and nervousness.

After freeing himself from home, he had ridden his bicycle to a nearby park where he tried to battle his emotions by pedaling hard around and around on the curved roadways. But in little time he had been drawn back to Juniper Lane.

Ty unsnapped his Eagles jacket. Although the October day was cool and gray, body heat had moistened his shirt. He breathed deeply, pushed his bike from the curb, and then rode around the block and back onto Juniper Lane. When he saw an elderly man— one of his customers—raking leaves on the sidewalk across the street from Marjorie's house, he U-turned quickly, raised his body, and sped from the neighborhood.

* * *

Returning to the Mulberry section about an hour later, Ty slowed his bike as he swerved onto Juniper Lane and searched the street with darting eyes. No one was raking leaves. Without hesitation, Ty turned his bicycle at a driveway and coasted along the sidewalk toward Marjorie's house. Neither his pounding heart nor his sweating armpits were about to restrain him. Whatever part of his emotional complex was in charge, it simply held control and moved his bike right up the walkway to the steps of Marjorie's house. Ty dismounted quickly, not allowing himself to think too deeply for fear that reasoning might produce restraint. He picked up his cycle and rammed it into a cluster of yews and hemlocks. Hurriedly mounting the steps, he grew frustrated with himself when the quivering returned to his legs. He gritted his teeth and knocked on the door. After seconds of pacing, he rang the bell and knocked again. He glanced about self-consciously, sighed, then whispered, "Please."

Minutes later Ty backed away. But, instead of retrieving his bicycle from the bushes, he spread the evergreens and pushed himself into the thicket. He moved behind the hemlocks and yews, squatted on the ground, leaned back against the house, and allowed his mind to wander into fantasies that bulged his jeans.

Within a half hour Ty peeked from the bushes and hurried to the door. Again his knocking and ringing went unanswered. Minutes later, as he began to walk away, he heard the click of the lock behind him. He turned, hesitated, stepped to the door, placed his hand against the wood and pressed ever so slightly. The door moved. Swallowing hard, he pushed it open and stepped inside, closing it behind him. He found Marjorie twirling lightheartedly in the center of the room. She was not dressed for afternoon, but for late evening. Her blue satin and sequins reflected candlelight, for she had set the scene by surrounding herself with candles—lighted candles on the piano, the mantel, the tables, the newel. Blue chiffon flowed from her like a giant, soft pinwheel, swirling up and cascading down as she turned. Sparks of light flashed from her rhinestone earrings. When she stopped moving, the giddiness vanished from her expression, replaced by her sultry, come-on look. She posed at the piano, one hand draped over the curved mahogany, and kept her eyes on Ty. Within moments she slowly approached him, removed his cap, pushed his moist hair from his forehead, smiled slightly and said, "Let me pour you a bubble bath."

* * *

Ty arrived home after dark to find his mother standing on the porch of their small, two-story house. Still wearing her Sunday attire, a deep blue dress with tiny white polka dots, Anna Scott stood in the glow of the porch light with her hands on her hips. She was usually slow to anger. This time, however, her displeasure exploded—a rare happening, indeed, that stung Ty as he wheeled his bike across the front lawn.

"Where have you been?" she snapped. "Your father's out there somewhere looking for you. What happened to you? We've been worried sick. Your dinner's still on the table—stone cold. I've never known you to miss dinner. It's not like you. What happened?"

"Sorry," muttered Ty, the usually considerate teenager who so often had surprised his mother by doing unexpected chores. He continued pushing his bicycle along the side of the house.

"Come back here, young man!" his mother demanded. She walked to the side of the porch, leaned over the railing, followed him with her eyes, and called after him: "You tell me where you've been!"

Ty stopped wheeling his bike, but did not look back at his mother. In fact, he stared at the ground as he said, "I had to help a customer."

"Help a customer? At this time? Why didn't you call?"

"Sorry."

"Sorry? Is that all you can say?" Anna had never before felt such distress as a result of Ty's behavior. She had often thanked God for his thoughtfulness, his agreeable nature and his sweet disposition, and fretted over the idea that she wouldn't live to see his middle years. Her only child had been a menopause baby.

Chapter Forty

Rob drank the rest of his bourbon and placed the glass on the coffee table near the crystal rooster, all the while keeping his eyes on Ty.

"I regretted coming home late that night," Ty said. "It caused real strain between me and my folks. It was never explained, and so they never understood. There was no way to explain it, so it just hung there like an invisible barrier. I still squirm a bit when I think of it. But that didn't stop me. I was drawn back to that house over and over again." Ty stared into space as his thoughts traveled. "I couldn't think of anything else. It was hard to concentrate on school. Sometimes I couldn't get to sleep. Other times I'd wake early."

Rob grabbed his glass and started toward the kitchen. "Don't stop. Go on."

Ty exhaled a deep breath, leaned back and gazed at the ceiling. "All my thoughts were on her, my next visit, how I'd get back there again. I hated it when we'd go away on vacation or something. I didn't want to go away. I lusted for her all the time. I would have gone to her every day if I could have."

Rob mixed his drink at the kitchen sink. "You want another brew?"

"No." Ty was quiet for a moment, but when Rob returned and sat across from him, he looked at his friend and spoke softly: "In time it became a pattern. She knew when I'd come. Always on Saturday—collection day. On other days, she knew when I was there in my secret place behind the bushes. I'd sit on the ground, lean back against the wall, and wait. She'd play the piano.

Always the same tune. I knew, then, that the door was unlocked."

Rob sipped bourbon, then asked, "Were there times when she didn't open the door?"

"Oh, yes. And they hurt beyond belief. I was in agony. I couldn't stand the feeling. I'd go home and lock myself in the bathroom."

"And all these years, you never told anyone?"

Ty shook his head and glanced down. "Not until now." He looked up and smiled weakly at Rob, as if expressing deep feeling for his buddy. "I'm sorry I cut you off the way I did. I just couldn't..."

"Hey, like I said, I understand. So don't bring it up again."

Ty looked away from Rob and allowed his mind to wander. "It was crazy. In school, I'd glance around at the other guys and tell myself they had nothing but silly, giggling girls their own age. I was way above and beyond that. I had the most beautiful woman in the Lehigh Valley. God damn! I think I will have another beer." He pushed himself from the couch and started for the kitchen.

"I saw her only once in those days," Rob said, "yet her image stayed with me always. So, I can imagine. I mean, what happened to you... Shit, it's unreal."

After a few clinks and bangs in the kitchen, Ty returned with a can of beer. He guzzled a swig before sinking into the sofa. "One time when I pushed open her door I saw all these dolls. They were sitting in the chairs, on the window sills, everywhere—all facing her as she played that tune on the piano. They were her audience."

"She was a nut!"

"No. No, not really. When you live alone all that time and don't see anyone... Well, she needed an audience. She liked to perform, but she needed an audience. I became her audience. And the dolls... Well, in time she didn't need them anymore."

"You became her doll?"

"I was her toy and her lover, I guess. Sometimes I'd have to attend a tea party before we'd go upstairs. At first they were fancy little tea-times, like the English might have in late afternoon. Later they were like kids' parties with balloons. I didn't want balloons. I didn't want kid stuff because I didn't do kids' things with her upstairs. I did men's things." Ty shook his head slowly as he conjured up images. "So often my anxious feelings were worse than impatience. I was on fire inside and wanted to go upstairs. Sometimes I'd be sitting at the head of the dining table and she'd walk around behind me, stand there, and rub my shoulders, kiss my neck and slip her hands under my shirt. Maybe she wanted me to beg. But I wouldn't say please no matter how much I silently pleaded inside of myself. I was always more than ready before I even entered the house. The suspense was agony. Once I lost it all in my pants at the top of the steps. That ended the tea parties. Though sometimes she'd still make me sit in the living room and watch her dance. She'd dress in ballet clothes, spin around and around, and then dramatically race up the stairs."

"She was always in control?"

"At first. For a long time, I guess. But not later on."

"What do you mean?"

"I grew to know that she needed me. I was her audience, her plaything, her everything. And I liked the feeling of being needed. It put me more in control. And she began to realize that. In fact, it got to the point where I'd let her perform or do whatever she wanted for a brief while. Then I'd just walk upstairs, get undressed, stretch out naked on the bed, and wait for her. She'd always come to me. I liked that."

"But maybe she was still in control. Do you realize that?"

"We were playing games. And she was letting me play my game. Is that what you're saying?"

"I think so."

"Maybe. But I always wondered if the turnabout led to her not wanting to see me anymore. Suddenly she just refused to open the door. Finally she left me a note and told me to go away. The hurt was unbelievable. I could never describe it. The sickness affected every part and piece of me. For months I knocked on her doors and windows refusing to give up. A couple times I hid in her bushes, fantasized and brought myself off, only to feel anger afterwards and fall into deep depression. Sometimes I'd actually vomit. I couldn't keep food down. My folks sent me to several doctors—even a shrink. It seemed that my life had ended at seventeen years."

Rob gulped the rest of his bourbon before he said, "It wasn't what you thought."

"What do you mean?" Ty stared directly at his friend.

"That's not why she stopped seeing you."

"How do you know?"

"I just know."

"What are you trying to tell me?"

Rob was unsure of himself. This seemed to be the point in the conversation where he was to spit out the tale of the garden skull and John Willow Doe. But to crack open the night with a lightning bolt seemed almost too enormous a task, especially in the wee hours of the morning. The push and pull within him—to tell or not to tell—battled to a stalemate. The uncharted path that stretched before him seemed too dangerous. He needed a clear head in the light of a new day. "Well, you see... Let me explain." Rob floundered. "It's hard to spell out, but, you see, Aunt Marjorie wrote a boxful of letters, all addressed to you. She had a thing about movie stars, so we thought they were notes to Tyrone Power and pushed them aside. We didn't look at them again until we found out everything else."

"Everything else?"

Rob struggled. He took a piece of ice from his glass, put it into his mouth and crunched it between his molars. "Well, you know. Those letters. I think they prove you're wrong. But you'll see." He looked at his watch.

"Rob, what are you trying to say?"

"Whatever it is, I'm not doing it very well. It's late. I can't think straight, so I can't talk straight. Hell, I've got to be at work in a few hours. And so do you."

"I'm not going to work. Cover for me, will you? Tell them I'm sick or something. I'm going to the hospital first thing. I've got to see Amy."

"Call me. I want to see you again tomorrow."

Chapter Forty-One

Ty hurried along a sterile, white corridor leading to the Intensive Care Unit on the second floor of Lakeside Hospital. He wore tweed trousers and a heavy, white, loose-fitting sweater, because temperatures had dipped during the night. His quick stride, which kept his bouquet of red carnations bouncing up and down with every thrust of his fist, had followed an impatient wait for the start of visiting hours. He raced by two empty gurneys just before reaching the ICU sign that projected into the hallway. Stopping abruptly at the doorway, he looked about, expecting someone to forbid his entry. Suddenly his shoulders gave way and he lowered the carnations, dangling them toward the floor. Worry weakened him as he stared at a cubicle within the ICU. Gone were the wires, the tubes, the monitor, and Sam Harrison. Fresh linen had been tightly secured over the hospital bed.

Glancing left and right, Ty stepped into the room where he saw nurses tending patients in cubicles at the far ends of the unit. But no one staffed the nursing station at the immediate right.

"May I help you?" asked a stocky, bull-faced, gray-haired nurse who came from the corridor and stepped up behind Ty.

Almost dropping the flowers, Ty spun about and faced the woman. "I'm looking for Mr. Harrison."

"Who?"

"Sam Harrison. The man who was over there." Ty pointed to the vacant cubicle. "He was there yesterday."

"I wasn't on duty yesterday." The deep-voiced woman brushed past Ty as she asked, "Are you family?"

"No, but..."

"If you're not family, you're not allowed in here. Wait right there." The thickset woman hurried to the nursing station where she scanned records and flipped pages of a register. Looking up, she said, "Mr. Harrison was moved to room four-ten. That's on the fourth floor."

"Does that mean he's better?"

"I presume so."

The carnations sprang up as Ty backed into the hallway.

* * *

Troublesome thoughts plagued Ty as he checked room numbers while walking along a fourth-floor corridor: If Sam Harrison were well enough to be moved, then he undoubtedly was well enough to converse with Amy and fill her with hateful ideas. Surely he had denounced Ty many times over, and condemned Amy for running away. Certainly he had sermonized, saying God had allowed the hand of the devil to strike him down because of sins committed by Amy with Ty.

The thoughts so distressed him that he almost turned away when he spotted Room 410. He stood motionless for a moment, then edged along the wall and stopped across from the doorway so he might see into the room. Amy's auburn hair alerted him immediately. Gathering his wits, he stepped into the room and stood just inside the door, holding the flowers in front of him with both hands. Her back facing Ty, Amy sat at the side of her father's bed, unaware of the visitor. Sam lay sleeping, his face turned slightly toward an empty bed on the window side of the two-person room—a typical hospital room with cream-colored walls, a TV set near the ceiling, adjustable metal beds and green divider curtains, at the moment pushed back and bunched at the side of each bed. A tube fed liquid into Sam's left arm.

Ty approached Amy gingerly, shifted the carnations to his side and tapped her gently on the shoulder. She started, turned her head and showed alarm in her eyes when she saw him.

Backing up a step, Ty quickly used the deaf sign for "Please."

Amy shook her head and pushed the air with her hands. She was telling Ty not to approach her father. Continuing to say "no" by shaking her head, she stood and pointed to the door. She followed Ty as he stepped back into the corridor.

Lifting the flowers, Ty moved his lips slowly as he said, "For your father." He repeated even more slowly, "For your father."

Amy raised her hands and began to sign with quick finger movement: "I don't want you to upset him." She could tell by the look in Ty's eyes that he had not understood. She repeated her signs more slowly.

Ty indicated that he understood, grasped her hand and wrapped it around the flowers. He pulled a folded piece of paper from his pants pocket, unfolded it, and handed it to Amy. She read the typed message: "Please believe me. It was an accident. I love you so much. Right now I'm hurting inside, as I know you must be."

Amy looked directly into Ty's eyes, but he could not read the message in her expression. For a moment he thought her eyes showed puzzlement. Or perhaps they pleaded. Or maybe they wished.

"Tell me," he signed.

"Father is much better," she signed.

"I'm glad. Tell me more."

"He explained what happened."

Ty was nonplused. He was confused by Amy's lack of hostility. Surely any explanation from her father would have deepened her distrust in him. With puzzlement molding his expression, he signed "What?" while speaking aloud: "What are you talking about?"

"My father is an honest man, no matter what you think of him." Amy moved her hands and fingers slowly in hopes that Ty would grasp most of her message. "He told me it was not your fault."

Ty failed to respond at first. He wanted to fully understand, and when he believed he did, he cursed himself for over-reacting to the point where much of his energy had been sucked away. He smiled, but allowed his smile to vanish, feeling that it might be inappropriate. As restrained joy seeped into him, he pointed to himself, to the flowers, and then to the room.

Amy shook her head again.

"Let me talk to him," Ty said while signing the words "me" and "your father."

Amy gave the carnations back to Ty, then signed, "He still doesn't understand. He still can't accept you." She looked down at the floor, then up into his eyes. "More than that, he's angry that he's here, in this hospital. You know how he feels about doctors. He blames me. And probably you." Suddenly she embraced him, squeezing tightly and crushing the flowers.

Ty's restrained joy became full-fledged joy. "I love you so much," he said as he freed his arms, dropped the broken flowers to the floor, and wrapped his arms around her. He kissed her on the neck and lips. "Oh, God, I love you so much!"

Though Amy could not hear Ty's words, she could feel their meaning.

Chapter Forty-Two

Emily, Rob, Jackie and a minister gathered near a cluster of sweet gum trees on a grassy slope in the cemetery and gazed on the casket suspended above a freshly dug grave. Only two sprays of flowers decked the mound of orange earth beside the hole. The Rev. Harvey Smothers, a tall, slender, youthful, dark-haired man, wore a black suit, as did Rob. Emily was thankful that the day was cool, for her high-neck, navy blue, worsted dress was winter wear. Jackie had chosen a black sheath and a narrow, gold-chain choker.

Services at the Oakview Funeral Home had been private. No newspaper obituary or paid notice had reported Marjorie's death. The casket had been closed throughout, because neither Emily nor Rob wished to view the body.

The autumn sun was bright, but not warm enough to take away the chill. It brightened the leaves remaining on some of the cemetery trees and set aglow clusters of colorful chrysanthemums at some of the gravestones.

Dressed in the red-and-black plaid of a lumberjack, Ty stood at a distance, unseen by the others, and looked down on Marjorie's grave site. He stayed behind a stone of gray granite crowded by azaleas that had grown too large for the small monument. Scattered maples, oaks, buckeyes and gum trees reached up from the slope between him and the casket, their sparse foliage allowing rays of light from above to streak and splatter the earth with brightness. A brown hare startled Ty as it darted into his view, stopped at a small stone of pink granite, sat on its haunches, perked its ears, twitched its nose, and then proceeded to nibble on weeds.

Stepping from behind the tombstone, Ty watched as the clergyman shook hands with Rob, nodded to the women, turned and walked away from the grave site. Ty moved slowly toward the hare, which froze briefly, hopped twice and fled quickly, darting here and there before disappearing into an evergreen thicket. Continuing down the slope, Ty zigzagged as he strolled among the trees, monuments and clusters of shrubs on his way toward Marjorie's burial plot. He kept holding himself back, fighting the pull of gravity, and at one point spun about and glanced at his van as if checking to make certain it was still parked on the upper roadway.

As the minister's black sedan moved slowly away along a curved drive, Jackie kept staring at Rob as if urging him to do something. She finally asked, "Shouldn't we each place a flower on the casket? Aren't they going to lower it?"

"I told them not to lower it until after we left," Rob explained.

"Why?" Emily asked. "Did you think it would upset me?"

Rob didn't answer.

"Well, I don't know about you, but I'm going to put a flower on the casket," Jackie said. She walked to the flowers on the other side of the grave and pulled a white carnation from one of the sprays. After placing it atop the coffin, she stared at Rob until he nodded. Then she fetched two more carnations and walked back to him and Emily. "Here."

Rob took a flower, but his mother turned away. As she did, she caught sight of Ty as he approached.

"Look," Emily whispered just loud enough for the ears of Rob and Jackie.

Ty went directly to Emily, grasped her hand, and squeezed it gently. He looked at Rob and shrugged his shoulders as if to say he wasn't sure why he had come. Then he took the remaining flower from Jackie and walked to the coffin.

Rob looked down at his carnation as he twirled it with his finger tips. He regretted that he had nervously pulled off a few petals. As he lifted his eyes and watched Ty lay his flower on the casket a strange sadness pervaded his body. He stepped to the side of his friend and placed his wounded flower next to Ty's.

"She died a long time ago," Ty whispered.

Chapter Forty-Three

Rob had tossed aside his funeral jacket, loosened his deep gray necktie and unbuttoned his white shirt. He sat next to Jackie on the love seat in his mother's living room, his left arm wrapped around her.

"Come on, Mom! Just stack the dishes for God's sake!" Rob showed his anxiety.

"Calm down," whispered Jackie as she patted him on the knee. "You have plenty of time."

"Once I start unloading it I want to get it all out," Rob said. "Let's face it, it's not the kind of thing you can break in the middle. I want to let it pour out and get it over with. And I'm counting on your help. As I go along, you fill in the gaps. Okay?"

"I'll do the best I can."

Rob pulled his arm from around Jackie, leaned forward and put his elbows on his knees and his fists in his cheeks. Seconds later he folded his arms and slouched. "Remember, I told Ty I'd meet him at Marty's later tonight. And that's important, too. In fact, that's more important than this."

Still in her funeral dress, Emily walked briskly into the living room carrying a tray of filled coffee cups and brownies. "I don't understand why Ty didn't come for dinner," she said while placing the tray on her coffee table. "You'd think a young man who lives alone would welcome any chance for a free meal." Emily sat in a wing chair opposite her son and Jackie. "I was so surprised when I saw him walking toward us at the cemetery. I suppose he showed

up for your sake, Rob. But I must tell you, I really was
dumbfounded. I had no idea he knew anything about Marjorie. I
never realized that you talked to him about your strange old aunt.
But then Ty is a special friend, isn't he? I suppose you do talk about
our private family matters with him. Do you?"

"Ty is my closest friend. And yes, we do talk. He's known about
Aunt Marjorie for a long, long time."

Jackie cringed at the thought.

"And remember, Mom," Rob continued. "We are living in Aunt
Marjorie's house. We can't very well hide that fact."

"So I suppose you'll tell the world about the weird recluse who
haunts your walls. Good conversation for a cocktail party, right?"

"Mom, will you stop it?" Rob struggled to control himself.
"She's dead. It's time to shake her off your back." He studied his
mother's expression of discomfort. "The truth is, the problem is
really inside of you. It's been festering inside of you for a long time.
Like I said before, none of it was your fault. You couldn't have
changed her. Believe me."

Emily lowered her eyes.

"Maybe you should let it all hang out and have a good cry," Rob
said. "Go ahead and bawl. Not because your sister died. But just
because of what was."

Emily glanced up at Rob. "You've seen my tears."

"Of anger and self-pity."

"Rob!" Jackie scolded. "You're out of line."

"It's okay, Jackie," Emily said. "He might be right." She shifted
uncomfortably, smiled weakly at Jackie and apologized: "I'm sorry,
dear. This really isn't your problem."

Jackie put her arm around Rob, held him tightly, looked kindly
on Emily and said, "Yes it is. I'm family now."

"Mom, I'm sorry," Rob said. "I didn't mean to be unkind."

"For a long time I never talked about these things." Emily's
eyes moistened. "Maybe I should have gone over there. To that
house, I mean. All those years, and I never did. Maybe I should
have. You know?"

"No, Mom. Believe me, it wouldn't have helped. For chrisake,
don't ever feel guilty about that."

Emily tried to shake off the feelings. "Here. Have a brownie."

Jackie lifted a cup of coffee. After a sip, she said, "Rob, please. Tell your mother."

Emily looked from Jackie to Rob with puzzlement in her eyes.

"Mom, please listen to me. You couldn't have changed things no matter how many times you went and knocked on her door. Aunt Marjorie lived in a fantasy world. She wouldn't have let you into it. No way. She only let one person in, and even that was to fulfill a fantasy."

"She would play-act and dance before her mirror," Jackie added. "She'd wear all sorts of beautiful clothes and jewelry."

"We found piles of rotting costumes in the basement." Rob explained. "Auntie would dress up like a ballerina and dance in front of her dolls. She'd perform at the piano, playing and singing, wearing long gowns, glowing in candlelight. She'd act out all sorts of parts. Aunt Marjorie was a star with a make-believe audience. She'd wear blue chiffon ballroom gowns, sometimes pink ones, and dance with imaginary movie stars. We found boxes of letters to stars she probably never saw on the screen—letters that were never mailed."

"She pampered herself, took constant care of her body," Jackie interjected. "She stayed young and beautiful well into her late fifties. Maybe longer."

"But then she deteriorated fast," Rob said. "Like a beautiful flower, she suddenly shriveled up. Partly because she wouldn't seek a doctor. She had no medical help, and when disease took over, it ravished her. But even at the end she tried to dress herself as Miss Liberty or something. I'm not sure what."

Emily shook her head slowly. Her eyes revealed sadness and wonder. Almost whispering, as if thinking aloud, she said, "Marjorie liked to dress up and dance, even as a little girl."

"Her dolls were real to her," Jackie explained. "She'd dress them up for daytime and undress them at night. She'd even nurse them. And when she figured they were dead, she'd bury them in her garden. Or sometimes wrap them up like mummies."

"How do you know all this?" Emily asked.

"She left evidence all over the house," Rob explained.

"And elsewhere," Jackie added. "We had to hunt elsewhere.

Rob put on his Sherlock Holmes hat and really did a job. And I didn't do so badly either, did I Rob?" She hugged him.

"How are you feeling, Mom?"

"Why? What do you mean?"

"Well, maybe you should grab a shot of whiskey and hold onto your chair." Rob frowned slightly as he rubbed his chin.

Emily looked warily at Jackie, then back at Rob. "Go ahead. Get on with it."

Rob said nothing until Jackie nudged him. "Well, you're not going to believe this," he began. "Aunt Marjorie had a baby."

Emily simply stared at her son.

"Did you hear me, Mom? I said Aunt Marjorie had a baby."

"Actually, two babies," Jackie added.

"Yes, she had two babies," Rob said. "Twins."

Emily frowned. Her expression denoted confusion. "You're talking about her dolls?"

"No, Mom, not her dolls. She gave birth. Understand? She gave birth to twins. We think they were both boys. We know one of them was. Or is, I should say."

"The one baby died at birth or right after," Jackie explained. "The other child still lives. He's a good-looking boy. We've seen him."

"This is some sort of a joke, isn't it?" Emily asked.

"No." Rob was emphatic. "No, Mom, we're serious."

"It's the truth," Jackie added.

Emily tightened her frown as she tried to read the expressions on the faces of Rob and Jackie. She shook her head in disbelief. Her incredulous stare was fixed on Jackie, then on Rob, then on Jackie again, then on Rob. "But that's impossible." Her whispery words were hesitant. "She was never with anyone. She was a recluse."

"But many men came to her house," Rob explained. "They delivered her food, her fancy clothes, her jewelry, her movie magazines. They cut her grass, checked her gas and electric meters, delivered her mail."

"She paid the mailman to take her baby boy away," Jackie said. "He left the baby on the steps of Willowood Hospital."

"My God," Emily muttered.

"You see, Mom, I was digging in her garden, and I found this skull—a baby's skull. And that started us wondering."

"A skull?"

"The dead baby. She buried it."

"You found a skull?" Emily stood and turned her back toward her son and Jackie. For seconds she continued to stand nearly motionless. Without turning, she finally asked, "Do you know the father? Was he one of the delivery men?" She spun about and studied the faces of Rob and his fiancée as she awaited a reply.

Jackie nudged Rob again.

"The paper boy," he said, the words nearly catching in his throat. He seemed almost embarrassed.

Emily did nothing but stare at her son.

"Ty," he said, fighting off his reluctance to utter his buddy's name.

"Ty?"

"Yes, Ty."

"Your Ty?"

"Yes."

"You mean Ty, who we just left at the cemetery?"

"Yes. Ty. My Ty."

Emily forced a laugh, which she cut off abruptly. "Your joke is stupid, sickening, morbid. Why are you doing this? And, good Lord, on the day of my sister's funeral?"

Rob figured it was only the second or third time he had heard his mother call Marjorie her sister. His tone was sharply convincing when he said, "Mom, do I look like I'm kidding? Look at me! Aunt Marjorie seduced her paper boy. Ty was her paper boy."

"You're serious?"

"That's right. Dead serious."

"My God." Emily moved nervously around the room, sometimes glancing at the ceiling, sometimes at the floor. "It's so hard to believe." Bringing her restive movements under control, she stood in the center of the room and glowered at Rob. "How long have you known all this?"

"We've known some of it for weeks," Rob explained. "But we're just putting the last pieces together now."

"No wonder you've been acting so strange, disappearing so

often, whispering behind my back. I thought it had something to do with your wedding. Why have you been so mysterious about it all? Why didn't you tell me before this?"

"Ty doesn't even know about his son," explained Jackie.

"I'm going to tell him tonight," Rob added.

"Why did you pick now to tell me?"

Rob breathed deeply, then said, "Well, the puzzle's pretty much complete now. We've located the boy. He's with foster parents. We can't wait any longer to tell Ty. So, if the boy becomes part of Ty's life, we want to make him part of our lives. And you're part of our lives, too. We couldn't very well lie about him." Rob looked down as he searched for words. When he lifted his eyes he said, "Anyway, there's more to the whole matter of truth. There's a lot of confusion and pain inside of you. I had no way of knowing whether all this revelation would bring more hurt, or help sort out everything and free you somehow. I had to take the chance, but not until the pieces were all in place. Truth was the only way to go. Besides, I wasn't going to live with all those secrets inside of me. Then, of course, there's Uncle Jack. Even though you always blamed Marjorie, there was always doubt, wasn't there? I thought maybe this would tell you something about your brother."

Emily smiled sadly. She walked to her son and kissed him on the cheek. After returning to the wing chair she said, "I'm always vacillating so. It's just so frustrating. This business of always asking Why? Why? Why? Why did Papa do this? Or why didn't Mama do that? Or why did I have a nut for a sister? Why do we always have these battles inside of ourselves about things in the past that we can't fix? If this. If that. Why do we fret over things that are long gone, things we can't do anything about?"

Rob stood and walked to his mother. She looked up at him and he smiled warmly. "Human nature, I guess," he said. He stepped behind the chair and put his hands on her shoulders. "As for Aunt Marjorie, I can't help but ponder the whys. Who knows what happens to a person who imprisons herself? Maybe she stayed a child in some ways, while growing up in others. How real to her were her fantasies? Maybe they could not erase her loneliness. Maybe she was secure only with someone very young. Maybe she was still playing house, or playing doctor, or whatever."

Emily shook her head indicating that she didn't want to be troubled by such thoughts.

Rob leaned down and kissed her on the cheek. "Will you be all right tonight?

"Of course." She lifted a cup of coffee and drank a little. "You go do what you have to do."

"Are you sure? I can change my plans."

"No you can't. Tell Ty what he has to know. I'd rather be alone anyway. Go on."

He took her hand and squeezed it. "Well, I want to get out of these funeral clothes before I head for Marty's."

"Then you'd better get going. Really, I'm okay."

Rob glanced at his fiancée and changed the subject: "Jackie's going shopping with her mom in the morning."

"Mother wants just the right dress for the wedding," Jackie offered. "It must be Wedgwood blue, no less." She stood, smiled at Emily and said, "Thanks for dinner. It was perfect."

"Why don't I stop over in the morning?" Rob suggested as he broke away from his mother.

"Come for breakfast," Emily ordered. "I'll fix French toast the way you like it. With powdered sugar. But don't come before I put on my face."

* * *

Jackie whispered into Rob's ear as he drove his car through the darkness on a residential, tree-lined street: "You're too kind."

"What do you mean?"

"About your dead, agoraphobic auntie. I mean, come on, now. Playing house? Playing doctor? I'd call her a vamp who craved the flesh of virgin boys. Or better yet—a closet whore who laid scores of imaginary boys before she took on Ty."

"I don't think Ty sees her that way."

Chapter Forty-Four

Office talk dominated the start of conversation between Rob and Ty at Marty's Tavern. Rob wanted to get a feel for Ty's mood before plunging into the tale of the skull and John Willow Doe. He figured Ty's state of mind was tied to Amy, and he was certain that the dialogue would move in Amy's direction sooner or later—probably sooner, simply because she was Ty's passion.

Weeknight patrons were sparse at Marty's. But, as usual, a few men played darts while others hung their heads over the bar. Rob and Ty sat in their familiar booth among memories of previous conversations. They both guzzled beer.

"Because of the funeral, I was in the office for only a few hours this morning," Rob said. "But I had a chance to see the paste-ups for the new puppy-chow brochure. Your drawings are great. You used Whiskers as a model for the cover, didn't you?"

"You noticed."

"How could I miss it? You did a super job. It has tremendous appeal."

"I'm proud of the eyes." Ty gulped some beer. "They really get to you, don't they?"

"They come right at you and tug hard." Rob drank beer to keep up with his friend. "Speaking of Whiskers, that old lady from the Methodist Home called. She was upset because she hasn't heard from you. She wonders what happened to Whiskers."

"Damn. My mind's been on everything else."

"In a span of two hours this morning we got calls from three of your causes. I think your do-good friends are about to converge on

Pure-Pup. A guy from the Little League called. And so did some woman from the Preservation of... of something or other."

"The Preservation of Our Natural Environment."

"Probably. That sounds right."

"I'm letting everyone down." Ty shook his head and bit his lower lip. "Maybe I'll take Whiskers to the old ladies home tomorrow night. In fact, maybe I'll take Amy with me."

Rob examined Ty's expression. "Does that mean things are better?"

"Much better. Amy knows it wasn't my fault. In fact, her old man told her so. But he still can't accept me. That's something I'll have to work on." Ty spun his eyes and lifted his brows. "Wow. You have no idea! It's like the weight of the world's been lifted from my shoulders. No. From my brain." He finished his beer, then wiped his lips. "Oh God, Rob, I really do love her. You can't imagine." Glancing toward the bar, he signaled the barmaid for two more taps. "I've thought a lot about the things you've said. And I figure it really doesn't matter why I feel the way I do. It's simply great that I feel that way. So what if I was drawn to her because I thought she needed me, or because I wanted to help her, or whatever. If that's what brought us together—fine. I don't think the cause is nearly as important as the result."

"I guess you needed an Amy after an overpowering force like my seductive auntie." Rob was deliberately trying to lead the conversation in Marjorie's direction. His eyes showed that he was searching for words. "Sometimes... Well, sometimes I feel to blame for what happened to you. Or that my family was to blame. Yet logically I know that's foolish. I guess what I really feel is a touch of guilt because I'm a member of that family."

"You still don't understand, do you? I've never blamed anyone, not even Miss Worth."

"Is that what you called her? Miss Worth?"

"I never called her anything. I guess I really didn't want her to have a name."

"What do you mean when you say I don't understand?"

"That woman gave me unbelievable excitement, and I kept going back to her. I mean, I was sixteen years old. I knew what I was doing. Sixteen isn't that far from eighteen, and I know guys who have married at that age. Let's face it, Rob, I wanted what I was getting. I was a small, underdeveloped boy, and I had something going for me that nobody else had."

"But I know how seductive she was. I was there once. I felt it."

"And that was part of the excitement. Rob, I wasn't a twelve-year-old being forced into something."

"And the years of nightmares?"

"Frankly, I didn't want the dreams to end. Until they tangled with Amy."

"Ty, listen to me. When you first walked up those stairs, you walked into a spider's web. And you couldn't get out."

"I didn't want to get out. I was in absolute misery when she closed me out. I was a lustful seventeen-year-old by then, and she just about killed me."

This was the time, and Rob knew it. He poured down an entire glass of beer as soon as the roly-poly barmaid placed it on the table. His face reddened. He wiped away the foam. "Ty, I've got something to tell you. Please bear with me. It's important."

Ty tried to read the message in Rob's eyes.

"She didn't close you out for the reason you think," Rob said. "I'm sure she still wanted to dance and play and lay with her paper boy. But you see—she became pregnant."

Ty showed no comprehension. He stared blankly at Rob as if totally confused.

"Did you hear me?" Rob asked. "Do you understand?"

"What the hell are you talking about?"

"I'm trying to tell you that you got her pregnant."

Ty's expression was one big question mark. He frowned slightly. "Is this some sort of a weird joke?"

"No, Ty. I'm dead serious. Aunt Marjorie not only got pregnant; she gave birth."

"This is insane."

"I found a skull in her garden."

"A skull? You found a skull?"

"But only one baby died."

"You're not making sense. I don't know what you're talking about."

"It seems that Aunt Marjorie gave birth to twins. One died at birth. The other one is still living. He's a fine-looking boy, heading for his fourteenth birthday. And you're his father. There's no question about that. He's the spit'n image of you."

Ty knocked over his glass, spilling beer that ran from the table onto his lap. "Jesus Christ!" He pulled his handkerchief from his pocket and began soaking up the beer from the table, ignoring his wet pants. He didn't want to signal for help in fear of disrupting the conversation. "Go on! Go on! How the hell do you know all this?"

"Are you okay? Here, take my handkerchief."

"I got it all! I'm just fine, man, just fine! Will you get on with it!"

"The garden bones sent me on a hunt. Jackie trailed along. I might say we did one hell of a job putting the pieces together. The kid's been shifted from foster folks to foster folks."

"You've seen him? This boy—you've seen him?"

"We've seen him. Like I said, he's you all over again."

"This is crazy! Are you telling me that I fathered a kid when I was a teenager?"

"Hey, when you're sixteen or seventeen those wiggly sperm are more lively and potent than ever. I don't know if Auntie was in menopause, but it obviously didn't matter."

"I don't believe this." Ty's lips quivered and his fingers nervously tapped the table. "This is unreal."

"Maybe Marjorie figured it couldn't happen at her age. Then again, maybe she wanted a real live doll-baby. But maybe later she couldn't handle it all and had the baby carried away."

"Is that what happened?"

"She paid the postman to carry him off."

"You know that?"

"I talked to the mailman who did it."

"My God." Ty slouched and stared at the ceiling, then sat up and tried to catch his breath. "Give me your handkerchief. The beer's soaking through my underwear." He stuffed Rob's handkerchief into his pants, then looked directly into his friend's eyes. "Do you know what you're telling me? You're telling me that I'm the father of a teenage kid."

"That's right." Rob smiled ever so slightly. "And we have a box of letters for you that make sense now that we figured it all out. The letters pretty much verify what we discovered." Rob reached across the table and squeezed his buddy's wrist. "Ty, listen to me. The boy looks mighty special. I don't think he'd be hard to love. We suspect he feels unloved, maybe unwanted. He does what he's told, but we figure he's just going through the motions. Then again, maybe Jackie and I are reading more into this thing than we should."

"I want to see him."

"I've already planned it. He's over in Maywood. I figured we'd ride over on Saturday."

"What kind of people have him?"

"Let me get us a couple more brews." Rob slipped from the booth and headed for the bar.

Ty put his face in his hands, then pushed his fingers through his hair. "I'll be a fuckin' monkey's uncle," he muttered. He fidgeted until the pressure of urine drove him to the men's rest room.

Rob returned to the booth with two glasses of frothy beer, positioned them on the table, sat back and waited for Ty while thinking of ways to explain Chester and Lana Oswald. As minutes passed, he shifted his buttocks a few times and drank half of his beer. Finally, he pushed himself from the booth and hurried to the men's room.

"Ty?" he quietly called while opening the door. "Are you okay?" He stepped inside the small, tarnished room, which contained one urinal and one stall, and found Ty standing in an awkward position trying to dry his pants under the humming blow-dryer.

"I don't know why I'm doing this," Ty said. "What's a little wet, sticky beer anyway." He straightened up against the wall and looked at his friend. "Do you think my reaction to all this is strange?"

"Frankly, Ty, I don't know what your reaction is," Rob answered, trying to speak above the hum of the machine.

Ty waited for the blower to stop, then said, "Come to think of it, neither do I. My thoughts keep jumping all over the place. First I think, 'My God, I'm a father. Maybe I can do something for this kid who looks like me.' Then I think, 'Holy shit, what will I say to Amy. How do I explain a son almost half as old as I am?' This is crazy, Rob."

"It'll sort itself out. And you'll end up with a gift from heaven. If this kid is hurting, you're the one who can heal his wounds. No one can do that better than you. You do it all the time with other kids."

"This boy may be more of a stranger than any. How wounded is he?"

"I don't know."

"These people who have him—who are they? What are they like?"

Rob leaned against a small, stained sink. "They have money, a nice house. I think Oswald wanted John, but lost interest. He's got a hot dish on the side. As for his wife, she doesn't want the boy. I see her as a hard, high-living chick who isn't interested in kids. I think any kid would get in her way. I'm not even sure she wants her husband. His money? That's a different thing."

"You called the boy 'John'?"

"He was labeled John Doe from the very beginning, although the press tagged him 'Baby Willow'. We call him John Willow or John Willow Doe for Willowood Hospital. That's where the postman dropped him off."

"God, there's so much I want to know. I guess my questions are hopping all over the place. But I can't seem to fill in the gaps." Ty put his hands behind his back and pushed against the wall. "How do you know I'll be able to see him? How do you know they'll let me have him if I want him?"

"We don't, for sure. But we've got everything we need to prove you're the father. And the foster-care agency in Philadelphia knows all about you. They want a blood test, but that's just perfunctory. If necessary, you could always have one of those DNA tests. But it's not going to come to that. This woman at the agency—she's got your picture next to John's in her files on the case. You look like clones—absolute clones."

"I can't believe all this has been going on behind my back. How long have you known? Why did you wait until now to tell me?"

"I had to be sure. No way was I going to tell you until the last pieces fell into place."

"Wow. And I said the Lady-of-Juniper-Lane died a long time ago, never realizing she left me a living legacy."

"I was surprised when you showed up at the cemetery. I thought you had painted her out of your mind."

"I was surprised, too. I don't know what made me drive into the cemetery. And even then I didn't intend to walk to the grave site."

Rob gave Ty a buddy-buddy punch on the arm and suggested, "Let's get out of here before someone thinks were playing with each other." He pushed open the door, glanced around the barroom, felt no staring eyes, and headed for the booth. Taking his seat, he waited for Ty to sit and face him, then explained, "We just gave the garden bones to the police so that the coroner could do his forensic stuff. Later, you might want to arrange a burial or cremation. That's up to you."

"This is unreal. It's like something out of the movies."

"The movies? Well, I suppose that fits. Knowing Aunt Marjorie."

Chapter Forty-Five

Jackie lunched with her mother, the 48-year-old, well-groomed woman whose poise and acumen had helped lift her husband to his company's upper echelon. They ate at a window table in the Green Crystal House, a restaurant replete with mirrors and plants. Because a glass wall faced another glass wall, the ferns, rubber plants and fiddleleaf figs reflected a thousand times over. Crystal chandeliers splattered the room with light, bringing movement to the plants and endless sparkles to the never-ending mirror reflections.

The glass walls also proved to Anne Harwood that she was well fitted, front and rear, in her camel-colored autumn suit—an Italian import. Green Crystal was Anne's favorite lunch-time stop on shopping days. She always ordered the same thing—crab and avocado salad—much to Jackie's dismay.

"Boring, boring, boring," said Jackie, who wore a smartly styled burnt ocher dress. She was about to dip into a crock of onion soup heavy with melted cheese. "We must do something about your unchanging patterns of life. You're in too many ruts, Mother. This place after morning shopping. The Adobe Grotto in late afternoon. Thursday night bridge. Friday night—what is it? Oh, yes, the symphony. What you need is lunch at a taco stand, a night at Great Adventure amusement park, a fat hoagie to munch on after a wild ride on a roller coaster."

"Now you're being silly."

"Not really. Rob's taught me how to live."

"I must say, he has changed you. I recognize that."

"Do you like the change?"

"To a degree. You're more assertive, more sure of yourself. That'll help you in the long run. It will help him, too."

"Oh, I know I'll be good for Rob, Mother. But not in the way you think. Rob's his own man. And I like it that way." She spooned some of her soup, fighting the stringy cheese. "What Rob and I did together this summer and fall—well, you have no idea how happy it made me. It took away all doubts. We proved that we can work and play together. He's incredible. And that's not blind love talking. Sure, he's drawn me out. But, more than that, I've learned to bounce with the bumps. And he's sharpened my wit. We have great give-and-take. To some extent, I owe thanks to that house, Rob's crazy old aunt and Ty Scott. When you solve problems together, you learn a hell of a lot about each other."

Anne toyed with her salad, then carefully lifted a small portion on her fork and slipped it into her mouth. A moment later she said, "I think you feel a sense of fulfillment. There's nothing like the taste of achievement."

"It's more than that, Mother."

"You feel joy having found the boy."

"That was fantastic. I can't believe we did it. I just hope everything turns out right for Ty and the boy. But I'm talking about a euphoric feeling that makes me twist in my sheets when I wake up each morning."

Anne placed her fork on her plate, fixed her eyes on her daughter, and said, "It won't always be there, Jackie."

"Spoilsport."

"Don't get me wrong. I'm happy that you feel that way. It's just that the dips will come. That's when it's important to remember the joy." Anne forked another taste of salad into her mouth.

"I didn't know you were a philosopher, Mother. Or should I say social worker?"

"There's a lot you don't know about me, and that's my fault. I suppose, now that you're about to marry, I suddenly want to tie a few knots between us. Isn't that always the way?"

Jackie struggled with her cheese-laden soup, but said nothing.

"Maybe I am set in some of my ways," Anne said. "But I do have ideas, believe it or not. And they're not all so bad. What I am today didn't just happen. Your father and I worked hard for what we have."

"That I've heard before."

"I'm not talking about material things only."

"You don't really have to worry about us. Believe me."

"I'm glad Rob gives you this... this... exhilaration, this love for life, or whatever."

"He'll make it, you know. He's the kind of guy who'll make it no matter what."

"Your father recognizes that, even though he won't admit it."

"And you?"

"I've always liked him, you know that. But when I heard him talk about Ty I was really moved. I saw something more."

"He's not just crazy and fun-loving like some people think."

"But his family doesn't have any money."

"Damn you, Mother!"

"I'm just teasing."

"No you're not! Anyway, we have our house, even though it annoys Father—the self-made man. If Father didn't have any money, then why fret over Rob?"

"I could say, 'Times are different', but that would only annoy you."

"You're right." Jackie looked for the waitress. "I've had enough of this soup. I need more coffee." She dabbed her lips with the corner of her napkin, unconsciously imitating her mother. "More and more Ty's introspective nature has rubbed off on Rob, adding to his love of life, without taking away his playfulness. Don't expect anyone to sing 'Because' at our wedding. Fanny Jones, the fat lady from the Spiritual Society, is going to sing 'The Bluebird of Happiness'."

Anne simply stared at her daughter. Though a secure woman, she didn't dare comment in light of the conversation and for fear she would look staid and set in her ways. "Well, to tell you the truth, I remember an old Jan Peerce record of the 'Bluebird of Happiness'. It's rather a pretty song. I didn't know you were familiar with it."

"I wasn't. And I'm still not very." Jackie waited as a pug-nosed blonde poured coffee, then said, "It has something to do with Rob and his father and happiness and sadness and birds and life and I don't know what all. Rob's father is coming to the wedding, you know."

"You said he might. I've never met the man. What can I expect?"

"Be gracious, Mother, no matter what. Okay?"

"Will he sit in the front with Rob's mother?"

"Well, he should. He's supposed to. But I don't know. Let's be surprised, okay?"

"I have funny feelings about this wedding."

"Don't worry, Mother. It won't be a circus. But it will celebrate life."

"What color is Emily Putnam wearing?"

"I don't think she's thought about it yet."

"Now tell me the truth. Did you like the way I looked in the slate blue at the Boutique, or the paler blue at Victor's?"

"You looked terrific in both."

"I think I like the darker one better. I just wish it weren't so busy around the collar. I suppose it could be altered." She drank coffee, then said, "I want Rob to call me Anne. I really don't want to be called Mother Harwood. And if he calls me nothing, then he'll end up calling me Grandma after your first child. I don't really want that." Turning her head quickly, she looked up at the passing waitress and said, "Please bring me a slice of chocolate fudge cake."

"Mother!"

"Maybe it's not a roller coaster, but it's living life! I have my secret desires. As I said, you don't know everything about me."

Chapter Forty-Six

An azure sky offered a bright autumn sun, dressing up Maywood in its October best. The approach of noon had shortened the shadows as the sun neared its apex. Varied rooftops of the many-styled houses of Maywood absorbed and reflected the sunlight, because the limbs of the tall Maples were nearly bare.

Rob needed the Maywood Middle School to orient himself. "From here I can find the house," he told Ty as he drove past the school. "Jackie and I first saw the boy back there, on the soccer field behind the school." He slowed the car as they approached an intersection. "She and I went out of our way, over the tracks to the river. I think if I turn here we'll end up in the right neighborhood."

Neither Rob nor Ty was dressed in his usual Saturday daytime clothes. Both wore navy suits and striped neckties—crimson and blue in Rob's case, mustard and blue in Ty's.

The broad leaves of the maples had coated the neighborhood sidewalks and lawns with brilliant yellow. Some of the leaves had been raked and heaped into huge piles in the gutters and on the grass.

Ty glanced left and right at the Tudor and Georgian houses. "Nice neighborhood," he said just before his eyes were taken and held by a trio of young boys playing in a pile of leaves on the lawn of a Dutch Colonial. The youngsters tossed leaves into the air, kicked them, laughed, and pushed each other into the heap. "It's good to see kids having fun," said Ty, who had talked little on the Interstate, chattering softly now and then. His only true discourse had been a lively depiction of his visit to the Methodist Home, including a glowing mention of Amy's elation when Hortense Williams took Whiskers into her arms. "I wonder if John Willow has fun in the leaves like that. God, I'm nervous."

"We're almost there," Rob said.

"Why am I so goddamn nervous?"

Why shouldn't you be? Hell, that's normal."

"Do you think it's strange that I have some kind of feeling for this kid, even though I've never even seen him?"

"Hey, you've been listening to me, and you've been stirring up all kinds of feelings over the past couple days. After all, you're aware that he's your own flesh and blood. Anyway, it's your nature to feel that way."

"But I don't even know him. And the most frightening thing is that he doesn't know me. Here I am thinking about holding him in my arms, playing catch with him, teaching him about toadstools and tree frogs and the moons of Jupiter. And, hell, he might not want to have anything to do with me. He's not mine, just because I got my jollies with your aunt thirteen years ago."

"You've gambled before, Ty. Aren't you the one who lectures about missed opportunities? About taking risks? Remember the first time you stepped up on Amy's front porch and pounded on her door?"

"But I decided to make that turn-in-the-road. Let's face it, I'm used to making my own turns. This is different."

"No it isn't. You could turn away. But you wouldn't do that, would you?"

"Well, I'm here. Right?"

"I didn't expect otherwise."

"I'm just so downright scared, that's all. The kid'll be wary. He'll be defensive. He won't accept me. I've seen it all before. Billy Wanjek wouldn't let anyone into his life. Only his dog. And when Chippy was killed by a car, Billy hanged himself from Joe Henry's wild cherry tree."

"I'm glad you're letting it all hang out," Rob said with a touch of sarcasm. Then, in a dead serious tone, he continued, "But I think your playing a defensive game with yourself. You were always Mr. Sunshine—that is, before the ups and downs of Amy. Now, the optimist is putting up a protective shield. Right?"

"Maybe. But that's okay. We don't climb every thorny locust tree in the same way." Ty slapped the shoulder of his buddy. "Anyhow, the optimist takes his dips. It's just that he always bounces back."

Rob recited with poetic beat: "For every cloudy morning there's a midnight moon above."

"From a poem?"

"No—from a song of my father's day." Rob turned the car at the next intersection. "This is the street. Pine Lane. The house is on your side. Right at the end of the block."

"God, why am I so nervous?"

"Ty, you have at least one big thing going for you. That boy can't look into your face without knowing you're his daddy."

Rob parked his car at curbside, directly in front of the Oswald house. Ty was quick to take in the view—the formal mix of yellow-painted brick and white trim, the lamppost, walkway and meticulously trimmed shrubbery.

"Do you think John Willow raked up all the leaves?" Ty asked rhetorically.

"How do you want to do this, now?" Rob asked. "You want to go in there alone? Do you want me with you? Or what?"

"I thought we'd agreed that you'd go with me?"

"Just making sure."

Ty waited until Rob stepped into the street before opening the door. When he joined Rob on the sidewalk he said, "You're description was perfect. I had this place sketched in my mind."

"It looks bigger in the sunlight." Rob stepped ahead of Ty. "Come on. Let's get this thing going."

In their well-fitted dark suits, Ty and Rob looked like a pair of Mormon proselytizers as they walked the pathway to the front door. Ty was about to lift the heavy knocker when the door opened. The man who greeted them was a far cry from Rob's mental image of Chester Oswald—an image of a tall, dark, businessman with well-groomed hair graying at the temples, a blue-chip stockholder who occasionally showed off his wife at cocktail parties attended by board-room types. Chester was a wide-shouldered mesomorph who could have once been a football player. His balding head held straggly yellow hair. He wore a loud, ugly-American type, short-sleeved shirt—a shirt with bold blocks of red, yellow and blue.

"I've been lookin' for yis," Chester said in a voice too high for his big body. His smile was almost a grin. "Come on in. The broad from the agency said y'd be here before noon. So I kept lookin' out the window. Nice day, ain't it."

Chester led his visitors through the central hall. Rob kept his eyes forward, but Ty glanced about, taking in the curved balustrade, the Ming vase, and all else. As they entered the spacious living room, Rob and Ty were bewildered by the incongruous scene. The sparsely furnished expanse was incompatible with the likes of Chester Oswald, who seemed totally out of place with the Georgian mantel, the rococo plaster work and rosettes, let alone the Chippendale chairs and settees, upholstered in brocaded satin. The chairs were widely separated, carefully placed here and there around the edges of the room as if each was on display in a museum. Chester looked awkward, uncomfortable and downright foolish when he sat on a chair near the fireplace. Spreading his knees wide, he then tried but failed to twist his right foot around a leg of the chair. He ended up extending his feet into the room.

"Sit down," he said. "Take the load off."

Rob took a chair to his far left, Ty to his far right. And the three men ended up widespread across an Oriental rug.

"The boy is home, isn't he?" Ty asked. "I did come to see the boy."

"Oh yeah, he's here, all right. I told him to stay upstairs till I was ready for 'im. Thought we might want t' talk things out first." Chester kept his eyes on Ty. "Y' sure look like 'im. I noticed that right through the window, soon as I saw y'. Said t' myself, 'Sure can tell which one of these guys claims to be Johnny's daddy.' What did y' say your name was?"

"Oh, I'm sorry. Ty Scott. And this is my friend, Rob Putnam. But I think you've met."

"No. 'Fraid I haven't met Mr. Putnam."

"That's right," Rob said. "It was Mrs. Oswald that I met on my last visit. Will she be joining us?"

"Nope. 'Fraid not."

Rob and Ty glanced at each other, then Rob said, "I hope you understand, Mr. Oswald, that Mr. Scott is simply here to see the boy. We're not taking him with us. Not today."

Chester looked Ty up and down. "I was kinda hopin' y'd be a fraud."

"Didn't the woman from the agency explain?" Ty asked as he shifted in his seat.

"Sure did. Said there was little doubt about you bein' Johnny's daddy." Chester wrapped his arms around the back of the chair. "But some sorta judge has t' make the final decision, ain't that right?"

"That's simply pro forma," Rob interjected while leaning forward and staring across the room at Chester.

"Pro what?"

"It's just routine," Rob explained while squirming undiscernibly. There was something uncomfortable about conversing across such a wide space. "Just a matter of course. No judge is going to deny custody to the real father in a case like this. After all, the boy's never been adopted. He's been shifted around from foster home to foster home."

Chester looked down between this legs. "S'pose you're right." He pulled in his feet, grabbed his knees with his hands and spread them wide, then focused on Rob. "Foster daddies don't have no rights, y' know. I went after this kid 'cause I thought I could do somethin' for 'im. I've made a lot of money—a real lot of money." He turned toward Ty. "I mean a fuckin' ton of money. Made it on root mulch—the kind of mulch that won't wash out of your garden patch. There's a lot of money in mulch today." After glancing around the room, he focused on Rob. "Y' see the stuff in this room? Cost a fuckin' bundle. It's all the real stuff. This chair I'm sittin' on—it's the real stuff. This guy from the Fairmount Gallery tells Lana that these chairs go with this house. I hate 'em. Hate them sofas, too. Y' can't lie down on 'em. I told Lana I'm gettin' myself a big recliner like they advertise on TV." Chester widened his cheeks with a broad grin that quickly slipped away. "I figured, with my money, that boy would stay forever. No way would they move 'im again. Not with my money. Not with what I could give 'im."

"Mr. Oswald, I'm glad that you've tried to do right by the boy," Ty said. "But we didn't really come here to discuss all this. I've never seen my son. Two days ago I didn't even know I had a son. Please, Mr. Oswald. I just want to see him."

Rob spoke before Chester had a chance to respond: "Does the boy know? Have you told him?"

Chester ignored Rob and kept his eyes on Ty. "How come all of a sudden you just came out of nowhere, Scotty? Where y' been all along?"

Ty wanted to tell Chester that such details were none of his business. But for fear of alienating the foster father of his son at a critical time, he offered, "It all started when I was a teenager. The birth was kept secret by the mother. I didn't learn about it until after she died."

Rob was less generous: "Mr. Oswald, it's up to the agency people to supply you with any pertinent facts, if they so wish. Mr. Scott is simply here to see his son."

"The agency won't tell me nothin'. Like I says, foster folks got no rights." Chester ran his hand through his hair. "I've put a lot of money into that kid. And I mean a lot of money."

Rob was seething inside. He stood and stepped toward Chester. Standing in the middle of the room, he forcefully said, "Please go get John Willow and bring him down. We want to see him."

Chester simply slouched in his chair, looked up at Rob and asked, "What's in it for you? I don't get it. What part do you play in all this? Y' gettin' somethin' out of it?"

"I'm not only Mr. Scott's friend; I'm the boy's cousin. John's mother was my aunt, my mother's sister. I'm the one who discovered the truth after all these years. But all of this really doesn't concern you."

As Ty and Rob felt their adrenaline pumping, the front door clicked, swished and banged. All eyes turned toward the hallway as Lana marched into the living room. Wearing a yellow, V-neck, jersey top, she posed just inside the room with her hands on her hips—well-pronounced hips covered by shiny, black, form-fitting pants. Heavy makeup added to her coarse look. Yet there was no question that she would turn a man's head.

"So what have you been telling our guests, Chester?" Lana asked. "All about the hundred dollar sneakers you keep buying the boy?" She offered a perfunctory smile to Rob, then to Ty. "Well I'll be a cross-eyed nanny goat!" she exclaimed after a double take in Ty's direction. "You look more like the kid's brother than his old man."

"You must be Mrs. Oswald." Ty stood and nodded.

"Call me Lana."

Chester didn't hide his displeasure at seeing his wife. His eyes kept sending her nasty messages that she ignored. "I thought you were going to stay at Tina's," he said while pushing himself from his chair.

"I changed my mind." Lana glanced from man to man, each now standing and staring at her. "Why, Chester, you didn't even offer drinks to our guests."

"We really don't want anything," Ty said. "I simply want to meet John."

"Oh my!" Lana exclaimed, looking at her husband. "You haven't even introduced them to Johnny?"

"We were talking business," Chester said in an unpleasant tone. "This has nothing to do with you."

"We don't have any business to talk about," Rob said matter-of-factly.

Lana fired back at Chester: "It certainly has everything in the world to do with me. Where's the boy?"

"He's in his room," Chester said.

"Well, I suggest we get him." Lana spun around, marched into the spacious entrance hall, lifted her chin toward the balustrade and shouted, "Johnny! Come down here!" Stepping back toward the living room, she didn't hide her sarcasm as she said, "Chester's a very busy man, aren't you sweetheart? He doesn't have too much time for Johnny anymore. Poor man. It's a shame. He has to sit up late and watch over his piles of mulch night after night." She turned again and yelled, "John! John, get down here, damn it! You got company."

Ty stepped toward Chester and quietly asked, "Did you explain me to the boy? Does he know? Does he understand?"

Ty's words brought Lana into the room. "You did tell the boy, didn't you, Chester dear?"

"I told him he might be getting another dad."

"You what?" Rob questioned. "He might think Ty's just another foster father."

"Not when he sees him," Lana said. She examined Ty from head to foot, then added, "Christ, you must have been twelve years old when you primed your pump." She winked at Ty.

Chester lumbered from the room and began to climb the stairs. When he reached the high balustrade he called, "Johnny," but continued toward the boy's room.

"I know what you're thinking," Lana said when her husband was out of earshot. "And you're right. But there comes a time when you just don't give a damn. That man has humiliated me. Believe me, I'd like to leave him tomorrow. But I'm not going without his money. I'll squeeze him where it hurts until I get everything I want."

Ty and Rob felt uncomfortable. Each smiled weakly.

Lana walked to the fireplace and ran her fingers across the mantel. With her back to Ty and Rob, she said, "I thought I was getting out of a mess when I married him. Instead, I got into one. My mama came from well-bred stock, but she took off with a free soul who couldn't hold a job stacking supermarket cans. She ended up raising me all by herself." Lana looked down at the Oriental rug. "I never had nice things." Lifting her chin, she forced a hard stare at her visitors. "Sure, I married Chester for his money." She burst into laughter, stopped abruptly, looked from Ty to Rob, and then said, "Sorry guys. You don't deserve this. You didn't expect to walk into a hornets nest, did you?" Putting her fist over her heart, she said, "Believe it or not, there's a softspot in here. I don't hate the kid. It's just that he got in my way. He cramped my style. And, for awhile, I blamed him for taking Chester away from me. But that was garbage. It wasn't the kid. To tell you the truth, he's kind of a mystery. I can't see myself getting through to him. Of course, I never really tried."

"He's not in his room," Chester shouted from the balustrade. "I can't find him anywhere up here."

"Jesus, what next," Lana muttered as she hurried off to check the downstairs rooms.

"Hold tight," Rob urged after reading uneasiness in Ty's expression. He sat and twiddled his thumbs while Ty paced the floor.

Chester entered the room scratching his head. "Can't figure it. I told 'im to stay in his room. One thing about that kid, he usually does what he's told. It don't make sense."

"Maybe we should look outside," Ty suggested.

"He was s'posed to stay in his room. Besides, no way he came down them steps. From where I was sittin', I sure as hell woulda seen 'im."

Lana sighed as she entered the room. "He's not in this house. Maybe he never went to his room." She glowered at Chester. "Did you see him go up?"

"I told him t' go."

"But did you actually see him go up?"

"No. But I told 'im to."

"He's probably with that Martin boy. I think that kid's his only friend."

"Freddie Martin's a no good weasel jus' like his old man. He's got a foul mouth, and he don't care what he smashes."

Lana saw question marks in the expressions of Ty and Rob, both on their feet and fidgeting near the fireplace. She explained: "Freddie comes from down near the river. Right near where Chester grew up. He's only got a daddy, and not a very good one at that. Chester doesn't like anybody down there across the tracks. Not any more. They remind him of where he came from. Thing is, he's still riverfront dirt. What is it they say? You can take the man out of the Maywood Riverfront, but you can't take the Riverfront out of the man. So maybe I did work in a canning factory when the Mulch King came courting. But at least my mama taught me the difference between 'don't' and 'didn't.' She'd slap me down for saying 'ain't'."

Chester ignored Lana, stepped toward the hallway, then turned and said, "It don't make sense. Johnny always obeys me. He's a good kid that way."

Lana scowled at her husband. "There comes a time, you know. There always comes a time. Once you're shit on too many times, you just don't give a damn."

Chapter Forty-Seven

Johnny and Freddie walked along the railroad spur track toward the old Kettleback stone quarry. Sometimes they walked the ties, often skipping some of them, particularly the well-worn ones that had broken loose from the rusty rails that snaked because of years of wear and missing spikes. At other times they walked along the edge of the gravel bed, kicking stones and cinders down the slopes and into the gullies. Johnny wore designer jeans and hundred-dollar high-top sneakers. His denim jacket hung unzipped, exposing his red-and-white striped, alligator jersey. As for Freddie, his soiled jeans were open at the knees and his dirty sneakers were split at the toes. The musty smell of his frayed sweater of black yarn was heavy with fuzzy pills.

"At least he buys y' things," said skinny, freckle-faced, redheaded Freddie in a voice yet to be fully lowered by puberty. "My old man would rather buy another bottle of booze." He kicked a beer bottle down the cinder slope toward a cluster of goldenrod yet to be zapped by the first frost. The moist gulches on each side of the track bed protected occasional clumps of autumn's late bloomers—goldenrod, toadflax and wild asters in shades of yellow and purple. The wild flowers and weeds shared the ravines with cans, bottles and other trash. High land beyond the slopes was thick with tall, beige-colored grasses with ripe seed heads and tassels. The expansive fields were broken here and there by outcroppings of rock and stubby clusters of sassafras and sumac, bared by the late October winds.

"You want these sneakers?" Johnny asked. "You can have them. I don't want them. When we get to the quarry, let's trade."

Freddie failed to respond with words. Instead he stamped on a prickly thistle struggling to grow in the gravel between the railroad ties.

The sun still shone brightly, but fingers of clouds reached in from a band of gray on the eastern horizon. A pair of crows swooped overhead, cawed several times and then perched atop a naked, crooked chokecherry tree that stood alone in the distance, silhouetted against the sky.

"He didn't even notice when I went out," Johnny said. "I started up the steps, then just turned around and walked out."

"Will he be mad?"

"I guess."

"What will he do?"

"I don't know."

"My old man doesn't care where I go. Till I get into trouble. Then he kicks my ass." Freddie stepped to the edge of the gravel bed, unzipped his fly, and peed down the slope. "Wait up." He aimed his stream at a jagged piece of green bottle-glass that projected from the cinders and stones. After a few shakes, he zipped up and kicked pebbles as he ran toward Johnny. "When we get to the quarry, y' wanna jerk off and see who can shoot the far-est?"

Johnny responded with a fiendish giggle. He punched his friend in the ribs.

With his arms stretched out for balance, Freddie walked the right-side rail, carefully placing one foot after the other. When he lost balance, he grabbed Johnny and tightened his arm around his friend's neck. Johnny punched him playfully in the chest, and then ran ahead as Freddie followed.

By mid-afternoon the fingers of clouds reached farther in from the eastern sky where the dark band of gray had widened. But the sun still shone brightly. Breezes began to send waves through the tall grasses as a crow cawed in the far distance. Ahead of the boys, the breezes stirred leaves still remaining on wild grape and poison ivy vines that draped gnarled trees at the quarry's edge—trees turned into odd shapes that had always fascinated Freddie, especially at twilight when viewed from deep in the quarry and seen as dark, ghostly images hovering above.

Migrating geese flew high above in V formation as Johnny and Freddie approached the quarry and the trestle that carried the railroad spur over the north end of the abandoned excavation. The boys stood near the tracks at the edge of the quarry and gazed down. The vast cavity of gray rock, invaded here and there by vegetation, always filled the young teenagers with excitement. Both glanced toward the south overhang to see if the older boys had staked out territory beneath it. They were both relieved to see that they had the quarry to themselves, though neither would say so to the other.

"Wanna walk the trestle?" Freddie asked.

"No. Let's go down."

The boys knew their route, for they had tested the steep inclines and drops many times. Scampering along a ridge on the west side, they slowed as it narrowed, then lowered themselves to a stratum of rock that sloped in the opposite direction. Here they walked gingerly on a narrow pathway that ended at a pillar of rock that projected toward the eastern sky—an outcropping that Freddie had named "the hard-on." Clinging by their fingers, they lowered themselves to a broad area where they sat and dangled their feet into the chasm.

"She doesn't want me around," Johnny muttered.

"Who?"

"His wife."

"Your stepmother?"

"Foster mother. But I don't call her anything."

"What's foster mean?"

"That's like people who get paid to take care of kids. They just want the money."

"You think your old man just wants the money? I mean, hell, he buys y' things. That's more than my old man does."

"Yeah he buys me things. Right after he does it to his secretary. He thinks I'm stupid."

"What do y' mean does it to his secretary?"

"You know."

"He fucks his secretary?"

"He tells me to play with the computers while he goes into his

238

back office with her. Afterwards he takes me shopping. We grab something real fast. Anything I want. Then he goes home and tells the blonde bitch that we were shopping for hours. That makes her hate me even more. But she hates him, too. They hate each other."

"Aaaa, forget 'em. Fuck 'em. Come on." Freddie slid his rump across the rock, grabbed the stump of a gnarled, dead cedar that protruded from a crevice, and lowered himself again. He secured his feet in a pile of loose stones and crumbled rock atop a fault-like projection that began a sheer drop. With care, he edged along the shelf, holding onto crags above his shoulders. At one point he slipped, but his fingers held as his biceps tightened, and he pulled his feet up and rammed them into sandy sediment on the narrow ledge. After inching along several more feet, he lowered himself to a wide but sloping stretch of rock on which he sat and slid his buttocks by carefully pushing with both hands. Within minutes he reached a deep, jagged, vertical crevice large enough to hold his body. Within the cleft he pushed his feet against the opposing walls and used the jags as steps to lower himself little by little until descending about 50 feet. He squirmed free, then jumped from the fissure onto flat rock that was the first of a series of step-like levels that took him down another 30 feet.

By the time Freddie reached the floor of the quarry, the fingers of clouds had caught up with the sun, and the dark band of gray had widened to cover half of the sky. He looked up at Johnny and watched his friend make the final leap to the bottom. Together the boys ran toward the center of the huge concavity, now and then zigzagging around boulders and patches of tall weeds. They headed for the deep recess under the overhang, but slowed to a walk long before arriving at the beer-drinking hangout of the big boys.

"Why didn't you want to stay and meet that guy?" Freddie asked as he walked shoulder-to-shoulder with his pal.

"I don't know."

"You might've liked this dude."

"It's always the same. They want the money. They don't care about me. Except maybe the Cuthberts."

"Who are the Cuthberts?"

"This other foster family. They tried, but they really didn't understand. I wrote to them once."

"What happened to your real dad?"

"I never had a real dad."

"That ain't possible. Y' hadda have one to get borned."

Johnny said nothing. He leaned over, picked up a stone, tossed it from hand to hand, then threw it toward the overhang.

"Didn't y' ever wanna find out about your real dad?"

"I'd rather have a dog."

"A dog?"

"The Oswalds—they won't let me have a dog. The Cuthberts—they had a dog, but not the kind you can pet, or keep in the house. Not the kind that'll sleep on your bed and wake you up in the morning. They just kept their dog tied up outside. I wasn't supposed to go near him. He was mean."

"What about your old lady? Your real one?"

"I got a letter from her once. The cops gave it to me."

"The cops?"

"Yeah, the cops."

"What the fuck y' talkin' about?" Freddie twisted Johnny's arm.

Johnny broke free and kicked his friend in the buttocks. "The cops were trying to find her. That's what this lady in Philadelphia told me. After that letter nobody could adopt me for some reason. So that's why I got these foster creeps."

"But this new guy might not be a fuckin' creep."

"Wanna bet?" Johnny started to run. "Race you to the overhang."

"So what did the letter say?" Freddie shouted as he ran after Johnny.

"Nothing."

"It hadda say somethin'."

When Johnny reached the recess under the overhang he began kicking the beer bottles and cans that littered the meeting place of the older boys. Freddie joined him seconds later and they both kicked and tossed with a vengeance, sometimes smashing bottles against rocks. At one point Freddie picked up a wet and moldy cushion, held it by a corner, and flung it into the open quarry. When he looked down again, he spotted a condom stretched over the neck of a beer bottle. He laughed fiendishly, then called out, "Get a look at this!" After giving Johnny a moment to stare, he kicked the bottle aside and made an obscene gesture with his finger. In time the boys sat on the ground deep in the hollow, leaned their backs against the rock wall and stretched their legs toward the paling sunlight.

"Why do you hang around me?" Freddie asked. "Nobody else does."

Johnny had never put into words his positive feelings toward anybody, so he struggled to answer. "You're the only... Well, it's because you're okay." He punched his friend on the upper arm. "You're okay. You're a cool dude. Know what I mean?"

"Fuck no!" Freddie pounded his fist into the ground between his legs. "The teachers at school—they hate me. I'm s'posed to be a bad influence. That's what they keep tellin' me."

Johnny kept his eyes focused on his knees. His body shivered when the words finally came out: "You're my friend."

Freddie squirmed, then scoffed, "Oh, sure."

"Then why did you ask?"

"Fuck if I know." Freddie picked up a sharp piece of rock, spread his legs, and scratched letters into the gritty soil: "YOU ARE MY FRIEND." As soon as he knew that Johnny had read the message, he rubbed it out with his hand as a squeamish feeling pervaded his body. He punched Johnny twice—once on the arm, once in the ribs. "You fuckin' faggot!" he yelled as he jumped to his feet. He ran toward a bottle, picked it up, and smashed it against the wall of rock. Dashing from under the overhang, he stopped suddenly and looked up at the sky. "A storm's movin' in. Sky's gettin' dark as hell." Minutes passed before he returned to Johnny and asked, "Did you ever have a friend before?"

Johnny toyed with the zipper of his jacket. "Sort of."

Freddie stood still and looked down on Johnny. "Whatcha mean by sorta?"

"There was this kid. When I was real little and living with my first foster parents. He lived next door. We played in the dirt under his back porch, making roads and tunnels and all. Sometimes they'd let me stay over. He had a dog that slept on his bed. I didn't want any more friends after him."

"Why's that?"

"I didn't like it when they took me away from him. I had to go live with these other people."

Freddie sat next to Johnny and began to rub the soil nervously with his well-worn sneakers. "So, what happened?"

"What do you mean?"

"Well, if you didn't want any more friends... So, how come... I mean, you know. How come, you and me?"

Johnny rolled a pebble between his thumb and his forefinger. He kept his eyes away from Freddie. "I don't know. It's just what happened, I guess."

"Yeah?"

"Remember in art class when the kids made fun of my painting? The one that showed a boy tied to a tree, and all those hands pulling at his feet? They didn't understand, and I couldn't explain it right."

"Your face turned red as hell."

"I felt awful when I left the room. And that big, fat kid—you know, Clarence—he laughed at me and pushed me. You came up and told him to get lost. Remember?"

"Yeah. Sure, I remember."

"Why did you do that?"

"He was an asshole!"

"That was the first time anybody... You were the first kid to ever... well, you know. The next day I caught up with you after school. We laughed about the worms you put in Miss Fredericks' desk drawer, and about Nancy Morgan's big tits. And from then on... well, you know." Johnny pushed wisps of hair from his forehead, stood and turned his big, blue eyes on Freddie. "But you got mad at me for following you. Remember?"

"Shit, no."

"Yes you do. Remember? I followed you home and saw your house and your father sitting on the steps."

"He was drunk!" Freddie leaped to his feet and hunted for another bottle. "And that house is ugly. It's a shit hole. I hate it." He picked up a bronze-colored beer bottle and smashed it against a boulder, then continued to try to conceal his embarrassment by dashing about smashing more bottles, squashing cans, and picking up stones and tossing them. In time he looked up at the sky again as winds began to sweep through the quarry. As a stiff breeze tossed his red hair, Freddie turned toward his friend and asked, "So, what are you gonna do? You gonna go back or what?"

"I don't know." Johnny looked down at his belt buckle. "If they make me go with this guy, I won't ever see you again." He felt thwarted and confused, not wanting to go home, yet not knowing where else to go. For a moment he wished that Freddie could hide him in that weather-worn, one-story house near the river, despite a drunken father. His mind even conceived of a forest hideaway to which Freddie would smuggle food each day. And he fantasized about hopping a freight train with Freddie and traveling to some far-off city where people would leave them alone.

Thunder rolled in the distant heavens as quarry-trapped gusts of wind swept sand, dust and debris into tiny twisters that spun here and there near the sheer inclines.

Before the sun began to set, it was covered by deep gray thunderheads. Darkness fell quickly over the quarry because the storm clouds joined the coming of night. Great sweeps of wind sucked pulverized rock from crevices and propelled coarse grit into strong gusts and whirlwinds. Thunder grew louder and flashes of lightening lit the sky. The rain came suddenly. Driving downpours swept in waves through the quarry as Johnny and Freddie huddled in the recess, somewhat protected by the overhang. In time, rivulets of water snaked their way down the side of the man-made canyon. Waterfalls burst forth here and there as ledges and projecting rocks deflected the widening streams. Water poured down from the overhang above Freddie and Johnny, building a curtain and obscuring even more an already blurred view of the craggy chasm walls when lit by lightning. The clumps of weeds on the quarry floor—already browned by autumn—were but pale, ghostly images as they bent, tossed and twisted in the torrent.

When the center of the storm neared, the flashes turned to streaks of brilliant lightning that cracked open the blackness and illuminated the entire quarry—widely erratic streaks followed immediately by explosive thunder that shook the earth and then rumbled away. Earsplitting blasts sent nerve-shocks reverberating up the spines of Johnny and Freddie. Despite the screen of water, the boys could see the trestle each time an electric discharge turned it aglow. They were spellbound by flashing images of the railroad crossover.

"Holy shit!" Freddie exclaimed when a streak of lightning bounced and skipped along the tracks and zigzagged down the vertical supports, jumping from one to another to another until reaching the ground. The accompanying blast of crackling thunder sent a shiver through Johnny, causing him to bite his lip as his heart pounded. He lifted his fingers to his mouth.

"Jesus, blood!"

"What?"

"I think I bit off a piece of my lip." He looked at the blood on his fingers. "What are we going to do?"

"Not a fuckin' thing right now."

"So, we just sit here and get killed by lightning?"

"You wanna go out there?"

"No."

"Then I guess we just stay here. I wanna know what you're gonna do afterwards."

"After what?"

"After the storm."

"I don't know."

"Well, y' better figure it out."

Pelted by the driving rain, puddles in the base of the quarry grew into large muddy, wind-driven pools. High points, boulders, heaps of sediment and clumps of vegetation soon became islands in a murky lake. A gnarled stomp of a dead cedar on the rim of the chasm broke lose and tumbled into the quarry, bouncing and splashing in the flash of streaking lightning.

"Sonofabitch!" Freddie exclaimed.

Johnny tensed his muscles, then shivered as he gripped his shoulders by crossing his arms over his chest. "I'm cold," he muttered.

Chapter Forty-Eight

The windshield wipers were on fast speed as Jackie brought her VW to a quick stop at curbside in front of Ty's apartment. The night had grown colder, making the driving rain a more formidable foe. No way would Jackie have ventured out on such a night if not for Rob's urgent plea. She had even canceled her plans with Nita Burleight, an old school chum and choice for one of her bridesmaids. Grumbling to herself, she lifted the collar on her trench coat, reached into her pocket to assure herself that the note was still there, and then grabbed her umbrella from behind the seat. With hesitation, she opened the door and projected the umbrella skyward as she pushed its automatic release.

Running toward the apartment building, Jackie splashed water in all directions. She avoided no puddles, thanks to her wintertime snow-boots. Remembering Rob's description of Sam Harrison's accident, she held the iron railing and stepped cautiously down the concrete steps to Ty's front door. She stood there for a moment, unsure of herself, as the water dripped heavily from her umbrella. Taking a deep breath, she pounded on the door, almost certain that no one would answer, and all the while trying to conjure up a means of arousing Amy.

Water at the base of the stairwell was halfway up Jackie's boots, and more water kept cascading down the steps behind her. After jiggling the door handle several times, she mumbled, "Damn it," turned and carefully climbed the steps. She knew that duty continued to call, so she stepped on the soggy grass in front of the building and aimed for the first of Ty's windows—those low, basement-apartment windows set partway beneath ground level, windows with deep wells and wide indoor sills that held Ty's dramatic house plants. Rain doused the back of Jackie's trench coat as she leaned far down and motioned at the window with her hand. Awkward to say the least, her off-balance position was worsened by the umbrella that she tried to keep above her head. Her efforts seemed fruitless, but she was encouraged by lights in the apartment.

The second window lifted Jackie's hopes, for its plant was a spiky growth with few leaves to block the view. Suddenly Jackie caught a glimpse of a young woman with auburn hair, dressed in a white bathrobe. She got down on her knees and moved her left hand back and forth across the window. Finally, she tossed the umbrella aside and allowed the rain to pelt her as she struggled to make various hand motions. But again her efforts failed. With a desperate need to straighten her backbone, she stood and stretched while the rain drenched her. Water ran down her neck, inside her collar. Her soaked hair was a dripping mop.

Within seconds, Jackie retrieved her umbrella, closed it, held it by its point, lowered its handle into the well, and swung it back and forth before the window. In a fit of frustration, she struck the window, then tossed the umbrella into an azalea bush. She leaned against the building, with her head just under a window box, and lowered her right foot into the well where she rubbed her boot against the pane of glass.

"Please," Jackie muttered as she withdrew her foot. She returned to her knees, and stared into the window. Her eyes looked directly into Amy's eyes, for the swinging boot had drawn the young, auburn-haired woman to the sill. Both women showed surprise, but Amy's expression also denoted fear of whatever it was that she could not discern in the darkness of the stormy night. Jackie put her hand—palm open and fingers spread—on the glass. Then she pointed toward the door in a constant jabbing motion. Hoping she had made her point, she stood, seized her umbrella from the bush, strode across the soggy grass and splashed her way to the stairwell entrance.

Again in ankle-deep water, Jackie moved close to the door and waited. Within a moment, the door opened but a crack, and Amy peered out. Jackie forced a smile to give notice that she was a friendly soul, prompting Amy to open the door another three inches for a better view of the drenched woman with the pleading eyes. The mysterious, nighttime caller was a pathetic sight, standing there in a pool of water, dripping from hair, nose and chin, carrying her umbrella instead of using it. But Amy's compassion did not erase the fear that showed in her eyes—soft blue eyes that scrutinized Jackie's face, glanced down at the muddy knee marks on the trench coat, and looked up again and studied the visitor's expression.

"Please let me in." Jackie moved her lips slowly with pronounced effort in hopes that Amy would understand. "I have a message from Ty."

Amy's eyes flashed at the mention of "Ty," but, nonetheless, she kept a firm hold on the door with her right hand while tightening her white terry-cloth robe around her neck with her left. The unrelenting wind kept blowing rain through the doorway.

Suddenly remembering the note, Jackie reached into her pocket, pulled out the folded piece of paper, and gave it to Amy. The fearful young woman struggled to unfold it with her left hand. A glance at the first sentence was all it took for her to release the door, back up and smile at her visitor. The words read: "I'm Jackie Harwood, Rob Putnam's fiancée." Amy immediately helped Jackie remove her wet trench coat. Carrying the coat and shaking her head apologetically, she backed into the coffee table, causing the crystal rooster to skip across the glass surface. She turned, jumped nervously, and raced between the table and the couch and disappeared from the room. But she was back in an instant with a thick, white bath towel. After wiping her visitor's forehead, she tossed the towel over Jackie shoulders.

Not until Jackie was seated on the couch next to a pile of books, with the towel wrapped around her head, did Amy reach into her bathrobe pocket and retrieve the note. Though still nervous and jumpy, she was thoughtful as she read: "Rob telephoned from Maywood to say that he and Ty would arrive home much later than expected. He said Ty couldn't get home in time to take you to the hospital as planned."

Amy looked at Jackie with questioning eyes, then took a felt-marker from her pocket and wrote "Maywood?" on the paper. She handed the note to Jackie and immediately dashed from the room again, returning from the kitchen with two legal-sized pads of paper and a fistful of pencils and pens that she placed on the coffee table.

"Why didn't he tell me he was going somewhere with Rob?" Amy wrote on one of the pads. She handed it to Jackie, pushed the books aside, and sat beside her.

"I'm sure he'll explain," wrote Jackie as Amy watched every move of her pen.

Obviously not satisfied, Amy frowned and slouched. Within seconds, however, she sat up and wrote on the other pad: "I'm sorry. It was good of you to deliver the message, especially in all this rain."

Jackie smiled.

"Tea?" wrote Amy.

Jackie nodded, and once again Amy scurried to the kitchen.

While she waited, Jackie reached for the books and glanced at the titles: Conrad's *Lord Jim*, Lawrence's *Sons and Lovers*, Golding's *Lord of the Flies* and Joyce's *A Portrait of the Artist as a Young Man*—obviously books from a college literature course.

Next, she glanced around the room, admiring Ty's artwork. Turning her head, she looked behind the couch and saw the portrait of Amy on the wall between the windows. Taken by its beauty, she pushed the books aside and rose slowly, holding the towel atop her head as she faced the painting. She was in awe of the likeness, though it was a portrait of a more youthful, childlike Amy. Without question, she thought, it had been painted from the heart. She pulled the towel from her head, walked around the couch, stepped close to the portrait and examined the brush stokes. Then she backed away and circled the room to get different, more distant views. Her eyes were held by the painting even as Amy entered the room and placed a tray of tea and cookies on the table—the tea in a copper kettle instead of a china pot, accompanied by coffee mugs instead of tea cups.

Forgetting Amy's deafness, Jackie finally looked at her and said, "It's just so beautiful!"

Amy succumbed to her feelings, reflecting all in her face. Her eyes became soft pools of wonder, of yearning, of giving, of accepting, of believing. Jackie saw and understood. Instinctively she took Amy's hand and squeezed it gently.

Within moments, Amy forced herself to break the spell, spun about excitedly, slid quickly onto the couch, and kept slapping the cushion next to her until Jackie joined her. She took the wet towel from her guest's hand, folded it neatly and placed it on a corner of the glass top table. Then, in deliberate, orderly moves, she put a pad and pencil in each of their laps.

Jackie's curiosity pushed her into pointing to the books, for she could not equate Amy's background with literary titles. She wondered if Rob had given her the wrong impression of the girl from Redrock Road. Perhaps Amy was not a totally deprived Cinderella. Jackie struggled to show nothing in her expression because of her fear of somehow revealing condescension.

Amy picked up the James Joyce novel, opened it to her place marker, and smiled as she pressed it against her bosom. She handed it to Jackie, then wrote on her pad: "Ty's books."

The fact that Amy could and would read such books only filled Jackie with more curiosity and wonder. She felt, however, that she neither had the finesse nor the right to probe.

Amy studied Jackie's eyes. She was discerning enough to guess the question, and wrote "I've always read, even books that my father told me not to read. I'd sneak them." Pouring tea from Ty's kettle, she motioned with her hand toward the small plate of butter cookies.

Jackie nodded, then lifted her mug and sipped tea.

"I love Ty," Amy wrote on her pad.

Such a simple, uncluttered statement, thought Jackie, who marveled at Amy's openness, thinking that it stemmed from her deafness, perhaps from a lack of worldliness not realized through books. "I know you love him," Jackie wrote. "I can tell."

Sudden seriousness gripped Amy. "My father expects a visit from me," she wrote. "Would it be inconvenient for you to drive me to the hospital? Perhaps if the rain stops?"

"I'll gladly drive you, rain or not," Jackie wrote.

Amy toyed with her pencil, then wrote, "My father is really a good man. He just doesn't understand. He tries to protect me."

The thoughts within Jackie were many, but she couldn't bring herself to express them. Around in her head spun ideas about Amy's innocence and vulnerability and perhaps a driving need to taste more of life, spurred on, perhaps, by a vicarious living through novels. But it was her vision of Ty as kind and gentle that finally moved her pencil: "Ty has so much understanding of people. He'll be good to you."

"He's so afraid he's taking advantage of me. He says I've known no other man. But he's the only man I want."

"I'm sure he knows that," wrote Jackie, marveling again at Amy's openness. Suddenly she understood the young woman's need—perhaps a burning need to shout her love from the mountain tops, or to at least tell somebody, for she had no mother, no sister, no girlfriend with whom to share her happiness.

"He's given me so much. I feel so safe when I'm with him."

Jackie took Amy's hand again and squeezed it.

Chapter Forty-Nine

Beams of light from each streetlamp pierced the dark night and caused glares to reflect off wet and shiny Pine Lane. The cold rain streaked diagonally and blew in sheets. Condensation fogged up the windows of the parked car as Rob and Ty continued to talk and breathe. Rob kept trying to clear the driver-side window with his hand, giving him a smeary view of the Oswald house across the street. He and Ty had been waiting in the car for more than an hour since shortly after telephoning Jackie from the diner where they had eaten dinner.

"We don't want to miss him," Rob said for the third time while wiping the window again. "Every time the wind tosses a bush I think it's him."

"We should do more than just sit here and wait," Ty said. "If they won't call the police, maybe we should."

"Chances are the cops won't consider the kid missing till he's gone overnight or longer."

"I don't know. This storm might worry them into action."

Rob looked at his wristwatch. "It's been an hour since we knocked."

"And got the door closed in our faces. How do we know for sure he's not in there?"

"Oswald knows we're here to stay. He wouldn't pull that. Besides, he has to give up the kid and he knows it. He likes to make noise, but I don't think it's really a big deal as far as he's concerned. Let's hold out a bit longer. If Willowboy doesn't show up within the next half-hour, we'll try to push Oswald into calling the police. He'll have more clout. The kid's not yours yet."

"He's such an ass."

"Who? Oswald?"

"Yeah. That line about his wife suffering dizzy spells from worry. Give me a break."

"She's too crafty and calculating to ever get dizzy."

"I can't figure her. She seems a contradiction."

"She's trying to be something she isn't."

"And John Willow got stuck with them."

"Count your blessings. Some foster kids really get knocked around. John may have escaped the worst."

"As far as we know."

Rob wiped the window again. "Christ, I can't stand this. I need air." He lowered the window a few inches, allowing a sprinkle of water to wet his face. "I think the rain's letting up."

"I wonder who this Freddie kid is, anyway."

"Sounds like an angry whelp that gives his teachers nightmares." Rob wiped the window. "Oh shit!"

"What is it?"

"It's him, I think. Looks like a drenched rat with blond hair."

"Where?" Ty stretched his neck.

"He just went under the light. He's heading for the door."

"Let's go."

"No. Let him go. Give him some time with the Oswalds. Let them explain. Then we'll go in. He's not going to disappear. Not if he came back in this rain. In fact, maybe we're lucky this storm hit. Maybe it drove him back."

"What's he doing now?"

"He's standing at the door. Hesitating. There he goes. He just pushed open the door."

"Did he go in? I can't see."

"Yeah. He's inside. The door's closed."

"I hope they don't turn him against me somehow."

"No way. The kid probably doesn't trust a thing they say. Besides, the woman's in your camp. She wants to get rid of him."

"God, I want him to like me."

"Give him time. Have patience."

"How many times have I told others that. Crazy, isn't it?"

"Christ, you're uptight."

"The boy doesn't know me, and I don't know him. Two strangers coming together. Easy stuff, right? And if I pull it off..."

"If?"

"I have to tell Amy."

"Will you get off of that? Face it when you come to it. Damn it, Ty, you were only a kid when Marjorie hit on you. She was an older woman. Your were seduced. It's not hard to explain."

"I don't see it that way."

"But you better tell it that way."

"Amy's different. She's hardly a part of this world. How will she understand? If only she could hear my voice, so she could hear my feelings."

Rob rolled down the window and thrust his hand out, palm up. "The rain's stopping. It's just a heavy drizzle now." He looked at Ty. "Are you okay?"

Ty gave Rob a friendly tap on the head. "Thanks, good buddy."

"For what?"

"For being here."

"Forget it."

"Sorry I held back."

"We've always been able to spill our guts. This one just got stuck in your entrails a little longer. The truth is, you should thank the burdock weed."

"The what?"

"The burdock that I pulled from Aunt Marjorie's flower patch."

"Oh." Ty slouched and put his knees on the dashboard. "The other baby. My baby, too. I hope you don't think this is strange, but... Well, I was wondering. Could we bury the remains in the garden where you found them? You know, where she buried her baby. Would you or Jackie mind?"

Rob looked at Ty. "No. We wouldn't mind. I know I wouldn't. And I'm sure Jackie wouldn't. I don't know about the laws regarding burial sites. If there's a problem, maybe we can get around it somehow."

"I think she wanted her baby there, among the irises."

"It's a deal. Even if we have to break a city ordinance." Rob squeezed his friend at the back of the neck. Then he made an effort to lighten the talk: "Just so you take care of me on my wedding day. 'Skinny-dip' Jones is coming down from Cornell to be an usher. You know damn well he'll team up with Smitty to pay me back for my evil deeds. Ty, are you listening?"

Ty nodded, but his thoughts were elsewhere.

Chapter Fifty

Soaking wet, Johnny sat halfway up the wide staircase with the elaborate balustrade. Chester had halted the boy's climb at that point, and now paced back and forth in the spacious, classical, peach-and-cream hallway. Lana stood at one side of the entrance hall, with her back against the handsomely carved woodwork at the opening to the living room.

"Let him change his clothes," she urged.

"You was messin' around at that damn quarry again, wasn't you?" barked Chester.

Johnny lowered his head, and Chester knew the answer.

Lana sighed, then repeated, "Let him change."

"Just a minute," Chester snapped. He stopped pacing at the foot of the stairs, looked at the boy and said, "It ain't like you to do somethin' like that. T' just walk outta here."

"But there comes a time," Lana muttered to herself.

"What do y' have on your feet?" Chester stared at the ripped and tarnished sneakers. "They ain't yours. Where're your good sneakers?"

"I gave them away."

"You what?"

"It's not important, Chester," Lana insisted. "Who gives a damn about sneakers right now? The kid's father is waiting outside." She looked from Chester to the boy. "He's your real father, understand? Your real father. He wants you. He loves you."

Johnny shot an incredulous stare at Lana. "That's nuts! He

doesn't even know me. Besides, whoever he is, he's not my real father. I don't have a real father."

"Look, he may be your real father," Chester began, "or he..."

"Of course he's the boy's real father," Lana argued as her eyes shot daggers at her husband. "And you damn right know it, Chester! You damn right know it! Tell the kid! Go on! Tell him!"

"Whatever, they're not gonna take you away right now," Chester explained to Johnny. "If they come get you, it'll be later."

"So, what are they doing out there?" Johnny asked.

"Lana wasn't feeling well, so I told them to..."

"That's a damn lie!" Again Lana switched her stare from Chester to the boy. "He wouldn't let them in when they came back from supper. They'll be knocking on the door any minute. Your father wants to meet you."

"If I have a real father, where's he been all this time?"

"He just found out about you," Lana explained.

"That's crazy!" Johnny snapped as he shivered so obviously that Chester and Lana noticed.

"The kid's freezing, Chester. Let him change."

"Why the hell would you go to the quarry in this weather?" Chester asked with a demanding squeal.

"It wasn't raining when I went."

Chester continued to squeal: "Did you go with that Freddie kid?"

Johnny looked down at Freddie's broken sneakers.

"You did, didn't you? You know what I said about him. And that quarry's dangerous as hell. You ain't got no sense!"

"Chester, stop it!" Lana insisted. "This is stupid. John, go up and change. Then come down and meet your father—your real father."

Johnny turned and began to scamper up the steps when the chimes rang and the knocker tapped. He stopped suddenly, stood still for an instant, then ran up to the top where he turned and looked down from the high balustrade.

Chester opened the door and said, "He's here. You can come in now."

Rob was the first to enter, and Johnny studied him well. When the boy's eyes turned on the other visitor they stayed there. Ty looked left, then right, then up. Within seconds his eyes were held by Johnny's. He and the boy stood still, transfixed. No one spoke, and no one seemed to move—not Chester, not Lana, not Rob, and decidedly not Ty or Johnny. The entrance hallway could have been an exhibition room of Madam Tussaud's wax museum.

Johnny moved first, but only to turn and look at himself in the massive gold-framed mirror that decked the upper-balustrade hallway. He looked into his eyes, then examined his nose, mouth, chin, ears. As quickly as he turned toward the mirror, he swung around, grabbed the railing and gazed down on Ty. Again he seemed statue-like, only to break his fixed stance suddenly and step toward his room.

"Wait," Ty called. "Please wait."

The boy stopped again, almost as if lassoed and held by an invisible rope. Within seconds he began to turn slowly. He riveted his eyes on Ty and watched.

Ty strode directly to the stairs and walked up without hesitation. He was decisive and even-paced in his ascent. At the top of the stairs, he looked directly at the boy and suggested, "What say we talk a minute? Okay?"

Johnny failed to talk or move.

"I'll tell you what," Ty said. "Let's sit right here on the top step and talk a bit." Ty sat on the floor, with his feet two steps down. He motioned to the boy with hand, finger and head movements, urging him to approach and sit beside him.

Still, the boy did not move.

"Come on," Ty said.

"What's there to talk about?"

"Well, I don't know. Maybe we can think of something."

Rob walked into the living room in a deliberate efforts to get Chester and his wife to follow. Lana watched Rob, then looked at her husband and whispered harshly, "Chester, come on." She slipped into the living room. "Come on, damn it. In here." Reluctantly, Chester sauntered from the hallway.

Johnny stepped closer to Ty, but remained standing, his hand on the railing.

"That fellow with me," Ty explained, "is my friend—a very good friend." Ty smiled as he inspected the boy from head to foot. "You did get wet and muddy. Quite a storm, wasn't it?" Holding the smile and keeping his kindly eyes on Johnny, Ty continued, "You were out there with a friend, weren't you? It's important to have a friend, isn't it? My friend Rob—he and I share a lot. We talk about all sorts of things. Do you do that with your friend?"

Johnny simply stared at Ty.

"Why don't you tell me about your friend?" Ty asked.

"Nobody likes him," Johnny blurted.

"But you do, right?"

The boy nodded.

"That's what's important," Ty said. "I guess you understand him better than others."

Johnny edged a bit closer. "Are you really my father?" The boy's cynical tone denoted skepticism.

"So it seems. It came as a big surprise to me. Can you imagine? Just think of what it's like to suddenly find out that you're the father of a kid that's just about to have his fourteenth birthday. Wow!"

Johnny's expression revealed heavy thinking. In fact, his thoughts were spinning loop-the-loops in his brain.

"See? We have a lot to talk about. Come on. Sit down."

John Willow edged a bit closer. Then with a burst of energy he sat on the top step beside Ty, but as far away as possible, right up against the balustrade.

"My friend Rob—he worked really hard to find you," Ty explained in soft, warm tones. "He's your cousin. His mom is your aunt—Aunt Emily."

Johnny shook his head, as if not allowing himself to accept the assertions of this look-alike stranger.

"I was just a teenager when you were born," said Ty, who sensed that Johnny was afraid to believe. "In fact, I was only three years older than you are now. But you see, I never knew you were born. If I had known, I would have come after you long, long ago." Ty wanted to put his arm around the drenched boy, but he held back, sensing that it was too soon and that the gesture would be rebuffed.

Johnny shivered, and Ty noticed.

"You're cold. Why don't you change, and then we'll talk some more."

"Are you going to take me away?"

"Well, I couldn't even if I wanted to. Not yet. Anyway, I don't want to take you anywhere. I would hope that, within time, you'd want to come live with me. I'd sure like that. You know, we could give it a try. See if it works."

Johnny didn't respond in words, but his tight mouth and darting eyes revealed his mind's gyrations.

"I realize this'll be a big decision for you. After all, you don't even know me."

"You mean I don't have to go if I don't want to?"

"Well, I suppose if you didn't want to come and live with me, I'd still try to be your dad one way or another. Do you want to stay here with the Oswalds?"

The boy didn't answer.

"Do you like living with the Oswalds?"

Johnny still did not respond.

"You can tell me," Ty whispered. "It's okay."

The teenager turned his head and looked at Ty. He waited until their eyes met before shaking his head.

Ty frowned slightly and asked, "But you're not sure you want to leave, is that it?"

The boy looked down at his feet.

"Oh, I think I get it," Ty said. "It's your friend, right?"

Johnny's weak nod was barely evident.

"I understand." Ty smiled knowingly. "What's his name? Freddie?"

Again the teenager nodded.

"I'll tell you something. If things work out and we get a chance to try living together—you know, to see if it works—well, you could invite Freddie over for visits. He could come to dinner. He could sleep over."

"He could?"

"Of course. He's your friend. Good friendships are meant to last."

Johnny shook his head again, as if unable to trust Ty's words. Suddenly he grabbed the railing, pulled himself to his feet, and charged, "I don't believe you. I don't believe that you're my father." Then he raced to his bedroom.

Ty felt deflated, but tried to tell himself that the boy was simply testing him. He stayed at the top of the steps, his head hanging, his elbows on his knees, his hands locked together in a vise-like grip, tighter than his preoccupied mind realized. Moments passed before he became fully aware of his pounding heart.

Silence reigned until Rob sneaked back into view and said, "I thought the talking stopped."

Ty shrugged his shoulders and grimaced.

"Hey, you gave it your best try," Rob said.

"You heard us?"

"Bits and pieces."

"I don't know why I'm so upset. It's exactly what I expected."

"What next?"

"Well, we shouldn't stay. He needs time to think. I planted the seeds. Now let's see how they grow."

Chester returned to the hall, this time ambling around the edge of the spacious entranceway. He cleared his throat twice to get attention, just as Ty began to descend the stairs and as Lana resumed her overseer's stance against the woodwork.

"We're leaving, Mr. Oswald," Ty said.

"Chester's not trying to rush you, are you Chester?" Lana uttered sardonically.

"It's okay, Mrs. Oswald, we are leaving," Ty said. "Really." Stopping at the foot of the stairs, he looked at Rob while he spoke to the others: "We'll be in touch soon. Thank you for your kindness."

"Yeah, thanks," Rob added while he and Ty walked briskly to the door as Chester opened it.

"Well, at least the rain's stopped," Ty commented as he followed Rob out of the house. He waited for Chester to close the door before saying, "What an asshole." He glanced back at the Georgian facade. "How did a guy like that get a house like this?"

"Root mulch," Rob shot back while racing ahead of Ty down the walkway.

Ty heard a window open, turned and looked up to see Johnny's silhouette against the bedroom light.

"Hey, mister," the boy called. "You got a dog?"

Ty thought for a moment, then replied, "Not exactly. But I know a dog named Whiskers who'd just love a young fellow like you.

UNDER THE BURDOCK WEED

And he's in bad need of a home." Backing down the walkway, Ty saluted John Willow, then turned and hurried toward Rob. He looked back and lifted his hand to wave, but the boy was gone. "God, I hope Whiskers is still at the shelter," he muttered in earshot of Rob.

"That should lift your spirits," Rob said while opening the driver-side door of his car. "We're late as hell. Let's move."

"Easy, man!" Ty ran, opened the opposite door, and pounced into the car as it roared. "I hope t' hell Jackie reached Amy somehow. If not, I got a big problem."

"Smile, damn it! The kid's already sprouting the seeds you sowed." Within seconds Rob was driving above the speed limit.

"Holy shit, just think of it. I might end up with Amy, a dog, and a fourteen-year-old son—all at once. My life is not just taking a turn; it's spinning a hundred and eighty degrees! If I pull this off, I'm a miracle worker."

"Why Mr. Goody-Goody Sunshine, what was it you used to preach about life? Something about relishing every chapter?"

"Chapter! As Chester Oswald would put it, 'This ain't no fuckin' chapter, buddy. It's a fuckin' saga!'"

"Saga? Chester wouldn't know a saga from a shadoof."

"What's a shadoof?"

"Hell if I know. I made it up." Rob brought the car to a sudden stop and turned his intense eyes on Ty. "You listen to me. This time I'll play Mr. Sunshine. It may take time. But in the long run there's no way you can fail with this kid. You hear me?"

"Why's that?"

"Because I know you." Rob punched his friend on the arm. "But there's something else."

"What's that?"

"You're stewing over Johnny and Amy at the same time. Shake off the guilt and it'll clear your head a little."

"Guilt?"

"I'm not stupid, Ty. I know you've been thinking that maybe you took advantage of a poor little deaf girl who didn't know the ways of the world."

"Now, wait a minute."

"No. You listen. I was wrong at first. Way wrong. It's so simple. I see it so clearly now. You and Amy moved quickly because you each had a desperate need. Both of you. Each of you. Hey, thank God you found each other. No regrets. Okay?"

Chapter Fifty-One

Sam Harrison lay sleeping in his hospital bed. Standing just inside the door in Ty's shiny black raincoat, Amy gazed on him for several moments before stepping closer. The television was on without sound, its picture constantly flipping and sending waves of light across Sam's bed. The green divider curtain hid the window-side bed, now occupied by a 70-year-old man suffering from cirrhosis of the liver. Moving toward the pillow, Amy looked closely at her father's face. His closed eyelids quivered slightly. She suspected that he was snoring, though she had never heard a snore in her lifetime. He lay on his back. His parted lips and heaving chest indicated labored breathing. She took the TV control from his hand and switched off the video.

Moving his head one way, then the other, Sam opened his eyes and looked directly at his daughter. Within seconds he focused on her, then struggled to sit up. Amy propped the pillow behind his shoulders.

Sam offered no "hello" or greeting. Communicating with his hands, he signed, "How did you get here? Did he bring you?"

Ignoring the questions, Amy used sign language to ask, "How do you feel?"

Her father continued the disjointed conversation with surprisingly fast-moving hands and fingers: "Where are you living? Are you back home?"

Again Amy disregarded her father's questions and asked him about his condition.

"How did you get here?" he signed.

"A friend drove me."

"Who?"

"A friend of a friend."

Quivers in the flesh around Sam's mouth revealed his frustration. His eyes flashed anger. "You're a sinner," he said in a harsh whisper that Amy failed to grasp. He translated it with his hands: "You sinned."

Amy backed away and looked down, but quickly gathered courage, lifted her chin, looked into her father's eyes, and with fast finger movements told him that she had no shame.

"Then it's true," he muttered to himself.

"You don't care that I came to see you?" Amy signed.

Sam looked away, toward the green curtain. Moment gave way to moment, and still he refused to gaze on his daughter. Amy walked to the foot of the bed where she stood for more than a minute. Then, in a sudden burst of energy, she hurried to the curtain side of the bed and turned her eyes on him.

With full-speed motions, Amy told her father that she intended to visit Dr. Anderson so she could hear the voice of the man she loved.

Sam raised his hand as if to strike her, and she fell back into the curtain and against the other bed, causing the cirrhosis patient to squeal and groan. Amy felt him move, but could do nothing until she recovered from the jolt that weakened her knees. Steadying herself, she stared at her father in disbelief, then gathered her wits and walked around the curtain and offered a few nods of apology to the thin, gray, sickly man in the window-side bed—a man who squinted strangely at her. Returning timidly to her father's side, Amy communicated nothing but questions in her eyes. Incredulity shaped her expression.

Sam turned his head and looked toward the door. Tightening her lips, Amy reached for her father's arm, but pulled back before touching. Within an instant she reached again, grasped his upper arm and tugged. Moments after she let go, he moved his head slowly and looked at her. It was not anger she saw in his eyes; it was sadness and fear. She sensed his pain, but not its meaning—until he made the signs for "loss" and "daughter." Then she knew that he was afraid of losing her, the child who had been his possession, and only his, for years. Her thoughts replayed his oft-repeated story of her mother's death, as willed by God, and the cloak of deafness that enclosed the inner spirit of the mother within the daughter.

Though skilled in sign language, Amy struggled in her efforts to explain her feelings. She wanted so much to tell him that she was thankful for the moral armor he had cast about her, yet, until now, so shielded by it that she couldn't see or feel the fullness of life. Even the spirit of her mother had been so heavily veiled that the lessons of childhood were almost gone, smothered in scrupulous righteousness. With desperation she tried to explain that Ty Scott had opened the treasure chest of her mother's teachings about fulfillment, love and joy. But her father couldn't grasp the meaning of her disjointed signs.

Amy tried to temper her anxiety and control her movements. Quoting from Ty, she slowly gave signs for: "If God gave us the intelligence to create, He meant us to use it. And that includes doctors who fix ears."

Sam moved his head slightly and gazed at the ceiling.

Attempting to position herself so that Sam might see her, Amy went on quoting from Ty, explaining that some persons must stay within the deaf culture rather than be split between two worlds. "But I want to be in his world."

Sam barely followed her signs from the corner of his eyes. He remained motionless, almost expressionless.

Amy wept in frustration. Tears streaked her cheeks. She wanted her father to understand, yet her efforts seemed in vain. Feeling thwarted, she walked toward the door, only to experience a touch of guilt and turn back and sign, "My friend is in the lobby. She was kind to bring me. I can't keep her waiting."

Backing away, Amy prayed for a warm goodbye. Instead, her father signed, "You should take me home. I don't belong here. If God wants my bones to heal, they'll heal without the interference of doctors."

Chapter Fifty-Two

"Cabbage and kale in a flower garden?" Rob pulled the telephone handset away from his face and stared at it comically, knowing full well that Ty was watching him from across the hallway.

"That's your only answer if you're serious about a November garden in this part of the country," Ty said.

Rob was sitting in his swivel chair at his crowded desk in his Pure-Pup office. He swung back and forth from his desk to his computer terminal as he spoke on the phone to his colleague, who was only 30 feet away. His office walls were a busy mixture of books and manuals on shelves, framed photographs of the Delaware River in all seasons, and a Ty Scott oil painting of a drunken elephant drinking beer from a fraternity mug.

He could see Ty simply by looking above the piles of papers and through two doorways. "I don't want a vegetable garden," he said while grimacing at the telephone. Stretching his neck, he squinted at Ty, who was sitting on a stool at his drawing board, leaning on his elbows, and dangling his telephone handset by its cord.

"You obviously are unaware of ornamental cabbage and kale," said the artist in a forced know-it-all tone. He waved to Rob and thumbed his nose.

"You're absolutely right. But, unlike you, I don't hang with young Four-H aggies who excite their gonads by growing Brussels sprouts."

"Drive out to the Collingswood Nurseries. I took some scouts out there yesterday for a load of pumpkins. See my friend Joe

Beazley. He's overstocked with pink, white and red varieties of cabbage and kale that have outgrown their containers. At this date, he might sell them at quarter-price. Hell, he might even give them away."

"Pink cabbage?" Rob looked at the ceiling and rolled his eyes. "I guess I deserve that. Anyone who plans a mid-November wedding deserves cabbage."

"Believe me, these things look like giant roses that hug the ground. They even survive the early snowstorms. I'll tell you what. We'll take my van and load up. Okay?"

"Hey, I like it. I like it. And I'll buy the pizza."

"It's a deal. But wait. Don't hang up."

Rob glanced across the hall and saw that Ty had tightened his hold on the phone and was pulling nervously on his ear.

"I'm going to tell Amy tonight," Ty said. "I'm uptight as hell."

"You'll be okay. I know it. So lighten up."

"I'm not so sure. She's not easy to read. It's hard to know how she'll react. She's such a strange mixture of romantic notions from novels, parts and pieces of her mother that are just surfacing, shackles from her father's iron hand, and my viewpoints, some of which she grabs and holds tightly."

"You're her man. She'll hang tight. Wait and see."

"I have a strange feeling. This is something far from her deaf world with Sam Harrison."

"But she's in your world now."

"Only partly. And I don't want to lose that part."

"You won't. No way."

"Let's face it. I could easily prove that Sam Harrison is right. Some of us out here in the big, bad world have evil ways. And sweet, young, deaf girls must be protected."

"I've seen you in action. You have good instincts. Just let it happen. You'll be okay."

"Amy suffers from some sort of Prince Charming syndrome."

"Oh?"

"I'm that guy on the white horse."

"And you don't want to get knocked off."

"She dreams of sweethearts whirling off on a fairy-tale

honeymoon. I'm sure she wants love in a castle on a hillside, or in a seaside cottage surrounded by tulips. How do I toss a fourteen-year-old boy into the midst of that?"

Chapter Fifty-Three

U sing a cookbook, Amy baked a ginger-chicken dish with orange slices and almonds—far from anything she had ever cooked in her father's house. She served it with Caesar salad and a blush wine, something she had never tasted in her father's world. Dinner was served on the new dining table at the end of Ty's living room—a Swedish blond table purchased to end Ty's bad habit of eating his meals hunched over the coffee table. Amy's joy in serving Ty was tempered by his nervousness and preoccupation.

Following dinner, Ty rearranged the table while Amy rinsed dishes in the kitchen. He removed the place mats and candlesticks, and substituted ball-point pens and pads of paper. In the past, he and Amy had usually huddled side-by-side when sharing written messages. But this was different. He wanted to sit up straight and look directly into her eyes no matter how inconvenient the passing of paper across the table.

After pacing around the room, he took his sign-language cards from his pocket and spread them on his side of the table. Again and again he silently rehearsed his words, but still found them inadequate, inappropriate, even stupid: *I have a fourteen-year-old son. I shacked up when I was only sixteen. I want my son. I was seduced by one of my customers. I was only a teenager. A woman three times my age took advantage of me. The truth is, I kept going back. I needed to prove something. Other than that I'm a virgin. I didn't know about the baby. I just found out.*

Still wearing his office shirt, Ty loosened his necktie with a sudden, fierce yank, and stiffened his chin as he grew more angry with himself.

Amy entered the room with a dish of strawberry ice cream in each hand. Her broad smile was quickly erased as puzzlement altered her expression. She stood like a winged statue, ice cream projecting left and right. But even with a frown she looked so fair and fine in her soft yellow blouse that Ty's eyes moistened.

Hurrying to her aid, he took the dishes of ice cream and made room for them at the table, then looked at her and pointed to her chair.

Though Amy's face brightened, she could not hold her smile as she signed, "What is it?"

Ty sat at the table, looked into his dish, and waited until she sat. He tried to eat his ice cream, but after one spoonful he pushed it away, lifted his eyes and sent signals with his hands: "You don't know me fully. There are things I must tell you." He struggled with the next sign, showed frustration, and looked at his cards while pushing them about with his fingers. He sighed, looked straight into her eyes and awkwardly signed, "I must write. I can't do it with signs. It's too complicated." His thoughts kept repeating Rob's words: "You have good instincts... good instincts... good instincts."

With little expression, Amy watched her ice cream melt.

Ty picked up a pen, but wrote nothing for a long, awkward moment. When he finally wrote, he did so slowly, with thought: "I'm aware that no one is obligated to discuss the secrets of his past life, even to someone he loves and intends to marry." He lifted his head, recognized Amy's perplexity, and used his eyes to ask for her patience. Then he looked down and wrote, "There is an exception, of course. That's when the past comes back to change the present or the future. Something I did many years ago has a bearing on today and tomorrow and my life with you." Ripping the top sheet from his pad, he then reached across the table and delivered the beginning of his message.

Amy's bewilderment failed to wane as she seized the paper and read his words. In fact, she shook her head to denote confusion while Ty raised his index finger and slowly moved his lips to enunciate, "Please give me time."

After tapping his pen repeatedly, Ty wrote: "I was only a teenage boy when it happened. But the sins of the child sometimes come back to haunt the man." He read and re-read his words, didn't like them, found them mawkish, but he wrote on: "The trouble is, I don't see my teenage adventure exactly as sinful, but I fear you might, considering your life and values." He was getting wordy, and he realized it, but he wanted to build a foundation. Again he looked across the table and tried to send warm vibrations. But he failed because of another confrontation with Amy's befuddlement.

"What is it?" she signed again. "Tell me."

Ty needed encouragement, some sign from Amy that their love would prevail no matter what. His thoughts went on another crazy rampage: *How different it would be with other women. Some wouldn't give a damn. So, I did more than jerk off at age sixteen. Big deal! So I'm not your virgin prince. Hell, most unmarried dudes my age have scored dozens of time. I was just a kid! Just a kid! Just a kid!*

Ripping off another sheet, Ty stretched and handed the paper to Amy, then wrote again: "I had a relationship with a much older woman when I was sixteen. I doubt that I would ever have told you this if not for my recent discovery that I have a son almost fourteen years old. He's a handsome boy who has been living in foster homes. I want to take care of him. I want to be his father. I knew nothing of the boy until Rob uncovered the facts. Please believe me."

Nervously, Ty tore the page from his pad and gave it to Amy. He grasped the spoon that projected from his dish and played with the melted ice cream. When certain that Amy had read and digested his words, he slowly lifted his head and looked at her. He was unable to read her expression. Perhaps her blank stare indicated shock. Or maybe she was deeply pondering the prospects.

Ty used his hands: "You don't want the boy. You want to fly off somewhere and make our own babies."

She continued to stare at him, almost expressionless, her eyes distant.

"Please," Ty signed. "Tell me something."

Amy rose from the table and wandered about the room.

"Amy," Ty called aloud, knowing she could not hear him. He stayed at the table and lowered his head.

Chapter Fifty-Four

Rob was aware that his lunch hour would give him little time to show Jackie his surprise. So he rushed her through a quick hamburger lunch, then sped her through neighborhood streets. Before his car reached Juniper Lane, Jackie returned the conversation to Ty and Amy, the subjects of their lunch-time tete-a-tete.

"So, the truth is, you're not sure what's brewing."

"I don't think Ty knows."

"Is she with him?"

"I don't know. Yesterday she was back at her father's house. Ty took her there."

"Maybe she just needs time to think. Mark my word, in the long run love will win out."

"Who knows how she thinks. Maybe she's not bothered by what happened years ago. Maybe it's simply John Willow. After all, she didn't expect a teenage kid."

"Is her father still in the hospital?"

"He was yesterday."

"I'll make you a bet. She'll be back at Ty's before her old man goes home."

Rob turned the car onto Juniper Lane, whose naked trees allowed the pale November sun to splash noonday brightness on the neighborhood.

"So when is he picking up John Willow?" Jackie asked.

"Now that Judge Weinstein has ruled, it's just a matter of paperwork."

Rob parked the car at curbside in front of his and Jackie's house. But he stayed behind the wheel, grasped Jackie's arm before she could open the door, and demanded, "Wait!"

"What's wrong?"

"Yesterday we stood and looked at the finished living room."

Jackie laughed. "And our bedroom. And the library. And the guest room."

"Are you scoffing at my suspenseful method of presentation? You left with a smile on your face."

"Suspense or not, I would have smiled. Last night in bed, I just kept seeing the rooms. They're beautiful. I love the books on each side of the fireplace."

"Well, I brought you back for another surprise."

"You found her money!"

"Hell, no! Will you stop that?"

"Just kidding."

"Like hell you are."

"So, what's the surprise?"

"This is something I told you was impossible in November."

She looked at him with perplexed but mischievous eyes. "Okay. So, what are we waiting for?"

He kissed her on the check and tickled her ear with his tongue. "Race you to the door."

"Only if you let me win." Jackie was out of the car before Rob, but he beat her to the door. "You're a nasty man!"

"But I have to go first. You don't have a choice." Fumbling his key, he still managed to open the door in good speed. "Stop. Wait. Close your eyes."

"You're an idiot!"

"Come on, now. Close you eyes."

"I don't trust you. You're trying to scare me. I know you. Don't you dare scare me."

"Come on. Put your hands on my shoulders and follow me." Jackie obeyed, but after a few steps she lowered her hands to his waist and tickled him.

"Stop it! Don't spoil things. I worked like hell to give you this surprise."

"Okay. I'll be good. But let me keep my hands down here."

"Don't squeeze or tickle."

"Lead on, my Romeo!"

"Don't cheat."

"I'm not. I'm not."

Rob led Jackie through the living room and into the dining room. She kept a tight hold as he stepped carefully along the east wall toward the garden doors. Halfway into the room, he took her hands in his. "Now, turn this way. And stay. Stay, now."

"I'm not a dog, damn it!"

"Don't look."

"I know exactly where I am."

Rob opened the double doors

"I know what you're doing," Jackie said in a childish singsong chant. "I know what you're doing," she repeated with even greater melodic embellishments.

"Ta-daaaah!" Rob trumpeted while gesturing dramatically with his arm.

Jackie unlocked her eyes, which widened as her chin fell. "Oh, my!" She gazed in wonderment at the display before her—a garden brightened by the noonday sun. She saw swirls and twirls of pink, creamy white and deep red rosettes in startling arrangements in the beds of the walled garden. Large groupings of each color had been arranged to contrast with each other—broad white splashes between irregular patterns of red and pink. Each "bloom" was like a fully open rose cradled in gray-green cabbage leaves.

"The plant-breeders have given us cabbage that will never see its way into the soup kettle"

"Oh, my!" Jackie could say little else. She began to stroll on the garden walkways. Finally other words came: "It's just so beautiful. I can't believe it. It's... It's... It's breathtaking."

"You didn't know I was an artist, did you?"

"I've seen these in city gardens. But not like this. Not these shapes and clusters. It's like a painting. It's spectacular."

"I'll have to confess. Ty laid it out on paper for me. I followed the pattern."

"Oh, Rob. I love it. And I love you."

"I didn't want to open the house to any wedding guests without the final touch—the garden."

"I thought we'd have to wait until spring." Jackie turned up one path, then down another. "I feel like I'm in a fairyland."

Rob remained just outside the double doors, smiling proudly as he watched his fiancée move about the garden.

"What's this?" she asked, pointing to a white cross between pink and red kale.

"That's where the iris will bloom in the spring when Aunt Marjorie's perennials break ground. That's where I found the skull."

Jackie stood still as she looked down at the cross. Her radiant smile slipped away. "Are we going to keep it here?"

"I don't know. I put it there for Ty. Do you mind?"

"No."

"I bought a small chest for the remains. It looks like a pirate's chest. I found it at Collins' Antique Shop."

"Is that what Ty wants?"

"I don't know. I took a chance. We'll see. Ty'll have to make arrangements with the Coroner's Office to get the skull and bones."

Jackie spun in a circle, and the brilliant colors brought back her smile. "Come here," Rob insisted. "Give me a hug."

"Why should I?"

"Don't I deserve it?"

Spinning again, she took in another overall look at the garden, then stood still, grinned comically at Rob, and marched toward him. "Will these cabbagey things keep till after our honeymoon?"

"Absolutely. They should last far beyond the first snow. Maybe all winter."

Jackie wrapped her arms around Rob and whispered into his ear: "You're something, you know it? You really are something. Think of what you've done—not only with this house, but for Ty. You're really very special. I'm mighty glad I'm marrying you." Suddenly, she shoved him away. "But the wedding's blowing my mind."

"Why's that?"

"It's not the ceremony itself. It's all the other things."

"Like the fat lady singing 'Bluebird'?"

"And maybe you and your father meeting after all these years.

LEE CARL

And that uncle of yours meeting up with your mother. And my mother sticking up her nose at strange deviations from the norm. And then there's your best man, Ty, whose going through some sort of metamorphosis. Not to mention your crazy ushers, Smitty and Skinny-dip, putting pebbles in our hubcaps, tying our clothes in knots, and... and... and doing whatever else you idiots do to each other at weddings."

"You love it all, and you know it," Rob said as he grabbed her. He kissed her neck, ear, cheek and lips, then picked her up and carried her into the house.

Chapter Fifty-Five

The day was cool and gray. Anxiety increased within Ty as he turned his van onto Pine Lane in Maywood. He drove slowly, as if fearful of the last 100 yards. The van coasted to a slow stop in front of the Oswald house where Ty's uneasiness grew to alarm. A "For Sale" sign projected from the lawn, and all blinds were drawn in the windows.

Petrified by the sight, Ty stayed behind the wheel as his chest thumped and cold sweat dampened his undershirt. The idea that the Oswalds had taken Johnny and run with him was ridiculous, he told himself again and again, but the thought wouldn't go away. "Don't be an ass, Ty Scott," he mumbled to himself. "They don't give a damn about the kid." Suddenly aware that he had spoken aloud, Ty tightened his lips, released his iron-fast grip on the steering wheel, opened the door and caught his foot and tripped as he got out of the van. After slamming the door, he took a few steps and then stood by the curb and stared at the sign. Within seconds he shook off the heavy weights that seemed to hold his feet and hurried up the walkway to the front door where he pushed the bell button and knocked.

No one answered.

Ty knocked again, harder. He fidgeted, then pushed the button repeatedly. Spinning about, he dashed down the steps, turned, backed up slowly, and scanned the house, looking from window to window. A moment later he charged up the steps as if attacking San Juan Hill and swung the heavy knocker with untamed force. Frustrated, he dropped his hands to his sides and stepped back.

Today was to be so special. Over and over in his mind he had
rehearsed his words. He had awakened early after a restless night,
and had lain in bed thinking of all kinds of things that he wanted to
tell John Willow—about father-son hikes in the woods, fishing
together, sharing chores, building model airplanes, throwing
Frisbees, eating ice cream cones, reading books, growing tomatoes,
helping friends, doing homework, going to the movies, eating hot
dogs at a Phillies baseball game, and scores more.

"Hey, mister," came a voice from across Pine Lane.

Ty spun around and saw his son standing on the curb with a
suitcase at each side. After two deep breaths, he attempted to
calm his nerves, then hurried down the walkway as the boy
crossed the street.

"Hello, there," Ty said as he continued his effort to assuage his
anxiety. "What were you doing over there? What's going on, anyway?"

"I was waiting at the Mitchell's across the street. They said it
was okay."

Ty instinctively reached out to embrace the boy, who
immediately pulled back. Dropping his hands, Ty forced a quick
recovery and matter-of-factly said, "Come on. Let's go. Hop into
the van." Without giving Johnny a second glance, he opened the
door, slid behind the wheel, rolled down the window and waited as
the boy watched.

Finally Johnny strolled to the van, with a put-on nonchalance, and
asked, "So, what do I do with these?" He looked down at his suitcases.

"Put them in the back. The door's open."

* * *

Neither man nor boy spoke until long after the van started
speeding along the Interstate. About five miles out of Maywood, Ty
decided to take a chance.

"I figured your foster folks would be there to say goodbye."

"Nah."

"I see they put the house up for sale."

"They had a fight. She hit him with a lamp."

"Oh?"

Neither spoke for the next half mile. Then Johnny offered, "The big mirror came crashing down. It woke me up. They were screaming at each other. I got out of bed, and I saw her hit him. Blood ran down the side of his head."

Ty was well aware that he should allow the boy to reach out and open up on his own. So he held back, unsure of how far he should probe. But when the minutes moved on, and Johnny failed to continue, he finally asked, "Where are they now?"

"I don't know."

"Did they say goodbye to you?"

"Sort of. I guess."

Ty decided not to ask more questions about the Oswalds, figuring Johnny would offer details in time. Besides, he felt it was vital to explain himself, his apartment and Amy before they arrived home. He struggled for the right approach, then asked, "Did you get my letter?"

"Yeah."

"Then you know about my job. And about my apartment. Like I said, it's big as apartments go. But it's still just an apartment. It's not anything like the Oswald's house. The kitchen's small. But the two bedrooms are large. I've been using one as my workroom and art studio. We're going to turn that into your room. I've pushed all my easels and work projects and tools to one end, just until I find a place for them. I put my single bed in there for you and got myself a double. The only double I had was a couch that opened up in the living room. Anyway, now you'll have something to sleep on in your room until we decorate the place. I figure we'll do that together."

Johnny looked curiously at Ty.

"We'll pick out what you like in the way of furniture," Ty continued. "Together we can paint the walls, fix up the room, and add some special touches that you like."

Such ideas were foreign to the boy. He wanted to believe, but his defenses toughened his hide, as was so often the case when he felt vulnerable. "Oh, yeah? So how are you gonna paint your pictures and make stuff?"

"Oh, I've got enough else to do right now. Besides, I can always use the office in a pinch. In time we'll get a bigger place. We're going to need it."

Two ideas completely alien to Johnny—designing his own room and Ty's plans for a bigger home—whirled him into heavy thought. Ty sensed the deep reflection and understood the youngster's ambivalence. So he drove on in silence, keeping his eyes on the road.

After riding quietly for several miles, Johnny softly asked, "You mean I can pick out things for my room?"

"Of course."

"Do you think I could have a bed on top of a bed?"

"You mean bunk beds?"

"So that Freddie could stay over?"

"Of course. That's a great idea. You'll be making new friends, too, and might want to have them over. Bunk beds would be perfect."

Again Johnny's mind traveled. About 10 minutes later he said, "Do you mean you'd really move for..." His lips and tongue couldn't seem to form the word, but it finally popped out with a squeak: "me?"

"When a guy's family grows, sometimes he has to get a bigger place. So maybe next year we'll go house-hunting."

Johnny had never thought in terms of years. He looked at Ty and questioned, "A house?"

"Maybe."

"Because of me?"

"And Amy, I hope. And maybe Whiskers."

"Whiskers?"

"Maybe. Just hold tight. I'll tell you about that later, if and when..."

Johnny looked puzzled but bright-eyed.

Ty took a quick look at his son and smiled, then concentrated on the highway. He hoped his perceptions were true. It was much too soon to expect even the beginning of bonding, but he felt vibes that heartened him. Maybe, he thought, it was time to suggest they break bread together. "Are you hungry?" Late afternoon traffic thickened as the dinner-time rush began.

"Not really."

"I think the excitement stole your appetite. Maybe we'll wait until we reach home. What would you rather do—stop at McDonald's or cook up something together at home?"

"Let's go right to your apartment. I want to see it."

Ty corrected him: "*Our* apartment."

Johnny's lips parted, but he said nothing.

Again Ty glanced at his son. "It's our home."

After another stretch of thought, the teenager asked, "Are you going to marry the deaf lady?"

"You mean Amy? I'd like to."

"I don't know any deaf people."

"Well, maybe it's time you did."

"Will she be at your apartment?"

"No. Not tonight."

"Do you think she'll like me?"

"Once she gets to know you. I'm sure she will."

"What if she doesn't?"

"That's not even worth thinking about. Don't worry. I'm not going to send you back."

Johnny stiffened. "Maybe I won't want to stay."

"Well, that's up to you."

Edging toward the door, Johnny began reading billboard signs aloud to free his mind from other thoughts, to fill the air with words, to help control his emotions.

* * *

The Blackstone Animal Shelter was located between a plant nursery and a miniature golf course on a two-lane highway just off the Interstate. Ty slowed his van as he approached the flat, red-brick building, and turned it onto the gravel driveway that curved in front of the white double-doors. He had a long-time, special relationship with Nellie Blackstone, allowing him borrowing privileges for his humanitarian causes. Now he hoped that no permanent home had been found for his favorite canine playmate.

"We're almost home," Ty said while bringing the van to a halt. "But I just want to make this one stop before we get there. Wait here. I'll be right back."

Johnny watched Ty leave the van and walk toward the entrance. Minutes later he also left the van, only to remain nearby and kick gravel, first with one sneaker, then with the other. Growing more restless, he scuffed here and there about the driveway, then wandered to a naked sycamore tree near the plant nursery and began to peel loose pieces of bark from its mottled trunk. As he was about to pick up a crooked stick, he saw Ty exit the building with a bundle of fur in his arms. He straightened up, gazed intently, but stayed under the sycamore, seemingly afraid to move while trying to determine the truth of his vision.

Ty started toward the van, realized that Johnny was not there, glanced about, then smiled as he saw the boy under the sycamore. He walked briskly toward the tree. As the teenager's face came into clear focus, Ty saw an expression of hope and awe tempered by suspicion—a look that seemed to say: Please, don't do this if it's not true.

"This is Whiskers," Ty said as he neared the youth and read the messages in the wide orbs that were mirror images of his own eyes. The dog barked twice and wiggled as Ty placed him in Johnny's arms. "Hold him tightly. He's got a lot of energy."

Johnny was stiff at first, holding the dog awkwardly. But when Whiskers reached up and licked his face, he melted and cuddled the dog. Whiskers licked again and again, and Johnny rubbed his cheek against the fluffy, tail-wagging parcel of curly haired fur. After squeezing the pup almost too tightly, Johnny suddenly froze again, then quickly thrust the dog at Ty.

"Hey, it's okay," Ty insisted. "Really. He's yours."

The dog nearly fell to the ground, but Ty caught him and secured him in his arms as Johnny backed off. Several yards away, Johnny seemed immobilized as he stared at Ty with an expression of anger frozen into his face. Ty took a leash from his jacket pocket, snapped it onto Whiskers' collar, and lowered the dog to the ground. When he looked up he saw tears running down the boy's cheeks.

"I would never do anything to hurt you, John. Please believe that. Whiskers is a wonderful friend who needs a home. I might be a fool to bring both you and Whiskers to my apartment at the same time, but I made that decision the night you called from your window. He's yours. But you must take care of him. It's up to you to feed him and walk him." Ty realized that the hurt within Johnny cut deep because nearly all things given to him at one time or another had later been taken away. He also knew from Johnny's expression that the best course of action was to keep talking. "They tell me he's housebroken. I've only known him to make one mistake. He piddled in my van one night during a long ride, but I think that was just a slip. Anyway, when he makes mistakes, chews on the furniture or whatever, it'll be up to you to scold him. You must also share him once in awhile with the little old ladies at the Methodist Home. I take him there sometimes. He gives them so much joy."

Whiskers kept pulling on the leash, as if eager to run toward Johnny. Ty finally decided to take a chance and allow the dog to win the tug-of-war. When the dog gave a sudden, forceful yank, he let go of the strap, and Whiskers bolted toward Johnny.

Instinctively, the teenager fell to the ground and grabbed the frolicking pup. He lifted him into his arms, cradled him, hugged him, petted him. Moments later, he placed the dog on the ground, held onto the leash, and raced around the sycamore. Suddenly he stopped, reined in the dog, held the tether tightly, and looked at his new-found father. Ty could tell that the boy wanted to say something. But the words wouldn't come.

"Tell me later," Ty said. "We better get moving. We've got busy times ahead of us. Come on. Bring Whiskers."

Acting decisively, Ty walked directly to the van without looking back to see if Johnny followed. He could hear the boy and dog as they scuffed and scampered across the gravel. Seconds later he glanced and saw them approach as he reached for the handle on the back door of the van. His opening of that door halted the teenager, though Whiskers continued to pull. Ty saw "no" written all over Johnny's face.

"Okay, if you insist," Ty said, interpreting the signals. "You can hold him up front if you must. But you have to control him. I don't want to ram us into any telephone poles." He slammed the door as Johnny lifted Whiskers and aimed for the passenger-side.

"If you like dogs, mister, then how come you didn't already have one?" Johnny asked as they settled into their seats. Whiskers pressed his nose against the window.

"Because I lived alone," Ty responded as the tires launched pebbles that pelted the underside of the van. "Dogs take care, and it's not fair to keep them locked up all day. I had a terrier named

Bingo when I was a kid. Even had a rabbit, but Mom shipped him off to the zoo after he broke loose and ate the neighbor's flowers."

"I went to the zoo once."

"I know. The Philadelphia Zoo."

"How'd you know that?"

"My friend Rob is a bit of a bloodhound. You wrote to the Cuthberts about the zoo. That was a nice thing to do."

"The Cuthberts were okay. They were always having these picnics for me."

"Did Mr. Oswald take you to the zoo?"

"No." Johnny struggled with Whiskers as the dog squirmed and wrenched. "It was a school trip."

"I hope we don't see the day when baboons and elephants are only in zoos," Ty lectured. "The earth belongs to them, too." Smiling at himself, he wanted to give the boy a friendly squeeze, but held back. "You'd better get used to me and my causes. I'm kind of hung up on certain things."

Johnny sank into thought. After the van passed a half-dozen utility poles, he said, "You're different."

"How's that?"

"You're just different, that's all."

"From whom?"

"Anybody I know."

As Ty drove the van along residential streets in suburbia, Johnny sat quietly and kept a tight hold on Whiskers, who grew more restless as youngsters and dogs darted here and there.

"By the way, I help out with the kids' sandlot baseball teams," Ty offered. "Do you like to play ball?"

Johnny was slow to answer. "Do I have to?"

"Of course not." Ty pictured Johnny in his bright green soccer uniform, standing alone, away from the other Hornets. "Only if you want to."

* * *

Holding Whiskers, Johnny stood at the top of the small stairwell as Ty opened the door to his apartment. He stepped down carefully when Ty summoned him with a swing of the head. Inside, he remained near the door and surveyed the room before lowering the dog to the floor. Moving slowly, he examined almost everything, piece by piece. He stopped in front of the portrait of Amy, while Whiskers continued to run, scamper and prance, dragging his leash and sniffing at the furniture. Suddenly, the living room seemed small to Ty, who walked toward an Oriental screen that he had purchased to separate the dining area from the rest of the living room. He pushed the screen back a few inches before turning to watch the boy.

"Is this her?" Johnny asked.

"Yes, that's Amy."

"You paint it?"

"Yep."

"You paint all these pictures?" Johnny glanced about the room, then returned his attention to the portrait.

"Yes, I painted them."

"She looks like a girl."

"She was younger when I painted her. That's when I first met her. At a carnival."

"Was my mother prettier?"

Ty was taken aback. "Your mother was beautiful. Perhaps the most beautiful woman I ever saw."

Keeping his eyes on the portrait, Johnny asked, "Did you love my mother?"

Again Ty was jolted. "I can't really answer that, John—not without explaining a lot of things. Give me time, okay?"

"You mean you didn't love her, right? You just fucked her."

Ty restrained himself, though the effort was difficult. He could feel his blood rush, but he knew that the wrong reaction might sever the tenuous linkage. In quiet tones he said, "Watch yourself. Look, I'll be fair with you if you'll be fair with me. Okay? Like I said, I was only a kid when I knew your mother. We'll talk about it later."

Spinning away from the portrait, Johnny looked at Ty and asked, "So, where's my room?"

Ty knew he was still being tested. "It's over this way. But first, grab Whiskers, take off his leash, and hang it on the door hook inside the kitchen closet. And don't forget your suitcases. They're still in the van."

Johnny did not respond. He walked to one of the window plants, pulled off three leaves and let them fall to the floor, then turned and stared at Ty.

Internally, Ty fretted over the ups and downs of the bridge-building effort. But he told himself that he was stacking three blocks for every one that fell down, and that encouraged him to hold his ground. He stared back at Johnny without a flinch.

"You can't make up your mind about me, can you?" asked Ty, who suddenly decided he had made enough gains to risk a frank approach. "I know that I have to earn your trust. On the other hand, I don't deserve your displeasure—not yet, anyway. Not until the day I fail. So give me a break, damn it. Give me a chance."

Johnny looked down.

"The dog is yours," Ty continued. "So, take care of him."

The boy turned away from Ty, hesitated, then chased after Whiskers, who raced around the room in a game of catch-me-if-you-can. Johnny cornered the tail-wagging, wiggly bundle of fur where the wall met the Oriental screen. In fact, Ty had to hold the screen for fear it would tumble and crash into the dining table.

Johnny laughed as he lifted Whiskers. While the laughter was brief, it tugged at Ty, for it was the first chuckle of any sort he had heard from the boy. Johnny hugged Whiskers, unfastened the strap, and let the dog go. Jumping at the youngster, Whiskers obviously wanted to romp. "No! Down!" Johnny ordered, but Whiskers continued to frolic. "No! Down! Sit!" Whether or not he knew the commands, Whiskers decided to sit, his paws shaking nervously, his tail still wagging, his tongue hanging out, his sad eyes looking beseechingly at his new master. "Stay!" A slight smile remained on the boy's lips as he looked at Ty, who motioned toward the kitchen.

Johnny found his way, and Ty heard the kitchen closet open and close.

"The red light on your phone is blinking," said the teenager as he stood in the kitchen entranceway.

Ty walked to the hanging wall-unit and pushed the "play" button as Johnny stood by and listened.

"Hello, Mr. Scott. This is Dr. George Anderson. Miss Harrison has come to me regarding cochlea implants in both ears. I've talked with her about the success rate, and I've scheduled her into the hospital for mid-November. I know how this must please you, considering our conversations, but please be cautious. She said the operation was for you as well as for her. At her insistence, I agreed to call you. I sensed a deeper meaning. I think she's trying to tell you something else."

"Well, I'll be damned!" Ty said as the telephone recorder beep-beep-beeped. "And I thought she'd have to meet you first, Johnny."

"What do you mean?"

"I think Amy just came back to me."

Johnny looked puzzled. "Is she going to get her ears fixed?"

"I guess she's going to try. But she has to understand her motives, and so do I."

Johnny looked even more confused.

"Come on," Ty said. "Let's see your room." He recognized a touch of anguish in the boy's eyes, not unlike the signs he saw when Johnny gazed on Amy's portrait. "Come on. I thought you wanted to see your room."

Ty led Johnny into what was once his studio-workshop. The bed immediately held the youngster's eyes because of its bold, boyish, wide-striped, quilted, red, white and blue spread—a brilliant comforter that took attention away from Ty's collection of easels, canvases, frames, sawhorses and power tools that had been pushed to the far end of the room and were partially hidden by a bamboo divider screen.

"It'll have to do for a bit," Ty said. "When you decide what you want, we'll change things. I set it up this way so you'd at least have temporary quarters."

Johnny broke his steady stare and began to look around the room. He soon put his legs in motion and began to touch things. While running his fingers across the top of the chest of drawers, he examined an oil painting on the wall above—a portrait of a sad clown holding a blue balloon. He moved close to be certain that it was signed by "Ty Scott" before turning his eyes on a companion piece across the room, above the bed—the same clown, smiling and holding a red balloon.

"Maybe we should reverse them," Ty suggested, "so that when you wake up you'll see the smiling clown."

"What if I don't want them in here?"

"That's okay. It's up to you."

Johnny looked down at a military-style footlocker at the foot of the bed. He glanced at Ty as if asking permission to open it, then went directly to the locker and threw back the lid as if suddenly deciding that he didn't need permission. A bright red Frisbee, a pair of high-top sneakers, a microscope in a see-through box, a pair of sports socks rolled into a ball, a book on dinosaurs, a fielder's mitt and a baseball rested within the small trunk. Johnny said nothing at first, and Ty wondered whether the boy liked the gifts or resented them.

"You buy me these?" Johnny asked. He picked up the Frisbee, spun it on his index finger, and tossed it back into the footlocker.

"I took a chance on the sneakers. They may not fit. I know the Oswalds were able to buy you a lot of things. This room isn't the greatest." Suddenly Ty realized that he was sounding overly defensive.

Leaving the lid open, Johnny sat on the bed, moved up and down to get its feel, and rubbed his hands across the quilted bedspread. "It's nice," he said.

"The bed?"

"All of it. I want to keep the room just like it is. Except for the other bed. Up there." Johnny pointed toward the ceiling.

Though he didn't show it, Ty felt an enormous release that sent a shiver up his backbone. He held back the sigh that should have issued from his mouth. "May I sit on your bed?" he asked.

"Sure."

Ty sat beside Johnny.

"I like the clowns. I never knew anybody who could paint like that. And to think you're my..."

"Don't say it if it doesn't come easily."

"I'm sorry about what I said in the other room."

"That's okay. Maybe I understand it better than you do. We're trying to get to know each other, and Amy's in the way. In a sense, she's competition for you, even though you might not fully realize it. I mean, the situation is tough enough without three-way complications, right? But you have to know, Johnny, that my relationship with you is special. It's one of a kind. That doesn't mean I can't relate to someone else, but in a totally different way. We all have room for different loves and different relationships." After a deep breath, Ty went on: "Then there's something else you should think about. Amy expected only me in her life right now. So she's got to come to grips with you."

The boy said nothing.

Ty organized his thoughts, then continued: "But I think there's another factor here. You have to understand that my relationship with your mother belongs to one point in time, while my relationship with Amy belongs to another part of my life. I suspect that deep inside your brain one pretty lady is interfering with the other." The portrait of Marjorie flashed into Ty's mind's eye, but he quickly quelled his impulse to show it to Johnny.

"She was a whore, wasn't she?"

"What?"

"My mother. She was a whore."

"My God no! Whatever made you say such a thing? No, no, never. She was a very beautiful but lonely lady, and she wanted to keep you, but couldn't. Don't ever think of her in that way. Please, John. In time I'll tell you all about her."

The boy said nothing, but his eyes showed that his mind was at work. Suddenly he seemed to shake off the heavy thoughts, as if needing to escape the pressure. He bounced again to test the mattress, looked about the room, sprang from the bed and headed for the door as he commanded, "You stay there."

After a few yips and yaps from the living room, Johnny reappeared with Whiskers in his arms. He went directly to the bed and sat next to his father as if putting together a three-unit family—on his bed, in his room.

Ty took another chance and placed his arm around his son. The teenager stiffened, but immediately gave in, softened and allowed Ty to pull him close.

"You may not realize this for a long time," Ty said, "but some of the lousy chapters in your life can be put to use. They'll help you understand other people and their problems."

"Like I know about Freddie?"

"Yeah, like you understand Freddie while others don't."

"He ran away from me when I said goodbye."

"Some guys have trouble with things like that. I guess he hated to see you go."

"But you said..."

"Yes, we'll invite him."

"Soon?"

"Well, we'll try. You want to talk about him?"

"He does bad things, but he really isn't bad. Like when he set a trash can on fire in Miss Wilson's class at school."

"Why do you think he did that?"

"That was the day his father burned his hand over the stove."

"His father did that?"

"Yeah."

"Then I guess setting the fire was his way of getting even—although with the wrong person. You see, when people are hurt and can't fight back, sometimes they take out their anger on others."

"We had these places we'd go. Now there's nobody to go with him. There was this old car in the dump. It was ours. We'd sit in it and pretend things. And we built our own fort out of tires down at the spillway. And we'd walk the tracks to the trestle and hang out."

"And the quarry?"

"Yeah. We'd go all the way down, and we'd do things. What's he going to do now?"

"Well, we're going to have to work things out. We're going to let him know he's welcome. Because he's your special friend." Ty squeezed his son, smiled warmly and deliberately changed the subject: "Hey, when do you celebrate your birthday? Rob and I tried to figure it out. We know it's around this time. Probably early this month."

"I don't care when it is."

"That doesn't answer my question."

"At the Oswalds I'd get a gift on November tenth. That's supposed to be when I was found at the hospital. Mrs. Cuthbert sometimes baked me a cake."

"Well, I think we can figure it out pretty close. Since I'm off from work tomorrow, maybe we should celebrate it then—that is, after we get you registered at school."

"School? Can't we wait?"

"I don't think so."

"Please?" Johnny entreated as Whiskers licked his face.

"I'll tell you what. Since we're declaring tomorrow your birthday, we'll put off school till the next day. But I have to work that day, so we'll have to hit the principal's office by eight-thirty. You'll have to get up early."

"That's okay."

"Tomorrow will be our day—together."

"What about Freddie?"

"We'll work out something as soon as we can. But let's make tomorrow special for us. Okay?"

"You don't have to buy me a gift."

"Why's that?"

Johnny pointed to the footlocker.

"But you're not adding things up right," Ty said with a facetious smile on his lips and a comical leer in his eyes. "Those things don't include your fourteenth birthday. If you add up the seven gifts in the footlocker, plus the footlocker itself, plus the bedspread, the two paintings of clowns, the chest of drawers, and the cactus in the window, the total comes to thirteen—for the thirteen birthdays I missed."

Johnny showed disbelief. His eyes widened and his chin fell.

"I've got to make up for fourteen absent years. Real fathers have debts that foster parents don't have. After all, if it weren't for me, you wouldn't be here. In a way, I'm responsible for what happened to you. But mark my word, I don't intend to spoil you. Be aware that you have to carry your share of the load around here. It's a partnership, and we have to work at it. Okay?"

"You really are different."

"Okay?"

"Yeah. Okay."

Whiskers squirmed away from Johnny, pranced playfully on the bed, then pushed his nose between father and son.

Chapter Fifty-Six

Hours before Ty had picked up John Willow in Maywood, Freddie had watched Johnny clean out his school locker and fill a duffel bag. He had remained in the school long after others left, hiding in the boys' lavatory and going from stall to stall carving his initials into each toilet seat. Later, he had returned to Johnny's empty locker and used an indelible purple marker to write "FUCK" on the locker door.

"Hey you! What are you doing?"

The voice of the guard had sent Freddie running down the shiny, empty corridor toward the west exit.

Freddie had spent the rest of the afternoon up-river in the Maywood freight yards, returning home after dark, at about the time that his departed friend and Ty and Whiskers were sitting on the red, white and blue comforter in Johnny's new bedroom. As usual he hung his head as he walked up the well-worn steps of the small, crooked porch of the four-room, one-story, river-front house—a weather-damaged, wood-frame house that had once been painted yellow. Freddie had lived in no other house during his 14 years on earth, and to him it had always been a mottled gray house with yellow flecks and streaks. Its shutters were long gone, adding nakedness to its look of decay. Hesitating at the door, Freddie unbuttoned his soiled denim jacket, exposing the shark's mouth and teeth that he had drawn in bold strokes on his T-shirt. He removed the jacket and flung it over his right shoulder before grasping the doorknob and pushing.

Inside the house, Freddie immediately encountered body odor mixed with the smell of whiskey. Two liquor bottles projected from under a sagging armchair, one of two threadbare upholstered pieces in the dingy living room—the other being a tan couch with dark spots of grease from hair oil and blackened arms from years of rubbed-in grime. A television set with rabbit ears rested against the wall, supported by a frail, crooked, metal bookstand. The room contained little else, except for clothes. Earl Martin's dirty workshirt, trousers and soiled undershorts were strewn across the couch, and a woman's panties and bra clung to one of the tarnished arms.

Freddie threw his jacket onto the floor and walked to the open door of his father's bedroom. He stood there briefly, looking at the naked man and woman sprawled unconscious on the big brass bed that filled most of the room. His thin, pale-skinned, red-faced father took up most of the bed because he lay on his back in the middle of the sinking mattress, his arms and legs spread wide. Earl's few remaining strands of unkempt red hair formed straggly wisps on the rumpled sheet under his shiny, balding head. The lumpish breasts and rolls of belly fat of Maria Gonzalez, part-timer at the Crossroads Diner truck stop on Rt. 14, were pushed up against the flowered wallpaper—yellow-stained paper that had peeled off the walls in two corners of the room.

Closing the door tightly, Freddie hurried to his room, a 10-by-12 foot space that held a mattress and a brown-painted chest flecked with green at the chip marks. Wallpaper had been stripped from the room, but the walls had never been painted or re-papered. Clothes were heaped in a corner, and an uncovered pillow shared the mattress with a stained, musty-smelling sheet. Freddie bared his underdeveloped chest by literally ripping off his T-shirt. It was as if he stripped himself of manliness or his macho image by destroying the shark's mouth and teeth, for immediately after he threw the torn shirt to the floor he began to cry. Tossing himself onto the mattress, he turned face down and shed tears into his pillow as he muffled uncontrollable crying. After turning over and gasping for air, he began to sob and heave violently. He twisted his body one way, then another as brokenhearted cries bellowed from his bosom. His surging sobs turned to moans and whimpers moments before his body began to shake and shiver.

In time, tears no longer came, but Freddie could not lift himself from his mattress. He lay there for hours, his mind groping aimlessly, hopelessly.

Sleep was but a partial escape, for his dreams brought a seemingly endless struggle to climb out of the Kettleback quarry. With each effort, rocks and earth gave way, and he slipped to the bottom. As dreams so often do, his nightmare shifted and changed. The quarry became a black abyss and then a whirlpool that sucked him down. Deep in the vortex a dark figure moved around and around. It was a distorted image of Johnny, his face elongated, his body stretched out as it was pulled by the force of the whirling blackness. Each time Freddie reached for Johnny, the force pulled them apart. In time the vortex closed in on Johnny and swallowed him up. Freddie awoke with a jolt. As the throbbing within his body subsided, he was returned to the painful thoughts of reality.

Freddie rose early, despite little sleep. Still in yesterday's jeans and Johnny's sneakers, he didn't wash or brush before retrieving his jacket from the living room floor, slipping it over his naked torso, and racing out of the house into the quiet 5:30 dawn. Suddenly aware of the pressure of urine, he unzipped and peed on the porch, brazenly facing the street.

* * *

The orange sun had lifted itself only slightly above the eastern horizon by the time Freddie saw the gnarled, vine-covered trees scattered here and there at the quarry's edge. Having shed all leaves, the vines resembled thickly entwined nets or giant cobwebs enveloping odd-shaped forms. Freddie followed the long shadow of his frail body—a shadow that rippled across the railroad ties as he walked between the rails, now and then tripping on the splintered wood. He slowed his pace as he neared the quarry, stopped briefly at the precipice and surveyed the scene, then continued onto the trestle. Sunlight had yet to move more than a few yards down the west wall of the rocky orifice that had ingested Johnny and tried to swallow Freddie in his dreams. As the bright morning sky constricted the pupils of the freckle-faced boy, the bottom of the pit appeared darker and deeper. The streaks of brightness and darkness struck his eyes repeatedly as he increased his speed, inducing a hypnotic effect. Freddie slowed, stopped, caught his balance, and sat on the edge of the trestle, dangling his feet into the chasm.

Defeated by his thoughts, Freddie pushed himself to his feet and began walking the ties again. Within seconds, he stepped onto a rail, extended his arms to gain equilibrium, and placed foot after foot, moving slowly to the trestle's halfway point at the deepest part of the quarry's north end. Keeping his balance, he stopped walking, but continued to sway left and right. He looked down, stepped from the rail and stood on the edge of the trestle, wavering as he scanned the depths. Minute gave way to minute, and still he stood on the brink, his eyes probing the darkness below. Sunlight had crept far deeper into the quarry by the time he stepped back and castigated himself aloud as his eyes moistened: "You suck, man. You really suck."

Angered by his ambivalence and fears, Freddie held his skinny frame erect as tears wet his freckled cheeks. Within moments, he stepped to the edge again, teetered, and moved backward, this time tripping over the rail and falling across the ties, bruising his left arm, leg and back. He scraped open his elbow. Blood trickled down his forearm. Gritting his teeth, he cursed Johnny and pushed himself to his feet and began searching for something. "Fuck you, Johnny," he muttered between sobs. "Why did you go away?" He looked east and west and circled about. Finally, he remembered the vines on the gnarled trees at the quarry's edge. He focused on the odd shapes on the eastern rim—shapes silhouetted against the brightly glowing sky and appearing even more grotesque because of his morbid mood. Skipping some of the ties, he limped while racing toward the bent and twisted trees that seemed veiled in fishnets.

The sun's rays had reached the tops of large boulders and jagged outcroppings on the quarry floor beneath the west rim by the time Freddie approached the nearest tree—a stunted hickory whose roots gripped the rocky lip of the chasm. A thick web of naked vines strangled and draped the half-dead, deformed tree. When Freddie stepped from tawny, matted, weather-beaten vegetation onto craggy terrain, he struggled to catch his breath, fell to his knees, pushed his hair from his forehead and looked up at the shrouded hickory. After a few deep breaths, he lifted one knee, paused, then pushed himself up and forward. He reached out and seized a thick vine and used it to pull his way toward the tree. Spreading the twines and ripping apart the tangles, Freddie shoved his way through the canopy of vines into open space around the tree's trunk and exposed roots, some of which reached out into the abyss as if grabbing for air. He lifted his eyes, and though his vision was blurred by tears, he searched for a long, free-hanging vine, not too thick, not too thin. As he slowly turned his head, he reached into his pocket for his penknife.

Chapter Fifty-Seven

The aroma of coffee and bacon filled the apartment. Eggs sizzled and crackled in a frying pan as Ty dashed back and forth between the kitchen and his dining area. Johnny had helped with the toast, but was now moving about the living room, closely re-examining his father's artwork.

"Who are these kids?" Johnny asked while Ty poured orange juice at the dining table. He stood close to the painting of the tattered slum children sitting in a row on a curb.

"Oh, they represent a lot of kids—faces I've seen here and there," Ty answered while dashing to the kitchen for the eggs.

Johnny moved to the steel-framed graphics on the opposite wall. Tipping his head one way, then the other, he seemed amused by the pinwheel designs. "Awesome, man. Awesome."

"Come on. I think we're ready." Ty set platters of eggs and bacon on the table. "I hope you like a big breakfast."

Johnny stepped around the Oriental screen. "Wow!" He stood and looked at the heavily burdened table, especially the heap of Danish pastry and cinnamon buns at center.

Hovering over the table-of-plenty, Ty began to chuckle. Within seconds his laughter grew to a hearty cackle that turned Johnny's smile into a giggle. "You think I overdid it?"

"Maybe we should give some to Whiskers. Shall I get him?"

"No, let Whiskers stay in your room. This is people food." Ty seated himself and tasted his orange juice. "Come on. Dig in."

* * *

The eggs and bacon were long gone, and Ty was drinking his third cup of coffee. Johnny's gulping had slowed to nibbling on his third piece of pastry. He sipped milk to wash it down.

"This is your day, Johnny," Ty said. "It's our day together. I really want it to be that way. But you'll have to excuse me for a couple hours first. There's something I have to do."

Johnny dropped his bun and looked at Ty.

"I have to see Amy," Ty continued. "I can't talk to her on the phone because she's deaf. So I have to go over there. I'll get back as soon as I can. And then the day will be ours. Okay?"

Johnny shrugged his shoulders. "I guess."

"You take Whiskers for a walk, and then give him some milk. Later we'll pick up some dog food. And I guess we should get him a bed. He can't always sleep on your bed like last night."

"Why not?"

"Don't you think he should have a bed of his own?"

"He likes my bed. You said he could sleep with me."

"Well, he can. But don't you want to give him a choice? Like I'm giving you?"

"What do you mean?"

"You want upper and lower bunks, don't you? I said okay. In fact, we'll pick them out today if you like."

"Does that mean Freddie can come this weekend?"

"Slow down. We'll invite Freddie, but not this weekend."

"Next weekend?"

"Maybe. Let's see how things go. Okay?"

Johnny toyed with a piece of his bun. "Could we give Freddie a birthday, too?"

Ty tried to read the boy's pleading expression. "What are you asking?"

"He never got anything for his birthday, even though he's got a real father."

Ty felt his throat tighten as he recognized compassion in Johnny's eyes. He smiled at his son. "Sure. We'll do something for Freddie. Don't you fret about that."

Johnny's eyes brightened. He pushed his chair back and said, "I'm gonna get Whiskers."

"Wait a minute. Since the rest of the day is going to be fun, let's get some serious stuff out of the way first. Okay?"

The boy's smile faded.

"I took two days off to be with you. Tomorrow I have to work. Like we agreed, I'm taking you to school early to get you registered. Now, when you come home on the school bus, Amy might be here. And I want you two to get to know each other. Whether she's here or not, you call me at the office so I know you're home. Okay?"

Johnny began playing with the bun again.

"I can't get home early because I have to testify at a late afternoon inquest."

"What's an inquest?"

"A coroner's hearing. You know what a coroner is, don't you?"

"He stores dead people in big filing cabinets."

"Well, he investigates causes of death."

"Yeah, like murder."

"That's right. Now, hold on to your seat and listen. I promised myself that you and I would have an honest and open relationship. I can't expect you to be fair and truthful with me, unless I'm that way with you. We can get to know one another better if we understand each other and ourselves. So, I want you to know who you are. And who I am."

"Did you murder somebody?"

Ty laughed. "No, no. This inquest is simply to judge the death of an infant born about fourteen years ago."

Johnny's eyes urged Ty to continue.

"It seems you were born a twin, John. We believe the other baby was a boy, just like you. He probably died at birth or shortly thereafter. We'll get a full forensic report tomorrow. You know, the kind of stuff Quincy always did on television."

The young teenager sat motionless, a stunned expression on his face.

"Are you with me?" Ty asked.

"I'm a twin? I had a brother?"

"That's why we were able to find you. Or I should say that's how Rob located you after he dug up the baby's bones in your mother's garden. Thank God for your twin." The look in Ty's eyes was a radiant mix of gratitude and hope. "Otherwise you wouldn't have come into my life."

"I don't understand."

"Well, let me explain..."

Chapter Fifty-Eight

Redrock Road was bleak but for on-again, off-again sunlight. Gone was the summertime foliage that had concealed a few rusty cars. Dry weed stalks and naked sumac projected from the roadside gullies. The Harrison house was in clear view long before Ty turned his van onto the lengthy, dirt, deep-furrowed driveway.

Bouncing and slipping in and out of ruts, the van was not yet halfway up the drive when Amy opened the front door of the house, dashed across the porch and leaped from the top step. She kept running toward Ty, her white warm-up suit reflecting the sunlight that streamed between fast-moving clouds. This was a morning of quick changes from dark to bright as fleecy puffs raced across a blue sky.

Amy ran directly toward the van. Facing her head-on, Ty suddenly braked without clutching and stalled the engine. He reached across the seat and opened the passenger-side door. Amy jumped into the van and threw her arms around him. She began touching and feeling him as a blind person might, not as a deaf person. After placing her hands on his cheeks, she moved them to his ears and neck, then ran her fingers across his forehead and down his nose. She kissed him forcefully on the lips while squeezing him with her arms, revealing her hunger to again experience what she had never tasted before Ty. In response, he held tightly and could feel the beat of her heart. Rubbing his nose across her cheek, he moved his lips to her neck and kissed again and again. He pushed his hands up under her soft, loose-fitting top and fondled her firm breasts. Seemingly desperate in their attacks on each other, Ty and Amy kept on touching and feeling with abandon.

Time passed, and still the fleecy clouds sped across the sky.

"I love you. I do, I do, I really do," Ty whispered rhythmically to the beat of his pulses, wishing that Amy could hear him. As he slipped his buttocks across the seat and lowered his torso, she pushed him down, forcing his shoulders below the window and pressing his head into the corner where the seat met the door. Continuing to surrender to impulses without restraint, Ty struggled to wrap his legs around her, all the time knowing they should go to the back of the van, but unable to pause during the feverish onslaught. Amy felt his body quake, his legs shake, his muscles quiver. A sudden spasm ended in a shudder, then total release, and Ty collapsed, falling limp. He looked into her eyes and wondered if she understood what had happened. Notwithstanding her deafness, he spoke aloud, "I'm sorry." She continued to kiss him with passion. Then, realizing his depletion, she stopped and lifted her head and gazed into his eyes. He shrugged his shoulders and gave a "couldn't-help-it" grimace. She pulled back, gently pushed his hair from his forehead, smiled and pecked a kiss on the tip of his nose. She was trying to tell him she understood. His problem now was a wet and sticky wad in his jockey shorts.

Amy sat up, and Ty slowly lifted himself, revealing discomfort as he moved to a sitting position behind the wheel. Using sign language, he tried to explain apologetically that not since his youth had he ever finished-off in his pants. He then loosened his belt and reached for his handkerchief.

* * *

Upper wind currents changed as Ty and Amy sat holding hands and leaning on one another, and the clouds dispersed toward the south. In time, Ty broke his hold and used his hands to acknowledge that they were obviously "a bit anxious" to see each other.

Amy grinned, then grew serious as she signed, "Tell me about the boy."

Explaining Johnny as a "wonderful son" who was "trying to adjust," Ty was stymied by his inability to make signs. He nodded his head, smiled crazily and whirled his hands in an effort to transmit the impression of happiness and confusion. "You'll like him," he signed. Then he struggled to explain that he wanted her to "meet the boy tomorrow."

Amy tried to hide her apprehension, but Ty was perceptive.

"He'll like you," Ty signed.

Shaking off the thoughts, Amy suddenly showed elation, grabbed Ty's hands, pushed them together and lowered them to his lap. Then she signed, "I know the doctor called you. Soon you'll be able to talk to me with spoken words."

Ty understood just enough to grasp her meaning. He hunted for a piece of paper in the glove compartment, found an auto-repair bill and a red felt-marker, and quickly scrawled, "I know I pushed you at first. But this is now. You must understand that it doesn't matter to me. If anything should happen to you I would never forgive myself."

"Don't worry," she signed. "I'm doing it for myself. I don't live in a deaf world; I live in your world. So I'm giving up nothing." She took the bill and marker from him and wrote, "The operation cannot hurt my ears, because I'm already deaf."

"But I don't want it to hurt any part of you," Ty said aloud, hoping that his eyes told the message. He pulled her into his arms and held her tightly. As the passing seconds flashed "hospital" into his mind, he thought of Sam Harrison and chastised himself for not having asked about him. Though he hated to broach the subject, he knew he must. Gently, he pushed Amy from his chest, then signed, "How is your father? When will he leave the hospital?"

Amy pointed to the house.

At first, Ty failed to grasp her meaning. Then suddenly he jumped and muttered, "Goddamn, you better be kidding!" He could not believe that they had spent passion on the front seat of his van directly in front of her father.

"Don't worry," Amy signed, somewhat amused by his expression of shock. "He's resting in bed."

Again and again Ty used the signal for "window."

"Don't worry. It's okay."

"Sure, sure," he mumbled to himself. "It's okay. It's okay." His on-going fear that Harrison would harm Amy instantly doubled. He tossed a mixture of signs at her in an effort to suggest that he take her with him now.

"No. I have to prepare my goodbye."

Again Ty twitched. And again his fear increased. But with Johnny waiting, he had no time to argue the point. He kissed Amy's left cheek, then squeezed a few more words on the back of the auto-repair bill: "Forgive me for the unromantic ending to our amorous reunion. I suppose if you can accept me when I'm so graceless, you must really love me."

She kissed him on the lips.

Chapter Fifty-Nine

The white, red-trimmed ice-cream parlor was a popular place that drew long lines of youngsters each day, especially after the final school bell. Its white bentwood chairs and round tables glistened underneath overhead fans with lily-shaped lighting fixtures. High-gloss cutouts of red tulips decorated the walls.

Ty and Johnny sat at one of the small tables enjoying maple walnut sundaes. The after-school crowd had yet to arrive, but a few patrons busied themselves spooning ice cream while three white-clad waitresses wearing red aprons relaxed and chatted with each other as they awaited the mid-afternoon invasion.

"Do you know what they are?" Ty asked, nodding toward the wall. He was obviously trying to keep the conversation going.

Johnny finished chewing a nut. "What?"

"Those cutouts."

"Tulips."

"Hey, you do know something about flowers."

"Not much. You go for that kinda stuff, don't you?"

"So, you've noticed my plants."

"Who wouldn't," Johnny slurred while eating and talking at the same time. "Can't very well miss 'em."

"Nature turns me on. Next summer, I hope we can hike into the fields and woods. Lots of things out there I'd like to show you."

"Freddie and I hike. We do it all the time."

"That's good. But maybe I can explain some things you haven't noticed."

"Like what?"

"Oh, some crazy tree-fungi, sassafras root, all sorts of mushrooms, skunk cabbage, tree toads, puffballs."

Johnny finished his sundae and gave his father a cryptic stare. "What's a puffball?"

"Oh, it's a fungus ball that gives off a cloud of spores when you step on it." Ty spooned the last of his sundae, then felt the urge to educate: "There's a balance in nature, you know. One creature eats another, then that one eats a plant, and they all change in time as the fittest survive. Of course man interferes and messes up the natural balance."

"You really are different."

"What do you mean?"

"You talk about things that other people don't talk about. It's kinda weird."

"Oh? And just how many *'other people'* do you know?"

The boy's only answer was a quizzical expression.

"You think maybe you've got yourself a goofy father, right?"

A slight smile turned Johnny's lips, but it faded quickly as a frown lowered his brows. "You into some kind of religion?"

"What do you mean?"

"Like church and stuff? The Cuthberts—they took me to this Baptist church. The Oswalds—they didn't go to any church."

"Well, I figure if there's a God out there somewhere, he's more interested in how we live than in how we worship. It seems to me He'd want everybody to help each other and take care of the earth, rather than fret over rituals and rites."

Again deep thought revealed itself on the boy's countenance. His active mind silenced him for many a moment. After parting his lips twice, he said, "This teacher at school—she said we should start thinking about what we want to be. I don't know what I want to be."

"That's okay, especially at your age. Follow the twists and turns and see where they lead. My motto is, 'Taste more, see more, feel more.' Some people are so set on some great thing they expect to achieve that they let the days pass without making the most of each." Ty was suddenly aware that he was sermonizing. He ended the lecture quickly: "I wonder how many people die without ever having seen a puffball?"

"Then why don't you tell me more about my mother? You don't like to talk about her, do you?"

Ty was taken aback. "I don't get the connection."

"You said I'm supposed to find out things, go after stuff. You know."

"I said we should make the most of each day."

"So, today I want to find out about her."

"Johnny, my promise is good. So help me, I'll tell you. But that has to come when I'm able to explain, and when you're able to understand."

Ty pondered the thought. After moment gave way to moment, he said, "Think of her as a beautiful butterfly caught in a web that lost its spider. She can't get out, but she needs a taste of life. She takes what she shouldn't have, at least by society's standards. So..." Ty cut himself off. He silently studied Johnny's troubled expression. Then he enlivened his mood and brightened his tone as he said, "That's your first lesson. It gives you something to think about. We'll build on it later, when we can. Okay? Now, you tell me what movie we're going to see tonight. It's got to be an early show. Remember, you have school tomorrow."

"What about the bunks? So Freddie can come?"

"That's next. Come on." Ty pushed back his chair and stood. "Then we have to stop home so you can feed Whiskers and give him his walk."

Chapter Sixty

Amy had sneaked out of the house with her heavy suitcases and slipped them under the front porch shortly after sunrise. She had returned to her morning chores, wanting to keep busy until noon when Nellie Nettlebaum, the neighbor in whose house she had first met Dr. Anderson, was scheduled to pick her up and whisk her away. Though dressed in her best white blouse and gray tweed skirt, she continued her kitchen work, fussing more than usual over little things, such as lining up pots and pans and rearranging utensils again and again, right up until 11:45, the planned moment of confrontation with her father. She pulled on the strings of her old-fashioned apron—one that had belonged to her mother—and then folded it neatly and slipped it into a drawer under a timeworn but clean counter.

Without hesitation, Amy marched through the scantly furnished but immaculate dining and living rooms. The well-scrubbed interiors contrasted sharply with the exterior of the house, though they held worn furniture from the early days of her mother's marriage—furniture moved from house to house as Sam Harrison slipped from job to job. In addition to sagging armchairs, the rooms held pieces that Amy cherished because they had been special to her mother—pieces that she cleaned and polished, in the same manner as her mother, but almost too often.

Amy climbed the stairs to the second floor, not faltering one step until just before reaching the door to her father's bedroom. Tightening her jaw and lifting her chin, she stepped inside the room and stamped her foot on the floor to get his attention.

Sam sat near the window, rocking in a green-painted porch rocker, wearing his burgundy-colored bathrobe. Amy broke his reverie. Turning his head, he looked blankly at her, then began to frown. "Why are you dressed like that?" he signed with quick hands and fingers.

"I'm going out," Amy responded with even faster movements. She had changed her clothes after serving breakfast and neatening his room—making his bed, arranging his brush and comb atop his old maple dresser, lifting his dark green window shade, dusting the framed photo of her mother that rested on the well-worn chest of drawers, and generally tidying up the austere room as she had done day after day for many years. "I want to make a new life for myself," she continued, her hands and fingers still in high-speed motion. "The doctor says you're well enough. Your concussion has mended and your ribs have healed."

"But my lungs are my cross to bear."

"They have been that way for a long time. I can't stay until God heals them. Or until you die, heaven forbid. But I'll always look in on you."

"You're leaving me. You're going to live with him."

"Yes. He will marry me. And the doctor will fix my ears."

"Honor thy father and thy mother."

"Don't start quoting Scripture. Anyway, I have honored you, always. And my mother is dead."

"Matthew, Chapter Fifteen, Verse Four. Honor thy father and mother, and he that curseth father or mother, let him die the death."

"Never have I cursed you."

"Genesis, Chapter Forty-Four, Verse Twenty-Two says that leaving the father would cause the father to die."

"Stop it. Please. Don't use the Bible to hurt me. Please."

Sam continued to rock back and forth, almost expressionless, staring at his daughter. "Numbers, Chapter Thirty, Verse Sixteen. These are the statutes, which the Lord commanded Moses, between a man and his wife, between the father and his daughter, being yet in her youth in her father's house."

"I'm not in my youth. And I don't intend to stay in my father's house." Amy stepped back into the hallway. "Don't do this. Please. I love you."

Sam turned his head and gazed out through the window. He continued to rock at an even pace. His steady back-and-forth movement added to Amy's frustration. She waited and watched for a moment, then fled, racing down the steps almost too fast, catching herself twice by grabbing the railing.

Heading for the front door, she stopped abruptly and glanced about the living room to see that everything was in order. She had cleaned and polished the aging furniture only hours before. Noticing a crooked antimacassar, she walked to an old armchair and straightened the embroidered tidy that had yellowed through the years. She placed her hand on it, and thought about her mother. Again she surveyed the room, her eyes resting on the pieces that her mother considered "good"—a kettledrum desk, a gate-leg table and a Hepplewhite chair, the last of what was once a set of four. After one last glance, she hurried to the door. Sensing movement, she quaked with sudden fright, spun and looked halfway up the stairs into her father's face. The expression on his face was disturbing to Amy, who was uncertain whether it showed anger, fear or pain. She reached behind her and grabbed the doorknob. Sam kept his right hand inside of his robe, as if hiding something. He walked down the steps and came toward her as she slowly turned the knob.

Outside the house, Nellie Nettlebaum waited in her old Ford coupe—a dull blue car spotted and streaked with rust. The small, pock-marked woman with the red, bulbous nose and spaghetti-mop hair had expected Amy to dash into her car before it had even come to a stop. She wiggled nervously and dug into her faded denim jacket for her cigarettes. Package in hand, she shook it twice, grabbed a cigarette with her lips and tossed the pack between the seats. "Come on, Deafy," she muttered. "Let's get the hell out of here. I don't need no trouble with your old man." Nellie had a soft spot for Amy, for she had watched her carry a heavy burden of chores. Amy's frequent walks to Nellie's house had been her chief contact with the outside world after her mother's death, her years in deaf school and her stay with her grandparents. She had often smuggled magazines back home and hid them under her bed. Over time she had learned that Nellie's rough hide covered tender guts—guts that were now churning as

Nellie waited in her car. Her cheek muscles twitched as she lit her cigarette with the car lighter.

Inside the house, Amy backed into the door as her father approached. He pulled the object from under his bathrobe, and Amy focused on it. He handed her the framed photograph of her mother—the one that had rested for years on his chest of drawers.

"No," Amy signed

Sam pushed the picture at her.

"No," she repeated. "It means so much to you."

He seized her hands and pressed them around the framed photo. Quickly backing away, he turned and walked toward the kitchen.

Chapter Sixty-One

Amy's frets about meeting Johnny had erased thoughts of Whiskers from her mind. Hence her total surprise after unlocking the door and entering Ty's apartment with Nellie and the suitcases. The dog kept jumping on both women, wagging his tail, yapping as he leaped, now and then racing about the room. At one point between jumps, Amy hugged Nellie and gave thanks with a look of warmth and a squeeze of the hands. Nellie winked, lifted Amy's chin, and waved as she left.

Alone with Whiskers, Amy tried to calm the dog by kneeling and petting him. But Whiskers wanted to play games. He pulled a knotted, red-striped sportsock out from under the couch and dropped it at Amy's feet. Ignoring it, Amy stepped to the couch, sat, glanced at her suitcases near the door, leaned back and breathed deeply as if trying to gather strength that had been depleted by emotion. But Whiskers was insistent. He picked up his play-time sock and again dropped it at Amy's feet. This time she leaned down and grabbed it, only to have Whiskers seize it and pull. The game was obviously tug-of-war. Amy played for awhile, then hid the sock under the sofa cushion.

Whiskers pranced, jumped and ran as Amy carried, pushed and pulled her suitcases through the living room and into Ty's bedroom.

As the time approached for Johnny's arrival home from school, Amy grew more and more nervous and annoyed with herself for allowing a young teenager to upset her to such an extent. She had tried hard to overcome her feelings of resentment, but they lingered, despite repetitive efforts to convince herself that she should be able to share Ty. Again she called herself selfish, "shouting" within her silence. But her dreams of a love nest always intruded. She told herself that she could have handled an infant far better than a full-grown boy just reaching puberty. Her thoughts skipped about: Was he a teen with bad habits that Ty hadn't seen? Would he hate her? Would he demand his father's time? What would her duties be? Would she be his mother?

Whiskers lay asleep under the coffee table. Amy paced back and forth, then went to the kitchen for paper. Quickly back in the living room, she placed pads and pencils on the coffee table and wrote "HELLO JOHNNY, I'M AMY" on one of the pads, ripped off the sheet and made a small hole in it, then buttoned the paper to her blouse. She was well aware that a meeting between a teenage boy and a deaf woman might be awkward under far less strained circumstances.

Ty's absence troubled Amy more and more as the minutes ticked away. He was the link, and he was missing. And that, Amy knew, was wrong.

She looked down at Whiskers and wondered if she should close him in one of the other rooms before Johnny's arrival. It took her but seconds to decide "no" in fear of Johnny's annoyance. Besides, she told herself, the dog might be a needed distraction.

As 3 p.m. neared, Amy became more anxious, kept moving about the room, and, at one point, checked the door to make certain it was unlocked. She scolded herself: Stop it, you fool! He's only a kid.

The door opened, and Amy turned to face a boy who appeared more youthful than expected—a blond, neatly dressed boy wearing gray corduroy pants and a blue-striped shirt and carrying a book under his arm. Though taken aback by his looks, she found enough poise to point to the greeting fastened to her blouse. Johnny seemed frozen in the doorway, but only for an instant thanks to Whisker's friskiness. Frolicking, jumping, wagging, the dog captured Johnny's attention, and the teenager was grateful for the diversion. He tossed the book aside, kneeled and romped with Whiskers, allowing the dog to lick his face. In time, he lifted his pet and held him firmly. Whiskers kept pushing his cold nose against the boy's neck and cheek.

Amy remained nearly motionless, watching the youngster and his dog.

Johnny finally forced himself to focus on her, realizing that he should greet her in some way. He nodded his head, not knowing how else to communicate.

Amy smiled weakly and again pointed to the words on the paper hanging from her button.

Smiling in return, Johnny immediately walked away. He carried Whiskers to his bedroom, leaving Amy feeling completely disheartened. Within an instant, however, the boy returned without his dog, and she realized that his intent had been simply to rid the room of frolic.

"Hello," he said, wondering if she understood.

Amy forced another smile. She was taken by Johnny's likeness to Ty. The resemblance nearly mesmerized her. She found the spellbinding similarity not only true of looks, but of actions—a tip of the head, a glance of the eyes, a push of the hair from the forehead. Right before her eyes she saw Ty as a teenager. Here was the image she had seen in photo after photo in Ty's albums from youth.

Suddenly, Johnny turned his back to her again. This time he hurried to the kitchen telephone to call Pure-Pup and report his arrival home. With a few fast words, he delivered the message to a secretary, deliberately avoiding conversation with his father for fear of too many questions about Amy.

Approaching Amy again, Johnny was ill-at-ease and she recognized his discomfort. He grew more and more uneasy as he stood awkwardly looking at her. She helped break the spell by moving toward him and pressing his hand. Pointing to the pads of paper, she urged him to follow her to the couch. Before moving, he watched her slide across the cushion and position herself, pencil in hand. Then, with little hesitation, he sat next to her.

Amy was the first to write: "It must feel good to find a father."

For some reason, Johnny could not respond. He toyed with his pencil, then finally wrote, "Do you have a real father?"

Small talk was gone before it started. Amy felt thrust into a serious exchange. She realized that Johnny was unaware of the pang caused by his question. Though she wanted to give a more insightful reply, she simply wrote, "Yes." Annoyed with herself, she reached for a thought, grabbed it, and penciled, "My mother died when I was a teenager. And it hurt so much. It still hurts."

Johnny looked at Amy with curious eyes. His empathic feelings unsettled him. When he wrote, he failed to follow his line of thought: "They think I had a twin who died."

"I know."

"Do you know a lot about me?"

"Not really. Just a few things that your father told me."

"Do you love him?"

"Yes. Very much."

"Are you going to marry him?"

"I hope so."

Johnny was troubled by his next thought. He could find no adequate way to phase it. He finally wrote, "Where do I fit in?"

Amy smiled, ruffled Johnny's hair, then wrote, "I think you and I have been fretting over the same things. Don't worry. We'll be a family."

"Does that mean Whiskers, too?"

"Of course it means Whiskers."

"You're okay."

"Thanks. So are you."

"What am I supposed to call you?"

"What's easy for you?"

"Can I call you Amy?"

"Sure."

Johnny glanced at Amy, then looked down. He started to write, but crossed out the words and began again. "Being deaf must suck. I'm sorry."

"Don't be sorry. I do very well."

"So why do you want to get your ears fixed?"

Amy smiled as she wrote, "Maybe I want to hear Whiskers bark."

Johnny laughed. "You want to be able to talk to him, don't you?"

"I think you mean your father. And the answer is yes. But I'd like to hear your voice, too." Amy flipped to the next page on the pad. "How did you and your father make out yesterday?"

"He talks about a lot of crazy things. He's different."

"We're all different."

Johnny thought about that. "Maybe. But if you don't know what a puffball is, you'd better find out before you marry him."

Amy shrugged her shoulders and drew a large question mark on her pad.

After tearing off his top sheet, Johnny began anew by changing the subject: "We bought bunk beds for my room, but they won't come until Tuesday. After that I can invite my friend Freddie to stay over. He's different, too. Nobody understands him. He seems bad, but he's not."

Amy thought she saw Ty's compassion within Johnny. Drawn to him, she wanted to reach out and touch his cheek, but she held back. Her affinity for him triggered a fuller response to his first question: "There are many kinds of real fathers. Yours is special. I like the word 'special' rather than 'different'. My father is hard to explain." She rolled her pencil between her finger and thumb as she sought the next word. "In his own way, he did what he thought was right by sheltering me. But your father opened a whole new world to me."

Johnny turned his head and kept his eyes on her.

Aware of his stare, Amy looked at him and read the mixed messages in the blue orbs so remindful of Ty's—messages of confusion and concern. The perplexity she could understand. But the concern astonished her. She sensed that he also felt affinity because she, too, was an imperfect person, like his friend Freddie, or perhaps like himself.

"Want to see my room?" Johnny wrote.

"Sure."

The teenager sprang up eagerly and started toward his room, only to stop, face the portrait of Amy, and grin broadly as he pointed to it. Then he spun about and bounced excitedly as he hurried, urging Amy on with quick motions as if about to show her the greatest of treasures.

* * *

It was nearly 6 p.m. by the time Ty pushed his way into the living room to be greeted by the aroma of cooked beef and onions and the laughter of Johnny who was huddled with Amy at the coffee table. She was writing and the boy was reading her words. They looked up at Ty with beaming faces.

"Well, look at this," Ty muttered to himself. Completely unsure of himself, he was well aware that he had taken a gamble in thrusting the two of them together without his presence. He stood there gaping, waiting for his nervousness to dissipate. But he was still highly keyed when he said, "Looks like you two are getting along just fine." The words seemed inadequate. And he was aware, of course, that they were heard only by Johnny, and that sent him hurrying toward them.

"Supper's ready!" Johnny exclaimed. "And I helped make it. Beef stew. I cut up the vegetables."

Ty loosened his necktie, stepped behind the couch, put one hand on Johnny's shoulder and the other on Amy's. He tried to communicate his gratitude with touches and squeezes as he glanced down at the pads of paper where notes were scrawled between games of tick-tack-toe. "Where's Whiskers?" he asked.

"Sleeping on my bed," Johnny said sheepishly.

"I don't think so. I think he's scratching at your door."

"Oh! I'll get him."

Ty pushed down on Johnny's shoulders and held him in his seat. "Wait. First, let me tell you about the hearing." Amy turned her head and scowled at Ty, letting him know that she disapproved of conversations that failed to include her, alerting him to a new problem. He immediately circled the couch, pushed himself between them as he sat, grabbed Johnny's pad and pencil, and wrote, "There's little doubt about your twin. The remains are being turned over to the Monroe Mortuary for cremation." Flipping to the next page, he continued, "County law says that even bare bones can't be turned back to the family unless they're being buried in a licensed cemetery. So, we'll get an urn of ashes." He stopped writing and spoke to Johnny: "We'll bury your twin brother in Rob's garden among your mother's iris plants." Amy looked puzzled, but Johnny retrieved his pad and translated the last sentence of Ty's message. But her perplexity remained, and Ty realized that all the holes in his past had not been filled to Amy's satisfaction.

Ty pushed the coffee table as he stood, walked across the room, faced Amy and searched her eyes. Her silent messages told him that he had to fill the remaining gaps, no matter how small.

Now Johnny looked confused.

Ty tried communicating to both at once by signing and speaking at the same time. He found it difficult, and signed almost every word twice as he spoke: "The beef stew smells good. Let's eat. After dinner, we'll have a three-way powwow and tie all the pieces together."

Chapter Sixty-Two

Saturday brought thin clouds, a hazy sun, chilly temperatures, and a rather pleased Ty Scott—pleased because his first, major, three-way discussion had not destroyed his budding family before it had a chance to blossom.

He dropped Amy and Johnny at a shopping center, chiefly to buy goodies for Whiskers, while he went to the office "just for an hour or two" to finish a layout to meet a printer's deadline. Two days off to get acquainted with Johnny had put him far behind schedule.

Rob and Jackie had decided to use Saturday morning to take his mother to their newly refurbished house—something Emily knew was coming ever since her reclusive sister had been carried out and deposited in that nursing home. Clowning like a couple of kids, Rob and Jackie raced up the walkway ahead of his mother. But then Jackie's curiosity about Ty, Amy and Johnny led to serious talk.

"Isn't he complicating things by moving Amy back into his apartment with Johnny there?" she asked.

"Probably," Rob answered while unlocking the door. "But you're talking about Ty, the miracle worker."

"What about the guilt she must feel? No one erases a strict background like that overnight."

"I think Ty's the one with the pangs of guilt." Rob pushed open the door and stepped inside.

"That makes no sense." She followed him into the house.

"Ty's trying to prove himself after a long hiatus. And Amy's trying to break loose. That's a volatile mixture. Very explosive. Boom, boom, boom."

As Emily approached the house with caution, Ty was in his Pure-Pup office surrounded by arts supplies and walls nearly covered by his graphic designs in all sizes and colors. Before opening his paste pot and turning on his computer, he decided to stretch out the morning newspaper on his drawing board for a quick look at the headlines. He smiled at a picture of a cow that had wandered into a suburban playground and was projecting her head from under the slope of a sliding board. Then a small, one-column headline in the lower left corner caught his eye. It read:

Maywood Youth Found Hanging From Trestle

A 14-year-old Maywood Middle School student was found dead yesterday, hanging from the spurtrack railroad trestle at Kettleback Quarry.

Police said Frederick P. Martin, son of Earl T. Martin of 19 Riverside Road, Maywood, apparently tied a vine around his neck, attached it to the tracks, and jumped off the trestle. His dangling body was sighted by three 17-year-old youths, who, according police, were drinking beer in the bottom of the abandoned quarry.

"Oh, my God, no," Ty muttered. He grasped the corners of his drawing board. "It can't be." He swung around in a circle, looked at the news story again, and struck the edge of the drawing board with his fist. His paste pot fell to the floor and rolled under his desk, and his pens and brushes flew in all directions. He reached for his telephone, but changed his mind. His next impulse was to drive home. But he remembered that Johnny was shopping with Amy. He had not planned to pick them up until noon. It was too early in the day for 'tyrob' talk at Marty's Tavern, but he knew he had to talk to Rob somewhere, somehow. Again he reached for the phone, and again he changed his mind. He stood gripping the handset as a heart-sickening feeling permeated his body. "Damn it! Why? It just isn't fair." His upper teeth were grinding against his lowers as he spun around and stepped on pens and brushes while hurrying to his office door.

Shortly after Ty raced down the hallway, Emily Worth Putnam stopped staring up into the tall trees in front of the Juniper Lane house and stepped toward the front door.

Rob stood just inside the doorway. "Come on, Mom. Wait till you see this living room."

"How the trees have grown," she said, still hesitating. Her ambivalence had been weighing heavily on her ever since her son had set the date. But she knew she had little choice but to visit the house before the wedding, certainly before Rob and Jackie returned from their honeymoon and began living as husband and wife. If she were to suffer any trauma, it would be better to do so now than at some future dinner party hosted by the newlyweds.

Rob stepped outside, took his mother's hand, tugged, and led her into the house. She stood next to her son and moved her head slowly as her eyes took in just about everything in the room. Immediately, she recognized a blending of the new and old. Gone was the clutter of trinkets, replaced by a few pieces of sculpture above the fireplace and books on shelving at each side, with Wedgwood blue plates on the top shelves. Gone was the flowered wallpaper, replaced by oyster white that created a contrast for artwork and other furnishings. Gone were the pink draperies, replaced by folds of gray-blue that matched the new carpeting. A few ornate vases remained, and the brass lamps still decked the piecrust tables.

"I must say it's beautiful," Emily said, "but it still brings back too many memories." She gazed at the portrait above the mantel. "I see you kept the oil painting of Mama."

"But we've decided it's yours if you want it, Mom. I didn't know Grandmother. To us it's a beautiful portrait. To you it must mean much more."

Jackie peeked in from the dining room and nodded in agreement.

Emily ignored the offer, looked at the stairway, and said, "I can see my brother running up and down those steps. He always took two steps at a time." Her eyes moistened. "I can see Marjorie, too. Standing on that landing. Crying. And Papa at the bottom, offering her another doll." Turning, Emily looked at the piano, but said nothing for many seconds. She shook her head slowly. "It was

Mama's. Not Marjorie's. 'Sweet Mystery of Life'—that's what Mama used to sing at the piano."

"Come on, Mom," Rob urged.

Emily walked to the dining room and stood with Jackie as she stared at the crystal chandelier that captured the morning sunlight and splashed the room with the colors of the rainbow. "When I was little, I never stopped marveling at that chandelier and the light and the sparkle and the colors on the walls."

"See how I waxed the table, Mom," said Rob, who stood behind his mother, peering over her shoulder. "And catch the shine on the tea service."

"If there's anything you want, please tell us," Jackie said.

Again Emily ignored the offer, ran her fingers across the table, touched the back of a chair, and said, "At dinner, I always sat across from Jack. We'd look at each other, wink, make faces. We knew what each other was thinking." Turning abruptly, she walked into the kitchen.

Emily barely recognized the newly refurbished kitchen, what with all new counter space and appliances. But she wasn't interested in the refrigerator or stove. She went directly to the back window, the one that overlooked a pair of sweet gum trees, under which no grass had ever grown, at least not in her memory. It was there on the hard earth that Jack and his boyhood friends had so often drawn a circle and played marbles. She envisioned Jack on one knee, propelling a marble by his thumb. Even the sound of agate striking agate echoed through her brain. But most vivid in her mind's ear was the boys' talk as it used to waft through the window screen on a hot summer afternoon. It was that give-and-take talk that had lured her to the window time and time again.

"Are you okay, Mom?" Rob asked after stepping into the kitchen. He suspected that his mother was crying, for he noticed barely perceptible shaking of her shoulders.

"He was such a wonderful big brother," Emily whispered. Her own words brought more tears. She tried to stifle her sobs, but to little avail. As Rob and Jackie stepped toward her and began to reach out, she wiped her eyes and turned to face them. "He should never have done what he did. I really wish you hadn't invited him to the wedding."

"Why?" Rob asked. "That makes no sense. He's made a new life for himself. He's successful. He has a family. You love him. You know you want to see him."

"I still wish you hadn't asked him," Emily said. She wiped her cheeks.

Rob frowned and shook his head. "But why?"

Staring directly at her son, Emily spoke forcefully: "Because he might not come."

Rob looked dumbfounded.

"Your mother means that if we hadn't asked in the first place," Jackie explained, "she wouldn't have built herself up for a possible letdown."

"I'm sorry," Emily said. "You must think I'm a silly old fool."

Loud knocking on the front door interrupted the kitchen conversation. Heavy and steady, the pounding continued without a break.

"I'll get it," Rob said. "Hold your pants on, damn it! I'm coming!" He hurried to the living room as Jackie used her handkerchief to wipe a smudge from Emily's cheek.

"My God, don't break the door down!" Rob shouted as he reached for the knob. He opened the door as quickly as possible and stared into Ty's intense eyes. "What the hell is it? Jesus, Ty!"

"You won't believe this."

"What is it?"

"Shit, man. Look at this." Ty thrust the newspaper at Rob and pointed to the Maywood story.

Rob read silently, then muttered, "Oh, God."

"How the hell am I going to tell Johnny? God help me. The kid's making big plans for his buddy's visit. I mean, why in God's name did this have to happen?"

"Take it easy, now. Come on in." Rob slipped the newspaper under his arm and backed into the living room. "Jackie's here. She's in the kitchen with my mother."

"How am I going to handle this, Rob?"

"You're asking me? Hey, you're the one who's practically a social worker."

"Well, I'm stumped this time." Ty closed the door and then

tossed himself onto the sofa. "He'll blame me for taking him away from Maywood. He'll blame himself for leaving. But he won't know exactly what he's feeling, except that it hurts so damn much. My God. It isn't fair. Hell, he may never trust me again."

"Hey, come on. You'll handle it. I know you."

"Damn you, Rob! Don't say that again, will you? Christ almighty."

Rob walked behind the sofa, put his hands on Ty's shoulders and squeezed. But he said nothing.

"This is so different," Ty said. "He's my son. And I'm the one who has to tell him. I'm the one who has to hurt him, to hurt him so very much."

Jackie stepped into the living room and was immediately aware of trouble. "What is it?" she asked while trying to interpret the grim expressions of Ty and Rob.

"Johnny's school chum killed himself," Rob said.

"Oh, no."

"Look, why don't you show Mom the upstairs while Ty and I toss things back and forth," Rob suggested. "Get her away from that kitchen window. I'll fill you in later."

Jackie backed away slowly. "I'm so sorry, Ty."

"I'm picking up Johnny and Amy at the shopping center at noon," Ty explained to Rob. "I've got to be ready. How about some heavy role-playing? Okay? I'll be the kid. Lay it on me, Rob. Hit me hard. I want to feel the impact."

Chapter Sixty-Three

Amy knew something was wrong from the moment Ty quickly ushered her and Johnny into his van at the shopping center. All the way home she felt his tension. Riding in the back, Johnny was unaware of his father's stress. He was busy sorting through the bags of toys and supplies for Whiskers.

After stopping his van in front of his apartment, Ty used his hands to tell Amy that he wanted time alone with the boy. He indicated the gravity of the situation and promised details later. With reluctance, Amy opened the door and stepped from the van. She moved slowly, keeping her eyes on Ty, who tightened his fingers around the steering wheel as his muscles tensed. Not until he heard the back of the van open did he break his hands free.

"Johnny!" he yelled as he saw the boy racing across the lawn, carrying the bags. "Come back!"

Stopping abruptly, Johnny looked at his father with an expression of puzzlement.

"Please, Johnny," Ty begged. "I have to talk with you. It's important. Come on. We'll take a ride."

Amy looked from father to son. She could feel the youngster's confusion and Ty's anxiety.

* * *

Johnny sensed disaster long before the van crossed the township line. His immediate fears were that he was to be separated from his new family and sent away somewhere. What else, he thought, could cause such behavior? For the third time he strained as he squawked, "What's wrong?" He soon became so seriously disturbed that the muscles in his neck bulged as he breathed. After houses gave way to fields and woods, he demanded. "Where are we going?"

"We'll park out here by Millview Ravine."

"Why?"

"We have to talk."

"Why couldn't we talk back there?"

"I don't know. I needed time to put it together. I had to think. I wanted a quiet place, I guess. Damn it, I don't know."

"Tell me what's wrong."

"I will. I'm sorry. Just give me a chance."

Slowing the van, Ty turned onto a dirt road and parked between fields of tall, dry grasses and weeds. Rolling slopes to the west led to the ravine and thick stands of naked trees and clusters of evergreens.

Ty put his hand on Johnny's shoulder, then ran his fingers through his hair. The boy shook off Ty's hand and pulled back. Looking directly into the young eyes, Ty struggled to speak softly but firmly: "Something terrible has happened. It's going to hurt you very much. I'm not going to ask you to be strong. Give in to your emotions and let come what may." He cleared his throat. "Your friend Freddie is dead. And I'm so, so sorry. I know you loved him." Ty could not keep his eyes dry.

Johnny gazed in disbelief, frowning, shaking his head, staring with anger. It was obvious to Ty that the boy was refusing to accept such a thought.

"Like I said, son. I'm sorry."

"Don't call me 'son'."

Ty reached out to touch Johnny, and the boy recoiled as he shouted, "You're lying to me!" His tone was defiant. "You don't want Freddie to visit me. You're lying!"

Searching for words, Ty shook his head slowly.

"Why would he be dead?" Johnny asked. "Youre lying. It doesn't make sense that he'd be dead. He's not dead!"

"I think you know I wouldn't lie to you." Ty paused to gather his thoughts. "Freddie must have been very sad. I guess he was just a very unhappy boy."

"What do you mean?"

"They found him at the quarry."

"My quarry? Freddie's and mine?"

Ty nodded slowly.

"He killed himself?"

"From the trestle."

"You're a fuckin' liar!" Johnny opened the van door and ran into the field.

"Wait!" Ty was quick to follow. He ran through the tall grasses and weeds and stopped when the boy turned to face him. They stood about 100 feet apart.

"Don't come near me! I don't want you! You're no good anyway. And my mother was a whore—an old dirty whore that you fucked. That's how I was made. Out of an old whore and you. Out of a stupid, dirty kid's fuckin' dick." Turning, Johnny began to run again. He zigzagged through the heavy, dead growth and headed for the ravine.

"Please, Johnny! Come back. Let's talk."

"I don't want to talk to you!" the teenager shouted as he ran faster and faster. "I never want to talk to you. I hate you!"

Ty stood dazed for a moment, then ran after Johnny, but the boy was a gazelle-on-a-tear—racing, leaping, turning, twisting. Soon the youngster was zigzagging among the trees on the rocky slopes of the ravine. When Ty reached the first of the tall, naked sycamores, he looked down and caught glimpses of the boy as he darted among the trees and leaped from one layer of rock to another. Deeper and deeper went Johnny until he was lost from Ty's view. The emotional pain within Ty brought him close to panic, but he kept going. A muscle spasm sent a sharp pang up his right leg. Stopping to catch his breath, he leaned against a tree, lifted his leg, shook it and pushed his foot against a chunk of granite. Again on the run, he dodged obstacle after obstacle on his way down into the ravine.

Later, in a partial clearing, he stood on an outcropping of rock halfway down. He could see the stream below as it meandered

LEE CARL

south and west and then disappeared into thickets of evergreens. In the far distance he saw glimpses of the water here and there as it flowed among the leafless trees of November. As a sharp pain in his chest subsided, he began to make his way down to where exposed roots of trees gripped the rocks. "Johnny!" he called. "Johnny! Johnny!" Again he stopped, pushed his back against a tree and slid to the ground. Because of the slope, he took hold of a young sassafras to secure himself, and began to plot strategy. Within minutes he was climbing back toward the fields and his van, trying his best to hurry by seizing trees and rocks and pulling himself up. At one point he looked back and thought he saw Johnny following the stream and vanishing into the pines and hemlocks.

* * *

Near a row of motel units shaded by oaks, Ty fidgeted nervously as he held onto the handset in a roadside telephone booth and waited impatiently for an answer.

"Hello."

"Rob, it's Ty. I really messed up. I mishandled it. Johnny exploded and took off. He raced down into Millview Ravine. I went after him, but I couldn't catch him. Will you help me?"

"What do you want me to do?"

"Together we might be able to cut him off."

"How? Where?"

"The ravine divides at Hammerhead. The south stream heads for Cloverbrook while the west stream flows to Harper's Run. I'll drive to Cloverbrook and wait at the falls where the path widens and ends at County Route Ninety-Nine. You head for Harper's Run. Park your car on Headwater Bridge and scan the narrows. If he comes out that way you won't miss him. He'll have to follow the path because of the steep rock wall on each side."

"What if he doubles back?"

"If he doubles back, he doubles back. He's not going to do that unless he changes his mind. And if he changes his mind... well, that's probably a good sign. But I figure he'll keep going. It's downhill all the way. Besides, he's damn upset. I don't know what he might do. I'm scared shitless."

"And if I find him?"

"I'm not sure. Just try to reason with him."

"I'm on my way."

Ty slammed the handset onto its hook and raced toward his van, which was parked on the highway near a utility pole. His fast-moving feet slipped and skidded on the roadside cinders and he fell toward the van, catching himself on the pole. He stayed there, holding on for a moment in an effort to shake off his turmoil, gain some control and organize his thinking. "Slow down, you idiot," he mumbled. He put his hands on the hood of his van and leaned his weight on them as he breathed deeply. Lifting his head, he gazed into the distance, across the stubble of harvested corn that stretched to a far-off cluster of pines, a white farmhouse, barns and silos. He straightened up, then struck the hood with his right fist and kicked the tire with his left foot.

* * *

Moistened by the spray of the waterfall, Ty paced back and forth on the broad, dirt walkway along the stream whose waters were directed into a concrete conduit under County Route 99. The van was parked far above him, on the road, up a steep embankment that was thick with autumn wind-burnt vetch, planted to halt erosion. The white water from the 50-foot falls churned until it neared the conduit where it turned muddy green and reflected sparks of sunlight that filtered through the heavy stand of trees.

Each time Ty spoke to himself his voice was swallowed by the sound of the cascading water. "I hope you're there, Rob. Come through for me, Buddy." He kept tightening his fingers around his thumbs, then pushing them through his hair. "Johnny, Johnny. Come on kid. Let me see you walk out of that mist. Please. Oh God, please."

Ty stopped pacing and looked up at the pathway along the falls—a steep path of stone steps that came down through the haze.

* * *

Rob stood on Headwater Bridge—an old, arched span of crisscrossed steel—and looked down on the Harper's Run narrows where the stream water rushed between steep banks of red-brown rock worn smooth through the ages. Dense thickets of November-bare vines and brush covered the earth on each side of the rushing stream. Leaning on and peering between the bridge girders, Rob scanned both sides of the narrows where pathways followed the turns of the watercourse, cutting through the autumn-dry vegetation after emerging from the distant woods.

Chapter Sixty-Four

Emily reached up and toyed with the chandelier prisms, causing them to tinkle. She glanced about the room and watched the colors dance on the walls. Then she sat across from Jackie and lifted her cup of coffee.

"Careful," Jackie warned. "It's hot."

Emily sipped with caution. "It's just fine. Thanks, Jackie."

"I wonder if they've found Johnny." Jackie's eyes wandered as she spoke. "Not yet, I suppose. The ravines are long and winding." She tasted her coffee.

"I haven't even met the boy yet, and he's run away. It's all so strange. So much has happened. This boy—he makes me think of my Rob when he was little, and how rebellious he could be sometimes." Emily drank coffee again. "I don't know why Rob wants to see his father. I guess even when you're mistreated you want to see for yourself."

"Mistreated?"

"Well, after all, the man never wrote to Rob, except for a few postcards years ago. I'll be very surprised if he shows up at the wedding."

"Oh, yes, 'The Bluebird of Happiness'."

"That's the most absurd thing... I mean, it's ludicrous. Believe me, Jackie, the title doesn't fit. Rob must be in his second childhood." She drank again. "And if that song is the only thing that Rob connects with his father... well then, there wasn't much there to begin with, was there?" Looking into Jackie's eyes, she recognized a touch of disapproval. "Oh, I'm sorry, Jackie. That was wrong of me. If Rob finds some connection with his father through that silly song, far be it from me to criticize."

Jackie finished her coffee and set her cup aside. "We all remember little things that bring back memories—a song, a sound, a smell, whatever. When I see a thistle I remember my father taking a thorn from my finger at a picnic. And that brings back a flood of memories—the fear I felt when I thought I was lost, even the ice cream that fell from my cone into the dirt. But mostly I remember his kindness as he wiped my tears and talked away my hurts."

Emily glanced around the room, but her eyes seemed to focus on nothing. "I have no conception of Rob's thoughts about his father. None whatsoever. I know that's wrong." She looked at Jackie. "Rob and I should have talked more." Looking down, she picked up her spoon and stirred her coffee.

"Are you okay?" Jackie asked.

"Yes. Forgive me when my mind wanders, but so much has happened so fast." She looked up and forced a smile. "Years ago I tried to close my mind to protect myself. All I did, of course, was keep the stew boiling inside. By doing that, I excluded Rob from things he had a right to know. And I hurt myself. But this house, your wedding, Marjorie's death, thoughts of Jack and so many other things have opened the flood gates. It's almost too much at once. Don't get me wrong. I'm not sorry."

Jackie looked at her wristwatch. "I wonder if they've found Johnny."

"Oh, dear God, I hope so. It seems wrong to be rambling on and on about all these other things while that poor boy is out there somewhere, hurting so much. But my mind—it just keeps hopping around."

"No." Jackie shook her head. "It's okay. We should talk. About whatever. We can't do anything else—except wait, of course." Keeping a steady focus on Emily, she said, "Have you thought much about the fact that you now have a nephew—a legacy from your sister?"

Emily's surprise approached shock. She had never thought of it that way. In fact, she had never thought of herself as being an aunt.

Suddenly conscious of her open mouth, she wet her lips and ran her fingers across them. "That seems odd. I guess—well, I simply hadn't put it together that way. Strange."

"The truth is, you're an aunt three times over, if you count Uncle Jack's children."

"Oh, my!"

"But it's Johnny who could become part of your life—if you let him. Because he's right here. That is, of course, if things go right today. And in days to come." Jackie offered a tight-lipped grin and rolling eyes to express the astonishment of it all. "Ty has no family left, so you and Rob are the boy's only relatives. Forgetting Uncle Jack, of course."

Emily tried to unscramble her thoughts. The only words that came were: "I do hope they find him soon. Maybe they already have."

Jackie watched Emily, whose eyes reflected deep thinking, but said nothing as moments passed uneasily.

"If you'll allow me," Emily began, "I'd like to explain something." With effort, she swallowed twice. "My husband was not faithful. Rob doesn't know. I'm not sure why I'm telling you." She studied Jackie's face, wondering about the future of her relationship with her soon-to-be daughter-in-law. "I suppose it seems more like woman-to-woman talk than mother-to-son talk. Anyway, I wanted you to know before the wedding. I just don't know what to expect if George shows up."

Jackie leaned forward. "But I thought you ran after your husband when he left. Isn't that why you deposited Rob with Marjorie?"

"Sometimes we hold onto those who hurt us. We adjust and put up with things. I was afraid to lose him, despite what he was. Besides, I blamed myself."

"You told Rob that you pushed his father away."

"He told you that? I'm surprised he would say that."

"Oh?"

"It's true, mind you. It's just that I didn't think he'd talk about it."

"Please, don't get me wrong. He said it with understanding."

"I did push George away. And I blamed myself for... How shall I put it?... for his... for his transgressions." Emily gave herself time to think by slowly drinking the rest of her coffee. "I told him to keep in touch with Rob. But he didn't. I don't particularly feel like seeing him, but it won't really brother me. I can't see why he would want to come. He hasn't cared all these years. Of course, he is Rob's father. Maybe he suddenly feels fatherly, or has pangs of guilt or something. Curiosity. It could be pure curiosity on his part. Anyway, I don't really care. It's different with Jack. I'm terrified when it comes to Jack." Emily stood and walked toward the living room. With her back to Jackie, she said, "The idea of seeing Jack again after all these years is so frightening, yet I'm scared to death that I won't see him. If he doesn't come I'll be devastated. But if he does, I'm not sure I'll be able to handle it."

"I suspect you'll find seeing him much easier than you think. His RSVP came. He says he's coming."

"Oh." Emily kept her back to Jackie. "Oh, my. Of course, he might change his mind. He still might not come. It's so unnerving."

"Outwardly, Rob acts and talks like his father is coming. Strange. It troubles me a little. The truth is, we haven't heard a word from the man."

Chapter Sixty-Five

Occasionally a car crossed Headwater Bridge, shaking Rob as it rattled the steel girders. The winding, rural road leading to and from the bridge carried little traffic. Rob stopped clinging to the beams and began pacing back and forth on the rusty span. In time, he seized the girders again and scanned the pathways on each side of the narrows. He grumbled, "Damn it!" just before the figure of a boy grabbed his attention and held him motionless. After emerging from the woods, the youth strolled along the west side of the stream, on a pathway between dense thickets and rushing water. Rob failed to move for several seconds, then suddenly broke his hold and hurried from the steel planks of the bridge floor to the broken macadam at the edge of the road where he began to work his way down the steep slope through a thick tangle of leafless vines. He was forced to turn, cling to the dense growth, and lower himself backwards.

When he reached the pathway, Rob turned to find Johnny standing about 30 feet from him, near a rock at the water's edge, staring at him. Rob stayed near the bridge, fearing that a rush toward the boy might frighten him away.

"Hi, there!" Rob called.

Johnny didn't answer.

Boy and man stood statue-still as a mallard flew overhead, quacking its way into the distance. A car sped by, and the bridge rumbled. Three yellow leaves fluttered through the air, landed on the water, spun in tiny whirlpools, and quickly floated away.

Rob raised his voice above the sound of the rushing water: "He's a good man, your father. He wants so very much to love you. I know you're hurt—terribly hurt. But please. Don't hurt him, too. He was so afraid to tell you. Because he cares so much."

Johnny didn't move.

"My father left me when I was your age," Rob continued. "Your father has come into your life. I'd rather have it your way. Even before my father left, I really didn't know him. I have only a weak image of him—a figure that came and went, and was mostly out of my life even when he was there. I remember a song—a song about happiness. I've held onto it. Maybe I'm kidding myself in trying to make that song the embodiment of him. But you have the real thing. You don't have to pretend or hope. Your father reaches out. He really and truly wants you, and he gives of himself. He's a beautiful person. Don't be a fool. Don't throw away something that I never had. You should run to him and let his arms wrap around you."

Still Johnny failed to move, except to lift his defiant chin. He kept his sad, angry eyes focused on Rob.

Taking a few steps toward the teenager, Rob said, "Cry for your friend Freddie. Mourn for him. Let it all hang out. But allow your father to be at your side. Let him share your sorrow."

Johnny remained motionless.

"I'm not here just to help you. I came here because my friend Ty is hurting. He's hurting because of you. He's hurting a hell of a lot. And you can help him, just like he wants to help you. Do you think he would have sent me here if he didn't care? Do you think he'd be out there looking for you right now if he didn't love you?"

Johnny pushed hair from his forehead, but his expression remained the same.

Rob went on: "People have always looked at me as a happy-go-lucky, crazy, fun-loving sort of person. And I guess that's the way I've come off during much of my life. But there was always something missing deep inside. I always covered it up. But your father taught me a lot of lessons about life and feeling and people. Hey, this past year has taught me a lot. Searching for you taught me a lot. You know, Johnny, you're a gift that sprang from almost nowhere—the greatest gift of your father's life. Right now he's along the stream at Cloverbrook hoping and praying that he'll find you. Come with me. We'll go to him. My car's parked right up here on the road near the bridge."

The teenager parted his lips as if attempting to speak, yet no words came.

"Come with me, John. Give me a chance to explain more about your dad. I know something about his dreams for you. Think of the Christmases that lay ahead, and the birthdays. He'll teach you how to make things with your hands. He's great when it comes to making and flying kites. You can run along the beach with your father, and hunt for sand crabs. He'll take you into the woods and explain why moss grows on one side of the tree and not the other. Come on. We'll talk more in the car."

* * *

Ty had walked close to the falls at Cloverbrook and now stood in the heavy mist—a mist glowing orange from the late-day sun. He kept his eyes on the flat stones that formed steps along the edge of the tumbling water, squinting as he looked up toward the top of the falls.

Johnny finished his downward struggle through the vetch, and then stood near the concrete conduit. He could see the figure of a man in the glowing mist.

Rob had remained high above, at the road's edge. He looked down on the boy.

Moving timidly at first, Johnny walked toward the falls. Not until his father turned and saw him did the boy begin to run, picking up speed as the mist thickened. Ty's heartbeat raced and his knees locked. Seconds seemed like minutes before he could free his feet and race toward his son.

Johnny threw his arms around his father and cried with deep broken-hearted sobs.

"It's okay," Ty whispered. But the boy's upheaval failed to wane. Ty held firmly in an attempt to comfort Johnny. Their tears mixed.

"Why did he have to die?" Johnny asked, his sobs breaking his words.

"I don't know."

"Because I went away."

"No, Johnny. You're not to blame." Ty continued his firm hold as he spoke softly into the boy's ear. "Lots of people go away from those they love. I guess Freddie suffered so much unhappiness."

"He didn't have anybody. If I hadn't..."

"Remember. You gave him a very special gift. You gave him your friendship. That was something he would never have had if not for you."

"But I left him."

"Maybe we can do something special in his memory."

Johnny's heaving softened slightly, but his tears kept flowing. He continued to hold tightly onto Ty, and in a barely audible whisper said, "I didn't mean what I said back there."

"I know. Forget it. It doesn't matter."

"You think Whiskers is okay?"

"I'm sure Amy's taking good care of him. Shall we go see?"

Chapter Sixty-Six

Rob and Ty had settled themselves in their usual booth in Marty's Tavern and were about to pour down their first beers of the night. After the clink of their mugs and a couple hearty swills, Rob asked, "So, how's the kid doing?"

"Just fine, most days," Ty answered. "It'll take time. He's upset at night sometimes. Once in awhile he wakes up from a disturbing dream."

"Hey, he may never get over it completely."

"He seems in great shape when he's busy, when his mind's occupied. But every now and then, when I catch him in an off moment, I see a fleeting touch of sadness in his eyes."

Rob guzzled most of his beer and wiped his lips, then said, "I guess that's to be expected."

"Thank God for Whiskers. What that dog does for Johnny you wouldn't believe. I tell you, it's unreal. They heap so much love on each other. Nothing—I mean it, nothing could be better for Johnny than Whiskers. What a godsend. Sometimes I wonder if he could have come through it all without that dog to hug."

"I'm ready for another brew. How about you?"

Ty gulped, then held his mug upside down. "I'm ready."

Rob signaled the barmaid.

"I don't know what all you said to Johnny that day at Headwater Bridge, but it had an impact."

"How can you tell?"

"Bits and pieces, now and then. Little things he says. One night, just before bedtime, he said, 'I'm glad I got a real father now instead of having one leave me like Cousin Rob's did.' And then sometimes he goes out of his way to do something for me because 'Cousin Rob explained things.' Whatever that means. I owe you, Rob. I owe you a hell of a lot."

"Hey, dude, I was just using the Ty Scott method."

"There's one thing I said to him that day at the falls that's been troubling me. He keeps bringing it up. And I'm not sure what to do."

"Oh?"

Ty waited until the barmaid placed frothy mugs of tap on the table before he explained, "I promised him something in memory of Freddie. I want to come through. But I'm at a loss."

"Paint something, damn it. That's your forte. Hell, the kid would cherish something you painted in memory of his friend. He'd cherish it forever. That's better than putting something on Freddie's grave, or giving something to his drunken old man. Damn, you're not going to build a monument to him in Maywood. And in Johnny's eyes that school was Freddie's enemy, so forget a plaque for the trophy room."

"What would I paint?"

"You'll think of something. You always do."

"I hate it when you do that. It really pisses me off."

Chapter Sixty-Seven

Amy knew the truth about Ty's trip to the office on Saturday. Johnny believed his dad was simply working overtime. To prepare for this full day of painting, Ty had made two trips to Maywood, returning each time with a pad full of sketches and a pocket full of film. He had also smuggled the portrait of Marjorie out of his apartment—first, pulling it from under a stack of canvases, keeping it wrapped in a blanket, then loading it into the van, all while Johnny was walking the dog.

Now the sketches and photographs were pinned on the corkboard that decked Ty's office wall near his drawing board and easel. The photos captured Kettleback quarry and the trestle from every angle, while the pencil drawings delineated close-up details of the trestle.

Johnny's rough sketch of a shark's wide open mouth rested on the drawing board. Ty had used subtle approaches and careful prodding to elicit a few facts from Johnny—facts that included Freddie's T-shirt design, his toothy shark trademark left here and there around Maywood, scribbled with an indelible purple marker.

Nervously turning this way and that on his stool, Ty was slow to start stretching his canvas and preparing his palette because of Marjorie. He wanted one last look, then another and another, before he covered her, concealing her for what he hoped would be seven years. He allowed minutes to pass before walking to his work table, unrolling a piece of canvas, measuring it with a tape, and cutting it to size.

Within minutes he was back at his easel, the canvas in one hand, a hammer in the other, and tacks in his shirt pocket. Standing next to his stool, he took another look at the portrait, then covered it with the canvas and began tacking and stretching with care, reaching the corners last.

The new painting that would cover the portrait of Marjorie had been forming in Ty's mind little by little over several days. In fact, it was still being conceived in his mind's eye as he selected his brushes and tubes of paint, mixed oil with thinner, and thought about preparing his palette. Almost everything was ready before he was. Sitting on the stool, he again glanced at the photographs and sketches, then stared at the blank canvas and tried to visualize his finished work over and over again. The shark's mouth, he thought, could be painted so widely open as to frame the rest of the picture, each tooth pointing toward the center of the canvas, toward significant aspects of the trestle and quarry, which would form the central interest. Details of the trestle would stand out sharply above a hazy quarry that melted into the distance.

Ty's real problem, however, was not the oil painting itself, but Johnny's acceptance or rejection. Would such a work of art stir up sad memories, even trauma? Or could it be the remembrance that Johnny wanted? Ty's hope was to give his son something that would evoke integrated memories of Freddie. He squeezed white and burnt umber oils onto his palette, then dallied, putting off his first brush stroke, waiting for the total picture to shape itself more clearly in his mind. Moving to his desk, he began writing the letter that was not to be opened for seven years:

Dear Johnny,

I asked you not to break the seal and read this letter until you turned 21. I'm sure you waited, and for that I thank you.

Please remove the frame from the picture I painted seven years ago in remembrance of your friend Freddie. Then carefully remove the oil painting by pulling the tacks one by one and gently lifting the canvas. Later, have it remounted. You'll find a second painting under the first—a portrait of your breathtakingly beautiful mother.

Yes, the woman in the painting is seductive because I painted her that way. Seduction was part of her alluring beauty, and for that reason I kept the portrait from you until now. I was so unsure of your reaction because of your teenage puzzlement about her nature. But I knew from the start that the portrait would someday be yours. You've come of age.

Love, Dad

Chapter Sixty-Eight

Ty had decided to present the painting to Johnny on the morning of Rob's wedding, though it had nothing to do with the occasion. His primary reason was simply that it was ready and he was anxious. The slower drying colors and his late touch-ups had lost all stickiness by Thursday. A day later—yesterday—he had secured the painting in a stark white frame that contrasted sharply with the dark colors at the edge of the canvas.

This morning—Saturday, the wedding day—he had surreptitiously moved the painting from his van and propped it against the corner post of Johnny's bunk beds while the boy was walking Whiskers.

Johnny was as excited as anyone on the morning of the wedding—a sunny but cool day with a few puffy clouds drifting across the blue. Never before had he seen a best man perform, and his father was the best man. Ty almost changed his mind about presenting the painting when he saw Johnny's buoyancy, surely the most exuberant happiness the boy had yet displayed. This was something not to be destroyed by thoughts of Freddie's death. Then again, perhaps Johnny's elastic spirit would envelop the painting, and he would receive it, as Ty so hoped, with the pleasure of warm memories.

Whiskers barely had time to finish spraying a hollybush before Johnny—dressed in his new Prussian blue suit—pulled him toward the apartment building. In fact, the poor dog's leg was still in the air when the boy yanked on the leash and commanded, "Let's go,

Whiskers!" Immediately annoyed with himself, he leaned down and rubbed Whisker's head. "Sorry boy." With effort, he restrained himself and allowed the dog to sniff around a spreading yew near the apartment wall. But then he hurried to the door-well, strutting proudly, shoulders back, obviously pleased with his new suit.

Inside the apartment, Johnny found Amy in a soft green dress that complemented her auburn hair. A strand of orange beads trimmed her neckline. She was busy adjusting an ascot tie under Ty's chin. The teenager beamed at the sight of his father in a cutaway coat.

When Whiskers pulled toward Ty and Amy, Johnny instructed, "No, boy. Not now." He lifted the dog, but held him at an uncomfortable distance to protect his suit.

"Don't go in your room, Johnny," Ty insisted. "Please. Wait for me. I have something for you. Why don't you tie Whiskers in the kitchen until we're ready to go."

Johnny seemed puzzled but headed for the kitchen as Ty rubbed noses with Amy, then silently mouthed the words, "I love you so much." Looking at Ty, Amy couldn't help but bubble up inside with visions of her own day at the altar—a day that was set to follow soon after her operation. She had told Ty that she wanted to hear the minister, the organ, the soloist, the chimes, and especially her groom.

Ty grimaced and pointed toward the boy, alerting Amy that time was running out. He moved quickly to his son's room, then called Johnny. "Come on. I want you to take a look at this. If you don't like it, we'll burn it."

"What is it?"

"Stand over there. Go on."

"A painting?"

"Don't stand too close. Back up a little so you can take it all in. Go on. That's it."

Johnny said nothing. He simply stared. And stared and stared, with little expression as Ty became more and more nervous. Finally, the boy turned and looked up into Ty's face, still giving no indication of his emotions. Then, all of a sudden, he wrapped his arms around Ty, yet continued to say nothing as his father felt vibrations of emotion in the boy's body. In time, Ty placed his hands on Johnny's shoulders and gently pushed him away and looked into his eyes.

"Do you like it?" Ty asked.

Johnny answered without speaking. He nodded his head and conveyed "yes" with his expression, then looked back at the painting as his father's eyes moistened.

"What does it mean to you," Ty asked. "What do you see in it?"

"The quarry, surrounded by the teeth of Freddie's shark. And that's Freddie and me." Johnny pointed to small silhouetted fingers of two boys crossing the trestle—figures that Ty had added only days ago, figures that turned the picture from a death scene to one of life.

"Do you really like it? Is there anything about it that bothers you?" Ty had troubled over the painting for days, seeing the isolated trestle, without the figures, as a grim reminder of fatality. On Thursday he had added the small silhouettes of playful boys, one pulling the other as they raced across the trestle, and he realized at once that he had transformed the painting, perhaps injecting it with joyful memories.

"With the teeth around the edge, it seems like we're looking out of the shark's mouth. Like we're looking at the quarry from inside the shark. Like you painted Freddie's shark's mouth backwards."

"Take another look. It's either way. It works both ways. The quarry and trestle can be inside the shark, or the shark can be about to swallow them. I see the shark as Freddie's anger and rebellion opening up to the good times that you and he shared."

This time, Johnny was beaming when he looked into his father's eyes. "Thanks. It's awesome."

"We have to move fast now, or we'll be late for the wedding."

Johnny kept looking at Ty. "Aunt Emily says she's glad I look like you instead of my mother. Didn't she like her sister?"

"Oh, it's a long story. But we'll get to it in time. Today, you might get a chance to meet your Uncle Jack."

"Jeez, I got a big family. And I thought I didn't have nobody."

"Anybody."

"I mean anybody." Again he looked up at his father. "I'm glad I look like you."

Ty smiled. "Well, I'm glad that you don't mind, since you're stuck with my looks. Eventually I want you to have a full picture of your mother. I don't want you to fret over gaps in your life."

"Now you sound like Cousin Rob. He's always trying to fill gaps."

"Lucky for us, eh? Come on now. We can't be late."

"The painting's awesome, Dad. It's really awesome."

"When we get home, we'll hang it."

* * *

The mother of the groom was dressed and ready long before her car was scheduled to arrive. Pacing back and forth in her living room, Emily wore a Paris blue street-length dress of satin peau de soie with a white orchid corsage. Now and then she pushed aside a curtain and peered through a front window. Each time she passed the mirror near the front door she glanced at her reflection and adjusted her matching blue picture hat.

Her mouth dry, Emily hurried to the kitchen for water just as the door chimes sounded. She drank little, trying not to smear her lipstick, and then hastened to the front door, thinking the car had arrived. After a deep breath, she opened the door and froze as she stared into the eyes of a man with a regal air—a white-haired executive type, an imposing, well-built, well-groomed gentleman wearing a black cashmere topcoat over a tailored gray suit. It took Emily but a moment to recognized her brother Jack. When she did, she stepped back and remained speechless as the seconds ticked away. Her chin fell, her lips quivered, her eyes moistened.

Jack tried to rescue her. Smiling warmly, he said, "You're beautiful in blue."

Emily still could not find words.

He tried again: "But then, just seeing you is beautiful. How is my little Emily?"

"Oh, Jack."

"You may not believe it, but you've never been far from my mind." His eyes begged her to respond in kind. "I'm sorry. I'm so, so sorry. I know I did a terrible thing."

Emily stepped back again.

"I wanted to see you first. I couldn't walk into that church without seeing you first. I had to know."

"Know?"

"I won't go to the church if you don't want me to. I'll leave town now if you want me to."

"No!" Emily shot back. The word was sharp, yet broken by a quiver. She threw herself at him, unmindful of her wedding clothes. "Oh, my God!" Grabbing him and clinging tightly, she gave no thought to the tears that smeared her carefully applied makeup.

Moments later Jack closed the door behind him, took Emily's hand and led her to a chair. He hung his coat on the newel, then sat on the love seat, leaned forward and studied her face. "I should have come long ago. But I didn't know whether I could look you in the eyes."

Emily rubbed her wet cheeks. "I've made a mess of myself. The car will be here any minute. I'll have to fix my face."

"Don't worry. They can't start the wedding without the mother of the groom. I'll talk to the driver when he comes. He'll just have to wait."

"This wasn't a good idea. I was so nervous anyway."

"You'll be okay. Better we take care of this here and now than at the church."

"I've missed you, Jack. You were... oh, God... everything to me. You were my wonderful big brother. Oh, how I looked up to you."

"Until then, right? Living with it has never been easy. It'll be with me until the day I die."

"I must say, you look like you've recovered."

"It's in here." Jack crossed his hands over his chest. "You can't see what's inside of me, Emily."

"I'm sorry. It's so sad, what Marjorie did to us."

"It's not easy to talk about Marjorie, especially with you, Emily. I suppose I could quote from today's sex counselors. What is it they say? It's an act of violence, not sex? Well, that certainly rings true in my case. I was an eighteen-year-old boy full of hate and frustration. What happened was aimed at him as well as her."

"At him? Do you mean Papa?"

"I was taking what he wanted."

Emily's eyes showed disbelief and asked questions at the same time.

"Surely you knew?" Jack asked.

She shook her head.

"I think you knew, but you denied it. You didn't want to believe. Come on, Emily. It was there for us to see all the time. Mama had to know. How could she not know?"

"Maybe I wondered, way back in my mind. Much later, of course. Not when I was little and so hurt by his obsession with her. All those dolls. I thought there was something wrong with me."

"I had not only committed a heinous crime. I had stolen what he wanted. His anger was doubled."

Emily looked away from him. "I suppose you told Rob about his grandfather?"

"I'm not spiteful. Believe me, when Rob came to me, I tested the waters before I swam. I wasn't going to destroy any images."

She looked into Jack's eyes. "Actually, there wasn't much to destroy. I had given him few or no images. So, he launched his big investigation. Frankly, I'm just learning to talk with him."

"I like him. I think you have a fine son."

"You have a nephew, you know. His name's John Scott."

"So I've heard. His father was Marjorie's paper boy."

Jack stood and began to walk around the room as Emily's eyes followed him and took in every movement.

"I remember so many things about you," she said. "I used to watch you when you studied. You'd sit under the lamplight in your room with that big geography book on your lap. I can still see you racing up and down the steps, and hear Mama tell you to slow down. And then there was the time you gathered so many pine cones for Christmas we didn't know what to do with them all. Remember? We sat in front of the fireplace, feeding them to the flames. I still have that polished rock you found by the river. You gave it to me, remember? I keep it in the top drawer of my dresser. I see it everyday, and it reminds me. My mind replays so many things over and over again. Like your playing marbles in the backyard with your friends. I think that's why I married George. Because he was always there in that circle of boys. He was part of the magic that was you."

Jack stood still. He smiled kindly at his sister.

"I was so scared. So scared to see you. But I was terrified that you wouldn't come. I don't know what I would have done if you hadn't come." She lowered her eyes, then looked up at him again. "Your wife? Is she with you?"

"No. I came alone. It had to be that way. She understands." Jack walked to Emily, took her hand and squeezed. "I have a son, too. And a daughter."

"I know."

"I want you to meet my family. When the time is right." He leaned down and kissed Emily on the cheek. "Maybe you and I can salvage something. We weren't given a fair break, you know. And it wasn't just Marjorie and Papa. Mama pretended all the time. She didn't want to see. She didn't want to believe."

Tears welled in Emily's eyes as the wedding car stopped in front of the house. "Oh, God," she muttered. "I'm a total mess. How will I..."

"It's all right." Jack took her hand as she stood. "Take your time."

* * *

Little by little the people had arrived at the church on Fairhaven Road, just outside the town limits. It was one of those white churches with a steeple and a tall spire. Resting on a slope dotted with pines, it was uncomplicated in structure, brightened by red doors, and half-circled by a cemetery whose old tombstones were worn and crooked. It looked down on a winding roadway now dotted with parked cars.

Inside, light filtered through narrow stained-glass windows and splashed touches of color on the oak prews. A center aisle led to a simple altar beneath a gold cross against a white wall. The pipes of the organ were in the rear, behind a choir loft where Fanny Jones, a large, big-bosomed black woman from the Spiritual Society, sang traditional and not-so-traditional songs in a resonant contralto voice of great range. The wedding was built of compromise. Jackie's mother, a bulwark of convention, had insisted on certain ingredients, while the bride and groom added dashes of fresh spice.

Anne Harwood had entered the church long before Rob's

mother, and now sat in the second pew on the left or bride's side. She wore a cocoa crepe dress with beige accessories, a beige orchid corsage and a wide-brimmed hat. She held herself proudly, just as she had when walking up the aisle, arm linked with Skinny-dip Jones, whose mass of curly, dirty-blond hair covered his ears. He looked uncomfortable in his usher's outfit. Thin and hollow-cheeked, the Cornell anthropologist could not remember when he last wore a necktie. He had always dressed for his classroom lectures the same way he dressed for an archaeological dig. Unlike Smitty, the other usher, he was doing his best to follow the rules.

Smitty (Oliver Quincy Smith Jr.) had his mind on nothing but getting even with Rob for wedding tricks, such as the Limburger cheese on the manifold of his car. Each time the short, wiry, spoon-nosed, brush-haired mischief-maker ushered someone to a pew, his mind plotted—pebbles in hubcaps of the honeymoon car, knots tied in Rob's underwear, a stink bomb emitting foul odor somewhere, sometime. Even as he led Rob's mother to her seat his thoughts pictured a dildo springing from a gift box at the reception.

Sliding into her pew, Emily smiled at Anne Harwood, then stared straight ahead and tried to calm herself. Jack sat in the pew behind her. He tapped her gently on the shoulder in an effort to calm her.

The last guest to enter the church was a sickly looking man whose pasty face held dark shadows under sunken eyes. Although six-foot tall, he appeared shorter because his head hung on slouched shoulders above a concave chest. His features, while short of flesh, were not unlike those of Rob. His eyes were the same blue-gray. No hair remained on his crown, but a thin covering of salt and pepper extended from his temples to the back of his head. His brown trousers were shiny from wear, and his brown tweed coat was out-of-style, thread-bare and frayed at the edges.

"Friend of the bride or the groom?" Skinny-dip asked.

The sickly man wanted to say he was the father of the groom, but he couldn't. He stammered, then said, "I'm a friend."

"Of the bride or groom?"

"The groom." He pulled away from Skinny-dip as he said, "I'll sit right here in the last pew. This'll be fine."

Dr. James (Skinny-dip) Harrington Jones stood motionless in the aisle, eyeing the strange man. Within moments he stepped back, just as Fanny Jones began to sing "The Bluebird of Happiness."

At first George Putnam didn't realize what he was hearing, though he knew it was familiar. Suddenly he started. A shiver raced through his body.

The words of the song echoed clearly and vibrantly through the church: "Be like I. Hold your head up high. Somewhere there's a bluebird of happiness."

Memories whirled in George's brain. Lifting his head, he tried to clear his vision. His mind's eye saw his teenage friends, gathered late at night around a radio, listening to the song they had requested by telephone. To their ears, it was unlike other songs of the time. They laughed. And after they had phoned the station again, requesting that it be played fast-speed, they laughed even more as they listened and called it "The Redbird of Hatred." Many years vanished before George thought about the meaning of the words recorded in his brain. He would often hum the tune, often sing the lyrics. His son, Rob, would ask about the song, smile and ask again, muse, gaze on him curiously.

Dressed in blue taffeta, Sally Lake, the maid of honor, and two bridesmaids took well-rehearsed hesitation steps down the aisle while George pulled a pen from his pocket, looked about, grabbed a hymnal from the rack in front of him, flipped to the first hymn, and wrote atop the page, "I killed my bluebird. I'm sorry, Rob." Immediately displeased with his words, he flipped several pages and wrote, "I couldn't see you. I was too ashamed." Again unsatisfied, he opened to hymn 416, "Blest be the tie that binds," and wrote atop the page, "Sometimes a father brings no honor to his son. I know you'll find your bluebird." George ripped the page from the hymnal, folded it, held it in his right hand, then turned and stood as the organ trumpeted the fanfare of Wagner's "Wedding March" from Lohengrin. His eyes and all others were on the bride as she started up the aisle, arm in arm with her father.

Johnny, next to Amy in the third pew, leaned far into the aisle to get a clear view. Amy smiled, knowing it was the boy's first wedding.

Jackie wore a full-length silk gown featuring a fitted bodice with a V neckline and low torso trimmed with French illusion, hand-detailed rose petals and tiny flower pearls. A crown of pearls held her fingertip four-tiered veil. She carried a cascade bouquet of white carnations and a white orchid. Her smile brightened her eyes.

Waiting at the railing with his best man, Rob glanced at his oncoming bride and then at his mother, who sat alone. "Damn, my old man didn't come," Rob muttered to Ty. Seconds later, he whispered to Jackie, "He didn't come. Damn him." The words were not the greeting Jackie wanted, and she knew immediately how Rob would react—by over compensating to cover his anger. She had seen it before—the high jinks, the crazy antics. Now she feared he would really skip down the aisle as he once threatened. She hardly heard the opening remarks of the tall, dark-haired minister with the piercing eyes.

Wearing his clerical gown and collar, the Reverend Clarence Cadwallader spoke in deep tones that carried well: "Dearly beloved, we are gathered together here in the sight of God and in the presence of these witnesses, to join this man and this woman in holy matrimony, which is..."

Johnny kept his eyes on Ty, waiting for his father's role to unfold.

"Robert, wilt thou have this woman to be thy wedded wife, to live together in..."

Johnny fidgeted impatiently until after Rob and Jackie said "I will." But again he prepared himself too soon for his father's role.

Alex Harwood gave away his daughter as the minister directed. He kissed her on the cheek, then joined his wife. Rob repeated the minister's words: "I, Robert, take thee, Jacqueline, to be my wedded wife, to have and to hold, from this day forward..."

In time, Johnny watched the transfer of the ring from his father. It was later, after the formal ceremony, that the boy saw his father lift a bottle and a brass cup from behind the railing.

Anne Harwood had controlled her butterflies until this moment. "They could have waited for the reception to do this," she whispered to her husband.

Ty popped the cork and, to the surprise of most, poured champagne while reciting a line from Petrarch that spoke of love as a "crowning grace" and a "golden link." He handed the cup to Jackie, who lifted it to Rob's lips. After drinking, Rob looked into Jackie's eyes and said, "You are the sparkling wine of my life." He raised the cup to her lips. She drank, then recited from Madam de Girardin: "To love one who loves you, to admire one who admires you, in a word, to be the idol of one's idol, is exceeding the limit of human joy; it is stealing fire from heaven."

After the newlyweds kissed, the music of Mendelssohn drew them down the aisle, Rob racing almost too fast for his bride. At the halfway point, he stopped, lifted her into his arms and began to carry her as some of the guests gasped softly. Others clapped as Smitty and Skinny-dip cheered. Rob's feet became entangled in the train of Jackie's wedding dress. He tripped, plunged forward and fell, pulling her with him. They landed in a twisted heap, his head buried under her gown. This time the gasps were many and loud as several guests rushed and reached out to aid the bride.

"It's all right, folks," Rob called out. "Just part of the act." He untangled himself, awkwardly pushed and pulled himself to his feet and joined with others in helping Jackie to hers.

"Don't touch me," Jackie muttered. "I know why you're doing this. So, he didn't come." She reached down to pick up her bouquet, but Skinny-dip grabbed it first and bowed from the waist as he presented it to her.

"I don't care," Rob whispered. "I really don't care."

"Yes you do."

"At least he could have written. He could have wished me well." Moments later, as the crowd pushed into the anteroom, George Putnam slipped the page he had torn from the hymnal into the hand of Smitty, who now more than ever was preoccupied with his schemes.

"Please give this to the groom," George said. He then walked toward the altar and found his way out of the church through the back rooms.

Smitty gave the note little thought, slipped it into his pocket, and forgot about it as his mind plotted tricks. He pushed through the crowd. In earshot of Rob he grinned and called out, "Yo, Moon! We're gonna get y'!"

* * *

Moon and his bride rode in the back of a limousine. Rob had invited his best man to ride with them to the reception "for protection" from his angry, sulking wife. Ty did so reluctantly, leaving Amy and Johnny in Smitty's hands. He actually sat facing the newlyweds, a bottle of champagne in a container of ice at his left.

"This is stupid," Ty said shortly after the limo left the church. "I'm not supposed to be here. It's against protocol."

Rob looked at Jackie's sour expression. "Lighten up, will you?"

"Did you see Mother's face? She'll never forgive us."

"Think of the future. You can always tell our friends about the time I dropped you in the aisle."

"You're impossible."

"Don't you love me anymore?"

"Of course I love you!" Jackie shouted in a mean, angry, almost vicious tone. "But I don't know why!"

"Because I'm so handsome?"

"Maybe if we had found lots of money in Aunt Marjorie's house you would've been worth marrying. I'm not so sure, now. Huh! I ended up with an idiot."

Ty glanced from Jackie to Rob, then said, "I know where she kept her money."

The newlyweds looked at Ty, eyes wide, mouths open.

"You what?" Rob questioned.

"But that was a long time ago," Ty said.

Jackie continued to stare in disbelief. "You've got to be kidding!"

"No. She often gave me money. I'd watch her go get it. Sometimes I'd even get it for her."

"You mean she paid you?" Rob asked. "Damn, Ty. You're telling us you were a sixteen-year-old gigolo. My God! A teenage gigolo!"

"I never thought of it that way," Ty said.

"I can't believe this!" Rob exclaimed. "So where did she keep her money?"

"Did you check the garden?"

"The garden?"

"Five bricks from the corner. Ten bricks up from the ground."

Rob and Jackie looked at each other. "Holy shit," muttered Rob. "Why didn't you tell us?"

"You didn't ask."

"Ty!"

"Well, I never thought of it till now. You never asked. So, I never thought of it."

Rob pointed toward the front of the big automobile. "Ty, tap on the glass."

The best man tapped, and the driver lowered the black glass screen.

"Driver, turn around," Rob instructed. "We're not going to the reception. Not yet, anyway. Take us to Juniper Lane."

* * *

Amidst the colorful array of ornamental cabbage and kale, Jackie held the train of her wedding gown in her arms as she and Rob stood on a pathway near the far corner of the walled-in garden. Standing nearly against the wall, Ty counted bricks, up and across, then pulled on one, but it didn't budge. He worked his fingers deeper into the crevices, but still the brick wouldn't move. His efforts, however, nudged a brick above and to the left. Quickly grabbing the loose brick, he wiggled it free and, with effort, pulled it from the wall. He pushed his hand into the hole and pulled out a fistful of money, including $1,000 bills.

Rob and Jackie gasped simultaneously.

Ty kept pulling more and more bills from the wall, allowing them to fall to the ground and scatter amidst the red, pink and white cabbages. Rob began to pick up the money as Jackie looked on, shaking her head in disbelief. Ty pulled out another brick and reached deeper into the hollow wall. He could feel the bills fall from above each time he grabbed a wad.

"My God!" Rob exclaimed. "I can't believe this. I just can't believe this."

In time, Ty pulled a yellow envelope from the wall. He held it up and turned to Rob. "Shall I open it?"

Rob hesitated, then said, "Sure, go ahead."

"No, here. It's not mine. It's yours. You open it. After all, this is your house."

Rob took the damp envelope, ripped it open, and slipped out a folded piece of limp paper. Opening it carefully, he read the short message silently, over and over again.

"What is it?" Jackie asked.

"It appears to be a will—the last will and testament of Marjorie Worth."

"What do you mean it's a will? You saw her will. It's already been probated."

Ty said nothing, but he stepped toward Rob.

"Well, it appears to be..."

"Does this mean we lose our house?" Jackie interrupted.

"No. The house isn't mentioned. It's very short. It's a codicil. That's what it is. It's a codicil to the original will. And it's witnessed by Harry Hedgepeth. Can you believe that?"

"Who's Harry Hedgepeth?" Ty asked.

"He's that retired mailman who carried Baby Willow to the hospital."

"I'll be damned." Jackie shook her head slowly. "Why didn't he tell us?"

"Who knows. Maybe he forgot, or didn't care. Maybe it meant little to him at the time."

"Incredible," Jackie muttered. Raising her voice, she asked, "So, what does it say?"

Rob read the codicil again, then turned his eyes on Jackie. "It's not our money to keep."

A quizzical expression spread across Jackie's face. "What are you saying?"

"This money—it all goes to John Willow."

"Johnny?"

"Yes. Johnny."

Ty was slow to open his mouth. "You're kidding?"

"According to this, all the money goes 'to my twin son who lives.' That's what it says. 'My twin son who lives.' Well, that's only right, isn't it? Johnny is her heir."

Ty was quick to make an offer: "We can split the money."

"No way!" Rob said emphatically. "It's the boy's money. It's from his mother. And that's the way it should be." He smiled at

Ty and handed him the codicil. "I think it's great."

"That's right, Ty," Jackie said. She stepped close to him and kissed his cheek. "It looks like a lot of money. It might even be enough to send Johnny to college someday. I think it's wonderful."

Ty's fair skin lost its color. He glanced from Jackie to Rob as he tried to shake off the jolt to his system. "Well I'll be a yellow-bellied sapsucker."

"I'll get a sack for the money," Rob said as he headed for the house. "Start picking it up."

Ty looked kindly at Jackie, but somewhat doleful at the same time. "I feel funny about this."

"Stop it, Ty," she insisted. "If this money were ours my father would never speak to us again. As it is, he thinks we didn't earn this house. Besides, all this green stuff would turn us into... into..." She looked down at the cabbage plants. "...into lazy old cabbages." After laughing at herself, she smiled comically and crossed her eyes. Then frowning in thought, she asked, "Why would Marjorie leave all this money in a garden wall? We might never have found it. Without you, we wouldn't have. In time it might have all rotted away."

"She ran out of time."

"What do you mean?"

"She never got around to moving it."

"What makes you think that?"

"She always stored things in strange places until she wanted them. She'd order me to move things for her. Her movie magazines. Even her clothes. One time she had me toss dance clothes into the coal bin." Ty turned and looked down at all the money scattered about him. "She just ran out of time."

"So only fate is giving Johnny his money."

"Only fate."

Rob stepped from behind the double doors and held up a brown paper bag. "Is this big enough?" He walked toward Ty and Jackie, but kept his eyes on his best man. His expression was serious as he said, "You're going to be a good daddy. In fact, you already are. My daddy didn't even come to my wedding."

Epilogue

The sound of a key turning in a lock.

A whistling teakettle.

Icy snow and sleet striking the window panes.

Tinkling bells.

The wailing winds of March.

A Christmas carol.

A robin's "cheerily, cheerily" song of spring.

Every sound was new to Amy. Each excited her. But most of all she cherished Ty's words, "I will," on an April day in the Community Church at Hickory Corners.

Now the month was June, but the May apples were still in bloom. Their green umbrella leaves hid their small white flowers. Thick patches of ferns reached out of black soil and rotting leaves. Ty led the way along the deep woods path, except when Johnny and Whiskers raced ahead to discover toadstools on a rotted stump or another cluster of puffballs. This walk was one of many for Ty, Amy, the boy and his dog. Each hike for sights and sounds grew more fun for Johnny as he discovered that he, too, could explain to Amy the chirp of a bird, the snap of a twig, the peep of an insect. Her thrill at hearing a new sound excited him, spurring him on to listen and seek.

"There!" Johnny called out. "Here it? Here the rat-a-tat-tat? That's a woodpecker."

"Where?" Amy asked excitedly, speaking too loudly and scaring herself, for she still had trouble with volume and pitch, let alone pronunciation. Often her words were ill-formed.

"There it is!" Ty exclaimed. "Over there. High in that swamp maple."

Amy ran like a little girl, stood under the tree and tipped her head as she listened.

"Look here, Johnny," Ty urged. "A jack-in-the pulpit."

Johnny's glance was quick, for Whiskers started to dig.

"Stop boy!" the young master commanded. "Come on!"

The shrill "klick-ik-ik-ik-iker" of the kingbird carried from the near distance. Amy glanced about excitedly, then hurried to Ty with questions in her eyes.

"It's a bird," Ty said.

She smiled and kissed him on the nose. "Th... thanks." She pointed to her ears. Then she wrapped her arms around her husband while listening to the sounds of dead twigs cracking under the weight of Johnny's feet as he and Whiskers raced around a dying elm.

* * *

The urn of ashes had been placed in the small pirate chest and buried by Ty and Rob among the iris tubers in the walled-in garden of Juniper Lane. Now, the irises were in bloom, their showy sky-blue flowers standing proudly among their sword-like leaves, surrounded by yellow and white daisies, pink roses and other blossoms of June. Rob stood on a pathway surveying the garden, another legacy of Aunt Marjorie, and feeling the warmth of a late spring sun that was about to bring summer. Never did he glance at the iris blooms without eyeing the gray piece of granite that had replaced the cross. Its inscription read: "Here Lies the Twin Brother of John Willow Scott. His Death Gave New Life to the Living."

The warmth within Rob came more from happiness than from the June sun. But it was still tempered by a touch of sadness, the kind he often covered with laughter.

Inside the house, Jackie hurried to the door when the postman knocked.

"Package for Mr. Putnam," said the stocky man in the blue uniform. "Sign here."

Jackie signed the yellow slip and took the package—a square box, about a foot deep, wrapped in brown paper.

"Who is it, Jackie?" Rob called as he entered the dining room through the garden doors.

"The mailman with a package." Ever since her honeymoon, Jackie had uncomfortable feelings about parcels that lacked return addresses. She especially despised boxes that released the odor of rotten-eggs into the bridal suite.

"Who's it from?"

"I don't know," Jackie said as she carried the package to the dining table. "It's addressed to you. It better not be another pair of copulating hippos, or a porno-pillow soaked in musk. If it's from Smitty again, so help me, I'll spray his house with skunk oil."

Rob was quick to rip off the wrapping and open the box. Digging into the tissue he found a ceramic music box that he lifted and examined. Standing atop the round base was a bluebird, its bright blue feathers slightly spread. Beautifully crafted in minute detail, the bird appeared to be in song, its head held high, its beak parted, its yellow breast expanded.

"It's gorgeous!" Jackie exclaimed.

Rob said nothing. He turned the tiny brass winder on the bottom and placed the music box on the table. After the first few tinkling notes, he recognized "The Bluebird of Happiness." Still speechless, he stepped back and watched the bird turn as his mind sang the words to the notes.

Jackie fished in the box and found a note. She read it to her husband: "Thanks for giving a piece of your wedding day to me. May you and your beautiful wife live the song of the bluebird—the bird that I allowed to escape from my life." Jackie looked at Rob. "It's not signed."

"It's from him," Rob said. "It's got to be from him. But it can't be. How could it be? How could he...? I don't understand. You don't think he was there?"